W9-BUO-413

TOO BRIGHT
TO HEAR TOO
LOUD TO SEE

TOO BRIGHT
TO HEAR TOO
LOUD TO SEE

JULIANN GAREY

Published by
Soho Press, Inc.
853 Broadway
New York, NY 10003
Epigraph is from the original C.K. Scott Moncrieff translation of *Swann's Way*

Library of Congress Cataloging-in-Publication Data

Garey, Juliann.
Too bright to hear too loud to see / Juliann Garey.
p. cm.
ISBN 978-1-61695-129-0 (alk. paper)
eISBN 978-1-61695-130-6
1. Manic-depressive illness—Fiction. 2. Self-realization—Fiction. 3.
Fathers and sons—Fiction. 4. Marriage—Fiction. 5. Psychological fiction.
I. Title.
PS3607.A744T66 2012
813'.6—dc23
2012026028

Interior design by Janine Agro, Soho Press, Inc.

Printed in the United States of America

10 9 8 7 6 5 4 3 2 1

For Michael, Gabriel and Emma

And, as ever
In memory of my father

We are able to find everything in our memory, which is like a dispensary or chemical laboratory in which chance steers our hand sometimes to a soothing drug and sometimes to a dangerous poison.

—Marcel Proust, *In Search of Lost Time*

TOO BRIGHT
TO HEAR TOO
LOUD TO SEE

FIRST

Willing suspension of disbelief. That's what they call it in the movies. Like the story about how each procedure will be over in less than a minute. And how you won't feel a thing. How you may be foggy for a while, but in the end you'll be better. You'll be whole.

I want that. So I suspend my disbelief. I let them hook me up. Willingly. And then they give me something. And when I close my eyes, I am neither asleep nor awake but rather suspended in the dark, somewhere between the two. Willingly suspended. Watching. I feel my eyelids being taped shut and hear the gentle hum of the electricity. I have no choice but to give in and let the story tell itself.

Los Angeles 1984. California is a no-fault state. Nothing is ever anyone's fault. It just is. Day after day. Until it kills you.

Automatic sprinkler clicks on at dusk. *SssstChchchSssstChchch.* Flattens oak leaves—yellowy, brown-veined—against stiff green lawn.

It is a warm September night when I leave my wife and eight-year-old daughter. I tell my wife I'm going out to the backyard to clean up the dog shit. It's the one chore I've never really minded. A couple of times a week, I use a long-handled yellow plastic pooper-scooper that came with an accessory—a narrow rake designed to help roll the turds into the scooper. I make my way systematically across the lawn in a zig-zag pattern. The dogs, a couple of beautiful overbred Irish setters who suffer from occasional bouts of mange, enthusiastically follow, sniffing as if hot on the trail of something other than their own crap. When the scooper gets full, I dump it into one of the black Rubbermaid garbage cans I keep in the garage. And when I'm done, I spray down my equipment with a fierce stream from the gun-like attachment I screw on to the green hose I use to top off the swimming pool. By the time I'm finished, the scooper is clean enough to eat off of.

"Jesus Christ, Greyson," my wife, Ellen, yells out the kitchen window, "it would be a whole lot easier if you'd do that during the day when you could actually see the shit." This is something she yells out the kitchen window almost ritually. But I always do it at night. I like the challenge.

Ellen accuses me of being antisocial. It's not true. My work as a studio executive demands a tremendous amount of social intercourse, the appearance of impeccable interpersonal skills, the ability to read the room better and faster than anyone, to negotiate every situation graciously and ruthlessly to my advantage.

I can hardly breathe.

I use the front door less and less these days. Want the ritual welcoming of the hunter/breadwinner less and less. Instead, most nights I let myself in through the little gate that leads to the backyard. I desperately need a solitary hour to catch myself by the scruff of the neck and stuff myself back inside that hollow glad-handing shell. *He* is all style and glitter and fast-talking charm. I cannot stand to be inside him when he does it. Now, the best I can do is stand next to him and watch.

I used to love my job. Didn't even mind the commute. After a cool rain or a good stiff breeze, the sickly yellow mattress of smog that hangs cozily over the Valley dissolves briefly. You can inhale without tasting the cancer in the air. That used to be enough for me. I have made the studio a lot of money over the years. My personal compensation—bonuses, stock options, gross points, profit-sharing—has been more than fair. I can't remember when exactly it was that the phone calls, the meetings, the glad-handing that once provided such a rush, ceased to be a source of pleasure. But through a combination of experience, luck, fear, and an excellent secretary, I have held on.

It is difficult to find oneself after pretending all day. Eventually you are nothing more than a suit, a car, and a business card. So at night I go straight to the backyard, strip off my Armani chain mail, and dive naked into the cool turquoise pool. The shock of the cold water reminds me—*my* body, *my* skin.

Without toweling off I put on a terry cloth robe and slip through the sliding glass doors into my study at the furthest end of the house. I want nothing more than to sit alone looking out through the glass doors, watching leaves from the big, twisted maple tree in the backyard fall into the swimming pool. The branches of the tree have grown so large that the shallow end of the pool is always in the shade. No matter how high I turn up the heater, it's still chilly to swim there. But I refuse to let Ellen have the tree people come to cut it back. I need to see the leaves fall.

All day, every day, there is so much noise. Everything seems so much louder than it used to. I just want to be left alone. My wife is not quiet about what she considers to be my increasingly reclusive tendencies. She wants more. I don't have what she wants.

So I've paid off the mortgage, signed a quitclaim deed putting the house and a trust in her name, and I've packed a small suitcase and locked it in the trunk of my Mercedes. Nameless, easily accessible off-shore accounts have been established.

Work is something else. I don't know where to begin. So I just leave it all—scripts half read, deals half done, foreign rights half sold. I want to apologize. Tell them we had a lot of good years. It's not you, it's me.

Truth is, though, the career of the average studio executive is slightly shorter than the lifespan of the average Medfly—those minuscule fruit flies being hunted by low-flying California Highway Patrol helicopters whose pilots spray insecticide over the Los Angeles basin at the height of rush hour. Best I could hope for at the end of my run is an indie-prod deal at the studio. A producer's office from which nothing is ever produced. That's if I'm lucky. I've seen better men than me leave my post with less. So, stay, go—the point is moot.

That last night—before dinner, before the dog shit, before I leave— I am sitting in my study watching the deadest of the leaves float on the surface of the pool and get sucked toward the filters at the shallow end. The pool man will be pissed off at the extra work. I am smiling at the thought when my daughter, Willa, walks in, small and blonde and long-legged. She has little circles of dirt ground into her kneecaps from playing on the black rubber under the jungle gym at school. She sits on my lap.

"I have a surprise for you," she says in a singsong voice intended to create suspense. Her breath is sweet and new.

"Oh yeah, what's that?"

"Ta-daa." She dangles the thing so close to my face that I can't see it. "It's a key chain, see?"

It's a heart cut out of cardboard and painted abstractly in the same primary colors that cling to her ragged fingernails and cuticles. Her school picture is stuck in the center. Elmer's glue has oozed out from under it and dried in hard, gray blobs. There's a hole punched in the top and a chain. It won't hold more than one or two keys without ripping.

"It's beautiful, thank you," I say, trying to mean it.

She looks at me for a while. I force an unconvincing smile and she looks away. She slides off my lap and onto the rug. I don't ask her what's wrong. I'm afraid she might answer.

Some people shouldn't be parents. I simply found out after the fact. I cannot tolerate the myriad responsibilities anymore—birthday parties and teacher conferences, soccer games and ballet recitals. And just as intolerable is the suffocating guilt of not attending those things. I cannot stand to disappoint. So better gone than absent. It is the only way to love her.

We look up when we hear Ellen talking to the dogs. She is walking across the Spanish tile in the kitchen and down the three steps to my study. She stands in the doorway and sighs heavily. She is barefoot and wears a pair of faded jeans with a hole in the right knee that gets bigger each time she washes them. She must have twenty pairs of jeans in her closet, yet she rarely wears any but these. Ellen gets attached to things—holds on to them even when they're torn and damaged and past their prime.

"There you are," she says, though she's clearly not surprised. "I don't know why we bother with the rest of the house." She looks from me to Willa. "What's wrong, Will?" Willa hugs her knees into her chest. "Did Daddy like his present?" She hugs her knees tighter, tucks her chin, and rolls backwards into a somersault.

"I loved it. I love it." I wring the enthusiasm out like the last drop of water from a damp washcloth.

"I told you he would," she says to Willa. "Come on you guys, dinner's ready."

The forced smile on my face twitches as Ellen heaps my plate with slices of meticulously prepared chicken paillard. She looks at me expectantly. This should be easy. I know what she wants this time, how to fill in the blank. But my hands are clumsy. I manage to slice off a corner of the chicken and lift it to my mouth. I think it is the best thing I have ever tasted and suddenly feel guilty that I am leaving on a good dinner night. Afterwards, I go outside to clean up the dog shit.

Then I leave.

If I'd waited until Ellen and Willa were asleep, I could have had a genuine Hollywood moment. I could have sat on the edge of my daughter's bed and stroked her hair. Tucked her in one last time. Or kissed my wife and had second thoughts and perhaps even gotten misty-eyed. It could have been classic.

Then maybe I wouldn't come off as such an unmitigated asshole. I might even appear sympathetic. Troubled. Conflicted yet caring. Someone the audience could identify with. I could have been box-office-friendly. But I don't do any of those things. I just leave.

On the way out of town, I stop by Hillside to see my mom.

Auburn hair. Green eyes through cat-eye glasses. Early death. Hated men like me. Then again, I do too. I wonder if we all feel that way. Men like me.

Al Jolson's enormous memorial is both the cemetery's mascot and its billboard. Climbing forty feet into the air with white Roman columns and a perpetually running waterfall, it rises high over the 405 Freeway. Ostentatious Hollywood wealth meets the looming specter of death.

Business hours are long over but there is always somebody on duty. I intend to make sure someone will be checking up on her. Frequently. I want the grass covering her grave to be lush and green, soft and well tended at all times. Fuck the water shortage. And she should have fresh flowers. None of that carnation crap.

I can tell right away the guy behind the reception desk is a hyphenate. A Hollywood hyphenate. As in actor-producer or writer-director. Or in this case, funeral director-actor. He is in his late thirties with an artificial orange tan he misguidedly thinks is going to get him in to read for late twenties.

"I'm sorry, sir. The grounds are closed."

I slide my business card and a hundred-dollar bill across the marble counter.

He slides me a flashlight and a headshot.

I hike up Abraham's Path to the top of the hill in the Mount Sinai section. My mother died before I could buy her a nice house. Being buried at Hillside is the next best thing.

If it were up to me, I'd have let my old man spend eternity in the cheap seats. Located in the shadow of the massive mausoleum walls with names like "Courtyard of Eternal Rest" and "Sanctuary of Isaac," those soggy little plots never see a ray of unobstructed sunlight. And still they fill up like seats at the opera on opening night. In this town, Hillside is the only place to be interred. To spend eternity anywhere else is proof your life meant nothing.

I look at my mother's grave and wish, as I did every time I came here for nearly 20 years, that hers was the one still vacant. I hate that her headstone has a year on it for when she was born and another for when she died but only a dash for the life she lived in between.

But now he's here, too. My father's dash was meaningless. But for some reason, which after all these years I still don't fully understand, my mother wanted him beside her. I made her a promise. So the man who spent his life putting her in the ground will spend eternity next to her on the top of the highest hill in the cemetery with a view of the green gold of the Santa Monica Mountains and the deep aquamarine of the Pacific Ocean.

I sit down beside my mother and decide to stay and watch the sunrise. And when the light begins to fight its way through the fog over the ocean, I get back in my car, merge onto the 405 and watch Jolson disappear in my rearview mirror.

It takes me awhile to realize I'm not headed out of town. Instead, I'm driving the other way, back through Culver City. I turn right on Pico, drive past Twentieth Century Fox, and keep heading east. I am only half interested in where my car will go next. My muscles go slack. It's kind of pleasant giving myself over to the care of a luxury German driving machine. The only thing missing is music.

I am up to my neck in the glove compartment looking for a Harry Nilsson tape when I hear the sound of tires squealing and metal meeting glass. I have run a red light. While I slipped through the intersection unscathed, the cars trying to avoid me slammed into each other. The hood of the smaller car, a little silver Alfa Romeo, has folded back like a piece of crumpled origami and its whole front end is nestled cozily into the collapsed passenger side of an old Ford pickup.

I pull over to the curb and watch the two cars pinwheel lazily together across two lanes, scattering shards of headlight glass before finally coming to a stop in front of a Der Wienerschnitzel. I appreciate the geometry their union has created. It seems to me they complete one another now. Like a set of vehicular Siamese twins.

And then it occurs to me that there are people in those cars. I know I should go check on them. As soon as I find the tape. I rummage around in the glove compartment, throwing one thing after another onto the floor under the passenger seat.

Then I pull up the armrest. It's been right here next to me the whole time. Well I'll be damned.

I'm taking Nilsson out of his case when someone starts knocking—loudly. Three someones actually, bent over looking into my window. Clearly this is going to take some negotiating. To begin with, it's important to know what one has to work with. Fortunately, it appears that no one is seriously injured. That could've fucked everything up for me. The first guy is Mexican. He has dirt under his fingernails and clearly belongs to the truck. There are gardening supplies scattered across the intersection—rakes, a leafblower, and something I think might be a Weedwacker. With any luck he'll turn out to be an illegal. There's a woman, early forties—small cut on her forehead, wearing a diamond wedding band. A big one. The guy with her is a good ten, maybe fifteen years younger, ringless, and has a supporting role on a new ABC pilot. This is my lucky day.

"Out of the fucking car this minute, you asshole!"

And suddenly the actor's hands are around my throat. I hadn't even realized the window was open. He has me by the neck and I'm fumbling with the door handle so when I finally get it open I fall into the street. They are *all* yelling at me. Growling and snarling and staring like a bunch of angry Rottweilers.

"Christ, I don't know what happened." Trembling, I stand. "One minute I'm fine and the next I'm dizzy and lightheaded, and then I think I blacked out."

The gardener starts shouting at me in Spanish. I nod. "Sir, I don't speak Spanish but I'm sure you're completely justified."

The actor is gearing up for his big scene. "I almost went through the fucking windshield," he says with feeling.

The woman puts a protective hand on his arm. "It's a miracle Dale and I aren't strewn all over the street in tiny pieces."

"I know, I know and mea culpa absolutely, but thank God you're alright. I guess we better call the police, huh?"

Silence falls over the group. They mumble incoherently. The woman shoots Dale a piercing look.

"I'm willing to take full responsibility. We'll just have to fill out the standard police report stuff: circumstances of the accident, names of drivers, passengers, where we were going, address, phone, employment information, social security. . ." I'm fairly sure I hear an audible gasp.

"Or . . . I can compensate you in cash right now and we can skip the paperwork."

"Bullshit," Dale says. "You don't have that kind of cash on you."

"Shut up, Dale," the woman says. Then she puts her hand on his. "Why don't you find a phone and call us a tow truck." Dale slinks off toward a strip mall across the street.

The woman turns to the gardener and begins speaking in rapid-fire Spanish. He nods. So I open up my trunk, unzip my special bag— false bottom, crisp bills in tidy, bound stacks, as if I just robbed a bank—and pay them off. Considering they have no leverage, I am very generous. Everyone leaves the scene happy.

No harm, no foul, no fault. Not in LA.

Back in my car, I pop *Nilsson Schmilsson* into the tape deck and pull into traffic. "I am driving this car, I am driving this car, I am driving," I whisper to myself and the beat of my pumping, pounding heart. But instead of heading toward the airport, I continue driving east. Toward the past. Into the past. Not my plan. But I sit back and watch. Suspended. To see what will happen next.

Yesterday, when I left, it was September, but here, in this now, it is April. I pull up to the curb and see that sticky purple jacaranda blossoms cover nearly every car windshield on the block. They hitch rides on rubber-soled shoes, bicycle wheels, and roller skates.

Suddenly everything old seems old again. Tinged with the sepia of fading Kodak photos. But I am in them. Where I was. Who I was. Yet I am fully conscious of my full-body flashback. I am was. How would I tell that story? There is no tense to describe it. Telling, though, is not my job. I am the audience—always watching, always suspended, always waiting for what comes next—burdened with both hindsight and self-awareness. Always present in my past.

Beverly Hills, 1957. I was twelve the first time I heard my father having sex.

Muffled laughter. Heads bumping against the wall. *Oh Oh Yes Oh Yes*. Unfamiliar voice. Sharp intake of breath. *YesyesyesNoDon't!* And groaning. Like a dying animal.

If he'd stopped to think about it, my father might have remembered that I was home sick that day; home alone with the chicken pox because my mother couldn't miss another day of work. She couldn't risk losing her job—not with four kids. I was the oldest; my sister, Hannah, was ten. We were closest in age so it fell to us to look after my brothers—Ben, six, who had a talent for getting into trouble, and Jake, two, who could get away with anything. Four kids was a lot of mouths to feed. It wasn't that my father was unemployed. Actually, he'd had more jobs than I could count. He just couldn't hold on to any of them for long.

His latest job was as a regional salesman for Tootsie's, a cheap line of children's clothing. He drove around to low-end stores in Los Angeles trying to interest buyers, managers, and owners in the newest line of stylish-but-affordable Tootsie attire. The back of our eleven-year-old brown Pontiac was home to a rack of Tootsie samples that completely obscured my father's view out the back window.

He hadn't stayed at one job for more than a year in as long as I could remember. Sometimes he quit, but more often than not he was fired. He'd come home ranting about how he'd been screwed or underappreciated or was overqualified for their shit job and fuck-them-he-could-do-better-anyway. Sometimes he just stopped going in. He had worked for Tootsie's for nine months. We all knew his days were numbered.

I found the woman in our kitchen bent over with her head stuck in our refrigerator. She was wearing a pink, fuzzy robe that didn't belong to her.

"That's my mother's robe," I said. It was the first thing that popped into my head.

She started at the sound of my voice, hit her head on the shelf, and finally emerged clutching a jar of pickles, a bottle of milk, and a jar of strawberry jam to her impressive chest. She hadn't bothered to tie the robe closed and now her hands were too full to do anything about it. She looked at me with panic in her eyes, but when she spoke her voice was as calm and sweet as Miss Lipsky, my second-grade teacher.

"Hi," she said, trying to sound like someone who wasn't using condiments to cover her virtually naked body. "I'm Lucille. I'm a colleague of your father's."

"I'm Greyson. I have the chicken pox. Why are you wearing my mother's robe?"

"Oh, the robe, well . . . *Ray?*" Lucille glanced over her shoulder trying to gauge the distance between her and the nearest countertop. "The chicken pox, huh? That's just awful. I had the chicken pox once."

Lucille's hands must have started sweating. She seemed to be having more and more trouble hanging onto her snack. Each time she lifted a knee to slide the milk bottle back into place or jiggled the pickles back into position, I saw more of Lucille—the outer curve of a breast, a flash of pink nipple, black hair between her thighs.

Now it was my hands that were sweating. I stood there gawking at her, both of us at a loss for words. Little by little, she was losing her battle with the pickle jar. She'd had it wedged between her forearm and the exposed part of her stomach. Now everything but the lid had slipped below her arm. She slid her right leg forward, trying to rest the jar on her bare upper thigh.

"How exactly do you know my father?"

"I told you, we—I—Ray and I are just—"

In midsentence her eyes dropped from my face to the tent in my pajama pants. She gasped. My eyes followed hers. The blood that rushed to my face did nothing to reduce the size of my erection. Seconds later, broken glass, pickle juice, kosher dills, globs of jam, and our milk for the week covered the floor and the front of my mother's robe. She turned away and started to cry.

"*Raaaayyyy?* . . . Raymond god*dammit* . . . *Ray-hay-hay . . .*"

"Coming, Doll," my father called from my parents' bedroom.

He dashed into the kitchen, looking lithe and graceful like one of those dancers on *The Lawrence Welk Show* and then turned two shades paler when he saw me, the mess, and Lucille crying.

"Greyson, what are you doing home from—"

"He has the chicken pox, you idiot. What kind of a father are you?"

Lucille was still hanging onto the counter facing away from us.

"Of course I knew he had the chicken pox," my father said defensively.

"You *knew*?" Lucille hissed at him.

Pop tried to whisper so I wouldn't hear.

"I knew he'd *had* the chicken pox. I was up and out before anyone else this morning. As far as I knew, Grey'd gone back to school today."

That was a lie. Today had been no different from any other. Pop slept in while everyone else cooked breakfast and packed lunches.

"Don't move," Pop told Lucille. "I'll get you some slippers. I don't want you cutting your feet."

My father left the kitchen. I didn't know whether to stay or go.

"Greyson?" Lucille said, still facing away from me. "I'm sorry about . . . your mother's robe."

"Yeah, me too," I said, backing into the hall and my father.

We stood there staring at each other, not saying anything. He cleared his throat.

"We were on a sales call," he said, beginning to lie again.

I looked at the wallpaper, trying to count how many brownish-gold fuzzy bouquets were in each row and then on the whole wall in front of me.

". . . so the manager of Sid's Kids trips . . ."

Two, four, six, ten, fourteen, twenty, twenty-eight, floor to ceiling.

". . . and spills his chow mein all over Lucille," he said.

. . . five, ten, fifteen, twenty . . . times forty-two left to right equals . . .

"Well, naturally she had to get herself cleaned up. So . . ."

. . . one thousand one hundred seventy-six.

I looked down. He was holding my mother's pink fuzzy slippers in his hand.

The ones that matched her robe.

I ran back to bed and crawled all the way under the covers. I thought about my mother and let myself wish she were home sitting on the edge of my bed, laying her small, cool hand on my forehead.

After lying to my mother, spending her money, or cheating on her, my father liked to play the good husband. He'd fix leaky faucets, give my little brother a bath, take a stab at the laundry. That night he cooked dinner.

I woke to the nauseating odor of frying onions and organ meats. I could hear Jake playing house with Sunshine, a ratty old doll Hannah had outgrown. I stuck my head out the bedroom door. My grandfather was snoring in his La-Z-Boy—his spindly arms protruding from his white T-shirt, his hand resting on his tiny bulge of a belly. He'd been almost as tall as my father before he started to shrink. Hard to imagine. Now he was barely as tall as Mom.

The door to the balcony was open and I could hear Ben and his friend Wallace playing cowboys and Indians in the cactus bed downstairs. In an effort to avoid gardening costs and unnecessary labor, my grandfather had planted thick, dull cacti out in front. Now their dry, dead tips had curled and turned yellowy-brown. "Ben, you and Wallace better not be breaking off cactus leaves," I yelled over the balcony.

"But they're dead anyway," he called back.

"You think that matters to grandpa?"

"Oh, *fine*," he said, and then screamed like a banshee and aimed one of his toy pistols at me. I made sure my father was nowhere to be seen and wandered into the living room. Hannah looked up at me. She stood up and put her hand on my head the way she'd seen Mom do a thousand times. "You look better," she said, "but you still have a fever."

I put my hand on my own head. "How can you tell?"

"I just can. Only girls can do it. It's Darwinian."

"Oh."

"Tyler McClaine got suspended for smoking in the alley behind the gym," she said, going back to her homework. She had perfect handwriting.

"Can they suspend someone for that? I mean isn't the alley off school grounds?"

"I don't know. I never thought of that," she said.

"Mom's late, isn't she?"

"No, she came home and then went out to the store," Hannah said. My stomach lurched.

"How'd she seem?" I asked.

"Huh?" Hannah looked at me blankly.

I turned and walked numbly into the kitchen. My mother was always fine.

I opened the silverware drawer and pulled out enough mismatched spoons, knives, and forks for the seven of us. My grandfather always sat at the head of the table. His place setting had to match. I looked at what was cooking on the stove, put the cover back on, and got a can of Campbell's Chicken & Stars out of the cabinet. I was sick. I could get away with eating soup. My brothers and sister would have to choke down the liver and onions.

My father came into the kitchen. I could hear the ice cubes in his scotch rattling around in the glass. I didn't turn around. He was nervous. I could tell without looking at him. I could practically feel him vibrating.

I turned around with a fistful of flatware and caught my father staring at the yellowing linoleum and pinching the bridge of his nose. He'd taken off his tie and jacket, but was still wearing his suit pants and short-sleeved sport shirt. I looked down at his feet: beige socks and cracked, brown leatherette slippers. He took the top off the pan, picked up a spatula and poked at the slimy purple globs swimming in onions. He saw me staring and forced a big, fat smile. I don't know why I smiled back, but I did. He seemed relieved.

He shouldn't have been.

He looked at the kitchen floor again and then at me.

"Hey, Grey?"

"Yeah, Pop?"

"You know I love you, son," he said.

As I folded the paper napkins, my stomach turned over and my mouth filled with saliva. Maybe I did have a fever. Maybe it was the smell of cooking innards.

My mother walked in the front door holding a gallon of milk. She looked exhausted and kicked off the navy-blue Sears Comfort Zone heels she'd worn for the last twelve hours. She had red marks on her toes from where they rubbed and pinched. My mom left the house every morning by six twenty to drive an hour and a half to her job at the Tarzana Public Library.

She smiled when she saw me. "Oh, don't worry about it, sweetheart. It's not as if you dropped it on purpose. It was an accident. Don't give it another thought."

It took me a second to register what she meant. And another to feel the sting of it.

She pulled me to her and put her lips on my forehead. I leaned in and put my arms around her waist. "Cool as a cucumber," she said. "I think you can go to school tomorrow."

I watched her from the hallway as she walked into her bedroom. The bed had been haphazardly remade. She stopped for a moment, looked at it, and straightened the bedspread. She walked to the closet to get her slippers, but stopped again when she stepped on something sharp. "Ow, sugar!" she said quietly. My mother never cursed. Staying close to the wall and with the ache in my stomach growing, I moved closer so I could get a better look.

She leaned on the bureau, lifted her foot, and pulled something round and sparkly off her heel. She turned it over in her hand examining it. Still holding the object, she limped to the bed, picked up a pillow, and, bringing it close to her face, inhaled deeply. Her shoulders sagged and she sat down on the bed and sighed heavily. After a few moments, she got up and tossed the sparkly thing into the trash basket. Then she put on her pink fuzzy slippers and walked past me into the kitchen to finish making dinner.

I found it under a bunch of used tissues, an empty bottle of Phillips Milk of Magnesia and an old issue of *Life* magazine. Lucille's brooch was shaped like a butterfly. It was covered in multicolored gems, three of which were missing. The gold paint was flaking off. I put it inside an athletic cup and shoved it in the back of my sock drawer.

I sat down to dirty looks from Ben and Hannah, whose plates of liver and onions sat untouched in front of them. My mother had a tight smile on her face. She tried to make pleasant small talk about the day. My father tried not to look at me. I was a ticking time bomb. In truth, I was a coward, but he didn't know that. I looked into my bowl of soup and watched the universe of chicken and stars swirl in front of me.

I hated him enough to tell, but I loved her more—enough not to. Besides, I thought, I could hold this over his head for years. It was my first lesson in strategic negotiation.

I was the last one to go to sleep that night. Since it was his house, my grandfather had the master bedroom. My parents had the smaller of the other two bedrooms. A bunk bed and a twin were crammed into the third bedroom that my brothers and sister shared. Normally I slept on the living-room couch, but since I'd gotten sick, I'd been sleeping in Ben's bed. Tonight it was back to the couch. I didn't mind though. It meant I had a TV in my room.

Once in a while, headlights from passing cars would shine into the windows of our living room—my bedroom. Sometimes they'd honk their horns because there was a three-way intersection on our corner and no one ever knew whose turn it was to go. I'd gotten used to the lights and the noise though. I pretended I was in the sleeper car of a train. Every night I'd go someplace different.

I lifted up the middle sofa cushion and pulled out my pajamas. I went into the bathroom to get undressed. I had a steady stream of pee going when I saw the little bunched-up ball of blue behind the toilet bowl. I tried to lean forward to see what it was, but I started to overshoot my mark and had to back off. When I finally finished, I got down on all fours, buck-naked ass in the air, and grabbed it. Them. Panties. They were lacy, sky-blue silk panties. My mother didn't have panties like these. And Hannah certainly didn't.

For a long time I just stood still, looking at them in my hand, feeling my heart pounding hard against the inside of my chest. Panic, desire, guilt, revulsion, lust—it was all coming at me too fast and too hard. I got dizzy and sat down on the toilet. I ran Lucille's panties over my legs and chest, and then somehow they found their way to my nose and I was breathing them in and imagining what Lucille would look like in them peeking out from underneath that pink—No! That was my mother's robe. That was disgusting. I was sick. I had a sick mind.

But not even the intrusion of my mother's bathrobe into thoughts of Lucille's musky-smelling blue silk panties could chase away my prodigious hard-on.

When I finished in the bathroom, I climbed into my bed-sofa and felt around under it for my flashlight and book. *The Catcher in the Rye* by the light of a Coleman See Bright. It was the best part of my day. I wasn't allowed to bring it to school—"not appropriate," our dumbshit principal, Dr. Bowen, said.

I got the book from my mom. She had checked it out from the Tarzana Library, where she was associate librarian. She said most people didn't appreciate Salinger yet, but someday they would and I could say I read him way back when. I tried to concentrate but felt guilty. By jerking off with Lucille's panties, I was cheating on my mother too. She was sleeping in that bed now. Which side had my father screwed Lucille on?

My mother was already gone when I woke up the next morning. We went to school just like it was a regular day. But I wasn't really there. By the time the bell rang at three ten, I'd almost convinced myself I'd made it all up. But my father didn't come home for dinner that night. He left a note saying he had to drive all the way out to Bakersfield to make a presentation to some new wholesale outfit. We all knew Bakersfield wasn't part of his territory.

This déjà *me speeds by in a breath and is gone. Because the speed of light is fast, but has anyone ever attempted to clock the speed of racing thoughts? Out of the gate there might be just two or three jockeying for position. But within seconds, dozens, scores, hundreds crowd the field, hurtling past each other, traveling back and forth in time, ricocheting off one another like pinballs, sending sparks flying; creating new tangents and fragments; sending reason running for cover.*

And now I am brushing sticky thoughts off my windshield, trying to clear my head. So that I can think, can drive—out toward the airport. I will stop at a used car dealership on the way. I will sell my luxury automobile for next to nothing and take a cab out to LAX. I have no plan, no idea what will come next. I just know I can't do what I've been doing. It has become too hard. Too exhausting.

I cannot pretend to be the person they think I am for one more day. Slowly, over time, like wallpaper, the face I have shown the world has peeled away. I am a building on the brink of being condemned. Of condemnation. I have tried for the longest time to hide it. To show only the best sides of myself in the most flattering light at the best time of the day.

Ellen kept my secret for as long as she could. She knew as well as I did that in this town, if people smell weakness, they will kill you, eat you, and spit your bones into a shallow grave in the Valley. And that's if they like you. Ellen didn't want that any more than I did. So we pretended. Long and hard. And then Victor found out. But only a little. Only the tip.

Part of me wishes I could tell Victor. Or just say goodbye. I know he will be hurt. And this matters to me. Victor is the closest I have come to a real adult friendship. But I will sacrifice my friend in order to save myself. I'm sorry, Victor. You may never understand. But I know if you were me you'd do the same. That's why we are friends.

I don't feel this way about my wife. Or my daughter. There was a time I thought Ellen would always understand. But at some point, she let go. And once I really started drowning, she became increasingly angry with me for not being able to swim. And Willa doesn't realize it yet, but I have been breaking her heart a little bit every day.

I have been gone for a long time. It just took me a while to work up enough desperation to leave.

I move through Alitalia security like a zombie, neither thinking nor feeling, simply going through the mandated motions. After this I must walk slowly, numbly to the Alitalia first-class lounge, where I will continue to feel nothing until I hear the boarding call for my flight. I must get from security to lounge. Lounge to gate. Gate to plane. I must fasten the seat belt around my waist. I must feel nothing until I feel the first first-class drink in my hand.

I give my ticket and passport to the security guard. I will get a new one with a new name on it once I have left the country. He looks at them and at me, nods, hands them back. I take off my Patek Philippe watch and place it alongside my Cartier money clip in the gray plastic tub on the conveyor belt. When the light overhead turns green, I step through the metal detector. Inexplicably, the alarm sounds.

"Change?" the guard asks.

I feel around in my pants pockets, but there is none. "No. Nothing."

"Lift your arms and spread your legs apart for me please," the guard says. His tone is casual, bored. I feel anxiety building. I try to sweep it away, wish it away, blow it away. Nothing. It's nothing. Feel nothing.

He takes his electronic wand and sweeps it up the outside of one leg and across my chest and the thing goes off like a siren. "Empty your jacket pockets please, sir."

I reach inside my breast pocket and immediately know what it is, though I have no idea how it got there.

"Sir."

No memory of putting it there.

"Sir?"

My throat closes as my fingers follow the rough, corrugated ridges up to the imperfectly punched hole. I roll the little metal chain between my fingers. A heavy, soul-splitting ache falls over me. I let my thumb pass lightly over her picture and can feel her face: dimpled chin, fine blonde eyebrows, small, impossibly soft ears. I am conscious of pain at the back of my skull, of pressure building behind my eyes, of the burning in my esophagus. I cannot swallow.

"SIR!"

"Yes. Yes," I say. Or try to. But there are tears where the words should be. And a very long line behind me. My head is bowed and I am dripping onto the dirty LAX airport floor.

No.

Please. God. Pleasepleasemakeitstop.

I do not realize that I have sunk my teeth into the inside of my cheek until I am forced to open my mouth, gasping for breath. A small spray of blood hits the floor alongside the other fluids I cannot seem to contain.

"Is there a . . . problem, sir?" the guard asks. "Are you . . . ill?" His hand is reaching for the walkie-talkie holstered at his side. I whip my head around and look at the exit doors behind me. Then back at the departure gates ahead. For several seconds all I can hear is the sound of my heart thrumming in my ears.

She is better off without you; you are no good to her; you are useless; go, just go; Jesus Christ, you weak piece of shit, just pull the fucking Band-Aid off.

And I pull out my handkerchief, blow my nose, and clear my throat. And I put Willa's keychain into the gray plastic tub.

"Allergies," I say. And I step through the metal detectors without incident. I smile pleasantly at him. "I'm fine."

The lie I have been telling for twenty years.

New York, 1994. I wake up feeling like shit. My head is pounding, every muscle in my body aches, and to top it all off, looking around, I have no idea where the fuck I am. That's not a completely new phenomenon for me, but usually I'm in an unfamiliar house and I've just gotten laid. I try to sit up, but the feeling that I've been hit by a truck changes my plan.

Days, weeks, months all carry the same weight and currency. I am beginning to get the feeling something bad has happened to me. What exactly, is a blank. But, as I look down at the hospital gown I'm wearing and the bloody IV shunt sticking out of the top of my hand, my surroundings begin to coalesce. As does the pain. And I begin to think it's probably more than just one bad thing. Maybe even several. I could ask someone. How did I get here? How bad off am I?

But then the shapes around me come into sharper focus. There are drooling morons and bedpans and plastic-covered monitors. I reach a hand up to touch my aching head and encounter a small patch of sticky, semi-dried gel. There is another just like it on the other side. I know now that I am far more terrified by the answers than I am by the questions. I close my eyes, slide down, pull the covers over my head and pray silently that this will all be gone when I wake up next time.

SECOND

The truth is technical, clinical, not well understood. Essentially, somewhere behind my overactive, often dysfunctional frontal lobe, my hippocampus is getting hot, and in the back of my brain, deep inside the little, almond-shaped amygdala, flashes of light are igniting a fire that burns through my memory like a box of random photos left for too long in a dusty firetrap of an attic. Some are vivid, bright, resplendent in the superior technology that preserves their detail, context, meaning. Truth. Others, many in fact, are so faded I can hardly see the contrast of negative on positive. I can barely remember the incidents, events, places, and people that were, for whatever reason, worth recording.

Where does the brain stop and the mind begin? Which part of my movie is merely mechanical, chemical? And how do fantasy, fear, desire, joy, loss emerge to become the story? If there is an answer, it's all in the editing.

For most of my life, my memories have been cut together, if not perfectly, then according to some system that has allowed me reasonable access to my story. To what I wanted to remember and how I chose to remember it. I had final cut.

Now they are a mess. A beautiful mess, cut and recut, and playing in no particular order across the insides of my eyelids, running both forward and backward in time as the electrical fire in my brain chases them down and ignites them.

I want to reach out my hand. I want to salvage one or two of my favorite frames. But memory is fast and my hands are strapped to this table.

Rome, 1984. I am in a giant Byzantine cathedral deciding whether to wait in line behind these pizza-eating American tourists just to get a look at Jesus' foreskin. Alleged foreskin.

Pigeons soar and dive overhead, disturbing the phantasmagoric comic strip told in stained glass. Sun strikes panes, illuminating the bloodshed. It is a cloudless day.

Across town, in the monastery of Vivarium, a rival foreskin lies in another heavily guarded, jewel-encrusted reliquary. It's been there for hundreds, maybe thousands of years. The guardians of the foreskins have more or less just agreed to disagree, I guess. Seeing all the tour buses, though, you get the sense there is a sort of Mets/Yankees feud that bolsters business for both parties.

I am not a joiner—an understatement—but wandering in Rome for some time without any purpose, feeling as if I should have a wife or a client or a life to meet up with at some museum or restaurant or set, I decided that a structured activity was in order. So I signed up for a day tour of the relics. I'm not sure what I was expecting—a little archeology, a little history. Perhaps something dark and self-flagellating to match my mood. But the tour has not lived up to my expectations. If I were in a room, I'd pitch it as "Jerry Falwell meets *Night of the Living Dead*." I guess I was hoping for the art-house version. The other relic-seekers don't seem the least bit disappointed though. Which is probably why *Police Academy* was so successful.

From what I've observed, relic pilgrims seem to fall into one of two groups. The first is the eggs-in-one-basket variety, who throw all their faith behind the relic they've designated as being authentic and eschew all the others—thereby cutting down significantly on the time they spend looking at crowns of thorns, threadbare shrouds, severed heads, and bones that leak saint juice. The relic hounds are more the cover-all-the-bases type. Easily taken in by anything boasting a bit of coagulated blood, they cannot take the chance that the one piece of ancient flesh, bone, or tunic they forego might in fact be the answer to their prayers. There are enough "authentic" splinters of The Cross floating around Europe to reforest the Amazon.

I'm told the best time to come here is really January first. Then, on the annual Feast of the Circumcision of Christ, the tiny tip is removed from its box, hoisted high on a velvet pillow, and paraded around all day. Some people plan their year around it.

This bottleneck is becoming absurd. "Jesus Christ, how long does it take to look at a fucking foreskin," I mutter under my breath. Or so I thought. The overly made-up girls in line behind me giggle. They are scandalized and titillated as only former Catholic schoolgirls can be. I turn and smile at them apologetically. "Save my place?" I ask. One of them reaches up and fiddles with the crucifix that dangles in her cleavage. She nods and giggles some more. She is from Buffalo. Or the Midwest. Same difference.

I step out of line and walk around the back of the cavernous church. There are a few old women in the pews crossing themselves and praying. Cross and pray, cross and pray. It reminds me of the pat-your-head-and-rub-your-stomach game I used to play with Willa. It is only midafternoon but there are already hundreds and hundreds of candles lit. There is something comforting and familiar about the smell. Hard to place.

I inhale deeply. Fill my lungs with the smell of dripping, pooling wax and the old stones beneath my feet. Leathery. Warm and cool. Musky.

I close my eyes and breathe in one more time. And then I know— the church smells just like our dogs' feet, like the warm, soft spaces in between their toe pads. I never would have known the pleasures of that particular comfort except that once Willa made me put my nose there. After that, I did it all the time. When no one was around. Dog huffing.

I try to inhale again, but I feel my throat closing and my tear ducts straining. I am going into emotional anaphylactic shock. I walk up to the giant altar of candles and discreetly hold my palm over one of the tickling flames. Just until the pain is unbearable. My throat dilates and the tears recede. I look over my shoulder at the endless line of penis pilgrims and decide life—even mine—is too short for this shit.

The afternoon sun is bright compared with the gloom of the church, and the piazza outside is too big, too busy, and too full of light and noise. The pulse of the square throbs in time with my blistered palm. It is both inside and out. Sound, color, voices—everything is both inside and out.

I turn onto a side street and, like a blind man, feel my way along the ancient stone buildings. It is blissfully quiet. I follow the wall around a corner. My eyes have not yet begun to adjust, but my ear picks up a faint and welcoming sound. Not English, but not foreign. Perhaps it is a stretch but I decide I am going to take it as a sign. And when I do, my heart slows its pace and I can take a full, deep breath again. Because I am missing home, in the form of my dimwitted, overbred Irish setters, and out of nowhere I have landed at the doors of an Irish pub—in the middle of Rome. The message couldn't be more clear: God wants me to drink. And I am only too happy to oblige.

Though the place isn't quite hopping at this hour, I imagine it must be the hub of the Celtic expat community, if Rome has one. Four big-screen TVs simultaneously play different soccer and rugby games. There are dartboards and billiard tables where half a dozen unattractive teenagers—boys too tall, girls too wide, all wearing the same navy blazers with Saint Something embroidered on them—are fooling around, goosing each other with pool cues. And in the back, there's a stage set up where live Irish music threatens to be played. I sit at the bar, order a pint of Guinness, a shot of Glenlivet, and promise myself I'll leave before any of that festive shit happens.

Frankly, it's a little too Saint Paddy's Day for my taste, but when I wrap my throbbing palm around the cold glass and take my first swig of the bitter brown stout, I forget all about Danny Boy and decide I've come to the right place after all. As I raise my glass and silently toast the dogs, I am interrupted by shouting and giggling coming from the pool tables behind me. I shoot the kids a dirty look. The man nursing his beer next to me swivels on his bar stool. "Come on people, I told you once already, if you can't keep it down we're going to have to split!" The guy, a few years younger than me but almost as tired-looking, swivels back, sighs, and stares into his nearly empty glass.

"They all yours?" I ask.

He smiles weakly. "They belong to me. I'm sorry for the noise." I reach my empty shot glass out toward the bartender.

"A couple more of these and I won't hear a thing." I'm not sure, but I think the look he gives me has some judgment, some holier-than-thou crap around the edges.

"You know, with six kids you really should be drinking something stronger than beer," I say, picking up the gauntlet. "Bartender! Two shots of Glenlivet over here."

"No, no," the guy says. "Thanks. But . . . I can't. It wouldn't be appropriate."

"And why's that? Are you driving?" I ask.

"No. I have to be a good role model. It's my job"

"That's a terrible job."

The guy laughs. "No, it isn't. I'm a good teacher. And a good Catholic."

"Oh," I say, as if I know what either of those things means. All I really know is that I'm pretty sure he could use that shot. So I motion the bartender to set it down between us and to leave the bottle. "So they aren't really yours."

"They're in my *care*," he says, trying to smooth a long, blond wisp of hair behind his ear. "Confirmation class trip. Saint Ignatius of Antioch."

I nod. "I don't know it. Him."

He shakes my hand. "Matt Gerson. We're from Billings. But he—the bishop—was martyred in Rome."

"Nice to meet you. Rick Blaine," I say, using my current alias. "And the kids—they get a lot out of this, do they?" We look over and watch as one boy uses another for a dartboard.

"I have a reputation for relating well with the . . . rambunctious kids," Matt says. "So I tend to get assigned the more . . . challenging children on trips like this. I try to think of it as a calling."

"I'd call it getting shafted, Matt."

"I take it you're not a religious man . . ."

"I was religious against my will. And then only briefly." But I tell Matt about it anyway.

Beverly Hills, 1958. I had no choice in the matter. Neither did my parents. The stucco duplex we lived in, built in the 1920s and designed to look like a Tudor castle, belonged to my father's father, who owned and ran a liquor store on Hollywood Boulevard. Twenty years ago, my grandfather, a man with virtually no education who read only Yiddish and spoke a garbled combination of the Old and New Worlds, had recognized a good investment. Since then, it had gone up in value tenfold—something he never missed an opportunity to remind my father of. "If my son was a real man," he'd say, as if Pop weren't in the room, "he could take care of his own family. Then I could sell this place for a bundle and retire."

It was my grandpa's grudging generosity that allowed us to live with him and to attend the best schools in the county. But we had to live by his rules. All of them. All the time. So when my grandfather decided I needed religion, my parents had to support the cause or risk eviction. I would now accompany him to Saturday morning and High Holiday services, and, I was informed, begin my studies to become a Bar Mitzvah. I may as well have been converting to Greek Orthodoxy.

I did have friends who were being Bar Mitzvahed, all at the very Reform Wilshire Boulevard Temple. The huge Moorish building had an interior decorated in gold inlay, black marble, and ornate biblical murals commissioned by the studio head Jack Warner. It had been built at the height of the Depression, when regular Americans were selling apples and jumping out windows.

I would be Bar Mitzvahed in one of the tiny synagogues in the Fairfax section of West Hollywood. I spent seventh grade playing Little League, studying for my Bar Mitzvah, and going to other boys' Bar Mitzvahs—all held at the members-only Hillcrest Country Club and the Beverly Hills Hotel and in huge private homes north of Sunset.

My friends' fathers all had jobs with titles—VP of Production, Director of Business Affairs, or Executive Producer. When their parents asked what my father did, I said he was in "business." A businessman. But "business" had nothing to do with "The Business," and when fathers with important jobs in The Business found out I was short an article, they did one of two things. Either they went off to refresh their gin martinis or they stayed to tell me the story of how they worked their way up from nothing.

"You know all of this is bullshit, right kid?" I was listening closely to my best friend Alan Rothman's dad, who was a senior agent at Franklin Morton. Alan knew pretty much everything about my family, which made me both more comfortable and more nervous talking to his father.

In fact, it had been Alan who'd broken the news to me in the first place. Well, sort of. I was eleven when I heard it from Alan who'd heard it from his brother who'd heard it from a kid in his grade who had a job there after school. But I didn't believe it. "That's bullshit," I told Alan.

We were playing catch on the playground at recess and I wound up and threw the ball hard. He caught it a few inches from his face.

"Hey, I'm just the messenger."

"Sorry. How the hell does this kid even know what my father looks like?"

"Apparently, your dad's been throwing your name around a lot. 'My son Greyson this, my son Greyson that. You know, proud father crap. Sorry, Grey."

But I needed proof. So at lunchtime we snuck past the teachers on monitor duty—which didn't exactly require a Houdini act—and biked to the Chock full o' Nuts all the way over on the corner of Sunset and Crescent Heights. I peered around the side of the building into the big front window.

Alan was right. He was sitting at the counter, drinking a cup of coffee. Pop's jacket was on the stool next to him. At some point he'd actually slipped his shoes off and the twice-resoled brown oxfords were lying on the floor under his feet. There was a hole in his left sock.

Alan put his hand on my shoulder. "Maybe he's just having lunch."

"Yeah, I suppose it's possible. But I bet the other businessmen aren't having lunch twenty miles from where they work. Or *say* they work." I remember that as the first day of feeling contempt for my father for the rest of my life. Of giving up trust and security and strength and replacing them with suspicion, cynicism, and resentment. And I think it was the beginning of my chronic heartburn.

"C'mon Grey," Alan said. "We have to get back."

"Alan?"

"Yeah?"

"Promise you won't—"

"Tell a living soul? On my mother's life."

Eventually, in bits and pieces, I'm the one who told Mr. Rothman—or let slip enough pieces of information for him to put the puzzle together.

"Sir?" I'd lost track of what he was saying.

"*This.* This exclusive, members-only crap," he said, gesturing around the main room at Hillcrest, which looked out onto the golf course. "They built it because the gentiles wouldn't let us join theirs."

"Right. I see what you mean."

"Everybody's gotta have somebody to step on. Makes 'em feel important."

"But there have to be better, more productive ways of proving your worth in the world—ways that don't involve crushing other people. Isn't that why we fought the war?"

He turned to me with a slightly surprised look on his face, which slowly melted into a smile.

"I sure as shit would like to think so, Greyson." Then he squeezed my shoulder. "Do me a favor, Grey?"

"Sure, Mr. Rothman."

"Keep being friends with Alan."

I laughed. "Of course. Why wouldn't I?"

"No reason. Just—you're a *mensch*, Grey. You know what that means?"

"I've heard—"

"It means you're a good person. A good man. In *here*," Mr. Rothman said, tapping on his chest above his heart. Then he drained his drink and looked around. "Look at these putzes . . ." He put his arm around my shoulder and rattled the ice cubes in his glass. "I think you may be the only one in the room," he said.

I have never before given much thought to that exchange. But for a moment, it makes me feel hopeful, optimistic. Mr. Rothman thought I was a good man. And then the moment is gone.

"It's never too late to start again," he says. "God will always welcome you back."

"Trust me, Matt, God wants nothing to do with me. I'm not a nice man." As if to prove my point, I nudge the shot glass closer to him. Because I feel like getting drunk. And I don't feel like doing it alone.

"Maybe just one," he whispers.

"Just one." I give his shoulder a squeeze. "They'll never know."

And come dinnertime, I'm happy to pick up the tab for all the Italian-Irish fish-and-chips those doughy, greasy-haired, pasty-faced Montana teenagers can eat. So Matt and I can get just a tiny bit shit-faced. And Matt tells me his story. It turns out he wasn't always so good.

"I was addicted to smack," he confesses when he's several shots in. "I mean, you know, before I was saved."

"Is that right?"

"Yes, sir. I was a young man in trouble. Drugs. Women."

"And look at you now," I say, slapping him on the back.

"I'm living proof, Jesus can save anyone."

"Trust me, Matt, keep Jesus and God for you and those kids and whoever else believes. Leave me out of it."

"Why? Because you think you don't deserve His love? What did you ever do that is so unforgivable?"

"Well, there were the drugs. They almost wrecked my marriage."

"We do stupid things when we're high. But you got clean—"

"Doesn't matter. There were nights . . . parties . . . business things . . . women. I'd stumble in the next morning smelling of alcohol and another woman and I'd kiss my wife on the mouth. And then I'd sit down at the breakfast table and eat Cheerios with my perfect little girl."

"That's the drugs," Matt says, coming to my defense. "You'd never do that now. And every marriage goes through difficult times."

"Does every husband rape his wife?"

Matt is silent.

I pour him another round. "It was the late seventies and people were getting high and fucking right out in the open. Right next to the buffet tables. I came home from a party one night—I had wanted Ellen there with me and she wouldn't come—and I came home all coked up, and I really wanted to fuck. I told her I'd spent the whole fucking night staring at a bunch of naked models, and I hadn't touched a single one. She asked me what I wanted, a fucking medal?"

I pour myself another shot and knock it back fast so I can feel it burn going down. "Well, you know what, Matt? I did want a fucking medal. Hadn't I made good on all my promises—my financial promises? And she liked it a little rough sometimes. Didn't she? Or maybe I did . . . Anyhow, she didn't make a sound during it. I don't know if she was trying not to wake our daughter or if she just didn't want to give me the satisfaction. But she bit her lip so hard it bled." I swallow another shot. "We never talked about it after."

The bartender is looking at me like I am scum and I can't tell whether he is repulsed more by my story or the fact that I have lured the Catholic school teacher into wanton drunkenness. But I don't care because I am undergoing a single-malt baptism. I also do not care that its effects will not remain—that when I wake, I will be a sinner once more.

"That's pretty bad," Matt says, "but if it makes you feel any better, I've heard worse. Billings is a shithole. Men put their wives in the hospital every day. Twice on Christmas." Somehow, the fact that I haven't fallen quite as far as the wife-beaters of Montana doesn't bring me much solace.

New York, 1994. I am standing unsteadily in front of the activities board reading the menu of options: Horticulture Club, Creative Writing, Collage, Current Events, Pet Therapy. The social worker assigned to me has encouraged me to participate in Group. On some wards Group is mandatory. Blessedly, here Group is optional. For some reason, none of these choices seems to appeal.

If, for example, there were a group like the table of patients I

eavesdropped on last night during dinner—the ones who were com-
paring the graphic details of their suicide attempts—the single-edged
razor blades, the cocktails of tequila, benzos, and Dilaudid—that
would be a group I could get behind. But nothing like that is featured
on the board today. And I don't feel like scrapbooking. So instead I
walk into my just-for-now private room and close the door behind
me, appreciating the just-for-now silence.

When I walk into the bathroom, I am again confronted by the
warning signs over the sink. The tap water in the hospital is contami-
nated with Legionella. Years ago, a dozen patients died from it. So now
we are instructed to shower with our mouths closed, and all drinking
and toothbrushing is done with bottled water.

We are not allowed to have dental floss or shoelaces and we must
be supervised while shaving. But giving us unrestricted access to a
deadly virus, that's okay.

Really, you wouldn't need much of a will to find a way out, would
you?

THIRD

"Try to relax, hon," Florence whispers. "There's nothing to be a afraid of." Florence, the ECT nurse, is short, fat, and maternal. She wears her glasses on a beaded chain around her neck and smooths my hair. As if I were a child.

"Pick a happy memory," she whispers. "Something that makes you feel safe."

Happy? Safe? I am drawing a blank. Florence, who has worked here since 1972 and has seen everything, sees the confusion in my eyes. "Or maybe just a really good day. Something nice that made you feel good about yourself."

They are all about building self-esteem here. And I know it hasn't been all bad. So I close my eyes and try to dredge up a piece of history. I do not expect miracles—am in fact prepared for failure. But the biggest surprise is how quickly real happiness rises to the surface.

Big Sur, 1982. I didn't become a real father until the year Ellen and I split up. The kind who knows that his daughter likes her peanut butter creamy, not chunky. The kind who knows that you never leave the house without Bunny, but Bear always stays home to babysit Piglet and Raggedy Ann. Unless you're going on a vacation, in which case they all have to come. So they did. I remember all of it.

Dancing across my eyelids: Faint blue veins on pale skin. Black sky breaks open, dumping yellow stars. Counting. Wishing. The soft flannel of her good-night.

I borrowed the giant luxury motor home from Leland Costa, a brilliant director infamous as much for his mood swings as for his propensity to spend studio money like it came from a Monopoly set. It was my job to keep Leland on an even keel and on budget. It was also my job to keep him happy. The two were mutually exclusive. So in order to keep him from being sued and to make sure he continued to win Oscars, I gave up on the happy part. And he threatened to fire me at least once during every shoot. Afterward, remorse would set in and he'd send gifts, which I'd send back.

"Leland, we've talked about this," I told him when he tried to give Willa a pony. "You don't have to buy me things and you don't have to apologize."

"It's not for you, it's for Willa."

So I asked to borrow his RV. And he was thrilled to be able to do something for me. Because Leland had once again gone from that place where he thought he was superior to everyone else to the place where he felt like he didn't deserve to be alive. I didn't need a map to get to either of them. So I was willing to forgive him—again—even when other studios were starting to toss around labels like "difficult" and "unmanageable."

The best thing I could do for him now was to take something he had to give. The RV seemed benign, a loan. Nothing permanent would change hands. I had rules—learned as an agent and followed ever since. Over the years I'd turned down countless free trips to Aspen and the Caribbean. But each time, I maintained and increased my authority, my credibility, my power.

I was bending my rules with the RV. But Leland needed to give and I wanted the freedom of traveling on I-5, of slowly winding our way along the California coast—pulling over to walk on a beach or ride a Ferris wheel; sleeping in campgrounds surrounded by redwoods. Until, eventually, we reached Big Sur. The excitement and terror of our first trip alone. So I bent the rules.

"Which one is that?" Willa asked, pointing to a random spot in the sky. We were lying in a sleeping bag on the roof of the motor home picking out constellations.

"Oh, that one?" I asked, pointing to nothing.

"No." She sat up. "There. There. The big one next to the little one."

"Ohhhh, that one," I said as she lay back down and put her head on my chest. I had no idea what she was pointing at. "That's Cassiopeia."

"Really?"

"Yup."

"Daddy?"

"Willy?"

She giggled. "Can we sleep up here?"

"Hmmmm. I don't know. What if we roll over in our sleep?"

"Do we have any tape?" Willa asked.

"Tape? I don't know. For what?"

"Well," Willa said, "we could tape ourselves to the roof and that way we couldn't roll off."

"That, Willa Todd, is the most brilliant idea anyone has ever had . . ."

"Really?" she asked, grinning from ear to ear.

"Really," I said. "Unfortunately, we have no tape." I made a very sad face and then a very happy one. "But, I have an idea!"

"What?"

"How about we have hot chocolate up here now, sleep inside, and in the morning while we're still in our pajamas we come up here and eat breakfast?"

"That's a great idea!"

"Really?" I asked.

"Really," she said.

Willa stood on her tiptoes watching as I stirred packets of powdered cocoa with dehydrated minimarshmallows into boiling water.

"Mommy makes it with milk," she said.

"Really? The directions say to use water." I showed her the box to prove I knew what I was doing.

"Well, Mommy says it's better for you with milk."

Apparently, I still had a few things to learn.

But even though it was a little thin and the marshmallows weren't fully hydrated and crunched under my teeth, that particular cup of hot chocolate was the best I've ever had, before or since.

The feeling is over too soon—sinks back beneath the surface before I can hit rewind. I would be grief-stricken and full of self-pity except that what shows up next is like tripping over a bald eagle or a polar bear or a platy-pus in your backyard: an endangered species—or at least nothing you'd ever expect to experience face-to-face in your lifetime. And yet, here he is, that long-gone version of my father—the one seen from the eyes of a boy who still believes in Santa Claus.

Beverly Hills, 1953. Seventy-five degrees. High in the sky, sleigh dusted with sparkling snowflakes, Santa and his reindeer had been flying over the intersection of Wilshire and Santa Monica since just after Thanksgiving.

The little white lights that covered the outside of the Beverly Wilshire Hotel and Saks allowed shoppers on Rodeo Drive to pretend they were in New York City, and when the temperature dipped below sixty-five and the matrons of Beverly Hills broke out their minks, you could almost believe it was true.

My father surprised me, showing up out of the blue when the bell rang at 3:10 P.M. There he was, chatting with the pickup mothers as if this was something he did every day. At first I thought something must be terribly wrong. But Pop wiggled his eyebrows and told me we were going on a secret mission. When you're eight, there's nothing better than a secret mission.

Pop wouldn't tell me where we were going, just stopped to buy us both ice cream cones at Thrifty Drug Store, where they had a scooper that made the ice cream come out square. Pop let me get a double— cherry vanilla and rocky road. We walked up Beverly Drive, past the hardware store and the smelly cheese shop and Harry Harris Fine Children's Shoes and Phil's Fish and Seafood, which was also pretty smelly. At the top of the block, outside the Beverly Hills Post Office, was a Christmas tree lot. That's where Pop stopped. And told me to pick one. I was so shocked I dropped what was left of my cherry vanilla, rocky road cone.

We'd never had a Christmas tree. We weren't allowed. In Beverly Hills, where most Jews saw a Christmas tree as nothing more than temporary interior design, my grandfather felt it was "a Christian invasion of his home." We weren't allowed to sing "Jingle Bells" or drink eggnog or even read *A Christmas Carol*. Not that my grandfather was a very religious Jew—despite his Passover zealotry, he didn't keep kosher and he worked every Saturday. He was just irrationally opposed to anything *not* Jewish.

My father picked up a circle of wood that had been sawed off the bottom of a Douglas fir and handed it to me. It was sticky with sap.

"Smell," he said.

I couldn't pull enough of it into my lungs. I pushed it against my nose, closed my eyes, and breathed in again and again.

"Careful. You're going to hurt yourself." My father laughed.

"Can I keep it?" I asked

The Christmas tree guy heard me and looked up.

"Sure. Take as many as you like. I'm just gonna dump 'em."

But I only kept the first piece. I didn't think the others could possibly smell as good. And then we picked out a tree. I looked at every single Christmas tree on the lot before I made up my mind. It was a pine—full and dark green, taller than me by an inch or two. And it smelled better than all the others. We carried it home along Wilshire Boulevard, past the white lights on the Beverly Wilshire and Saks, and under Santa and his reindeer. Every block or so, someone would honk at us and wave, and Pop would yell "Merry Christmas!" at them.

When we got home, Pop picked a spot in the far corner of the backyard, dug a hole, and planted it. Sort of. Grandpa never noticed. He kept the liquor store open on Christmas. It was a big day for him, so he left the house early. As soon as he was out the door, Pop and I dug up the tree, brought it in, and decorated it with strings of popcorn and cranberries, candy canes, and tinsel. Then we put all the presents we'd bought for everyone under the tree—mostly just little stuff from Woolworth's, like a Matchbox car for Ben, bubble bath for Mom, a stuffed rabbit for Hannah.

When everyone woke up, we had Christmas at our house—just like all the other Jews in Beverly Hills. We even drank eggnog. And when the living room floor was covered in wrapping paper and my brother and sister were playing with their new toys and my mother was dabbing her new rose water on her wrists, my father put his arm around me and kissed the top of my head.

"Mission accomplished," he said.

I remember that Christmas as part of the time when my father's behavior was what people referred to as eccentric, unconventional. Or less generously, unreliable. But also lovable. I remember he had time to coach Little League. He wasn't the robot in the suit and tie my friends' fathers were. I didn't know then why he had so much spare time. Or why my mother was always so tired. When I figured that out, his eccentric behavior became a lot less endearing. But until then, it made him seem special to me. Different from the other fathers. It was almost like he knew something important that they didn't.

Like the day we caught the fish. I've never known what to do with that memory. Mostly I've spent my life wishing it would go away. But it doesn't. That day will always keep me from hating him as completely as I want to.

I was seven, Hannah was five, Ben had barely been born—to us he was inconsequential. We hadn't yet realized the world had just changed radically. But we knew Mom was exhausted. Pop was in a good mood, so he took Hannah and me to the Santa Monica pier for a whole after- noon to get us out of her hair. We rode the merry-go-round and the Ferris wheel and ate hot dogs and cotton candy, and then Pop rented a fishing rod and Hannah and I took turns holding it and being bored and complaining. Until one of us got a bite. Which one of us that was, depends on who you ask and who's telling the fish story.

I don't think either of us actually expected to catch anything. And neither of us knew what to do. It was our first fishing expedition. Our family wasn't big on nature activities. No fishing, no camping, no hik- ing. Sometimes we barbecued. And then ate outside. Hannah and I were in way over our heads.

We gripped the rod with twenty white knuckles—like we were fighting a marlin or a whale.

"Gently, gently. You have to use a light touch," Pop said like he knew what he was doing. He took the cheap little rod from us and started turning the reel, letting out more line before he realized he was turn- ing it the wrong way. Any fish with half a brain should've been able to free itself by then, but something was still thrashing around under the blue-black surface.

A group of easily impressed city folk was beginning to gather, ooh- ing and ahhing and cheering my father on as he performed what was apparently a Herculean task. Hannah and I stood by his side beam- ing. For once it was our father who mattered, who was important and admired. It was a feeling of elation I will never forget. And it was extremely short-lived. None of my Cub Scout badges had prepared me for the bleeding, bug-eyed, flailing trophy my father held up for the cheering crowd.

"Neat-o," Hannah said, sticking her finger through the gaping hole the hook had torn in the fish's lip.

"Stop!" I screamed. "You're hurting him!" I pushed her and she stumbled backward.

"Put him down!" I yelled at my father.

"Calm down, Greyson," my father said, laying the fish down on the pier where it flopped around frantically. "Fish don't feel pain."

Hannah wiggled her bloody fish finger in my face. "Yeah, stupid, everybody knows that."

My father raised one eyebrow at her. "That's enough, Hannah."

I squatted down next to the fish. I was starting to cry and my tears were dripping on him. "Look at him. He can't breathe."

My father sighed heavily, then started looking around. "I'll be right back," he said. "Don't move."

Hannah squatted next to me. "He's not going to be breathing when we eat him either," she said and poked it.

"I said stop it! And we're not eating him."

"He's my fish too," she whined. "I caught him just as much as you did."

"Well, I wish we hadn't caught him," I said, feeling a mixture of nausea, panic, and anger.

"Fine, I'll cook my half and you throw your half back."

"Go ahead and try." I shoved her hard and she fell back onto her butt.

She just sat there for a minute. Then her eyes teared up and her chin started to tremble. "You got my shorts all wet . . . my bottom's all wet."

And then a shadow blocked the sun and I looked up and saw my father standing over me with a janitor's bucket.

"Go get some water. I'll take the hook out."

"Water?" I asked lamely.

"Salt water," he said, pointing to the seafood restaurant at the end of the pier that kept live lobsters in a tank.

"Hurry," he said, pulling me to my feet. "I don't think our friend here has much time."

I sprinted down the pier and asked a man who was wearing black rubber boots and an apron that looked like my yellow rain slicker to fill my bucket. I could hardly lift it, but I made it back and Pop scooped up my wounded fish and dropped him in. I felt like I could breathe again too.

But when a feathery cloud of blood began to trail through the water from the hole in the fish's lip, I started to cry. "Oh God, Pop, look what we did to him. He wasn't doing anything except swimming around in the ocean and we . . . we tore a hole in him." I was sobbing and I couldn't stop. I couldn't ever remember being so sad or feeling such regret over something I had done.

My father pulled me to him and hugged me hard.

"It's gonna be okay, sweetheart."

"No, he's gonna die and it's going to be my fault." I could hardly breathe, I was crying so hard.

"Greyson's a sissy," Hannah teased. "A boy crying about a stupid fish. I'm going to tell everybody you cried about a stupid fish. Right after I cook it."

Pop turned to her. "That is enough, young lady. Not one more word out of you. Do you understand me?"

I'd never heard him yell at Hannah, not like that. Her chin quivered and she started to cry.

"Well, do you?" my father asked.

"You said not one more word," my sister said in a tiny whisper.

"Alright," my father said, stepping between my sister and me. "Whaddya say we put our friend back where he belongs?"

Hannah and I nodded silently and followed my father to the edge of the pier where he handed me the bucket.

"I'm really sorry," I whispered. "I hope you feel better." I dumped the fish and water over the side and watched until the splash disappeared and there was only the slosh of the blue-green water on the mossy leg of the pier. Then Pop reached into his pocket and pulled out two nickels and told Hannah to buy us a couple of snow cones from the cart nearby.

When she was out of earshot, he held my arms tight so I was looking right at him—so tight it almost hurt. "I don't know if you're going to understand this, Greyson, but I'm going to tell you anyway. You should never be afraid to cry."

"But boys—" I started to say.

"No, not just because it's okay for boys to cry too. But because, Greyson, you are very lucky. Not everyone can feel things as deeply as you. Most people, their feelings are . . . bland, tasteless. They'll never understand what it's like to read a poem and feel almost like they're flying, or to see a bleeding fish and feel grief that shatters their heart. It's not a weakness, Grey. It's what I love about you most." Then he hugged me. Hard. And I'm not sure, but he might have been crying.

That short, unsullied time when I simply thought he was special has a sense of place and a smell all its own. It is a tiny shred of my father that, like a child's blanket, I am both attached to and embarrassed by. And that I would be devastated to lose.

I suppose that irretrievable time is as much a piece of me as it is of him.

New York, 1994. "Mind if I sit and talk with you for a few minutes?"

The voice, with its heavy outer-borough accent, is at once cheerful and timid. I look up from my tray of uneaten, inedible food—colorless, tasteless, but unfortunately not odorless. I did not realize I was staring down at it; do not know for how long I've been sitting here alone at this lunch table.

The young woman stands next to the orange plastic chair beside me waiting for permission. She is dressed neatly in cheap clothing— the kind secretaries and receptionists who earn next to nothing buy at Kmart and J. C. Penney in order to achieve the look of an acceptable professional. The poor woman's facsimile of her boss. This woman's slacks and matching blazer are gray polyester and her blouse is made of some kind of shiny, no doubt highly flammable acetate. She is clutching a clipboard to her chest. She takes a step toward me and I can hear her polyester-covered thighs rub together. I wait for her to finally get up the nerve to "axe" me a question.

"I'm Yolanda," she says, offering me her hand. I make a good faith effort to raise mine, but it is just too heavy. So she pulls out the chair and sits down.

"I'm Yolanda," she says again. "I'm a nursing student here and I was hoping we could talk for a few minutes."

A nursing student? I look around to see if there is any real staff person who can help me get rid of this well-meaning pain in the ass.

"Mr. Todd? Can I get you something?" Yolanda asks, trying to meet my eyes.

"No, I'm just very tired today."

"Oh, well, this won't take long."

"What won't?"

"Well, as you may or may not know," Yolanda says, sounding like a telemarketer, "this is a teaching hospital and part of our training as nursing students involves interacting with the patients and learning how to take a proper history."

I look at Yolanda again and instantly know her history. She's from one of the boroughs, first in her family to graduate college. City, Brooklyn, maybe Hunter. She's probably first generation—Puerto Rico, Dominican Republic, Santo Domingo. Something like that.

She must have done well to get in here. Competitive program. Her parents must be over the moon. Father probably drives a cab. A cab with Yolanda's picture and the Virgin Mary stuck to the dashboard. Mother probably waits tables or cleans houses or works as a seam-stress at a dry cleaners.

"I'll talk to you," I say.

"Thank you, Mr. Todd," Yolanda says, smiling. She sits ready with her pad and pen. "Just tell me your story."

"My story?"

"How you got here, when you first became ill."

"But Yolanda," I say, truly disappointed at having to disappoint her, "I haven't a fucking clue."

FOURTH

Florence says things go best when I am relaxed. When I close my eyes and breathe deeply. When I remember something good. Something happy. So I am trying. To remember. What came before. But I have run out of Christmases and fishing trips. That well was shallow and ran dry quickly. Almost as soon as it saw me coming to take a drink. But there are other things. They come in different flavors—some are whole, some are just bits and pieces, some are bright, shining flashes. And some of the most vivid are also the most joyous and exhilarating. And yes, I suppose I could use those. But I am ashamed of them. Because they are not my wedding day or the day Willa was born. They come easily, and when they do, I feel a rush of guilt and shame that my happiest memories were moments of pure narcissism. Before I knew that was a bad thing.

Los Angeles, 1974. The awards were over and all bets were off. The sweet smell of anticipation and optimism that filled the Dorothy Chandler Pavilion at the beginning of the Oscar ceremonies had turned fetid with the stench of disappointment and resentment the moment the few became winners and the many became bitter. And after sitting through three and a half hours of acceptance speeches for Best Achievement in Sound Editing, five full-length musical numbers to remind us of the nominees for Best Original Song, and the annual memorial montage, all three thousand attendees wanted to be first out the door.

But how long it took to exit the overcrowded, poorly designed auditorium was largely dependent on the relative weight you carried in the industry. Nominees in the documentary and animated short subject categories usually got out just after the janitorial staff.

"Jesus Christ, these people are savages," Ellen said, watching one A-list actress nearly decapitate little Tatum O'Neal as she leapfrogged over three rows of seats. We'd been caught in the bottleneck for twenty minutes when an enormous Inuit dressed impeccably in a Christian Dior tuxedo appeared—deus ex machina—in front of us.

"Mr. and Mrs. Todd?"

"Yes, and you are . . ."

"Hugo. Angela invites you to come with me."

Angela Glass was my client—brilliant, neurotic, innovative, visionary, high-maintenance. Actually, that description only narrowed the field of my client list by half. Physically, Angela was a tiny woman, but tonight she'd become a heavyweight. She'd won big. And I was her agent, which meant over the course of this three-hour ceremony, I had become the holder of the keys to the castle. In fact, I now held a lot of keys to a lot of castles. It was my turn to jump to the head of the line. And so the incensed crowd shut up and parted like the Red Sea when they saw the Inuit bodyguard escorting the newly minted A-list agent and his beautiful wife. We were whisked out of the building and into Angela's waiting double-stretch limousine.

Hugo opened the door for us and a huge white cloud erupted from the car. Inside the limo visibility was near zero. Ellen doubled over coughing. She grabbed my arm with one hand and bunched up her Valentino with the other to keep it from dragging on the asphalt while she hacked up a lung.

Shit. Water. "Hugo, could you—"

Suddenly, there was a miniature bottle of Perrier in my hand. Ellen downed it in one go, wiped her mouth with the back of her hand, and fixed her smudged mascara. She looked at me with a wide grin.

"I just got so totally high."

She slid her arm through mine. "Shall we?"

Someone—couldn't see who—slid over and made room for us. Then a pair of tanned, sinewy arms came shooting through the white cloud.

"Grey! Ellie!"

The rest of Angela dove across the lap of our movie's nonwinning Best Supporting Actor nominee. He was bent over, snorting lines when we got in, and didn't look up even when he slid over to make room for us. Ellen braced herself just as Angela threw an arm around each of our necks, squeezing us into her sweaty armpits.

"Thank God you're here! I couldn't do this without you two. Can you believe this *fucking night?* We fucking did it, Greyson."

"You did, Angela. You made a great picture. Against all odds."

"Bullshit. I'd be nowhere if it weren't for you and you know it. Right, Ellen? You know I'm right, Barry. He's not an agent, he's a fuckin' alchemist. You know I never wanted you for this picture, right?" she said to Diego Lazarus, who'd just won for Best Director.

"He convinced me. It was all Greyson. He said you were the only guy out there with balls big enough to do this script justice."

Diego put his hands together in prayer and bowed his head in humble Hollywood thanks. Angela turned back to Barry.

"Grey's a genius, Barry. You better fuckin' make him a partner before someone else does," Angela yelled into my boss's face.

"I'm not arguing, Ange," Barry said through tightly closed lips. A couple of seconds went by and we all watched Barry's chest expand and his eyes bug out. Then he let go and a blast of white smoke exploded out of his mouth.

"You did good, Greyson, real fuckin' good. We'll talk business tomorrow."

The Inuit bent down and stuck his head inside the car.

"Angela?"

She looked at him blankly. "Oh shit, of course. Grey, give Hugo your car keys."

"What? Give who . . ."

"Hugo. Give him your keys. He's going to drive your car home."

"Ange, that's not nec—"

"Oh cut the shit Grey. Come on, we're gonna be late to our own goddamn party."

Our goddamn party was being hosted by Sydney Freeman, president of production for New Vision Pictures and the guy who'd gotten us greenlit. I liked him, which of course made me instantly suspicious of him. I handed the keys to my brand new Jaguar to an Eskimo I'd known for twenty minutes, and before I could close the door, "Band on the Run" was blasting from the tape deck and the limo driver was screeching out of the parking lot.

The inside of the limo had the square footage of a small apartment. There were at least a dozen of us seated elbow to elbow.

Angela intercepted one of the lacquered trays that were being passed around.

"Line?" she offered as if she were holding a plate of pigs in a blanket.

The long, evenly spaced white stripes were elegant, almost graceful against the black background.

"Maybe later," I said.

"Ellen?"

"Thanks, not just yet, Ange."

"Something else? Pot? Ludes? A little Valium?"

No doubt she'd ingested them all before breakfast. Twice. And I was tempted. But I knew better. From experience. A couple of lines would lead to a half dozen more and a dozen more after that. After that, I wouldn't need the coke to get high. Once my switch had been flipped, I'd stay up for days, overflow with creative brilliance, share with my colleagues in the middle of the night, spend forty or fifty grand like it was nothing. Eventually, the inevitable would come. And how bad was a matter of how high I'd been and for how long. The higher the high, the bigger the crash. So, I passed on the coke. Ellen jumped in.

"How 'bout a drink?"

Thank God for my wife.

"Booze it is!" Angela clapped her hands, relieved we'd finally agreed to consume something at least vaguely mood-altering.

"Somebody get the Todds a couple of vodka tonics!" she screamed over the din.

Ellen smiled and squeezed my hand. I fell back against the leather seat and let my head loll from side to side. She leaned in, still grinning, and kissed me, and then laughed into my open mouth.

"Jesus," I said. "I guess I'm a little—"

"Shit, Grey, who wouldn't be?" She twisted around to face me. "They thanked you. They said your name. On national television."

"I know . . . I . . . know."

"God, I just—shit." Ellen leaned back next to me grinning.

"Yeah. Fuck. It's a little . . ."

"Of course it is."

An actual conversation would have been redundant. I was twenty-nine years old and had brought the agency the property, writer, director, cast, and producers that had just resulted in this year's Oscar for Best Picture, Best Director, Best Screenplay, Best Actor, and Best Supporting Actress. All the major players were our clients. I had handled the conflicting demands, pacified the volatile tempers, and anticipated and circumvented the irrational tantrums. The fundamental tools of agenting—lying, manipulation, and negotiation—usually acquired over decades—were skills that came naturally to me. It was what I'd done to survive growing up in my father's house.

But for once it hadn't hurt. For once it actually felt fucking brilliant.

The limo driver took the turn onto Laurel Canyon doing at least sixty and the huge car veered violently to the right, crushing Ellen and me under the combined weight of our seatmates. As we headed toward the opposite slide, I reached out and grabbed Ellen, hoping to keep her from falling into the nonwinning Best Supporting Actor whose only verbal contribution during the forty-five-minute ride had been to yell "Fucking cunt!" out the window as we passed a billboard advertising his ex-wife's new movie.

Unfortunately, I grabbed mostly Valentino and not very much Ellen, and with nothing to hold on to, she fell face-first into loser actor's crotch. The cocaine tray should have been there to keep her from coming into direct contact with his leather-clad balls, but during the badly executed turn, the tray had also gone flying, dumping the coke onto the limo floor.

Ellen wiggled around trying to push herself off him while the limo continued to speed along the windy road, coming precariously close to the canyon edge. A smile spread across the actor's face. He then put a gentle hand on the back of Ellen's neck and pushed her back down. That was it. I stood up as best I could and pulled Ellen off him.

"Eric, what the fuck do you think you're doing? That's my wife!"

He looked down at Ellen, then up at me. He shrugged.

"Way to go. She's fuckin' hot, man. Mind if I fuck her?"

I wanted to beat the living shit out of him. But I knew I should laugh it off and treat the guy like the poor, pathetic loser he was. Like the guy whose wife threatened to divorce him unless he went into rehab and then left him while he was in rehab.

So I decided to let Ellen make the call.

"What do you think?"

"About what?"

"Eric. Should I hit him? To defend your honor?"

"Don't be ridiculous, Greyson. It would be like kicking a three-legged dog."

"Cool, so can I fuck her?"

"Fuck who?" Angela asked, her head emerging from a thick cloud of smoke.

"Me," Ellen said. "Eric wants to fuck me."

"Oh I wouldn't do that if I were you," Angela said as if Ellen were seriously considering the possibility. "His dick is actually registered with the CDC."

"Fuck you, Angela," Eric spat at her. "You've had the clap so many times your pussy gets a standing ovation every time you spread your legs."

Angela burst out laughing and the Perrier she had in her mouth shot out onto Eric's leather pants.

"That was very funny, Eric, very good. But nice Jewish girls do not get the clap. And I am a nice Jewish girl. My pussy is completely disease-free."

Ellen looked at me and whined, "Are we there yet?"

I leaned over and looked out the window but all I could see was asphalt. The driver downshifted to gain some traction as the double-stretch resisted the climb up the ridiculously steep hill of Sydney's private driveway.

The limousine stopped at the top and, like couture-wearing, coke-snorting clowns, our impossibly large group tumbled out of the car. Dresses and breasts were adjusted, lipstick freshened, flies zipped. Angela stayed behind. She was going to make an entrance.

"Holy shit! Grey, Ellen, you've got to see this."

Angela was standing with her toes hanging over the edge of the canyon. Or part of it, anyway. The view was jaw-dropping. Three hundred and sixty degrees. All of L.A. Lights blinking, swimming pools glowing turquoise, headlights, taillights, skyscrapers, the ocean, the studios, the mountains. And behind us, Sydney Freeman's three-story glass house with wraparound balconies on every floor, where the most powerful and famous names in Hollywood stood smoking, drinking, and kissing each other's asses.

"Sydney's got balls, you gotta give him that," Angela said, looking the house over.

The place was Sydney's "fuck you" to God. Five years ago, the neighborhood had been decimated by an earthquake that registered over 6.5 on the Richter scale. Lots of people had run *from* the hills after that, buying in Beverly Hills, Brentwood, or the Palisades.

"I suppose that's what makes him a good executive," I said.

"No," Angela said, sniffing one armpit and then the other. "What makes him a good exec is that he's a greedy son of a bitch. Shall we?"

And linking one of her arms through mine and the other through Ellen's, she hauled us toward the house. A few yards from the door, she left us behind, hiked her strapless gown up over her nonexistent chest, put on her best shit-eating grin, and walked through the front door and into a standing ovation.

The living room was so crowded it was hard to find the bar. There were models and actresses—all of them under thirty, all of them willing to do whomever to get the next great part—draped across low white couches. Three actors I had scripts out to were sharing a joint on the balcony. I still hadn't found the bar.

I heard a splash and looked out the back window to where dozens of glowing white candles and gardenias had been floating in the enormous pool. Eric had just canonballed off the diving board. I turned around just in time to see him climb bare-assed out of the pool. Behind him—or rather unfortunately for the bartender, in front of him—was a bar. Thank God.

I walked past Eric en route to my martini.

"Put some clothes on, Eric."

"Don't be such a tight ass."

I leaned in so he could hear me. "Eric, as a representative of your agency, trust me, if you ever want to play a leading man you'll put your pants back on."

I found Ellen sitting on Freeman's kid's swing set, deep in conversation with Kate Davis, wife of A-list actor Victor Davis. Victor had grown up dirt poor and had married Kate when she was a secretary and he was painting houses. Since he had no tolerance for prima donna actors or for Hollywood bullshit in general,

I wondered why they'd shown up to the party at all. But I didn't dwell on it for long. I was too busy being happy that Ellen had found Kate and was making the most of it. Even if she didn't think of her burgeoning friendship that way. Lots of her friends just happened to be the wives and live-in girlfriends of my clients. In this town, there was no separation between work life and social life. There were no boundaries. Unless you were locked in your bathroom taking a crap, you had to be on. But sometimes, like tonight, it worked out nicely for me.

"There you are!" I kissed Ellen as if we'd been separated by oceans and wars and decades. She looked at me quizzically.

"Hi, I'm Greyson. The husband."

Kate laughed. "Kate Davis."

I handed Ellen the martini I'd spent the last half hour risking life and limb for. "I brought you a drink."

"Thanks, babe," she said and toasted me with her margarita, "but I got one. Two actually." And she and Kate giggled. I'd known a long time ago that I wanted Victor as a client. This was perfect. I saw intimate dinner parties in our near future. Maybe even a weekend away for the four of us—Santa Barbara, Palm Springs.

"Well, I will leave you two ladies to your fun." I discreetly gave Ellen a thumbs-up. She rolled her eyes. I wandered back into the house and upstairs, stopping to have my own ass kissed by at least a half dozen executives, directors, and actors who, before tonight, considered me to be somewhat of a pisher. It was a novel and altogether pleasurable experience.

When I got to the top of the stairs, I found myself staring at a pair of large, dark nipples. They were visible to everyone but the legally blind through the ultra-sheer dress worn by the woman to whom they were attached. I followed the nipples up the plunging peach-colored neckline, past the leathery, freckled chest, up the wiry neck to the heavily made-up face and frizzy blonde perm. It was possible at one time, a lot of booze and many tubes of Bain de Soleil ago, this woman had been pretty. She was swaying back and forth, but not, I realized, to the sweet strains of Gordon Lightfoot's "Sundown." She was just having trouble standing.

"Hi there, any idea where Sydney keeps his upstairs bathrooms?" I asked from the top stair.

"Sure do, sweetheart," she slurred and then pitched forward, planting her hands on my shoulders.

I flailed and teetered but it was useless. With a martini in one hand and nothing behind me, I went down with her. Fortunately, it was only two small, white shag-carpeted stairs down to the next landing. She landed on top of me. And stayed there for far too long. She smelled like a combination of Chanel No. 5, rumaki, and day-old cigarette butts. And an entire bottle of Dom.

"I was just on my way," she whispered an inch from my face. "Follow me and we can go together."

And suddenly I felt a hand cupping my balls. Instantly, I rolled out from under her and then—chivalrously, I thought, considering—offered her my hand and helped her up.

"Thanks, but you can go first. Need my privacy." I picked the carpet fuzz off the olives from my spilled martini and tossed them into my mouth. "Pee fright."

"Aw, the poor wittle guy," she said, bending over and talking into my crotch.

I pulled her up by the shoulders and propped her up against the closest wall.

"Hey, where're you going?" She stuck out her bottom lip.

"I don't believe you have any intention of showing me where the john is. I'm betting you don't even know yourself. I'm striking out on my own."

"Fuck load you know." Suddenly, Nipples was no longer a happy drunk. "I know this fucking house like the back of my fucking hand."

She spit out the words like she was trying to physically expel the resentment and bitterness that produced them. And all of a sudden I recognized her. Nipples was Theodora (a.k.a. Teddi) Bacon. Fifteen years ago she'd been an up-and-coming young actress whose career had peaked and then quickly plateaued when she devoted herself to playing the part of Sydney's longtime mistress for nearly a decade. After putting in all those years, she naturally expected to become the second Mrs. Freeman just as soon as Sydney's divorce came through.

Instead, she found her presence requested at the marriage of Sydney to his current wife, Nikki, an up-and-coming young actress fifteen years her junior.

By way of a consolation prize, Sydney bought Teddi a condo in the Valley and got her a part playing the mother in one of the *Herbie* movies. Shortly thereafter, Sydney built the house Teddi had helped him design for the two of them on the land Teddi helped him pick out back when they were together. As dictated by the rules of the game, they all agreed to be friends. As if Teddi had a choice.

"You're right," I said, "I don't know shit." I put my arm around her waist and she tentatively let go of the wall. "Why don't you give me the tour?"

She smiled and looked up at me. "Should I start with the bathroom?"

I steered her down a hallway, opening doors, looking for a bed. "Actually, I was thinking maybe someplace you could lie down for a while might not be a bad idea."

"Are you trying to get into my pants, young man?"

My eyes dropped down past her nipples. "You're not wearing any pants, Teddi."

She attempted a girlish giggle. "You can tell?"

Then she took an unsteady step back and studied my face. "Do we know each other?"

"We do now."

"I mean from before, Mr. Smarty Pants. How do you know my name?"

Shit, I didn't want her to know I knew she was infamous for being humiliated.

"You told me."

"I did? Did you tell me yours?"

I pretended to think for a moment.

"How rude of me. Greyson. Todd. It's a pleasure."

We continued down the hallway.

"So are you in the business, Greyson Todd?"

"It's an Oscar party. Is anyone here not?"

"Don't be a smart ass."

"I'm an agent. I can't help it."

"Really. An agent? Represent anyone big?"

"I do okay."

"You know, I might be able to help you."

"Help me?"

"Meet people. Make contacts. I know a lot of major players."

"That's very generous of you, Teddi."

We reached the end of the hallway and I pushed open the double doors of what was obviously the master suite. The interior decorator had been given free reign in here and the results were mixed. Immediately upon crossing the threshold, Teddi and I were attacked by a monstrous light fixture. Its chrome neck grew directly out of the ceiling, and attached to its bulbous head were dozens of bouncing tentacles—metal springs of varying lengths—each of which had a glowing white probe on the end. There was a matching zebra-skin love seat and armchair in the sitting area, and a black-and-white horse from an old carousel had been installed in the ceiling and floor, stirrups and reins still attached.

"Can you believe this shit?" Teddi teetered as she leaned in to whisper in my ear. "Mrs. Nikki fucking Freeman wouldn't know good taste if it bit her in that tight little aerobicized ass of hers."

"Oh look, Teddi, the bed!"

The bathroom door opened and two young women came out giggling. Nipples went in. And took fuckin' forever. By the time my turn came around, I had to pee so badly I was already unzipping my pants as I walked into the enormous black-marble john. So it was a shock to find the bathroom occupied.

"Shit, I'm sorry . . . I thought . . ."

The man was bent over the marble counter snorting huge lines of coke through a gold straw. Nearby was another pile that looked like the top of Mount Fuji.

"Don't be sorry. I mean I guess this is the designated coke bathroom, but I think it was originally intended as a place for people to pee . . . and, you know, go number two."

I couldn't see her—she must have been behind the privacy wall hiding the toilet and bidet—but I knew the voice. Raspy, tough, with a trace of Brooklyn in it. But young. Kind of like a prepubescent hit man. With strep throat.

It belonged to Christie Donovan, Academy Award-winning twelve-year-old actress. Apparently she was hanging out, perched on a toilet lid in Sydney Freeman's bathroom while her daddy/manager snorted cocaine. Three years ago, Mick Donovan and his model-actress-wife Kathryn had waged an ugly and very public battle for custody of Christie. Mick and his lawyer pulled out all the stops and trumped up enough evidence to have Kathryn declared an unfit mother. After that, it wasn't long before she became what he accused her of being but had never been before. A drunk. A high-priced whore. A junkie. So Mick was the good parent. Poor fuckin' kid.

Yes, he was scum. But I happened to have a script that was perfect for her. I turned and locked the bathroom door. My bladder could wait.

"Mick Donovan, right?" I asked, sticking my hand out before Christie's daddy could stick the straw up his nose again. "I'm Greyson Todd. With Franklin Morton."

He returned my handshake limply. "Yeah?"

"Touchdown!" A pile of magazines—Architectural Digest, Variety, Esquire—slid across the marble floor from behind the wall. Then Christie appeared, waving what looked like a calculator over her head.

Dressed in a perfectly fitted, miniature tuxedo complete with cumberbund and French cuffs.

"Mr. Todd, if I may, congratulations on your success this evening," she said, extending her hand. Her cufflinks were monogrammed.

I looked over my shoulder to see if she had an audience—why she'd suddenly become a tiny adult. But it was just me.

"Uh . . . thanks. Thanks, Christie. Great outfit. I'm guessing it's not off-the-rack."

"I have a spectacular tailor. Very old school. I'll give you his number."

"Why not? Hey, what is that?" I pointed to the calculator thing.

"This? Oh, it's just a game."

"Can you show me how it works?"

It didn't take long before she was chattering away. She'd probably been bored out of her mind for hours, desperate to engage in anything that didn't have to do with fucking or drugs.

". . . So this one's *Electronic Football*. I also have *Electronic Auto Race*. They're not even gonna be on the market till next year but Mattel wanted to create a buzz so they gave them to a few kid actors. Can you believe how small it is?"

Mick picked up a razor blade and concentrated on chopping the coke as if he were defusing a bomb.

Christie looked at him and quickly looked away. "Hey, so you had a pretty kick-ass night." With tremendous effort, she hoisted herself up on the bathroom counter. "How does that feel? To suddenly become hot shit. It's weird, right?"

"Oh, I don't know about that. I think if you're fortunate enough to have your career go a certain way—"

"Bullshit."

"Bullshit?"

"Yeah. Bullshit," she said, staring me down. "It's weird for anyone it happens to. Weirder for me because I'm a kid. But if it changes your life, that's weird. And if you say it's not, you're lying."

We continued to stare at each other.

"You're right."

She arched one eyebrow at me. I had seen that look with those ice-cold blue eyes in more than one closeup. It was very persuasive.

"Okay, fine. It's weird. Very fuckin' weird."

She grinned. Then she turned her eyelids inside out, stretched her mouth apart with her thumbs, and touched the tip of her tongue to her chin.

"Lovely, Christie. Real leading lady material."

We both looked up when we heard pissing. Very loud, very sustained pissing. "Ugh, that's disgusting, Daddy."

"Where the hell else do you want me to piss?" he barked.

I had forgotten how badly I had to go. Until now. My work here wasn't nearly done. Maybe if I could talk to Christie alone first. Get her out of here and make my pitch. Mick turned around, zipped, and adjusted himself. Then he offered me the gold straw.

"Help yourself, man. Celebrate. Apparently you're hot shit."

"Thanks. I'm cool for now."

"Okay, then what the fuck are you doing in here? We're not looking for representation."

"I'm not trying to steal Christie from ICM. Although frankly I could do a lot better for her than the limited range of opportunities Jeff's been—but that's a different conversation."

Christie shook her finger at me and smiled. "You're a very bad man."

"Seriously, Mick, I didn't come here with an agenda tonight. But I'm representing this truly exceptional script—and the female lead—Christie was made to play this part."

"I hear that once a week," Mick said, opening a bottle of prescription pills.

It was a testament to Christie's talent that this moron hadn't ruined her career.

"You've never heard it from me and you've never heard it about a Raymond Scotto project. Angela Glass is producing."

Mick popped some little pink pills in his mouth and stuck his mouth under the running faucet. He stood up and wiped his mouth with a guest towel.

"Mick, Jesus, she won Best Picture tonight for Chrissake."

"I know. And no."

"What? Dad, Raymond Scotto."

"I've heard about this script. We're not interested."

"Why? What's it about?"

"It's a career-making role, Mick," I said, "a serious part. She can do this and you know how sensitive Raymond will be with her—with the material. He adapted the book himself. Just give it a read."

Christie jumped off the counter and tugged on my tux jacket.

"What. Is. It. About?"

I started to answer. "It's this completely gripping story about a young girl and a—"

But Mick jumped in. "It's about a ten-year-old heroin addict and a psycho Vietnam vet."

"It's about loneliness and isolation—two outsiders. And she's thirteen."

"Who's playing the guy?" Christie asked.

"It's out to Pacino. Hoffman, De Niro, and Jeff Bridges are also possibilities. But that is all off the record."

Christie nodded. "Interesting. I want to read it."

"Great, I'll get it over to—"

"Don't waste her fuckin' time." Mick picked up the razor blade again.

Christie raised the football game in the air, about to throw it against the wall next to Mick. Then she stopped and gently put it down on the counter.

"Don't listen to him," Christie said calmly. "He gets very grouchy when he does too much coke. Send the script to the house. I'll read it after school tomorrow."

A couple of barely dressed models somehow managed to unlock the door and push their way in. The bathroom was suddenly very crowded. "Awesome," one said, as she bent over Mount Fuji and snorted while the second one held her friend's long blonde hair out of the way.

"Help yourselves, ladies." Suddenly Mick had become much more generous.

"But Daddy . . ." Christie pulled at the sleeve that held the arm attached to the hand holding the razor blade. "You promised we could find some food. I'm starving."

Mick grabbed her by the arm and spoke to her through clenched teeth. "This is business. These are potential clients—"

"Why don't I take Christie downstairs to the buffet?" I said, stepping between them. "You come meet us there when you've wrapped up your work thing here."

Mick was already face-down in the coke again. "Fine, sure," he said, without looking up.

Christie and I ate burgers and fries and shakes made to order. I took off my shoes and socks and we ate sitting with our feet dangling in Sydney's brightly lit pool.

"Is this how you usually woo your clients?" she asked.

"Okay, no, and since when did twelve-year-olds start using the word 'woo' in casual conversation? And by the way, I'm not wooing you as a client. Just for this one script. Though I do think we'd make a fabulous team."

"So why are you being so nice to me?" she asked. "You're not some creepy pervert, are you?"

"No, I'm not some creepy pervert." I cleared my throat and looked off across the pool into the anonymous black-tie crowd. "You and I have more in common than you might imagine."

Christie looked at me, tilting her head from one side to the other. "Hmmm. Well, you're not an Oscar-winning female child actress," she said coyly.

I managed half a smile. Still avoiding her eyes.

"As far as I know there's only one other thing I'm famous for," she said, putting her burger down.

I didn't need to ask and she didn't need to answer. She stared down into the pool and made figure eights in the water with her feet.

"So your father's a fucking asshole too?" she asked, quietly.

"I—uh—I don't think he meant to be . . . means to be," I said. And it was probably the nicest thing I'd said about Pop in years.

"But that doesn't really change things, does it?" she asked.

I forced myself to look at her. "No. It is what it is. Just don't . . ."

"What?"

"It's none of my business, but—"

"You're an agent. I thought it was your business to make everything your business."

"Funny."

"Well, I should get home. School night." She swung her legs out of the water. I stood and helped her up.

"Don't waste your time trying to please him. He'll disappoint you," I said before letting go of her hand. "Over and over."

She looked at me with a sad smile. "And I deserve better."

"Yes. Much, much better."

"Sound advice, Mr. Todd." She stuffed her socks in her pockets and put her shoes on.

"Should I get . . . your father?" I asked.

"You're kidding, right? Like I'd get in a car with him behind the wheel. I have a driver. It was a pleasure meeting you, Greyson," she said, extending her hand. "I'll look for that script tomorrow."

I took the pale little thing and shook it. Her grip was exceptionally firm. I don't know why I was surprised. As I watched her seek out Sydney and politely say her good-nights with more grace and good manners than most of the guests in attendance, I had no idea what all of this would do to her later in life, but I couldn't help wishing that I had been as strong at such a young age.

All I remember from that time is the weakness and the naïveté. And the fear. The resentment came later.

New York, 1994. "Greyson, Mr. Todd, *shhh,* it's okay."

I wake up in the middle of the night to see Frankie standing over me. "You were having a nightmare."

I touch my face. It's wet and there is a dark, damp circle on my pillow. "Was I—?"

"Crying?" Frankie nods in a gay, sympathetic, nurse-like way that couldn't be more humiliating, unless perhaps I had actually wet the bed.

"But I don't remember anything," I say, genuinely baffled. "Nothing."

Frankie nods his gay, nursie nod again. "It's very common. We don't really know why. The ECT just seems to stir things up."

I lay on my pillow, nodding, knowing he doesn't know fuck all about what he is saying but appreciating his concern nonetheless.

"The important thing for you to know is that it's perfectly normal. Now how about a milligram of Ativan so you can get back to sleep?"

"Two?" I ask

He clucks his gay, nursie tongue at me. "One and a half."

"Deal," I say and turn my pillow over, tear side down.

FIFTH

"Okay, hon, ready for another little trip?" Florence whispers in my ear. Her breath is a mix of sour hospital coffee and Licorice Nibs.

"Where to?" I say with quiet menace. Just the way the character in the movie did.

"Someplace nice."

"Florence, Flor . . . have you ever seen the movie?"

"What movie's that, hon?"

"Where To?"

"Oh sure, the little heroin addict girl and the disturbed Vietnam veteran. It's still on cable every once in a while. Now I need you to count backwards from a hundred."

"The whole point of the movie is that—" and then the warm sensation is in my chest and stomach and arms. I stare into Florence's eyes, refusing to give in. Willing them open.

"Come on, hon. Quick trip. Someplace nice." My eyes close without my permission. I twitch slightly. Just a tiny myoclonic jerk—the kind babies have in their sleep. That sleep-induced feeling of falling left over from when we were monkeys and hung from trees by our tails.

I am under before I can tell Florence that the point is that there is no someplace nice. There's just the place. And then the next place and the next. And the motion in between.

The Negev, 1987. The road snakes back and forth along the wall of
the giant crater without, it seems, any particular goal in mind.
One switchback brings me and my rented Peugeot toward the top
of Mitzpe Ramon—which in Hebrew translates to something like
"huge fuckin' hole in the ground." The next leads me down a steep
hill into the belly of the beast—splayed open, gasping and arid. Yet
a third gives me an unobstructed view of the rusted-out cars that
lie at odd angles at the bottom of the canyon. The Israeli Ministry
of Transport hasn't bothered to install guardrails on this desolate
desert road. Or reflectors. Obviously, the Israeli MOT believes that
God will provide.

No lights, no guardrails, no people—just an endless expanse of
purple-brown rock. This road, this desert seems to go on forever. Nice
place, but I wouldn't want to visit. Occasionally a little puff of sand
rises suddenly and swirls like a miniature tornado. Then after a minute it collapses and dies. At least the Sahara, with its great drifting
dunes, shape-shifts overnight. There I would wake up with a view
that resembled the Great Pyramids, and by happy hour the following evening I'd be staring at the back of an impossibly sexy woman,
sprawled languidly on her side, the curve of her lower back smiling
at me sweetly, her hips and ass jutting out into the desert. I haven't
been to the Gobi, but in the interest of fairness I'll have to go. For
comparison's sake.

Every ten kilometers or so, there is a yellow sign. CAMEL CROSSING,
it says, in Hebrew and in Arabic and in English. Under a picture of a

camel. Every ten kilometers, another sign. But so far, no camel. Just more desert. More nothing.

The friendly woman at the air-conditioned visitors' center back in Avdat—a ruin on the spice route, which once did very well in the frankincense and myrrh business—told me this drive was not to be missed. I believed her because she spoke English and because the bathrooms in the visitors' center were clean and because she used a highlighter on the map when she showed me the route. Next time I'm in Avdat, I'll have to kick her ass.

My rental car and I finally reach the bottom of the crater, and, as if it were possible, it is even less than I expected. I get out of the car to look around and the heat sucks the air out of my lungs. Chalky rocks give off prodigious amounts of dust punctuated by dry, brown beds of dirt out of which sprout sad, withered growth that aspires to be vegetation. Who the fuck would fight over land like this?

The wind is blowing, which should be a relief, but here just means sand. A lot of it. In your eyes. I can't see shit. But I can hear. It sounds like a shriek, only not human. Then something nudges me. In the crotch.

"What the fuck?"

I take a step back and bump into the car. It keeps coming. I close my eyes against the blowing sand and swat blindly at whatever it is. I pray they don't have coyotes in Israel. I feel fur and then a warm, wet tongue and then it bites me. Hard.

"FUCK!"

The wind and sand stop blowing and I see my attacker. A goat. And he has backup. Two others flanking him. They are nibbling at desiccated shrubbery but they clearly have his back. I look down at my hand, which is dripping blood. I seriously doubt these goats have been properly vaccinated.

The girl who comes over the rocky hill in the distance makes me forget about the rabies I may have contracted. She almost makes me forget about the desert. Except that she *is* the desert. She is almost biblical. In a central casting kind of way. Filmy fuchsia cloth winds around her waist and covers her legs like a sarong. The rest of her, including her head and most of her face, is covered in thin black fabric. In one hand she holds a tall, gnarled staff.

Her willowy silhouette standing there, backlit on the top of that hill. I couldn't have designed the shot better if I'd hired David Lean.

And then come her goats. At least a dozen of them. And my perfect Bedouin princess opens her mouth and makes a noise somewhere between a yodel and a gag and starts knocking the goats in their knees with her staff and they start running straight at me.

She takes her time coming down the hill. From ten feet away I can see her face is as beautiful as the rest of her. Dark-brown skin, huge copper eyes, long eyelashes, full lips, and dark hands with long fingers and pink palms. She walks up to me without hesitation, takes my wounded hand in hers, and gives the guilty goat a nasty whack with her staff. Then she pulls a canteen from underneath the folds of her black scarf and pours a little pool of water onto my wound. The blood washes away and we can see where the goat teeth have punctured my skin. After that, the beautiful Bedouin girl makes a great guttural hacking noise in the back of her throat and launches a giant loogey onto my open wound. She massages it into my hand and I feel slightly light-headed. Until she reaches down and lifts the bottom of her skirt over her knees and halfway up her surprisingly muscular brown thighs, bending her head so she can catch the hem in her teeth and make a rip in the sheer fabric. She tears off a strip of fuchsia and ties it around my slimy, spit-soaked goat wound.

Then she speaks to me quickly in some language that may be Arabic. Or not.

"English," I say. "Sorry."

She rolls her eyes, walks around to the passenger side of my car and gets in. I stand there like an idiot until she honks the horn several times. I get in.

Drive, you moron, she gestures.

I pull onto the road slowly and the goats fall into line behind us. I point out the back window, smiling. She rolls her eyes again.

Bedouins are such cynics.

We putter along the main road for a while until, just as we reach another camel crossing sign, the girl grabs the steering wheel and turns us onto a dirt road that eventually disappears under an arch created by two enormous boulders. Not a road you'd find on any map. The goats follow. And, without warning, a camel.

Clearly not the brightest of species, the thing tries to stick its head into my closed window. I see a flash of teeth—uglier, yellower, and more crooked than I would've thought possible—and then the window is smeared with camel spit.

I finally understand the need for all the signs.

Obviously, every camel in Israel lives in this Bedouin camp. There must be hundreds of them—grazing in the wadi (which in Hebrew translates to something like "huge fuckin' patch of dirt"), standing crammed in barbed-wire pens, and wandering freely, crapping at the entrance to sleeping tents and near cooking fires. Goats, on the other hand? My girl seems to have the exclusive. I can't help wondering, where's the money in camels? Goats I get. Goat's milk, goat cheese. But even in this godforsaken place I can't see camel dairy products flying off the shelves.

I slam on the brakes when one particularly ugly beast steps in front of the car. Through the windshield all I can see are four long, knobby-kneed legs. And the long, slow string of camel saliva that drips from above onto the hood of the car. My girl throws all ninety-nine pounds of herself over the gearshift and leans on the horn, and our roadblock moves off with all the speed of a hermit crab. She speaks to me in that language again and points to an area off to the left, which I assume is the designated parking area. So I park.

I suppose there is a certain *Lawrence of Arabia*-ness to this Bedouin settlement. If you can ignore the burning piles of garbage, ancient school bus, and swing set sitting on squares of dingy Astroturf held together with duct tape. Naked and half-naked children run around the makeshift playground kicking a soccer ball. Women sit on rugs inside the tents nursing babies and drinking tea. Some weave rugs on huge homemade looms. The yarn has been dyed vivid shades of pink, green, blue, and orange, and I wonder where the hell they found the materials to come up with anything other than brown. Old men smoke water pipes and play some kind of game with dice.

The girl pulls me into one of the bigger tents. Like the others, it is constructed somewhat haphazardly mostly out of the black tent's original material but reinforced and repaired with whatever works. This one has corrugated aluminum on one side. My shepherdess consults briefly with a woman who's been winding skeins of wool. She is maybe forty-five and missing a couple of teeth, but not as many as the camel. The woman smiles at me. "So, you want real Bedouin experience?"

I obviously look as confused as I am.

"Real Bedouin experience. Includes tour of camp, tea with real Bedouin family, and camel ride. Sixty shekels."

I look over at my girl and shake my finger at her. "What's her name?" I ask.

"This one? She is Neela, my granddaughter."

"I'm happy to give you the sixty shekels, but could you tell Neela that since it was her goat that bit me, I think the least she can do is invite me to tea herself."

Neela's grandmother starts yammering away at her.

"Yeah, yeah. Fine," Neela says and rolls her eyes.

Other than yelling at me to take off my shoes when I start to enter her dusty tent, Neela says nothing as she prepares our tea. I sit on the rug and watch her, wondering what I have done to piss her off. It is almost as if we are married.

She moves around the tent at hyper speed, stooping, bending, squatting, opening jars and canisters and boxes of exotic-smelling plants, flowers, and spices, tossing them into a big copper kettle. When she's done, she reaches her hand down her shirt, pulls out a key, and goes marching out of the tent, kettle in hand. I watch her unlock the metal cage around the faucet the Israelis have provided— the only source of water in this village they have forced these people to call home.

Neela boils the tea on one of the smoldering cooking fires, and when I see her head back to the tent, I hurry back to my place on the rug. She pours tea into tall glasses filled with crushed mint leaves and slips the glasses into brass holders. When she walks toward me, I think she is going to hand me a glass of tea—or pour it on me. Instead, she lowers herself into my lap and brings her lips together, gently blowing on the tea to cool it. With her other hand, she reaches up and unwinds the black scarf from her head and then her shoulders until it falls away completely. Underneath she is wearing a thin white tank top. It has a picture of Madonna and the words "Material Girl" written on it.

She is stunning. And younger than I had imagined. However young that was. She takes a sip of the tea, leans forward, and, as she kisses me, lets the hot, sweet tea run into my mouth and follows it with her tongue. I forget hot and dry and thirsty. There is only warm, sweet, wet. The tea has long since been swallowed, so it must be her taste. Or some alchemical combination of the two. Does it matter? The tip of her tongue runs across the roof of my mouth. And then I realize, it does.

Reluctantly, almost painfully, I disengage my mouth from hers just enough so I can use it for speaking. "I wasn't expecting . . . I was going to give you the money. You don't have to. . ."

"I don't *have* to do anything," she says, the corners of her mouth turning up almost imperceptibly—less a smile than a parenthetical.

She lifts her "Material Girl" tank top over her head and lies back against a pile of rolled-up rugs. I have never seen skin the color of hers. She is cinnamon and cocoa and bittersweet chocolate. And suddenly I am ravenous. Neela reaches her arm out, dips her finger into my tea and then slips it into my mouth. The tea is cooler and even more fragrant than before.

Then she takes the glass from my hand, tilts her head back, and lets a tiny trickle of liquid pour from the glass. The drops land on her exposed throat and run down, pooling in the hollows on either side of her clavicles. I stare mesmerized, watching as the perfect stream runs between her perfect breasts and collects in her belly button before continuing on its course.

"Drink your tea," she says.

I sit up and my heart is racing. My mouth is dry. The thin cotton mattress on which I've been sleeping and the muslin sheet that covers me are cold and damp. I shiver in spite of the stifling heat. At first I can't remember where I am. Only fragments of a dream. Willa. And a gun. And I am running. Trying to stop something terrible from happening. Running but getting nowhere. I have a pounding headache.

My eyes adjust to the darkness. I remember that I am in Neela's tent. But Neela is gone. So are my Patek Philippe watch and my wallet. The little snake charmer has been thoughtful enough to leave me my passport. My luggage is in the car, so I put on the same dusty, sweaty clothes I wore yesterday. I tentatively stick my head outside the tent, and though I have no idea what time it is, I can tell by where the sun is in the sky that I have slept through most of the day.

Between the hallucinogenic dreams I had last night and the Rip Van Winkle experience I'm having now, it's becoming more and more obvious there was more than tea in my tea. As I walk toward my car, I notice that the camp is much quieter. The pickup trucks are gone. The bus is gone. The goats are gone. My car and luggage are gone. There are still children playing on the Astroturf and old men smoking hookahs in a tent. I jog over to the men and feel a lead weight land on my head with each step.

"Neela?" I ask vaguely, stupidly.

A few of the old men turn to me for a moment and then go back to their game of dice

"Neela? My car? Where is my car?" Now I am yelling.

Something registers with one of them. He reaches out his hand and I help him up. He hobbles over to Neela's tent, disappears behind it, and is gone so long I think he too has deserted me. But then I hear yelling—in Arabic. Or something. And he comes out leading a recalcitrant, fully saddled camel.

"Car," he says, grinning. "Your car."

Because Neela is not without a heart. She has left me transportation.

I ride the thing to the nearest camel crossing sign and wait for the next lonely bastard to come through. This, I think, is the real Bedouin experience.

Seduced, screwed, conned, robbed, and left sitting on a camel. Neela would have made a terrific agent—in a non-Bedouin setting. She and I have a lot in common, but to her I am no different from any other rich Jew. Like those rich, entitled Hillcrest Country Club Jews were to me. And, absurd as it may sound, that is a revelation. Because

I never saw myself as anything but being on her side. Growing up on the outside. Wanting in.

Beverly Hills, 1961. December was when all the juniors had their preliminary college counseling meetings—the ones where the guidance counselor, Mrs. Di Carlo, told students like Stacy Aronson she should be aiming for, say, Tarzana Junior College rather than Harvard. I was not looking forward to mine.

Nine thirty and already it must have been ninety-five degrees in Di Carlo's office. Her beige bra straps were sticking out from under her sleeveless lime-green blouse. There were dark half-moons of sweat under her armpits and her short copper curls sat like coiled Slinkies, plastered to her scalp.

Every couple of winters, without warning, a vengeful current of air called the Santa Anas came rushing through the desert, dumped a load of scorching heat on L.A., and took off. For days on end there was just heat. Pure and unrelenting.

"You have a real shot at Stanford, Greyson," she was saying. "And Yale isn't out of the question."

I knew I shouldn't stare, but I was fascinated by the way the loose, wrinkled flesh under her arm undulated as she fanned herself with the brochure from Mills College. She looked down at my file.

"Your grades are stellar. You're active in student government. You've done a little community service work." Her finger tapped the manila folder. "You might want to take up a sport, though," she said. She looked up and studied me. "You're tall," she said. "How about basketball?"

I was a lousy athlete. The only varsity team I stood a chance of making was debate. "Yeah, great idea," I said, getting up to leave. "Well, I've got math now, so . . ."

"Greyson, college admissions committees also tend to be impressed by students who've had valuable work experience. If you'd like, I could speak to some of our alumni . . ."

"Uh, yeah, thanks. I'll think about it and let you know, okay?"

"Alright, dear," she said, "but remember, he who hesitates is lost."

"I'll remember."

August Van Gilder was not an alumnus of Beverly High. He was the man who owned the Chevron station at the corner of Robertson and Third. I stood across the street for a while just watching the petroleum fumes hang in the sweltering air around the station as if they were afraid to wander too far from their home. The glare from the sun beating down on the shiny black patches was almost blinding. Cars had been dripping motor oil in the same spots on the same asphalt since 1947 when the station opened.

A woman rushed out of the station's ladies' room with a sour look on her face. She held the door open with the tip of one finger and waited impatiently as a little girl wandered out. The woman quickly yanked her finger away. The metal door must have been hot. Then she spit on her finger and wiped it on a handkerchief. Hot and dirty.

The woman pulled the little girl toward a light-blue Eldorado convertible. A man, as pleasant-looking as she was sour-faced, waited in the driver's seat. A boy—I couldn't really tell how old—eight, ten, twelve—sat in the back, his face buried in a Green Hornet comic book.

I took a deep breath and choked on the gas fumes. How long had I been standing there? Five minutes? Twenty? A man came out of the ladies' room carrying a suitcase. He cut across the black asphalt to the city bus stop and sat down on the bench.

Both the male and female patrons who stopped here to use the facilities had to use the ladies' room. The toilet in the men's had been clogged for years. Even if the proprietor of the Chevron, Mr. August Van Gilder, made an effort to keep the restroom clean (and quite obviously, it wasn't a priority), two hundred and fifty people probably used that toilet in the course of one business day. And like the man with the suitcase, probably half those people didn't even buy any gas.

I'd been one of those freeloading Chevron-toilet-users enough times to know. Not that I went out of my way to relieve myself here. A person only took a leak at the Chevron out of sheer desperation. Mr. Van Gilder must have thought his mechanics had more important things to do than mop up urine and refill the paper towel dispenser all day. But that would be my job now. Probably not what Di Carlo meant by valuable work experience.

I filled my lungs with another airless breath and forced myself to walk toward the body shop. There was no door on the dingy little office inside. A guy in his twenties with an Adam's apple that made him look like he'd swallowed a hamster stood behind the counter. He was sifting through a little metal box filled with dirty, dog-eared index cards. A rusty old fan was blowing behind him. It wasn't doing much, just rustling the invoices tacked to the bulletin board next to him. An orange rag covered in grease hung out of the pocket of his mechanic's jumpsuit. I rested my hands on the counter and noticed how clean my fingernails were.

The guy—Wes, according to his jumpsuit—did not look up. I opened my mouth to speak but Wes held up his hand to stop me. Wes continued to alphabetize. He'd put "Scott, Philip" before "Schwartz, Dave." I stood there, obediently. I would be lower down the food chain than Wes. Wes, the mechanic with the freakish Adam's apple who couldn't alphabetize.

Maybe I'd just tell Wes to go screw himself, I thought. I'd tell August Van Gilder, "Thank you very much but I've been elected junior class representative to the Beverly Hills High Student Council. And between that and tutoring those foster kids, Mr. Van Gilder, I'm just not going to have time to pump your goddamn gas and clean your goddamn ladies' room. You see Mr. Van Gilder, I have a real shot at Stanford. And Yale's not out of the question."

Wes finally looked up at me.

"I have an appointment with Mr. Van Gilder," I said.

My interview went well. Van Gilder hired me on the spot.

I walked around back to the ladies' room and changed into my jumpsuit.

On the way home, crossing the hot black asphalt at the intersection of Doheny and Olympic, I pretended I was walking across some snow-covered quad. I imagined I was surrounded by Gothic buildings and girls in Fair Isle sweaters.

I didn't see the Mercedes turn into the crosswalk in front of me. The guy driving didn't care that I had the right of way. He leaned on his horn, stuck his head out his window and yelled at me, "Stupid little pisher!"

I flipped him off, but it was too late. He was long gone. My fantasy had gone south too. Best-case scenario: I'd get a free ride to UCLA, live at home, and work at the Chevron. Eventually, I guess you got used to the fumes.

New York, 1994. I don't remember coming back from shock this morning. I know it must have happened. I must have awakened, heavy-headed and confused and no doubt nauseous in the ECT suite. That's what they call it—a suite. Someone in the hospital's PR department must have spent quite a while paging through a thesaurus in search of that gem. That euphemism. There are no expensive little soaps in the ECT suite; no minibar stocked with Stoli and Perugina chocolate and six-dollar cans of Coke. I've spent a lot of time in hotel suites over the last decade, but not one of them had a bed made up with rubber sheets or came with an in-room defibrillator or a guy in the next bed who thought he was Jesus.

I wonder if I am the only ECT patient who's noticed. I've come to realize lately that if you're really crazy most people assume you're also really stupid. They either speak to you in a quiet, slow voice as if speaking to a retarded child or enunciate and yell as if addressing a hard-of-hearing, demented senior. Either way, I resent it. True, I can't always remember who's president when they ask me after I wake up in the suite. Or what day it is. Or the name of my doctor. But is that really a fair assessment of my mental acuity? I don't think so.

I think that when I have the energy I will put a slip of paper into the suggestion box at the nurse's station. I will suggest they change the word "suite" to "lab" or "chamber" or "electric fun house." Just to let them know I know.

Somehow I got from there to here. My room, my bed. My head feels dull and thick—like the time I tripped on bad mushrooms in Yemen. Only, then, I awakened next to a naked girl. I can't tell you who's president, but I remember every detail of that blow job like it was yesterday.

I lie back on my Styrofoam pillow enjoying the memory, recalling the fine points that might be gone tomorrow. Heat, sweat, scent. I feel myself getting hard and try to locate my dick inside the complicated folds of the hospital gown and the oversized paper pajama bottoms

I'm required to wear to ECT. You'd think the scavenger hunt would be enough to lower my flag, but if anything, I've gone from half-mast to full. I don't know, maybe it's the residual electricity floating through my bloodstream, but ECT always makes me horny. So much so that I've taken to hoarding tubes of the good lotion and hiding them in my night table. I have a feeling Milton, the Jamaican orderly in charge of the linen cart, knows what I'm up to. Lately he's been handing me two or three tubes at a time and winking at me. Milton knows a man has his needs. Even when he's locked up having his brain lit up like a Christmas tree three times a week.

I have managed to pull the enormous tent-like pants off and toss them onto the floor along with the sheet and blanket and have hiked the hospital gown up onto my chest. I am treating myself to an expert double-fisted hand job.

I am in Yemen, in Thailand, in Santiago. I am remembering—girls with skin the color of coffee, of saffron, of cinnamon. I am remembering how they smelled and tasted and felt as my dick slips and slides up through my left hand and circles down through my right in an endlessly delicious loop.

And then there is a sharp knock at the door, followed, without pause, by the swift banging of the door opening against the opposite wall. And then Milton is backing into my room, pulling a wheelchair.

"Mr. Greyson Todd, please to be meeting Mr. Tyrone Washington, your new roommate," he says before he turns around. And when he does, turning the chair with him, he is rather stunned by what he finds. The kid in the chair—tall, skinny, black, catatonic with depression—does not even register what's in front of him. His wet lips and slack jaw hang slightly open. His hands, palms turned up, sit curled in his lap, looking like sick birds. His ECT shunt sticks out of one wrist. And still, I am hard as a goddamn brick.

And having worked fucking hard to get to the exquisitely painful point of eruption, I have no intention of stopping now.

"Milton," I say through gritted teeth, pumping myself once or twice to show him I will not be intimidated, "a moment if you wouldn't mind."

Milton looks from my face to my dick.

"Please," I plead.

He chuckles and slaps the Formica table. "Lord." Then he whips Tyrone's chair around. "You got five minutes."

Later that night, I look over at Tyrone lying in a fetal position—all six feet three inches of him curled into a ball—in the bed next to me. He is nineteen and wears a hospital gown and his basketball sneakers. He is a child.

I can't sleep and it occurs to me to jerk off again. I wonder if he would notice. I know he wouldn't say anything. But that is not the point. I don't want to be rude. There are rules of etiquette, even here.

SIXTH

I have never been into being tied down. Until now. Lately I am so anxious to be restrained that this morning I actually grab an ankle strap out of the orderly's hand and start buckling myself to the table. "Aren't we the eager little beaver this morning," says Florence, perennially cheerful. But it's not so much that I can't wait to be zapped. If anything, it's the feeling that being bound and gagged is the only thing that will stop the sensation—that I am the third rail; that I am filled with a kind of buzzing, humming energy that keeps my knees bouncing and toes twiddling. I am chewing the insides of my cheeks and yanking out strands of hair. And so, while God knows I'd much prefer my first voluntary experience playing the M in S&M to be shared with a highly experienced, leather-clad dominatrix—the kind who makes house calls and comes equipped with her own bag of tricks—I have resigned myself to the fact that my first priority is ridding myself of the feeling that my flesh is about to come flying off my bones. So hospital-issue restraints, a paralytic and generic knockout drops will have to do. When I am finally, completely strapped down, the relief is immediate. The restraints provide a kind of counter-pressure I have not been able to give myself. In being secured I finally feel secure. I haven't told anyone about this, though I admit it's been hard to hide. I just tell them I'm nervous. If I told them how I really feel they'd think I was out of my mind.

Tarzana, 1965. When I got to my parents' house Pop was in front of the TV—where he'd been since my mother had died. He didn't look up when I walked through the living room, and I didn't say anything. Without her in it, the house itself felt like a coffin. I wanted to do what had to be done and get out. I felt what was becoming a familiar fermenting anxiety begin to roil around the worries I was normally able to handle with ease.

I was acutely aware of the beating of my heart in my chest. I felt as if some giant hand had wrapped itself around my throat and squeezed until I was choking. Eventually I did what I'd been doing since my mother had suddenly stopped existing at the age of fifty-three, having expired in the stacks of the Tarzana Library without even making it to the hospital. I wrenched myself free, swallowed the fear, and did my best impression of an acceptable version of me.

I found Hannah sitting in the back of my mother's closet. The floor was littered with empty black plastic garbage bags, labels, and markers. She looked up at me with puffy, red-rimmed eyes and smiled.

"What took you so long?"

"Sorry," I said. "Traffic."

Hannah looked up into the clothes hanging over her and tears began to fall. She threw her arms around my legs and buried her head in my knees.

I stroked the back of her head. "I know. Well, I'm here now so let's get this over with," I said, smiling. "They're just clothes, right?" She looked up and nodded halfheartedly. My heart was racing. I felt dizzy and nauseated. I smiled again.

There wasn't that much—dresses, pants, the same simple skirts and blouses my mother had worn to work year after year. It was mostly crap from Sears. The Salvation Army would get almost everything.

I went to the shelves where Mom kept her sweaters neatly folded and began looking, but I couldn't find what I wanted. I started tearing through them.

"Greyson, stop it. What are you—?"

Hannah, on her hands and knees, tried to collect the sweaters as fast as I threw them to the floor.

"The blue one she wore on Thanksgiving . . . the blue cashmere sweater I—"

"Relax." Hannah shoved an armful of acrylic and wool at me, reached over the top of the shelves, and brought down a box.

"She kept it hidden up there."

"Hidden."

Hannah hesitated. "Well, Pop always had kind of a thing about this—"

"Stop. You know what, I don't think I want to know."

I didn't make much more working as a summer law clerk in San Francisco than I had working afternoons at the Chevron station when I was in high school. Ellen was basically supporting us by working as the executive secretary to the president of one of the fancy department stores in the city, and she got a thirty-percent discount, so we managed to bring my mother some little present every time we came to visit. A light-blue cashmere cardigan warranted a special trip down to L.A. Ellen said she'd never forget the look on my mother's face when she first touched that sweater. What I remember, what will never cease to give me pleasure, is the look on my father's face. It was a perfect mix of anger, humiliation, and the desperate attempt to hide both.

I sat huddled in the corner and carefully lifted the lid off the box. The original tissue paper lay over the sweater. I was taking this home with me.

Hannah laughed.

"What?"

"You look about as old as you were the night you hid in the closet and they couldn't find you."

I was seven. They were coming home from a party. I don't remember why but I thought it would be funny to play a trick on them and hide. I didn't realize how scared they'd be. And when they were, I was afraid to come out. I wanted them to find me. But I was too afraid to come out myself. Afraid I would get in trouble. For hiding. I started to cry. I didn't want to hide anymore. I was tired. And I could hear my mother crying. I think I finally made enough noise so that my father came to look in the closet. He was furious. But my mother just wanted to know why I had been hiding. I said I was afraid everyone would be mad if I came out.

"You knew about that?" I said.

"Are you kidding? Mom was so panicked when they couldn't find you she practically tackled me in my sleep," Hannah said.

"I made her cry." I felt a dull, empty ache.

"Oh," Hannah gasped, "She looked so beautiful that night."

Closed eyes brought shifting kaleidoscopic fragments—high heels standing in the closet doorway, full skirt silhouetted in the yellow light of their bedroom. A turned cheek, red lipstick, a smudge of black mascara.

Hannah jumped up off the floor and quickly rifled through my mother's clothes.

"She wore this," Hannah said, holding an outdated dark-blue taffeta dress against her. "I loved this dress. She made it herself. I remember going to Fairfax Fabrics with her to pick out the material." Hannah held the dress tighter, then slowly lifted it to her face. Tears formed in her eyes and fell down her cheeks. As if it were a baby, she gently passed the dress to me.

"Go on," she whispered, "take it." When it was safely in my arms, I buried my face in it. At first I smelled nothing, maybe a little mustiness. But with the second and the third and the fourth breath, my head began to spin. Because the folds of that faded piece of cloth were replete with the ghost of my mother's special-occasion perfume. An alchemy of gardenias and orange blossoms, of dances and bright red lipstick, of holidays and all my mother's best Saturday nights.

For a split second, the anxiety receded and in its place there was just her.

And then suddenly everything—every last shitty housecoat—seemed important. Nothing was disposable. And nothing was the same. Nothing was ever the same.

The words roll around in my head. And eventually a red flag goes up. Nothing was the same. Is this where it happens? I think something bad happened. I think. I remember thinking: I'm guessing it was more than one thing. Who was it that said that? Who was that?

The words roll around in my head. Crazy. "Crazy," they call me. Sure I'm crazy, sure I'm crazy . . . Sure. I'm. Crazy . . .

And that's how it happens. Like a broken record, warped and scratched. Once I was music, now I am just noise.

Palo Alto, 1965. By then it was happening every day. The panic spread out like a late-afternoon shadow. I became aware of a dull ache in my stomach, of a thick metallic taste in my mouth that made it hard for my throat to open and close, of the irregular thrumming of my heart.

An air conditioner. A car with a flat tire. A refrigerator. A whirring. Usually soft at first, always low—almost guttural. Mechanical. It is safe to say the sound was mechanized. Safe to say. Relentless.

I left the apartment, the library, the student union to get away from it. The sound only got louder. I walked downtown and seemed to head straight into it. I ran in the other direction, and it followed me. And got louder still. As if I'd made it mad. By then it had swallowed all the other sounds outside. I fought against the tide of cheerful students, and mothers slowed to the pace of their toddlers. Stupid and naïve, they shopped for dinner and passed out political flyers and listened to the Raiders play the Saints on their transistor radios. All I heard was the air-conditioner–flat-tire–refrigerator whirring. Were they deaf?

I began to understand that the only way I could prevent the sound from swallowing every last synapse in my brain was to talk. To myself. Out loud. I had to scream to hear myself above the whirring. That's when the people on the street stopped shopping for dinner and passing out flyers and listening to the game. And started staring at me. I stared back. They looked away. I took a step forward. A woman grabbed her child by the hand and yanked her out of my path. I had become a man who ate children.

I found my way home, stripped naked, and lay on the bathroom floor, the cool tiles pushing up. Keeping me from falling.

I didn't know how long the floor would hold me. I prayed Ellen would come home before it gave way. I felt one hot tear leak out of each eye and run down the sides of my face. If they hit the floor they'd dissolve the grout that held the tiles together. I tried to wipe away the tears but I couldn't lift my arms, couldn't move at all. Someone must have drugged me. Or poisoned my food. Someone who worked in the law school cafeteria? Someone from my study group? Could it have been Ellen?

I became furious thinking that my wife could betray me like that. Furious and devastated. The grief was overwhelming and I began to sob. I could see my tears fall to the floor and begin to eat through the marble like acid. I heard the hissing and burning of rock turning to ash and I saw light coming through the spaces where gaps had opened up. If I didn't get control, the whole thing was going to crumble and I was going to slip through one of those gaping holes and fall. And keep falling. There would be nothing and no one to catch me. I would die.

That was exactly what Ellen wanted. Well, fuck her. I stopped crying. I forced myself to stop hyperventilating. I wasn't going to give that bitch the satisfaction. I counted six long seconds for every inhalation, ten seconds for every exhalation. I was going to get control of this. I don't know how long I lay there—breathing and counting, breathing and counting, carrying on a running conversation with myself in which I articulated and repeated every thought that entered my mind, every tiny action my body (of its own volition) performed. I was spinning. I was the plastic dial on a game board—rigid, whirling, dizzy, and finally, inevitably, broken. Pointing toward Ellen.

I felt something drip on my forehead. And then on my nose. And on my chin. Drops of water were falling from the ceiling. Rain. It was raining from the bathroom ceiling. And the drops were burning holes in the bathroom floor. I was going to fall through the floor and die and there was nothing I could do to stop it.

"Grey, are you home?"

Thank God, Ellen was home.

No, that was wrong. That was bad. She'd come home early to kill me. She was going to make me drink bleach. No, not bleach. That knife. She was going to skin me alive with the electric carving knife we'd gotten as a wedding gift. It made sense. She was the one who'd wanted it, who had insisted we register for it along with the china and silver and all the other crap, most of which no one bought us. We didn't have any cereal bowls, but we did have an electric carving knife. And now she was going to use it to kill me. Suddenly I felt horribly nauseous, not just at Ellen's betrayal, but at my own stupidity. She'd been planning this for over a year. Lying flat on my back, I nearly choked on the bile that rose up into my throat.

"God, I'm sorry about the mess."

She was in the living room, just outside the door. She wasn't alone.

"He's not usually such a slob."

"Don't apologize. We're painting—our place is a disaster."

It was Larry, our neighbor who lived upstairs with his boyfriend, Ian.

"Help yourself. I'm going to go see if Grey's taking a nap."

A minute later the door opened. Larry stood above me with a beer in his hand.

"Oops. Ellen, I found him," Larry sang over his shoulder. "Sorry, Grey, I didn't know you were . . ."

He stopped smiling and knelt down next to me.

"Greyson, are you okay?"

My mouth opened but nothing came out. Larry tossed a towel over my crotch.

"Did you fall? Hit your head?"

I managed a weak, airy "No."

"Ellen, I think we've got a problem."

"Don't touch me!" I screamed at Ellen as soon as she appeared over Larry's shoulder. Suddenly I was able to move and I scrambled backward, wedging myself between the toilet and the bathtub.

"Greyson, what's wrong?" She was pushing past Larry, moving toward me.

I pleaded with him. "Get her away from me. She's trying to kill me."

"What? Greyson, this isn't funny."

"I said get the fuck away!"

She reached out to touch me and I slammed the heel of my hand into her chest. She flew backward into Larry and lay on the floor breathless. Ellen lifted her head and looked at me with the stunned, confused eyes of an animal that had been stalked and cornered—like she was looking at a stranger, a predator.

"Don't. Touch. Me," I growled. "I know what you did."

Larry helped her up, never taking his eyes off me.

"Go call the doctor," he said. "I'll stay with him."

We didn't have a doctor. Ellen and I were healthy twenty-year-old newlyweds. We didn't get sick. Ellen went to student health for her birth control pills, so she called them. The physician in charge didn't seem all that surprised. Stanford was a pressure cooker. It wasn't uncommon for a couple of students to crack every semester. The previous year, a med student had dissected his own neck the night before his anatomy practical.

I was doing my final year of college and my first year of law school at the same time. On top of that, my mother had just died. As far as the doctor was concerned, I was textbook. He told Ellen that I was suffering from sleep deprivation and academic burnout, that I needed to be sedated and brought in to the university hospital to rest for a few days, that he would send a nurse right away.

Our apartment was small. I could hear Ellen hang up the phone and start to cry. It stopped me for a moment, hearing that—hearing my wife cry. I'd known her long enough to be able to recognize that this was the sound of her crying with her mouth closed, of her trying to contain and extinguish her sobs, of her trying not to cry. I knew this was the sound of Ellen crying out of pain, not out of anger or frustration. Because I knew what that sounded like too. What I heard sounded familiar. Intimately, painfully familiar. And very far away.

"Ellen," Larry called into the living room. "Not right now if you can help it."

"I'm sorry, I just—"

"I know, sweetie," he said, studying me, "but I think it might upset . . . the situation even more."

I heard her pull two tissues out of the box and blow her nose.

"Okay, I'm fine," she said.

Ellen left my favorite jeans—a soft, faded pair of Levi's I'd had since high school—and a Stanford Law School sweatshirt just outside the bathroom door and Larry tried to get me dressed. But I refused to put on any of my own clothes. I was convinced that Ellen had saturated them with something—rat poison, cyanide, battery acid, cholera, polio, smallpox, oven cleaner, the possibilities were endless—that would seep into my skin and kill me. I was naked, covered in sweat, and shaking. Larry was very patient.

"Okay, Greyson, I . . . understand your concern—not that I agree, but I understand."

"You do?"

"Sure. So let's put our heads together and come up with a solution to this."

"W-w-why?" I asked, my teeth chattering.

"Why? Because (a) you can't spend the rest of your life in this bathroom and (b) you're freezing your dick off."

I looked down at my dick. "Oh, okay."

"Good," Larry said. "Now we're on the same page. How about this . . . how about you wear my clothes?"

I was six foot two, 180 pounds. Larry was five foot eight, 170 pounds.

"Okay."

Larry stripped off his purple paisley bell-bottoms and canary-yellow guayabera. My hands were shaking, so he buttoned me into his shirt and zipped me into his pants. He patted me gently on the ass and sighed.

"I've always thought Ellen was a lucky woman, Greyson, but I have to say, sweetheart, you're making me reevaluate."

When the doorbell rang, I was fully, if absurdly, dressed. Larry was wearing nothing but his black bikini underwear and turquoise socks. It had taken the nurse two hours to get from student health to our apartment located less than a mile off campus. Then again, it had taken Larry almost that long to get me dressed. I'd been in the bathroom for nearly four hours.

The nurse from student health had not come alone.

"Hi, hon," she whined. "I'm Nurse Warren." Her voice was brimming with insincere sympathy and trumped-up compassion.

I looked at Larry, panicked. "Who's here?"

"Uh . . . just some friends."

"What friends? I don't want to see anyone."

"And this young man is Mr. Terrell, my work-study student."

"Come in, I'm Greyson's wife."

Mr. Terrell was Lester Terrell, a linebacker on the Stanford football team.

I was confused. "Am I on the football team?"

"No, sweetheart," Larry said gently.

"Then why—"

"I'll explain later. You mind?" he asked, picking up the pants I refused to wear.

"Don't!" I screamed.

"Could you please hurry? He's in the bathroom," Ellen said from the living room.

"It's okay," Larry said soothingly. "I'm . . . I'm willing to bet you Sunday brunch at the Bay Street Café that there's nothing wrong with these clothes."

"You are?"

"Yes."

"How do you know?"

Larry was struggling to close the buttons on my Levi's.

"Because I know Ellen loves you and would never hurt you."

He put my sweatshirt on and his hands disappeared into the dangling sleeves.

"Bullshit!"

"Could we get a little help in here?" Larry called over his shoulder.

"Be right there, just as soon as Mrs. Todd fills out these forms."

Larry rolled his eyes. "You have got to be kidding me." He turned, threw open the bathroom door and stormed into the living room.

"Sweet-Mary-Mother-of-God! First it takes you over two hours to respond to an emergency—*an emergency*—and now you want her to waste more time filling out paperwork while you sit here with your thumb up your ass instead of doing something to help that boy?"

It was very, very silent after that. Eventually Warren spoke up. "University policy," she said flatly, no longer pretending to care. "Be sure to sign all three copies of the liability waiver."

After that everything started to sound as if it were being filtered through cottony, cloudy marshmallows. The adrenaline had finally receded and a fuzzy kind of exhaustion was taking its place. It was like all the sharp edges had been filed off my panic. It wasn't that I thought I wasn't going to die, just that maybe it wouldn't be so bad.

Obviously, I fell asleep, because when I opened my eyes Lester Terrell was sitting on me and Nurse Warren was yanking Larry's pants halfway down my ass. Instantly I started thrashing. Instantly it became clear how well suited Lester was to this particular work-study assignment. I felt a sharp pinch in my hip followed by a painful burning sensation. Warren stood up and I saw the empty syringe in her hand.

After that I didn't even try to resist. It was over. I'd been had. By Ellen, by Larry, by Lester Terrell. Ellen stood in the doorway with tears running down her cheeks. Her shoulders were shaking. One hand covered her mouth; she was hugging her middle with the other.

I couldn't tell if she was laughing or crying.

The first time I woke up in my room at the Stanford University Hospital, Ellen was sitting at my side holding my hand. Bad call on her part. I was drugged, but I had not forgotten. I was out of bed and screaming within five seconds.

"How did you find me?" I screamed at her, frantically scanning the room for the exit. Ellen jumped out of her chair.

"Calm down, Greyson. You're safe. You're at the hospital."

Fuck, Ellen was standing in front of the door. "They said they could protect me!" I screamed.

"Who? Protect you from what? I'm your wife. I love you. I would never hurt you."

"Liar! You're lying!" I picked up the chair she'd been sitting in, lifted it over my head, and hurled it at her. My aim was rotten and I missed her by at least a couple of feet, but she was shocked enough to make her way back to my bed and pull the patient panic cord.

Almost immediately, two orderlies and a doctor, having already heard the screaming and furniture rearranging, burst through the door ready for battle. The doctor was carrying a loaded syringe, and the orderlies—a tall gangly kid with an Afro and a pink-faced giant with a crew cut and yellow teeth—each carried a pair of leather straps. The big one tackled me and I felt the familiar pinch of the needle and heard Ellen cry out before I even hit the floor.

The next time I woke up, things were very different. Looked different. This wasn't student health. Also, I was tied to my bed by those leather restraints. Hannah was there. And Ben and Jake. And, of course, Ellen. But I was so drugged—on something worlds away from what they'd been giving me—that I hardly recognized my siblings or cared that I couldn't move.

Eventually I figured out I had been transferred to the university hospital psychiatric ward. After ten days spent mostly asleep as a result of the drugs they were pumping into me almost hourly, my psychosis seemed to be clearing up on its own. There was still no diagnosis. The doctors threw around "schizophrenia"—which often manifested around my age—or maybe it was some rare form of epilepsy, or perhaps a brain tumor. In other words, they had no idea. And I was so drugged I could not be very helpful about what led up to the "episode." Not that I really knew.

On day eight, Jason Randall from my study group came by to visit. Randall had miraculously gotten into Stanford Law after spending four years surfing his way through UC Santa Barbara. He knew his was probably the last acceptance letter to go out, that he was one lucky son of a bitch, so he worked twice as hard as the rest of us just to keep up. He was an excellent note-taker and he brought the beer to every study meeting.

"Grey, look who came to visit," Ellen said much too enthusiastically.

He came in with some wilted carnations and pulled a chair up next to my bed.

"I'm going to try to find a vase for these and leave you two to talk," she said, kissing me on the forehead like I was a fucking five-year-old home from school with the flu.

When she was gone, Jason leaned in conspiratorially. "You know," he said, like he was about to tell me he'd just gotten laid, "some people are saying this was a genius move, Todd, fuckin' genius."

I tried to fight my way past the drugs to understand what he was saying.

"And I thought so too. At first. I mean, there's no way they can get you now. It's documented. You're textbook Section 8. From what I hear, you were very fuckin' convincing. You must've been planning this for months."

I was slow but I finally understood. So that was the story. I'd faked a complete mental breakdown. To avoid the draft.

"But if anyone needed to pull something like this, it's me," Randall went on. "Of any of us, you were the shoo-in to make JAG. I mean, editor of *Law Review,* top of our class. You didn't have shit to worry about. And now—I mean after something like this . . ."

He lifted up one of the leather straps still attached to the bed but no longer to me just as Ellen walked back into the room. "Forget about politics. I mean, there's no way you're ever running for office. Even a judgeship will be out of the question with this on your—"

"Get out," Ellen said, calmly dropping the water pitcher of carnations into the trash.

"What? I was just saying he should maybe have thought this through before—"

"Get the fuck out of my husband's room."

Jason looked from Ellen to me back to Ellen. "Okay, buddy, you rest up and we'll see you real soon, okay?" He smiled awkwardly at me and walked toward the door, pausing when he got to Ellen.

"I never thought—I mean, we all just assumed . . ." Jason glanced over his shoulder at me. The look on his face was no longer conspiratorial. It was an expression reserved for limbless vets and children with cancer. I think they called it pity. "Christ, I'm sorry," he said, turning back to Ellen. "I mean, Greyson, man, he's the last guy you'd think—"

"You really are as stupid as Greyson always said." Ellen opened the door for him.

"He said that?" Randall looked genuinely hurt.

Ellen just raised her eyebrows and shut the door behind him.

"FUCKING ASSHOLE!" she screamed at the top of her lungs.

But it was too late. The drugs had clouded my thinking, my vision, my ability to look ahead to the long-term consequences. Not that I could have done anything differently, but to have the bomb dropped like this was—like having a bomb dropped. Suddenly everything I had worked for . . . my horizons had just narrowed considerably.

Ellen sat down on the edge of my bed. "He doesn't know what he's talking about. This doesn't have to mean—"

"Yes!" I yelled. "Yes, it does. He's right. I will never be able to do what I . . ." Ellen put her arms around me and I wept silently into her shoulder.

"Home," I whispered. "Want t-to go home. T-today."

"Yes," she said. "Home, absolutely."

"No m-more d-rugs," I managed.

"Definitely. No more drugs," she said. "Not these anyway. These people are idiots."

"I-diots," I nodded into her shoulder.

At home I lose track of how many days, weeks, maybe longer I have been unable—or simply unwilling—to get out of bed. I lie on my back, staring at the insides of my eyelids, some days paralyzed by crushing despair, others trying to survive the panic that threatens to engulf me. I swear I can hear it. The panic that comes to get me breathes. It has a pulse and teeth. I am sure one day soon it will eat me alive. And then the despair returns. God's idea of a reprieve.

I spend much of that time making lists in my head. Actually putting pen to paper would require a feat of superhuman strength and endurance. But so does bathing and dressing and eating. Now breathing exhausts my physical capabilities. And frankly, I resent having to do even that. I want to be relieved of the responsibility. I am no more up to the constant inhaling and exhaling than I am to running a marathon. Or leaving the house. I sleep as much as I can; pretend to be nervous even when I'm not so I can take the pills that send me off to the warm, dreamless place that is pure nothing. But the doctor won't let me take many of those. He says that kind of sleep isn't restorative. I say fuck restorative.

When the pills run out, he refuses to give me any more. So I lie on my back awake, categorizing and cross-referencing and alphabetizing, making endless versions of lists of the things I have, over the course of my life, lost or hidden or buried. I count among these things regrets, opportunities, disappointments, school elections, trust, loved ones, a favorite sweater, my dignity, childhood treasures, and various and sundry pieces of myself. When I am done, there is virtually nothing left. Except the despair and the panic. And so I start again. But the beginning is never where I left it.

Beverly Hills, 1960. John was a bootstrap kind of guy. As in, pull yourself up by them. I didn't think about the irony at the time—that John and Pop worked side by side at the Florsheim factory, cutting leather to make shoes. Only that they had nothing in common and Pop had no business working there.

John and heavy machinery, on the other hand, were made for one another. John was second-generation Polish. Thick-necked, barrel-chested, blond and blue-eyed, he looked like he'd been bred to spend his life in a hard hat. At thirty-two, he'd already swung a pickax in a West Virginia coal mine, sawed cows apart at a meatpacking plant, and killed a bunch of Japs during the war.

Pop was tall, long-limbed, and smooth. He always had clean fingernails. He was a talker, a seller—a schmoozer. He'd spent his war duty procuring things from behind a desk on a base in San Diego. On a good day Pop could charm anyone into anything. Like this job. My father had never used anything sharper than a steak knife in his entire life, but he'd convinced the Florsheim guy he was the only man in Los Angeles qualified to operate a room full of razors, electric blades, auto-drills, and industrial tanning ovens. That year, from May through August, Pop was—second only to John—the most productive guy on the line. He mastered not only his own dangerous job but every detail of production. He worked double shifts and graveyard shifts and never seemed tired.

He was also the most fun guy at the factory, hands down. John thought Pop was hilarious. And for a while, John came over for dinner every Tuesday when his wife went to visit her mother. Grandpa was skeptical of John. He told me all the most famous concentration camps were in Poland. Lucky for John, his courageous relatives back in Ciechanovietz had risked their lives hiding Jews in their hayloft. The Poles, John told me, were great friends of the Jews during the war.

But in late September, Pop started getting sick. At first it was just once in a while. Then it was once a week. Then by November, whole weeks at a time. Pop was no longer anyone's favorite employee. In the beginning, John did his best to cover. He came in early and stayed late and put Pop's name and number on the extra pieces he cut. But on the third Sunday in a row, when Mom called to tell John that Pop still wasn't up to coming in, John told her enough was enough. He said he was coming over and hung up before she could tell him not to.

My mother took her time answering the door. We all watched as she slowly put down the onion she was slicing and washed her hands and wiped them on her apron and checked her hair in the gleam on the handle of the refrigerator door. She startled when he knocked again. Harder and louder. But then she looked at us and smiled.

"Who's there?" she called out.

"Geez, Willa, it's John. Come on already."

She crossed the living room at its widest point and gently pulled open the door. But she didn't let him in.

"I'll tell him you stopped by," she said pleasantly.

"What?"

Sensing the mounting drama, Hannah, Ben, Jake, and I rushed to my mother's side and filled in the spaces around her. "He'll appreciate the thought," she said. "Really."

"Is that right?" John spread his feet wide apart and crossed his arms over his chest. He wasn't going anywhere.

"I'm sorry you made the trip over for nothing," my mother said, her voice light. But I could see her shoulders tighten.

"If it were up to you, you wouldn't even tell him I came."

"What do you mean if it were up to me?"

"I want to talk to him." John pushed past my mother, stepped around Ben and over Jake, and just kept going. My mother ran after him and caught him by the arm.

"Please, don't. You're going to upset him. He doesn't want to see anyone. He's . . . not himself."

"Not himself? Then who the hell is he?" John's neck was bright red.

When she saw the startled look on Jake's face, my mother stopped, took a breath, and walked over to him. She ran her hand over his head and let it trail down his cheek.

"He doesn't feel like seeing anyone," she said quietly.

"He's tired," Jake whispered in his tiny toddler voice. It's what he'd heard us all say. Over and over.

"Yes. That's right," my mother said, still holding on to Jake. "He just needs some rest. Undisturbed rest."

John just stood there shaking his head. "You're not helping him, Willa."

"I'm sorry?" my mother said.

John leaned in closer, hoping, I supposed, to keep some of the conversation between the two of them. But I heard it all.

"I know you think you are, but you're not. You're making it worse. The way you're treating him, he's never going to be a man again."

I used to like John.

"I think you should do what my mother says," I told him. That made him laugh.

"Some example you're setting."

"I don't know what you're implying, John, but—"

"You want him to turn out like Ray?" John said, squeezing my shoulder. "Is that what you want?"

My mother was speechless.

"You have to put your foot down. And if that doesn't work, you kick him out. He's not going to snap out of this until he hits bottom."

"I'm not like him," I said.

"I didn't mean it like that, Grey," John said, slapping me on the back. "Your dad is a good guy. He's just weak right now. But we're going to help him."

Then John walked past my mother, down the hall toward my

parents' bedroom, and, without knocking, opened the door and stepped into the room that for weeks had been off-limits to us. And my mother just stood there staring after him. Maybe she was too shocked or maybe she just wanted to see what would happen. I think maybe she wanted John to be right.

I wanted to know what was in there. I'd heard him crying in the middle of the night, pacing up the long, narrow hallway that ran outside the bedrooms, out into the living room, and then—always as if for the first time, remembering I was asleep on the couch—cursing to himself and pacing back down the hallway. The noises he made didn't really sound human. I'd been listening to them night after night for weeks. I wanted to know what he looked like. I wanted this to make things different even if it didn't make them better. Anything but more of the same.

"Christ, Ray, smells worse than my Aunt Tina in here."

He opened the blinds and all the windows and pulled back the bedcovers. Something that vaguely resembled my father was huddled in a ball against the headboard.

"Don't you think we all feel like crap sometimes, Ray?" John was saying.

I never imagined this. My father looked like a sick nocturnal animal desperately seeking cover—like something in pain looking for a place to die.

"Shit, Ray, you don't think Frank would rather just crawl under the covers and pretend those beautiful little girls of his aren't crippled because he took 'em to a goddamned public swimming pool? What the hell do you have to complain about? Four gorgeous kids and a woman who'd give her life for you. I'd say you got it pretty good, Ray."

"I don't think you're making him feel better," I said quietly.

"I didn't come over to make him feel better," John said, making sure my father could hear him. "I came to give him a little dose of reality—to remind him he's got it pretty fuckin' good compared to a lot of people we know. People with real problems."

I couldn't stand this.

"Jesus, Mr. Polikoff. John—okay," I whispered. "I think he understands."

"I know you *think* you got problems, Ray, but you don't." The louder John's voice boomed, the smaller and more wasted Pop appeared.

"You are just giving in to whatever is in your head. I came over to tell you it's time to stop. Don't give in. You get up, you strap on your fucking balls, and you go out and do your job. Don't look in the fucking mirror, Ray. Don't think about it. You think too fucking much, Ray. You read too much and you think too much. That's your problem."

Pop said nothing. Seeing him huddled against the headboard, I almost expected him to slip down into the crack between the bed and the wall and disappear. But he didn't. Instead, he looked up at me—unshaven, eyes wet with tears, begging.

That kind of misery had to be contagious. I turned and walked out of the room.

I lie in bed at home, and it's like I'm falling off a cliff, only I never hit the ground. I just drop further and further and further, my stomach seizing, unable to move beyond the involuntary, normally temporary wave of panic that comes from hearing a loud noise or losing your balance.

I lie in bed and feel too light. I need weight. I need gravity. So I lie down on the floor. But that's not enough. I imagine the ground rushing up toward me. I can see myself connecting with the sidewalk, or the smooth black asphalt. Almost like scratching an itch.

When I was sixteen, our neighbor, Mrs. Bronfman, threw herself out the window of her tenth-story apartment. Hannah and I heard her body hit the sidewalk. But, since we didn't know that the sound—almost like a gun going off—was Mrs. Bronfman's life ending, we continued to argue about which one of us was going to get stuck scrubbing the huge cast-iron pot grandpa had used to make chicken paprikash.

A half hour later, my mother walked in. She closed the front door and leaned against it. No smiles, no hugs. My father looked up at her from where he sat in grandpa's recliner, feet up, sipping his scotch. He studied her face. None of us had ever seen the expression she was wearing. He put his scotch on the side table and walked toward her.

"Willa?"

She had one hand clamped tight over her mouth, and although she didn't make a sound, I could see her shoulders begin to shake.

My father wrapped his arms around her, and as soon as he did, she fell against him, crying into his chest.

"Sweetheart, come on, tell me what happened."

My mother stood on her tiptoes and, trying to catch her breath, whispered into his ear.

"Oh God, Jesus Christ," he said. His knees buckled slightly and for a moment my parents fell against one another, propping each other up with their grief.

Two days later, I heard pots and pans banging and loud voices coming from the kitchen. I wouldn't have been surprised if it had been my father. There were times when he yelled a lot. But it was my mother, so I knew something was really wrong.

"It's cruel and hypocritical. It's disgusting."

I'd grown out of sneaking around and listening behind doors a long time ago.

I walked into the kitchen and saw my mother in a dark-blue dress. There was a Bundt cake sitting on the counter. The plastic wrap had been peeled off. My father, wearing a suit, was leaning against the counter across from her, eating a slice.

"What is?" I asked, walking into the room.

My mother's eyes were red. I could tell she'd been crying, but she looked much more angry than she did sad. Neither of my parents said anything.

"What is?" I asked again, this time looking at Pop.

He put the cake down on the counter and brushed the crumbs off his hands. Then he looked at my mother and nodded.

"I think he's old enough."

"Mrs. Bronfman's family won't be sitting shiva for her," she said. There were tears leaking from her eyes, but I'd never heard her sound so angry.

"They're not even giving her a real funeral. They're just dumping her in the ground. In an unmarked grave in a public cemetery."

"Why? I mean, I don't understand. They're her children. And her grandchildren. They were at her house all the time. I don't—"

"She killed herself, Greyson," my father told me quietly.

"I know. It's terrible. They must be—"

"As far as Jews are concerned, suicide is just another form of murder. It's a sin. You understand? She's a sinner. So they're punishing her."

I think about Mrs. Bronfman a lot lately. I think I can safely say she didn't give a shit where she was buried or whether anyone came over with casseroles or Bundt cakes. I think she probably just wanted something to push against. Something solid to end the fall.

Occasionally I am aware of the light changing at the edges of my peripheral vision. The wet, grey dawn is suddenly the bright midmorning, the orangey late afternoon, the purple-brown dusk, and then the yellow-black of late at night. I know it's late when Ellen turns on all the lights. I know she is desperate to make the sun shine inside.

I always wondered how I would know when I had hit bottom. Somehow, the perpetual terror of dangling after the bottom had fallen out always seemed more obvious—a step beyond and more self-evident than hitting it in the first place. Especially the first time.

Because the first time, you always think it could be worse. You always think maybe you're just tired. Or coming down with something. Or under a lot of stress. Or overthinking things. Or secondguessing yourself, doubting the choices you've made. You always think you just need a break from work and friends and the phone and your family. That you just need a rest.

You think you should have an answer to the question, "What's wrong?" You wish you knew. No one can understand how much you wish you knew. You know you must be horrible to live with, to be around. Because you cannot stand to be you—to be in your own skin. You think you should be able to promise it will stop a month from last Friday. You can't imagine it will ever stop. You would do anything to make it stop. Instead you say maybe you just need a day to lie in bed. And then you take another and another and another and twenty more. And think you'd rather not get up at all. Ever. Over. You want it over. You would do anything.

And before your wife goes grocery shopping she asks if it's okay to leave you alone. And you look at her like you don't know what she means but you do. And you laugh and say, "Of course, don't be ridiculous."

But that was yesterday. Now you're standing in front of the medicine cabinet and you're insulted that she didn't believe you because she's emptied it of everything but Q-tips and Tampax and cotton balls. You thought you meant it. But that was yesterday. And yesterday is a whole world away from this pain. Today, you're tearing through the kitchen drawers with more energy than you've had in weeks. You wonder where the hell she could have hidden everything because spoons and butter knives and rubber spatulas are the only utensils left. And you catch yourself running your thumb over the impotent edge of a butter knife, wondering how much damage you could coax out of it. You imagine yourself, like an animal caught in a trap, gnawing away at your wrists with that little butter knife. How undignified. How pathetic. And then you think: *No, I am not my father.*

You are not your father. Because even old Mrs. Bronfman could get it right but he couldn't. He couldn't even do this right.

Because there was a hole in the bag. And he didn't swallow enough pills. So when you found him, it was almost like he was napping, sucking the plastic bag in with each thick, drug-induced breath and blowing it out with each raspy, snoring exhale. You wanted to leave him there. For a minute you hated him so much you even thought about plugging the hole. It was what he wanted, wasn't it? But you couldn't leave him. Because then someone else would find him. Your mother or your sister or one of your brothers. And that would be worse. So you ripped the bag off his head and dragged him into bed and let him sleep it off. And then you washed his piss out of the rug. And you hated him. For failing.

You are not him.

And you throw the butter knife back in the defanged drawer and slam it shut.

You were just browsing. Just browsing. And that is not the same thing at all. So you cross that option off the list. For now. Because when the time comes, yours will not be some half-assed attempt, some pathetic bid for attention. You will mean it. But you are not quite there yet. Not quite.

So you go back to the old routine: panic and despair, panic and despair in endless succession—or worse, at the same time. Until it does become routine. Your routine. Her routine.

And as soon as she leaves for work, or even sometimes when she's home and you're in the shower—on the rare occasions when you have the energy to take one—you hear heaving, open-mouthed howls of breath-stealing grief. And realize when you gasp and choke on the saliva and snot running down the back of your throat that you are the source of the screaming. And then you stop.

You close your mouth and swallow it all and pull yourself together because you know that you're just tired or coming down with something. You know there are people out there with real problems. You know it could be worse. You have a wife who loves you and a good job. You know you're lucky.

So you stand up and you strap on your balls and you go out there. You smile. And pretend you can feel the bottom under your feet.

New York, 1994. I wake to Cooper's soft melodic voice floating across the hall. I have never seen Cooper unhappy. She is always smiling, often laughing at jokes only she can hear. At every meal she asks the attendant for five oranges, and every time, when the attendant shakes her head, Cooper laughs.

"Okay, then four! Three!" she yells giddily. Then the lunch lady rolls three oranges onto Cooper's tray.

Cooper loves food. Tall and slim with narrow hips, broad shoulders, and a smooth, bald black head, she is always first in line when the food truck is wheeled in. I can only assume she tastes something the rest of us do not.

Tonight I listen as she describes a recipe. She is giving instructions.

"So good, such a nice dish. Couscous with raisins, braised leeks, and little onions, baby onions. Add chopped cilantro and little pieces of white sausage."

At first I think she must be talking on the pay phone just down the hall. A request for homemade food from a family member. But then suddenly the conversation changes. Now she is onstage in front of an audience introducing her next number.

"It's a four-minute song," she says, "just about four minutes." And she begins to sing. Soft and sweet. It is just the tonic I need to soothe my raging post-shock headache. I take my pillow and lie with my head at the foot of the bed, a little closer to Cooper's room. I can make out what sounds like a Top 40 love song. I can't hear the words but I can fill them in myself. I imagine her dancing in front of the aluminum mirror in her bathroom, like a teenager singing into a hairbrush. She is both audience and performer. Cooper's voice can make it better, I think. Cool and soft, there is safety in its meaningless melody.

SEVENTH

"It'll be over before you know it, son," the tall, grey-haired anesthesiologist says, without much conviction. Not long ago I knew his name.

But that line, I remember. It is the same line he used on me the last time—and probably the time before that. And on the patient before me.

Over before you know it. For a split second I think about that. Does he mean quick and painless? Or that I will no longer possess the brain cells required to participate in the act of knowing, an activity I have taken for granted until recently. When I wake up—assuming I wake up—knowing itself will be different. Less painful? Or just less?

How will that feel? But now I can't ask. Can't move. So the panic and mounting claustrophobia I feel are silent, evidenced only by the increased frequency of the beeping on their machines.

"BP's going up," the old guy says. The stern young doctor pauses, stops adjusting the dials and buttons on the dashboard in front of her.

"Heart's fine. Just anxiety," the old guy says.

"Shhhhh. Happy memories," Florence whispers. I can smell the sour hospital coffee lingering on her breath. "Or just imagine you're on a beautiful sunny beach somewhere."

Typhoons, hurricanes, tropical storms, monsoons—the sunnier the beach, the bigger the storm.

Thailand, 1989. Bangkok looks a lot like Dallas. Or Atlanta. Or any other relatively charmless modern American city. Except in Bangkok there are four hundred Buddhist temples sandwiched in between the skyscrapers.

Tangles of intersecting highways. City of a thousand generic office buildings. And low to the ground, red roofs, gasping for air, praying.

I suppose if I were walking along the shore, looking out at the Chao Phraya River—its water taxis, ferries, and fishing boats churning through the rough mud-brown water—maybe I'd feel like I'd gone somewhere.

But I am standing on the deck of a converted rice barge, surrounded by a bunch of rich Western tourists like myself, staring across the river at a bunch of office buildings. I am nowhere. This is not what I expected. And I am all about expectations—dashing and disappointing and not living up to them. That's me. On a good day. I am bored too. And I know that what lies between boredom and the self-indulgent navel-gazing, which quickly leads to wallowing in self-pity, is a very narrow and slippery slope.

I perk up when I see the waitress—young, thin, beautiful, dressed in something Asian-themed that stops just south of her crotch—coming around with a tray of drinks. I down the rest of my lychee martini just in time to swap my empty glass for a full one as she passes. She stops for a moment, looks back at me and winks.

"You naughty boy. I keep my eye on you."

Then she tosses her ass-length, stick-straight hair over her shoulder and chortles as she walks away, swinging her tiny hips to the Thai disco beat.

All that attention because I stole a drink. On an all-inclusive dinner cruise. I am growing tired of the endless hard sell here. There is no seduction. No seducing. I think I'm beginning to feel cheap.

"Breathtaking, isn't it?"

There is a slightly southern lilt to the voice. Southern American. Georgia? Virginia?

I feel the vacant air next to me change as she moves into it. She smells expensive. She rests her arms on the railing. Our elbows touch.

"Spectacular," I say.

I turn to look at her, but the sun behind her is still too high and bright. She is a shadow. I shield my eyes with my hand and squint. And now I am able to make out certain essential details: crow's feet around the eyes, lips notched by decades of smoking, slightly sunken cheeks—proof that she never eats more than half of what's on her plate and attends step class religiously. I'm sure she has a lovely figure. For a woman her age.

"Excuse me," I say, and walk away before she has time to introduce herself.

I am seriously considering swimming back to shore. Instead, I find the waitress and subject myself to another chortle in exchange for another drink. I'm beginning to like lychee.

By the time we return to the dock in Bangkok, I am so drunk that I have thrown up twice. Once over the side of the converted rice barge and once all over the chortling waitress.

"I guess I really am a naughty boy," I say by way of apology.

She does not chortle.

I don't remember anything after that. Somehow, though, I wake up in my bed in my hotel room in a Pan Pacific Bangkok robe.

The pounding in my head feels record-breaking. History-making. There is a bottle of aspirin and a glass of water on my night table. And a note:

Mr. Lee Majors:

Please take two of these white pills to feel better. You may also call the front desk for assistance at any time.

—Ina

I love Ina. I have no idea who she is, but right now there is no one I love more than Ina. I pop the top off the aspirin and swallow four. I lie there for another twenty minutes and wait for the aspirin to kick in. Then I take a long shower just to be sure that when I get outside I'll be able to tolerate the sunlight. I dry off, toss the towel on the bed, and draw the blackout curtain.

"Motherfucking-Jesus-fucking-Christ," I say much too loudly, yanking the curtains closed. Naked, I sit on the edge of the bed and dial the concierge.

"Yes, you too . . . Listen, what would be very helpful is if you could send someone into the gift shop." I picked up the note on the night table. "Ina maybe? Fine, whoever, and pick out a pair of Ray-Ban sunglasses for me—aviator style, very dark—and send them up as soon as possible. Just charge them to the room. Excellent, thank you."

Lying by the hotel pool on a chaise under the shade of an umbrella with my new Ray-Bans, I am almost beginning to turn the corner.

And then, "Eh mate, this one taken?"

I move my eyes as little as possible, but he is hard to miss: middle-aged, beer-bellied, Australian. He doesn't wait for a response. After he's taken off the plaid terrycloth-lined top that matches his trunks and gotten comfortable, he reaches over to shake my hand.

"Jimbo Jackson," he says, loud and proud.

From there everything pretty much goes to shit. For me. Because I'm not looking for a friend or playmate. Not one with a dick anyway.

But he is persistent.

And chatty.

"It's love, mate. I'm in love."

I don't feel the declaration warrants a response. Jimbo has made it half a dozen times over the course of our forty-five-minute relationship.

So I do my best to ignore him and continue silently enjoying my breakfast. I don't know what it's called, just that it's fruity and liquid and heavily alcoholic. And like everything else on the menu at the Pan Pacific Bangkok—the food, the décor, and especially the entertainment—it is a traditional Thai specialty.

"She is too," Jimbo continues. "I mean it's real. Really fuckin' real. I mean she washes my feet before we make love."

I chuckle. Barely. I don't mean to. I know it will only encourage his pathetic filibustering, but I can't help it.

"I know. Sweet, right? Thai women are different, mate. You'll see. They know how to take care of their men. They enjoy it."

I turn to look at Jimbo. Just for a second. So I can see if he's fuckin' kidding me. But lying back with his hands clasped behind his head and a big stupid smile on his face, Jimbo appears to be entirely sincere. The soft, hairless undersides of his snow-white arms are turning pink. I think about saying something.

I hear a splash and turn. The diving board is still bouncing. Beneath the surface of the water a girl flutters across the length of the pool. She surfaces at the shallow end just in front of my lounge. She is a local girl, eighteen or nineteen years old, and when she gets out of the water, her tiny white bikini is completely transparent. She twists her long dark hair, wringing out the water, and slips her feet into a pair of four-inch Lucite stilettos. I would like one of those, please. I nod at her and a slow smile spreads across her face.

As she walks toward me, I realize my eyes have been filming her—this scene—in slow motion. I am disappointed in myself. Such a cliché. Such an obvious choice. But then Bangkok itself is a cliché. I knew that and I came anyway. That was the point. So maybe I should stop fucking resisting and just enjoy fucking the cliché.

"You likey more?" the girl asks. She is standing so close to my chair that water from her still-dripping bathing suit is falling onto my belly. When I turn to look at her, my eyes are level with the crotch of her see-through bathing suit.

It takes until then to realize that the girl from the pool is the same girl who brought me my alcoholic breakfast drink. Just like all the waitresses and bar girls and dancers in Patpong, she is for sale—for an hour, for a night, for a week, or, like Jimbo's girlfriend, for as long as she can keep her man in love with her. Thai women know how to treat their men.

I gently tug her wet ponytail so she has to bend down further. "I would like you," I whisper hotly in her ear.

She takes my face in her tiny hands and turns my head to the side. "See barman. He make date," she whispers, and then darts her soft, wet tongue inside my ear before walking away.

I see barman. He make date. It turns out, however, that Suchin, my girl of the see-through bikini, is very popular—kind of like the hottest restaurant in town. But with only one seat. And so, despite offering to triple her rate, I will still have to wait three days for my turn at her table. I can't help but think that if this were Hollywood she'd be paying to screw me. But it's not. And oddly enough, I find being on the other end of the fucked-up sexual power dynamic not only frustrating but kind of a turn-on. When in Bangkok, I guess.

At about four o'clock, two women of indeterminate age—forty? fifty?—wearing satin pants embroidered with birds and flowers and matching quilted satin jackets, lead a ragtag group of barely post-pubescent girls dressed in bikinis, halter tops, and miniskirts or ridiculous-looking disco dresses into the pool area and line them up as if they're next in line for a firing squad. This is clearly a tourist-class outfit, so what are they doing *here*?

"It's about fucking time," says Roy, the man on the lounge to my left. I glean from the conversation that has taken place over me between Jimbo and Roy that Roy is from somewhere in Texas and has come to Bangkok on an all-inclusive sex tour booked for him by a travel agent in Dallas that specializes in such things (and that the Pan Pacific is not above participating). And in general, as things that are included go, the younger, the better.

I have tried to do as little talking as humanly possible—to project an air of "leave me the fuck alone." Now, though, I am too curious. And if something worse than Roy and Jimbo and their conversation over my chaise is going to happen, I want to know now.

"Time for what?" I ask.

"The pussy parade," Roy says and throws Jimbo a look that clearly says, *Where'd you find this hayseed?*

Jimbo leans over and educates me patiently. "Those women are madams. The girls work for them. If you see one you like, you tell one of the madams and they make a date for you."

"Does she chaperone too?"

They ignore my sarcasm because things are getting serious. One of the madams climbs on the diving board of the pool facing our lounges and yells, "Okay, who want pussy? Who want sucky dick? We got best girl. You want see? Come on."

Then she gestures to the line of girls and they walk toward us.

"Lemme see your titties," Roy says to the first girl. She is nowhere near eighteen. Not even close. The girl reaches up with one hand and pulls at the strings tied behind her neck. The two little triangles flop down and rest on her pale stomach. Her breasts are tiny—hardly worth covering at all. She has a mole on her left nipple.

Roy dismisses her with a wave of his hand. I'm sure I hear her sigh with relief. The next girl, who cannot be more than thirteen, moves to the foot of my chaise. With one pull at the strings on the side of her bikini bottoms, she is standing before me bare-assed. She has the figure of a ten-year-old boy and is completely smooth, hairless.

It occurs to me that, despite my leaving home long before having to endure the humiliating awkwardness of Willa's transition into womanhood, I am still possessed of enough paternal instinct to feel healthy amounts of shame and disgust at being offered the services of a girl so young I cannot tell whether she has had her pubic hair removed or whether it simply has not yet taken root. Suddenly eighteen seems completely reasonable. Hell, even seventeen. Any hesitation I might have had about Suchin has been banished thanks to this pornographic middle school assembly. I lie back in my chaise feeling downright upstanding.

The girl knows instantly that I am not interested and ties her tiny string bikini bottoms back into place. The smile drops from her face. Nothing personal. She is just taking advantage of the second or two between sales pitches to rest her facial muscles. She steps to the left.

This is Roy's fourth sex tour. He is full of advice.

"If you're going to do parlors, you want the ones off Chi Cha-am. The girls are less experienced, but they're a lot tighter. You won't even want to fuck 'em in the ass. But you want to get there by three or four. They don't have the endurance the girls in Patpong do."

I am afraid to find out what Roy might mean by "less experienced"—that "the ones off Chit Ha-am" might in fact turn out to be daycare centers doubling as brothels—so, not having booked a "date" at the hotel for tonight, I head to Patpong in search of some empty but prurient adult deviance.

"You want fucking show? You want cheap beers? Hello, handsome man, welcome please."

The man calling me handsome is small and jaundiced, feeble and asthmatic. I've been walking around Patpong for nearly an hour and either I'm going in circles or there is a species of sex show barkers that all look alike. I know I will go upstairs and participate or at least observe one of these fabled shows—I'm here, I have to—but I can't decide which one. So I keep walking.

"You like pussy shoot balloon?" This is by far the most interesting pitch I've heard.

"Sure, I like pussy shoot balloon," I say. The little man smiles and his teeth look like the cracked yellowed mah-jongg tiles my mother used to play with. I like him. And his teeth. He takes my arm and we walk into the bar, past the patrons, past the dancers, all the way to the back and up a set of narrow, steep stairs, at the top of which long strands of red and silver beads hang in a doorway.

"You have good time," he says, pushing me toward the beads.

"How much?" I ask and reach for my wallet.

The man pushes harder. "Cheap. You pay after. You like. You have good time. Very good pussy show. Best in Patpong."

There is nowhere to go but through the beads. So I go.

Call me crazy. Watching a woman smoke a cigarette with her vagina has never been real high on my list of fantasies. Certainly never made the top twenty. Or top fifty, for that matter. Okay, truth be told, the thought never even occurred to me. When I was at the studio, I once green-lit a Vietnam movie that used Bangkok as a stand-in for Hanoi

and the director came back with lurid stories of "Ping-Pong shows."
At the time, the idea of a woman shooting little balls out of her vagina
seemed exotic. At least to me. Ellen was less intrigued. Particularly
when I suggested she give it a try.

But that was years ago—and in comparison with what I am seeing now, it was amateur night. Vaginal Olympics have clearly come a
long way since then, I think, as I sit in the audience at Charlie's, which
turns out to be in fact one of Patpong's most established sex show
venues.

When I first arrive, the girl on stage is dancing—bored, expressionless, topless. Then, without any fanfare, she stops gyrating, pulls
off her gold lamé bikini, and walks to the edge of the stage where an
old lady, simultaneously shoveling rice noodles into her mouth and
operating the boom box, hands her a cigarette. And a lighter.

After that the girl disappears. More or less. She lies down on
her back, knees pulled into her chest, and becomes a disembodied
vagina. Only when she reaches around, inserts the cigarette into her
bald pussy, and, lighter in hand, uses her inch-long red thumbnail to
flick the Bic and light the smoke do I remember that the pussy has a
woman attached to it. And now her pussy is, it seems, puffing away.
Of its own accord. It's wild. In a *Ripley's Believe It or Not* sort of way.
It's fascinating in much the same way I found some of the more complicated exhibits at the science museum where I once took Willa to be.
I tilt my head to one side and then the other, trying to get a better view
of the mechanism. I fully expect to see strings or a carefully hidden
set of hydraulics, or maybe a tiny little man—a Tom Thumb-sized
version of the chain-smoking, mah-jongg-toothed guy who brought
me here.

Fascinating, but not the kind of thing you want to fuck. I wonder if
it's just me. I look at the men sitting at the tables around me, trying to
see if I can spot a single erection in the group. But it's dark and many
of the patrons seem to be preoccupied with the waitresses who—topless but wearing numbered badges so they can be identified—wander
through the audience trying to negotiate "dates" for the night.

After the girl finishes smoking the cigarette with her vagina, she
plucks it, like a flower, from between her lips and the bidding begins.

The winner will get to keep the cigarette. Even smoke it if he so chooses. After that the girl pulls on her bottoms, slaps on her badge, and walks off the stage. She is replaced by another girl who squats as if she is going to use the toilet but instead pops the top off a Sharpie. She shoves it into her cunt with all the eroticism of a mechanic inserting a dipstick, and then uses it and her vagina to draw a portrait of one of the drunker, richer patrons in the audience. When she is done, it looks a lot like Baby Huey. He pays a hundred dollars for it. The next girl peels a banana with her pussy. The one after that opens a Coke bottle. And for the finale, the last girl lies on her back, reaches two fingers up in there, and yanks out a string of razor blades that must be three feet long.

After that the show is over. No balloon. I am slightly disappointed, but the truth is I've had enough of watching underage women use their twats as substitutes for household gadgets.

The mah-jongg guy is waiting for me outside the beads.

"Good pussy show, yeah? What I tell you?"

"There was no balloon," I say, trying to sound more annoyed than I am.

"What? No balloon?" He does a terrible job of acting shocked and appalled.

"No. No balloon."

"She do cigarette in pussy?"

"Yes," I nod. "She did the cigarette in the pussy."

He slaps me on the back and winks. "That a good one. You like?"

I shrug.

He looks at the dirty tiled floor for a while. I think I am supposed to think he is deep in thought.

"You want private pussy balloon show?" he says, raising his index finger. I think I am supposed to believe this thought has just occurred to him.

"Maybe another time," I say.

"You want date?" He winks again.

"Just the check, thanks," I say, sounding irritated. Because I am.

Mah-jongg guy stops winking and smiling and trying to make me happy. He hands me a tiny piece of paper covered in Thai scrawl and says I owe him $150. Entry fee plus drinks plus government tax. I could argue with him but I don't. I just want to go.

I wander aimlessly around Patpong for a while, passing bar after bar.

"You want fuck show?"

"You want see pussy smoke cigarette?"

I look from one side of the street to the other and then over my shoulder. I'm nowhere near Charlie's. The man yelling at me has perfect straight white teeth. Apparently, in Bangkok, pussy smoking is not an uncommon skill. For some reason this makes me sad. I keep walking, trying to ignore the fact that suddenly it all makes me sad— the women, the pussy show barkers, the tourists, the smell of the food carts, the old men who sell greasy noodles and unidentifiable meat on a stick, the flashing neon lights, the sound of the Vespas, the thick black exhaust from the cars, visible even at night.

The drop is sudden, extreme and frightening. Like going over a waterfall you didn't know was there. One minute you're floating on calm water in a canoe. The next you're tumbling, plunging . . . Now it is just you and the churning water and the rocks just beneath the surface. No one and nothing can help you. Your only consolation is that you've been here before. But try telling that to a drowning man.

I am startled when I feel a hand on my arm. She is young and at first glance pretty.

"Mister look sad."

Then I notice the acne scars. And that she is missing her right thumb.

"Mister want date? I make Mister happy," she says, stroking me with her thumbless paw. "I know how suck goooood."

It's still early. Not even midnight. I could hire a prostitute if I wanted. But I don't. Mister not want. So I put fifty dollars in her good hand. Then I hail a cab and tell the driver to take me back to the hotel. I want to sit at a normal bar and get picked up by a relatively normal woman. I'm rich, I'm American, and I am in possession of all my digits. Is that too fucking much to ask?

I walk into the giant lobby of the giant Pan Pacific and feel the panic pull up and park in the empty space next to the sadness. The hustle and bustle, coming and going, to-ing and fro-ing—even at midnight—is overwhelming. And everyone here seems to have a destination.

Normally, I like big, anonymous hotels like the Pan Pacific. Sixteen hundred rooms, Jacuzzi bathtubs, monogrammed slippers, and room-service cards that get collected by some nameless, faceless housekeeping staffer at three A.M. and magically produce eggs, bacon, and hash browns at your bedside anytime you fucking please.

Ellen loved—loves—bed-and-breakfasts. The kind of place where each room has a name. And a theme. And more often than not, a stuffed bear. Once a year—usually on her birthday—I would indulge this perversion. She would pick some overpriced gingerbread Victorian in the wine country and we would spend the weekend sitting at some elderly couple's dining room table making small talk with strangers over egg soufflé and cranberry quick bread served only between eight and nine fucking thirty.

At ten thirty we'd be nodding politely while some chick with a nose ring explained why her soil was so much better than that of any of the other vineyards in Napa. Then we'd swirl, sniff, sample, and spit.

By eleven I stopped spitting so I wouldn't have to pay attention to their shit or notice that their wine all tasted the same, and by noon Ellen would wrestle the keys to our rental car away from me and insist on driving. I miss those trips.

I am feeling very sorry for myself, and thinking about Ellen has made it worse. I am not tired and I don't feel like watching porn. The giant circular lobby bar, open twenty-four hours a day, is centrally located so as to make it nearly impossible to avoid. Exactly halfway between the hotel's front entrance and the dimly lit Club A-Nan Roi-Yim (Club of Endless Smiles) where hotel guests or whoever is willing to pay can see elaborate floor shows featuring traditional Thai entertainment of the non-pussy-smoking-cigarette variety. "Smiles," as it is known on the premises, offers only PG-rated, family-friendly fare. Which is to say that penetration of any human orifice—whether by another human, animal, or inanimate object—is not part of the lineup.

The first night I was here—too jet-lagged to leave the hotel—I took advantage of my Pan Pacific guest discount coupon and went to the Smiles dinner-theater show. I sat alone at my table in the dark, smoke-filled room, surrounded by mostly Western tourists and a few Thai businessmen, eating my traditional Thai six-course meal. On stage, lovely young women wearing traditional Thai period costumes narrated an abbreviated history of their country while stripping down to their G-strings and then pole dancing to traditional Thai folk music. It was like going to see a titty show at the Smithsonian.

I haven't been back to Club of Endless Smiles. I much prefer the impromptu little entertainments inadvertently staged by the guests at the lobby bar. Chrome, black leather, and mirrors all the way around, it emits a comforting corporate blandness. The lobby bar is always the path of least resistance—which is always my favorite kind of path.

I sink onto a squishy barstool and order a vodka. I feel the panic recede a millimeter or two. The first icy-cold sip slides down my throat, past my esophagus, and into my stomach, where I feel a painful but pleasant burning sensation. Physical pain is not only preferable to the other kind but often welcome. Distracting, soothing—pain I can sink my teeth into.

The couple is already arguing when they sit down on the barstools to my left. She is very tall and icily blonde and everything about her is long—her legs, her fingers, her hair, which she gathers up into a self-knotting bun.

"I'm happy to lie to you if that's what you want, Donald, but eventually you're going to have to—"

"Catherine?" His voice is soft and sad and his suit is black. He is blandly handsome in a forgettable Brooks Brothers sort of way. "Please try not to be a bitch?"

She shrugs and takes a long sip of her drink. She puts her hand on top of his.

"I'm not trying to be mean. He was my friend too."

Donald yanks his hand away. "No, you sat at the same desk. You exchanged information about commodities and currencies." Donald is yelling, or at least raising his voice enough to give me sufficient excuse to look over and make eye contact with the woman.

"Donald, come on. Stop yelling," she says, gripping his sleeve.

"You were colleagues. You were not friends," Donald says quietly.

"Ben was my friend. And I know him. I knew him. He was having a genuinely good time. It was the right move. He was happy. He wouldn't have . . ."

I can't tell yet whether they are married or just good work friends in mourning. They say nothing for a while. She orders another drink. And one for him.

"He was crazy, impulsive," she says, turning to look at him. "That's not the same thing."

Donald bangs his glass on the bar. "He hated working at Lehman. You're saying quitting makes him crazy?"

Catherine bangs back. "No, I'm saying . . . because he left in the middle of the night . . . without telling any of us. And why did it take him almost six months to get in touch?"

I know I am staring but I can't look away. I am riveted by Ben's story and by their differing versions of it.

"And fine. Yes," Catherine says in a tight, angry whisper I have to strain to hear, "because *my* friend Ben—who I shared a desk with for *four years*—was not the kind of guy who would just jettison his MBA and a VP job to live in a shack on the beach and teach econ to a bunch of stupid rich kids who couldn't get into a decent college back home."

And it is at this moment that I realize that is *exactly* what I want to do. I am tired of wandering. I want a home base. Or at least a shack base. To be part of a community for a while. Of bikini-clad coeds. Suddenly I realize that everything happens for a reason. Everything is connected. Everythingisconnected. Everything. Is. Connected.

Donald stares down at the bar, shaking his head.

"Ben wouldn't kill himself. He wouldn't do it."

I decide to become part of Ben's story.

"It's really none of my business." I am on a mission to make their business my business. "But what's the point of torturing yourself over questions you'll never have the answers to?"

Donald thinks and nods. "You're right, not that you know fuck all about it." Catherine leans around Donald to look at me.

"Uh . . . excuse me, but who the hell are you?"

Here, I think, is my opportunity. But it is fragile. These two are grieving, which makes them vulnerable. But they are not stupid. This will not be easy. But I do not like Bangkok. I would much rather be on a secluded Thai beach. With . . . a job? A job. Yes. Ensconced in faculty housing. Students. Colleagues. Purpose. I will serendipitously show up at just the right time to fill the position left by the tragic and untimely death of . . . shit, what was his name?

"You're right, I'm nobody," I tell Donald apologetically. "And I'm sorry, your friend, his . . . the way he . . . passed. None of my business. Guess I've had one too many. Probably a little starved for conversation. But that's no excuse."

"No worries," Donald says. "Don't sweat it."

"Thanks," I say. "And really, I'm sorry about your friend. Sounds like he was a good guy."

"He was. He really was."

"Yeah," Catherine says wistfully, "Ben was like—no bullshit. He always told the truth. How many people can you say that about?"

Ben. Right.

"Too few," I say. "Too damn few." I call out to the bartender for another round. When he brings it, I raise my glass.

"To Ben," I say. "No bullshit."

Catherine and Donald raise their glasses. "Ben," they say, and, misty-eyed, we down our drinks. It is the beginning of a beautiful, if brief, friendship.

I entice them into playing hooky from work so that we can take a day trip to Kanchanaburi, where we tour the wildlife sanctuary, ride the train along the Death Railway, and have lunch with the monks. At night we get drunk at upscale clubs filled with Westerners and expats. By day five of our lovefest, I know the names of their bosses and their bosses' bosses, the brownnosers, the wimps, the backstabbers, and the decent guys in the Lehman Brothers Bangkok office. I don't care but I act like I do. They need to think that I do. Because we tell each other everything. Our friendship has the intensity of bonds made at summer camp and in freshman dorms. We reveal our most intimate secrets. Mine are lies tailored to suit Donald and Catherine's particular needs. I research and fabricate a résumé just imperfect enough to make me the perfect candidate for Ben's job. When I leave, Catherine gets teary. We all promise to stay in touch. Really.

Two weeks and a five-hour train ride later, I am sitting in a chair opposite Tim, the dean of McCarthy College, who is younger than I, American, ginger-haired, and freckled. There is a surfboard leaning in a corner behind his desk. I stare out past his balcony on to Cha-am, the most beautiful beach I have ever seen, as he peruses my fabricated résumé and letters of recommendation from two senior vice presidents at Lehman Brothers Bangkok.

When he finishes, he looks up at me and shakes his head. "Professor Conrad—"

"Oh, please, call me Joe."

"Alright then, Joe—you are a godsend. Seriously."

"Well, I certainly didn't know Ben the way Cathy and Don did, but I do know he loved it here. I've wanted out of the city for a long time, so—I didn't want to take advantage, but as you can see, Don and Cathy seemed to feel Ben would approve."

"I know he'd be thrilled," the dean says. "He was that kind of guy. Generous."

"And no bullshit," I add.

Tim nods. "Exactly."

I am surprised at how quickly, how seamlessly I slide into this life. And how much I enjoy it. The nondescript but tidy modern campus has all the amenities its 3,500, largely American students and faculty could want. And I have classes, faculty functions, office hours. Suddenly, I have a life. Not my own, but a life that I am living. Every day. And I feel normal. Every day.

I awake expecting not to, but I do. I wait for the other shoe to drop, but it doesn't. The sun shines on the ocean and I realize I am happy to be just where I am. I begin dating a colleague—Karen, from the poli-sci department. When, after some months together, she suggests we move our things into one bungalow and cohabit, I am stunned at how quickly and happily I agree.

Whatever was wrong with me (which seems to have happened an eternity ago), I think, must be gone. Because I am happy. Again and again. Every day.

And then, without warning, a tsunami hits our little island, taking with it everything I hold dear. Except I am the only person whose life is lost. Karen tells me, as she is packing her things, that there were plenty of warnings. That she herself issued them, as did Tim, my best friend. But I refused to listen to anyone. She tells me she loves me but cannot live with me anymore; cannot be with me anymore.

She tells me I need help. And Tim—my friend, my boss—says he cannot cover for me any longer. That he has to let me go. I don't remember doing anything terribly untoward, but when he goes over the laundry list, it is long: coming to class drunk, not coming at all, hitting on students, starting fights with deans, more drinking, conducting drug deals on campus, punching a student. It begins to sound familiar. To wash over me in sickening waves.

I am my own personal tsunami. I have wiped out my life again. The debris floats around me, reminding me that this was no cure, just a happy hiatus.

Now it's back. I am back. So I leave. Filled with more dread for what lies ahead than I have ever felt before. Because this was good. For a long time. And I don't know what I did to fuck it up or how the hell to get it back. And that is a new kind of terror.

New York, 1994. In general, I dislike coming to the dayroom. Two weeks in, I got bored with the circus animals that lie around here throwing their crap at each other. Now it is just irritating. And depressing. I can't decide which is worse. But when a guttural scream comes from the dining area, I know there's at least a chance that something entertaining might happen.

"How can you even think of not coming tomorrow? I cannot go one more day without my own clothes!" It is Glenda—manic, psychotic, paranoid, and generally unpleasant—she arrived a few days ago. And has been a one-woman show ever since.

By the time Glenda was brought in—tiny, wild-haired, raving mad—she hadn't eaten or slept in weeks. Her skin was almost translucent except for the deep gray moons under her eyes. Any normal human would have been half dead with exhaustion, but Glenda had an energy that was like watching gasoline burn. And despite all the drugs, she has not settled down. She is like watching Twyla Tharp interpret a six-car pileup.

Her mother sits next to her knitting, not even blinking as Glenda screams at the top of her lungs.

"I am completely dissatisfied! I am unimpressed with your church! I hope you die cleaning their kitchen like the slave cunt that you are!"

"I am going to pray for you," Glenda's mother says quietly without looking at her daughter.

"You are an old woman and you don't know anything! You are ignorant and uneducated! I don't need you to pray for me! I need my fucking clothes!"

At this point Glenda begins to yank off her hospital top, revealing a lacy lavender bra.

Her mother continues to knit, silently absorbing the vitriol.

At this point, there is no show I would rather be watching. Unfortunately, Glenda catches me. "What are you staring at, you fucking pervert?"

"You," I answer. "Because you're undressing in public, you fucking pervert."

Glenda stands and screams again as she upends the flimsy Formica table she and her mother have been sitting at. I'm guessing Glenda is somewhere in her late thirties. Her mother, in her late fifties. I wonder how many times they've played this scene on this set before. Glenda's mother continues to sit there knitting as two or three orderlies come running.

"I don't need you in my life, you bitch!" Glenda screams as she is being restrained. But Glenda is stronger than she looks and reinforcements, in the form of the two New York City policemen whose job it is to protect the fancy hospital and its mostly white doctors and patients from the surrounding immigrant neighborhood, enter through the double-locked doors. It's not the first time the staff has summoned the men in blue since Glenda arrived here. As she is being escorted to the Quiet Room, she looks over her shoulder at me.

"You see how I treat my mother? Don't even think about messing with me. It'll be a thousand times worse."

Nurse Frankie pats me on the back.

"She'll be fine when her meds kick in. She's actually very sweet."

That's too bad, I think, she's so much fun just the way she is.

EIGHTH

What if this is the end? What if this time I don't come back?

Maybe I'd deserve that. Maybe not. Regardless, I will have brought it on myself. That much is clear. I can't argue—though I have tried to on countless occasions with an impressive array of doctors, law enforcement officials, and more women than I can count—that my behavior over the last ten years has been to varying degrees . . . inappropriate.

So maybe it would be justice, I think, the panic slowly rising as I go under. Maybe this is karma coming around to vindicate the victims of my bad behavior. Karma coming around to bite me in the ass.

Santiago, 1991. I tell lies. Everywhere I go, I am someone else. Every country, every day, every woman, a different lie. There is a speedy thrill to it—losing track of myself. But I'm starting to get bored. Twitchy. I roll over in this king-size bed with its massive head- and footboards made out of trees ripped from the local rainforests and stare at Miren, the lovely young woman I have been fucking and pretending to care about for the past two weeks.

She has round hips and a substantial ass and big, heavy breasts. But what I like best about Miren is the enormous black thatch of ungroomed pubic hair between her legs and the little tufts under her arms to match. My passion for female armpit hair is a relatively recent development. I might have come to it sooner if I'd had the opportunity, but you don't see a lot of fuzzy pits coming down the red carpet or signaling for the check at the Ivy. If only those women knew what a huge turn-on it is to wander the sidewalks and markets here and to feel as if every woman who hails a cab or opens an umbrella is flashing me, allowing me to steal a glimpse of her little pocket-sized vagina.

After we fucked for the first time, I told Miren the women where I come from shave or wax most of their pubic hair off.

"And you think it look nice, these womens with the little baby cunts?" She made a thoroughly disgusted face. "And the mens, they rip the hairs off their balls too?"

"No, the mens get to keep their pubic hair," I told her.

"Dats fucked up," she said.

And cultural differences aside, I couldn't disagree. Miren is Basque, twenty-three, and was traveling through South America with friends when we met at a bar nowhere near my five-star hotel. I watched her in the bar for a long time before I approached her. I've learned by now that watching them, deciding what I like about them, helps me decide who I am. What lies I will tell.

With Miren there was a lot to like. I liked how she pounded her fist on the bar after every shot she drank. How she lifted her thick, dark curls off her neck and fanned herself. And I liked how she held her girlfriend's hips from behind and swayed with her on the dance floor. And most of all, I liked how her wide, deep laugh reverberated in me. How it bounced around in my empty spaces. I liked the kind of man she made me. By the time I bought Miren her first drink, we were already intimate.

Five days ago, Miren sent her traveling companions—three girlfriends from university and a couple of charmless, unwashed German boys—ahead, choosing instead to stay here with me in Santiago. This trip is supposed to be Miren's last bit of frivolous fun before she starts working as an au pair for a family in Greenwich, Connecticut.

If Miren has made any assumptions, they are her own. I did not encourage nor discourage her choices. I never do. Despite that, she's angry when I tell her I'm leaving. When Lee tells her. Lee Majors, hotel security specialist.

"East Africa, Lee!" Miren yells over the noise of the shower. "Why don't you just put a gun in your head? Do you know what's happening in there? AIDS, civil war?"

The doors of the enormous three-headed shower are completely transparent, so the only buffer I have between me and this irritating whining is the water and whatever steam I'm generating (which isn't much since Miren has the annoying habit of leaving the bathroom door open). Still, I refuse to engage.

"Got to go where the jobs are, babe," I call out cheerfully, making sure to keep my back to her. Rules of nonengagement. Rules to live by. I know she is standing out there yelling at me completely naked, probably with her hands on her full, fleshy hips. Miren is completely unselfconscious.

"That's bullshit, Lee. No tourist with any brains is going to go in there now."

I turn off the water, and as I step out of the shower Miren chucks a towel at me.

"Thanks."

I dry off absentmindedly as I walk past her into the dressing room, dropping my towel on the thick vanilla-colored carpet and pulling one of the hotel's three-hundred-dollar terry-cloth robes out of the closet. As I slide into it, I think how very nice it would be to be alone right now. I look across my deluxe suite at the clock and wonder how quickly I can get rid of Miren. I feel the need rise in me like dirty flood water—murky, violent, impure.

She has followed me out of the bathroom and I can feel her standing behind me—stiff, angry, lips pinched. "Goddammit, don't just walk away."

I ignore her, fill a glass with bottled water from the minibar, and stand in front of the mirror drinking it down while she stares at me, fuming. I am buying time. Because what I'd really like to do is turn around and slap her. Hard enough to make her shut her fucking mouth. I see my hand pull back to gain momentum, watch it fly through the air toward her face, and feel a sharp, painful sting as I make contact.

Miren gasps. "My God, Lee. You are fucking crazy."

Like a dog's electric collar, the pain reminds me of my boundaries. I would never do that. The drops of blood on the carpet are mine—a shard from the glass I slammed onto the marble counter is stuck in my palm. I would never hit a woman. That would show a lack of control. An unseemly weakness. And Lee Majors is not that kind of man.

"Hey, Miren, sweetheart?" I say with great tenderness.

"Yes, Lee?" She looks at me expectantly.

"I could pretend to appreciate your concern but I really don't give a shit what you think, so let's just skip to the end, okay?"

Her mouth falls open and experience tells me I have less than forty-five seconds before she picks up something and throws it at me. The ubiquitous hotel Bible is a popular choice.

"Just what the fuck do you think you can be doing?" she spits at me.

I move to the in-room safe and spin the combination while I talk to her over my shoulder.

"What I mean is . . . you are a smart, funny, sexy woman. And you are going to do great things in life."

"That is not an answer. Answer me, you *kabroi hori*."

I am standing beside myself. Watching this scene. Enjoying the comic absurdity of the hysterical, chubby naked girl with the full bush screaming at the cruel, unfeeling bastard.

Twenty, maybe twenty-five seconds left on the clock.

Her eyes are darting around the room. I grab the envelope from inside the safe where I've kept it since I made my purchase yesterday. "I have something for you." And before she can make a move, I put it in her hands. She is wary but carefully tears it open and peeks inside.

"You are paying my ticket to JFK?" she says, stunned.

I look into her eyes and gently caress her cheek. "I think you're a good investment," I say softly and know I've just closed the deal.

She throws her arms around my neck and I can almost hear the door closing behind her.

"Thank you, Lee," she whispers in my ear. "I never forget this. Or these weeks we spend. Or you." She kisses me, and without bothering to put on underwear, throws on her clothes, grabs her backpack, and bolts. Just like I knew she would. Because she doesn't want me to find out what I already knew when I bought her $875 coach ticket—that her Greenwich employers sent her a plane ticket when they hired her. And that she's rushing out to cash in the one I gave her for U.S. dollars.

I straighten the sheets, lie down on the bed, and aim the remote at the TV, speeding through the Spanish-speaking channels on my way to the universal language of porn. I sigh with relief. I am alone. Lee is alone. Lee is alone. Lee . . .

I try to concentrate on the girl-on-girl action, but a disturbing feeling of weightlessness has begun in my ankles and is creeping up toward my colon. I'm aware of my heart picking up speed in my chest. I get up and walk slowly to the hotel safe, hoping maybe I won't realize I've begun to panic. The safe is still open. I take out my old passport and examine it carefully. Surname: Todd. Given name: Greyson

Harold. Date of birth: 4 August 1945. I take my wallet out of the safe and dump the contents on the bed, examining the defunct credit cards, expired driver's license, ancient AAA membership. I recheck the passport. Todd, Greyson Harold. I check the picture against my image in the mirror. Close enough.

The panic recedes and I climb back into bed. I call room service, order a bottle of Ketel One, and go back to the porn. Relieved. Greyson is alone. Greyson is alone.

And then—I am staring at a blank screen. I wait. For something. For some synapse to fire. For neurotransmitters to distill into pixels which will consolidate into interpretable images. But for what seems like the longest time, there is nothing. I have the impulse to get up—to walk across the room and bang on the top of the TV. But I can't move. So I lie there waiting to reboot. When I do, I have no idea how much time has passed. All I know is, it is all wrong. The picture is clear enough. I am more or less where I left off. Santiago. Hotel bathroom. The shower. Water running. And yet it is all wrong. Because the editing has been botched.

The poor bastard in the shower is not me. And at the same time, in some other space, he is—a black-and-white image set against an otherwise Technicolor memory. He is fifteen years old, soaking wet and dressed in the tux I wore to my first Oscar ceremony. He stares out of the shower at me, lost, terrified. He is a memory, out of his depth, drowning, clearly yanked from some black-and-white montage I had stashed away somewhere in my temporal lobe, where he was minding his own business.

I realize, as I have dozens of times in my career, that it's all in the editing. Even now. Someone, I think, should put this kid out of his misery before he gets where he is going. Before he ends up in this hotel room. In this shower. In color. Before he ends up on this table. Watching this. Like me.

How great, I wonder, is the divide between fate and memory? Between playing the game and Monday morning quarterbacking? Being old enough to know better and being a better man? Does choice exist or is fate biologically predetermined? The question becomes an association, followed by an image which quickly morphs into montage. And in the flutter of an eyelid the scenery has changed.

Beverly Hills, 1961. When I woke up, I found Pop sitting in the La-Z-Boy, legs bouncing, hair greasy, standing up in the back, still wearing the short-sleeved sport shirt and wrinkle-resistant slacks he'd put on two mornings ago. He hadn't been to bed in nearly three days; he'd been up scribbling ideas for a new business venture.

There was an empty liquor bottle under the coffee table and another more than half-empty on top. When he got like this, though, even the booze didn't slow him down. Nothing did. He didn't even seem to notice when there was another person in the room.

"Hey, Pop." I approached him tentatively. Like you would an unpredictable wild animal. I watched him carefully arrange scraps of paper in rows and then change his mind and sort them into piles. "Get any sleep last night, Pop?" I asked. He didn't seem to hear me, but I knew the answer. I'd been right there next to him all night with the pillow over my head, trying to block out the noise.

"Got the idea off the TV," he blurted out as if we were already in the middle of a conversation. Then he clapped his hands, like he was all ready to get to work. "Except the guys on the show completely missed the boat, whereas my way—"

My mother walked in with Jake and Ben sleepily trailing behind her.

"What's going on?" my mother asked, trying to hide her nervousness.

My father ignored her and continued talking. "Let me tell you something, boys," my father said, suddenly on his feet pitching to Ben and Jake. "The biggest success stories in our nation were risk-takers—Thomas Edison, Howard Hughes, Henry Ford, Charles Lindbergh—great men who weren't afraid to take chances."

Ben and Jake stared at him, wide-eyed.

"Am I right?"

They looked at each other and then nodded. "Smart boys. Of course I am."

I could feel disaster hovering like a huge blimp above our house. Again.

"Well, what do you think would have happened if those great men had played it safe?"

Ben's hand shot up in the air. I put my hand on his shoulder and whispered, "Ben, you're not in school and Pop's not Miss Lipsky. You don't have to raise your hand."

"Ray, sweetie," Mom asked, "what's going on? Something I should know about?"

"When the time's right," he said without looking at her.

Last week Pop had stayed up drinking scotch, ransacked the kitchen, and found the Blue Chip Stamps my mother had painstakingly collected. He still wouldn't tell any of us what he'd ordered. "When the time's right" was all he would say. In the meantime, all we knew was they were gone. All of them.

"Willa, baby, have I ever let you down?" he said, coming up behind her and roughly massaging my mother's shoulders.

"No, sweetheart, of course not . . ."

"Then you leave the financial matters to me," he said and winked at me. "Every good entrepreneur knows you got to spend money to make money. Isn't that right, Grey?"

After twenty minutes Pop had hardly paused to take a breath. "You have to diversify, which means investing." I looked at him—dirty, ranting, stinking of booze and sweat—and thought of the crazies and the winos I'd seen staggering around Hollywood Boulevard near my grandfather's store. I wondered for the first time if they had children.

"Pop," I said loudly but calmly. "Pop, enough, okay?" But like a politician on some marathon filibuster, he just kept talking.

"And investing means spending. And that's where the government bonds come in. Because I've figured out something no one else has—a way to manipulate the interest. All on the up and up. I think. And it all starts with credit."

"Credit?" Suddenly my mother turned pale and sank to the floor.

"That's right, by George." Pop was practically beaming with pride now. It was almost as if he owned Diners Club outright; almost as if, without giving a thought to finance charges and monthly interest rates, he had charged well beyond his limit without bothering to pay a cent of it. Without even thinking about the fact that after his card was revoked it would take my mother two years of working overtime and weekends to pay off his debt. It was, in fact, almost as if my father's confidence increased with the length of his unemployment. It was almost as if it had never happened before.

"What the heck?" Hannah had just appeared at my side.

"He's . . . It's bad, really bad," was all I could say.

"Hannah," my father boomed at her, "did you know that credit is one of the things that makes America great?"

A short-term, high-interest loan, he'd called it on more than one occasion.

While Pop was still talking, my mother slowly got up and pulled a chair over to the front closet where we kept the suitcases. "Greyson, could you help me please," she said, her voice tight.

I took down all four suitcases. All four of the little gold locks had been pried off. Her handbags had been ransacked. Anything of value—silver candlesticks, my grandmother's pearls, anything, everything—it was all gone. My mother collapsed onto the floor again, her face a blank mask except for the single tear running down her cheek.

"What else, Ray? Just tell me now. How bad is it?"

"It's not bad, Willa, don't you see? This is it—this is our big chance. I've figured it all out, all the angles. And sure it's risky, but no risk, no reward. Right? Am I right? I'm right. This is an investment in our future. You trust me, don't you, baby? I need to know you're on my side."

"I'm on your side, Ray," my mother whispered.

"It doesn't sound like you mean it," my father bellowed. "Say it like you mean it."

"I'm on your side," she said again, almost letting her anger seep out. But not quite. Because she knew where that would get her. I clenched my jaw until I thought my molars would break.

"But I need to know," she said, trying to keep her voice from shaking. "How much have you spent? What did you buy? Who did you give . . ." Her voice caught and she swallowed a sob. My mother knew by now that getting emotional when Pop was like this just made things worse. "Who'd you give our credit card numbers to? And did you give away anything else? We have a stack of bills that just keeps getting taller and taller and I don't know how much longer I can—"

"What? What the hell do you know? I knew you'd crap all over my idea. You always do. You don't know shit about business. You don't know shit about anything. If it weren't for you, I would have made my first million by now."

"You know that's not true, Pop," I said. "You're just exhausted. I'm going to get you cleaned up and then you're going to rest for a while."

"Bullshit! I have work to do. So if you're not with me, get the hell out."

Pop sat back down on the sofa and started organizing the napkins, empty potato chip bags, torn pieces of newspaper, and labels from the scotch bottle that he'd scribbled his notes on. He looked up at me, then at my mother.

"Are you deaf or just stupid? I said get out. Jesus Christ, the woman can't do anything except breed."

"Hannah, take the boys in the other room," I said.

"What the hell are *you* staring at?" my father screamed at me.

"I think you owe Mom an apology," I said through clenched teeth after they'd left.

"Oh yeah? Is that what you think, you little smart-ass piece of shit?"

My mother rushed toward us. "Raymond, please, he didn't mean—"

"You shut up, I'm talking to my son!" he screamed. And then he hit her. Hard across the cheek. She fell onto the floor, too stunned to cry.

"There's your fuckin' apology. Happy now?"

He sat back down in front of the TV with his notepad and bottle of scotch. It took me that long to realize what had just happened. I pulled him off the sofa and started pummeling him, punching him over and over. He was still bigger than me—broader, heavier—but he was drunk and his reflexes were slow. He wasn't even fighting back. I didn't hear my mother begging me to stop until I'd broken his nose.

The room was very still for a moment after that. Then he left. Mom called after him but he didn't turn around. He was still wearing his slippers.

That was on a Wednesday morning.

On Thursday, a truck arrived from Sears. Hannah was home with the boys.

"You signed for it?" I said, staring at the garage full of boxes. "What were you thinking?"

"Well, no one else was home and the driver said 'signature required.'"

"Who gives a damn what the driver said? We don't want this crap!" Now she was crying. And it wasn't her fault.

"I'm sorry for yelling," I said. "You're not the one I'm mad at."

On Friday, our neighbor, Mrs. Hoffman, saw another Sears truck outside the house. Knowing no one was home, she dashed across the street and took it upon herself to sign for another eight cartons. The final inventory consisted of: tents (5), power lawn mowers (3), cases of Spackle (10), ironing boards (4), TV sets (5), wheelchair (1), set of matching luggage (1), canoes (3), radial tires (8), motorcycle (1), boxes of copper pipe, rubber tubing, aluminum siding (12).

My mother took it better than I thought she would.

"Well, I'm very familiar with the Sears return policy," she said, arms crossed over her chest, looking into the nearly full garage. "Full refund if returned with a receipt within thirty days. Of course, they'd charge an arm and a leg to come pick it up. And we can't wait thirty days. I can't have these charges on Lord knows which card."

She turned to look at me. "Greyson, do you think Mr. Van Gilder would let you borrow his truck for a few hours this weekend?"

"This weekend? I'm working Sunday . . ."

"Saturday then . . . tell him it's just for a few hours."

I looked at the garage and knew it would take more than a few hours. Cleaning up Pop's mess would take most of the day. The day I was supposed to have my first real date with Ellen Goodman. I'd had a crush on her since the first day of European History class when she walked in and sat behind me. Her family wasn't rich and they weren't poor; they were in the middle—"comfortable," as my parents would say. And she was smart. Smarter than I thought any girl that pretty could possibly be.

Alan was having a pool party and Ellen had agreed to go with me. Now I was going to have to cancel. She'd still go. Just not with me. I don't think I ever hated my father more than that morning when I was loading those boxes into the back of Van Gilder's flatbed.

Two days later, Pop reappeared in a light-blue convertible Cadillac Eldorado. He pulled up in front of our building and leaned on the horn until the neighbors yelled and my mother came running out in her bathrobe. He sat in the front seat wearing a brand-new shiny blue suit.

"Well, what do you think?" he asked, spreading his arms as if he were offering her a world he had to give instead of a used Caddie leveraged against wedding silver and college funds, bought by a crazy drunk on a Sunday morning.

Run. Run, is what I thought. Before it's too late.

To be anywhere else.

Santiago International Airport, 1991. I am having trouble sitting still. I know I cannot rely on my limbs to remain within the space allotted them by the FAA. So I buy two first-class seats for the flight to Entebbe. At first the woman behind the British Airways counter in Santiago is confused. She wants to know the name of the second passenger. I try to explain about my arms and legs, but she doesn't understand. I can feel my skin getting hotter with my frustration, my irritation. She is ineffectual, useless. I put my hands on the cool Marbelite counter and lean in to get a look at her plastic ID badge. She backs away, startled.

"Pillar," I say, closing my eyes and lowering my forehead to rest on the cool counter, "do you think perhaps I could speak with your boss or whomever you think would be kind enough to take my goddamn fucking money?"

She says nothing and I don't look up, but I do hear the sound of her ridiculously high heels receding and then returning with her supervisor. Though she has demonstrated no understanding of it herself, Pillar seems to be explaining the situation to her boss. She is bilingually incompetent. She talks for forever. At least thirty minutes.

There is a huge clock over the entrance to the departure gates set to Santiago time. And another set to Tokyo time and one to New York time and one to Paris and one to Moscow. All of them indicate only nine minutes have passed since I arrived at the first-class ticket counter; only three since Pillar began her soliloquy. But I know that's a manipulation. Something the airport management does to trick you into thinking you're not waiting as long in line, or for your luggage, or to get on a delayed flight as you really are; that Pillar is not really as incompetent as in fact she is. Assholes. I'm surrounded by assholes.

I have to get out of here. Now. Where I go and what time I get there are largely irrelevant. I am never in the right place. The present, *here*, is just an anxious pit stop I make between memory (which is to say regret) and the dreadful anticipation of hoping *there* will be better but knowing it won't.

Many people—usually the happier ones, apparently—spend the bulk of their lives living in the here and now rather than continuously running the stoplight at its intersection. And judging by the number of self-help and talk-show gurus around, many more are looking to buy in the neighborhood.

I, on the other hand, speed through, running lights and stop signs, causing one accident after another. I know this is not the way happy people live. I've tried to make *here* matter. But for whatever reason, I can't make it count, much less make it last.

Unhappy people think like this. Like me. But I try not to dwell on it. It's a buzzkill. And inevitably leads me down a road paved with nooses and guns and toxic combinations of sedatives, vodka, and oven cleaner. It's better just to move on.

"Señor?"

I turn toward the voice and see the supervisor calling me from halfway across the ticketing area. I've been pacing. Restless. Uncooperative limbs. Unaware. Beware, small children, animals, the elderly and infirm.

"Señor?"

"I heard you the first time," I call back testily. I stride purposefully back to the counter and bark at the supervisor. "This had better be important."

The little mustached man is totally baffled. "Sir . . . ? Señor?"

"You pulled me out of a meeting. What's so urgent?"

He takes a small step back, nods slowly and smiles.

"I apologize for the interruption, señor. You would like to purchase two first-class tickets?"

"Yes."

"But you are the only passenger?"

"Yes?"

"You would like to spend the additional 4,600 U.S. dollars to have the empty seat?"

"Yes."

The supervisor begins clicking away on the computer keyboard in front of him. "How would you like to pay for that, sir?"

New York, 1994. "Hey there, welcome back." Slowly, Dr. Knight's round, friendly, goateed face comes into focus. His brow knits behind his little gold-rimmed glasses.

"How're you feeling?" He looks worried. "Can you tell me what year it is, Greyson?"

I shake my head but stop when the intense throbbing registers.

"How about the president? Can you tell me who's president?"

"No," I say, barely able to dig my way out of the fog. "What happened?"

"Apparently you gave 'em a little bit of a scare. Didn't want to come out from under. But you're okay. Wasn't anything major."

Out from under. Where. "Dr. Knight?"

"Yeah?"

"Shaved or unshaved?"

"Excuse me?"

"Women's armpits?"

"I . . . uh . . . well, geez, I don't exactly . . ." Knight is trying hard not to laugh. "Which do *you* prefer?" he asks.

"Don't give me that shit," I croak. "We need to agree on this. If we're going to be able to work together."

Knight knocks me lightly on the head with my file. "Get some rest. I'll come by later."

"I'll give you a hint," I yell slurrily as he's leaving. "One of 'em looks like a beautiful little twat and the other looks like a whole lotta nothin.'"

NINTH

I do not believe in God. Instead I believe in the power of Family. And occasionally, when I'm feeling optimistic, in free will. But blood is a force to be reckoned with. God, for example, can't give you an excellent head of hair. Your family can. They can also give you cancer. And heart disease. Nothing kills like Family.

I see my past stretched out in front of me—one flawed, damaged, beleaguered ancestor after another. The secret. The tragedy. The unfulfilled promise. The one success that got away.

My present is a conglomeration of the mistakes, missteps, dubious additions to the gene pool, and bad investments made by my parents, grandparents, great-grandparents, and great-great-grandparents.

But after that, there is my future—what is left when the Family has left the building. Has finished fucking with me. It's not much to work with, but it's mine.

Thank God for free will, right?

Uganda, 1992. Nearly everyone in Africa is black. This, for some reason, is a complete revelation. Maybe it's the effect of crossing four time zones in two days. Or possibly the heavy, steady flow of alcohol and sedatives into my system. Or the relatively few hours of sleep I've clocked over the last week or two. Or eight.

Or maybe it is just the truth—that compared to the rest of this continent, the passengers coming off my flight, myself in particular, are pasty, lifeless, bleached. That we look as if something integral has been removed. The part essential to the whole extracted from us in the night by space aliens or flesh-eating zombies. Or Jerry Falwell.

Deposited into this crowd of brown, I feel the sudden desperate urge to disappear into it.

Like a single drop of milk stirred into a cup of coffee.

Two tall, thin men in light-blue jumpsuits unload our baggage from the plane and wheel it over to the baggage area. The cart only holds six or seven suitcases at a time. After forty minutes of watching the two men go back and forth, I see three of my four bags make it onto the trolley. I am tired of waiting. Whatever was in the fourth can't be that important.

As I stand in front of the airport scanning names on the dozens of cardboard signs held by dozens of black men, all wearing African-print shirts and Ray-Ban sunglasses, I feel a momentary impulse to break into one of Johnny Carson's monologues. I imagine reciting the names on the cards as if they were jokes. Then I see my name. The impulse passes. I walk toward my driver and hand him my baggage.

When we pull up to the hotel, I immediately regret allowing the travel agent in Santiago free rein. She was a British expat in her sixties. She'd been working at the American Express Office for more than twenty years. She said she knew just what I'd like and that she'd take care of everything. And she reminded me of Rene, my secretary at the studio. Except that Rene was from the Bronx. Rene took care of everything.

I have not completely broken the bad habit of delegating my life. Not that there is anything wrong with the beautiful five-star colonial hotel set among five acres of tropical gardens. In fact, it is perfect. But perfect is a lie. That much I know. Especially in this part of the world. We have that in common. I decide to stay and enjoy the perfect lie for a day or two before moving on to look for the awful truth. Or at least a more imperfect lie. One I can live with for a while.

I take the concierge aside and slip him too many Ugandan shillings to set me up with a non-government-sanctioned tour guide. I want someone who will take me places the guests in this hotel will never see. Nikudi, the concierge, says he will have no trouble finding such a person and that he can guarantee I will be taken places meant only for locals. He cannot, however, guarantee my safety.

"Do you understand, sir?" he asks.

"Yes," I say. "That's fine." The prospect of putting myself in harm's way only adds to the adventure.

"This is not going to be a tour out of *The Rough Guide.* Once you go off with this person—who is, I assure you, quite trustworthy—I will have no idea where you will be and no way to contact you."

"Sounds good to me," I say.

At eight the next morning, I meet my tour guide, Kwendo.

"So you and Nikudi are friends?" I ask after seeing them embrace warmly.

"Brother-in-law," he says, walking ahead of me so fast I have no choice but to follow.

"You're Nikudi's brother-in-law? Are you a tour guide?"

"I take you on tour" is the closest thing I get to an affirmative answer, but I cannot make myself care about his credentials.

"Where are we going?" I ask as I climb onto his motorcycle behind him.

"No problem," he says, "I take you real Uganda." And he is out of the gate so fast that the heat slaps me across the face and leaves me breathless.

The colors, sounds, smells, and heat of Kampala are overwhelming. At first it is like a circus or carnival. Swerving in, out, and between trucks spewing putrid exhaust and carrying live animals—chickens, goats, alpacas, and bicycles that double as taxis and a means to carry loads of bananas and bags of rice to market—is a dizzying ride. The relentless onslaught of swarming crowds and mixing smells of dung, cooking meat, sweat, and earth make my head feel as if it is going to explode.

I am relieved when we leave the city. The roads are unpaved, unmarked, an endless expanse of rust-red dirt. Women carry huge bundles on their heads. Women and girls as young as nine or ten. Little boys trail behind them, dirty, naked, trying to keep up.

"Where are the men?" I ask.

"Dead. AIDS," Kwendo says.

"Not all?" I ask stupidly.

"Of course not. But many. Too many."

At the Kalangala market, Kwendo has me buy several bottles of *waragi,* the local moonshine.

"This the best," he tells me in his heavily accented English. "Made from cassava. Not like that sugar cane shit." I nod like I know what he's talking about. I also, as directed, buy several kilos of meat the seller claims is goat, bags full of cassavas and bananas, sacks of rice, and some kind of soft bread. Then we stuff it all into leather satchels that hang from Kwendo's motorcycle where my legs used to go.

Kwendo climbs back on the bike and motions for me to get on. We drive for several hours with my legs wrapped around Kwendo's waist. He drives fast. No one here wears helmets, and on several sharp turns I have to squeeze my thighs together to keep from becoming roadkill. The experience is everything I'd hoped for. Thrilling. Exhilarating. Anonymous. I am lost now and there is no going back. I have not a single relationship or responsibility. I have no history. I am my actions and then only insofar as they linger or I leave.

There is a boat waiting for us when we arrive at Lake Victoria. A sort of all-purpose barge with a motor and a bamboo canopy, it easily accommodates Kwendo, his motorcycle, our provisions, and me. It is the complete opposite of any boat you might come across in a hotel brochure for a luxury or even economy tour of Lake Victoria.

The captain and Kwendo embrace briefly—a quick but sincere chest-bump and backslap. The tall young man, who wears a very sharp, long knife tucked into his jeans, turns out to be another relative of Kwendo's and of the concierge at my five-star hotel. I don't know why, but I am beginning to feel as if there is another agenda at work here, that my off-the-grid sightseeing adventure is not at the forefront or even background of today's plan. That, at best, I am along for the ride and have paid several hundred American dollars for the privilege (goat meat, moonshine, and cassava not included).

Every decision I have made today, from the minute I climbed onto Kwendo's motorcycle in front of my hotel, has been risky and reckless. It would be appropriate to be frightened at this moment. I know this. Intellectually. But I am not. I have no feelings. I cannot connect my actions with any consequences they may or may not have. The concept simply does not exist. I only want to see what happens next. Lake Victoria is enormous. It takes a very long time to cross even a small part of it.

"This is quite a tour," I say, trying to remind the two men who've been talking to one another nonstop in what I can only guess is Swahili that I am still on the boat with them. "So, where we going?" Again, I am ignored. As tour guides go, they leave much to be desired. But I don't mind. This is not that kind of tour.

We're pulling into a makeshift marina, and as the captain steers the boat, Kwendo throws me a line. "Tie up your side," he says. "Can you manage that?"

Little by little, over the course of the day, it has become clear that, while I may be the one with the money (which I am expected to spend freely), Kwendo is the one with the power. He calls the shots. I listen and obey. "Sure, no problem," I say, having no clue what to do. When the captain cuts the motor, I imitate Kwendo as he jumps off the boat onto the dock and then wraps the line around the ragged-looking iron moorings sticking out of the dock.

"We go to supper now," Kwendo announces.

"Great, my treat," I say. "By the way, where the hell are we?"

Kwendo and the captain exchange a look.

"Kenya," Kwendo says.

We have left Uganda and entered Kenya. I have no passport. Not even a fake one. No one has asked any questions. My kind of people. "We have been invited to dine with family," he says, as if this simple statement explains our journey.

Obviously we have brought dinner for the family. And breakfast and lunch. For at least the next month. The agenda has revealed itself. I wonder how the three of us and the food are all going to fit on one bike. Fortunately, the captain ("Call me Richard," he finally tells me) has his own motorbike.

The road signs indicate we are heading toward Kisumu city center, but just as we get close, Kwendo veers off in another direction. "Where are we going?" I yell into his ear, my thighs locked in a death grip at his waist.

"The whites and Asians live in the city," Kwendo yells back. "The Luos live here." Luo, I think, and make a mental note. Luo, not Swahili. Big difference. Wars have been fought over such differences—tribal, linguistic, territorial—it's all the same.

I look around. The "here" he has indicated is a slum. A big one. Row after row of huts made of mud and aluminum siding. Occasionally a concrete slab. Sewage is directed via some kind of primitive aqueduct into the lake. Scenic Lake Victoria: toilet of the impoverished and unplumbed.

"This is my sister's house," Kwendo says, stopping in front of one of the tiny concrete squares surrounded on all sides by mud huts. The front door opens and four small children come running out. The oldest maybe eight or nine, the youngest just starting to walk. A pretty but exhausted-looking young woman follows behind them. It is nearly impossible to guess her age. I look more closely: still pretty but probably once gorgeous. Her limbs are long and very thin. She might look emaciated were it not for the basketball-sized pregnancy she is carrying.

Richard and Kwendo drop their packages and each pick up two children, hug them, spin them around. Standard-issue uncle behavior. Then they embrace the woman. She cries and hugs them. For the first time today, I wonder what the fuck I am doing here—in a Kenyan slum, voyeur to this surreal family drama. A feeling? I can't be sure, but I suspect.

Next time you say you want to see how the locals live, be careful what you ask for.

"Greyson Todd," yells Kwendo from inside the house, "bring in the packages!" Of course, I think, looking down at the load of bags lying on the ground, I am now the Sherpa. And am I really going to argue? Fine, but not before I have a drink. So I pop the cork out of one of the bottles of waragi and take a long swallow. And regret it immediately. It is like drinking moonshine mixed with turpentine with a splash of triple sec. I recork the bottle and start hauling.

Oma, Kwendo's sister, lives in two rooms with a dirt floor. There is a sofa and an armchair, both leaking foam rubber filling. I cannot imagine where they all sleep. Oma is cooking dinner over a small fire.

But the place is neat and the decrepit kitchen table is covered with a lace cloth. Care has been taken. The paradoxes confound me.

"Where is the father?" I whisper to Kwendo.

"Dead. AIDS," he says.

"What about your sister? How will she manage with all these kids?" I ask, feeling like an idiot for being so shocked at something that should be no surprise.

"She will have to marry her husband's brother," Kwendo says. "He will inherit her."

"Inherit her? Seriously?" I ask, allowing my Western judgment to ooze out all over the dirt floor.

"It is tradition," Richard says coldly. "Her brother-in-law will take care of her."

"But I mean is she . . . what if she has . . ." I don't know how to ask the question delicately.

"Is sick?" Kwendo spits the words in my face.

"Well . . ."

"I don't know," Richard says. "She does not want to know. Probably she is. And the baby as well. But that's the tradition. And she'll give it to him and he'll give it to his other wives and so it goes." He spits on the floor, his anger and frustration landing on the red dirt next to my judgment. "Any other questions?"

Probably, but if I'm stupid enough to ask, I don't remember.

This is what I remember of the rest of that night: that goat tastes better than I ever imagined it could; that Oma dances with me to drum music that seems to come from nowhere and then everywhere, one hut at a time; that I drink toast after toast of waragi with Kwendo and Richard; that I develop a taste for it by the time I reach the bottom of my first bottle; that I have never smelled anything like Oma's skin—grassy, nutty, pungent, sweet, and dusty with sage and the red dirt floors of her house. And that I tell her she doesn't have to marry her brother-in-law.

"If I do not," she says, "I will be thrown out of the family and the community and they will take all my property from me. I will be homeless."

And after finishing the second bottle of waragi I lie down next to her on the old stained mattress out back behind her house, listening to the drumming, smelling the dirt, feeling so foreign that none of the rules apply.

"Do you have a condom?" she asks.

"No, but I'll just run down to the 7-Eleven."

"Don't be stupid," she says.

"I'm not stupid," I say, sliding my hand up her dress and into her panties. "I'm reckless."

"You have choices," she says, her breath catching, beginning to speed up, keeping time with the movement of my fingers. "I don't."

"I am giving you a choice, and," I add, stopping what I am doing and withdrawing my hand, "you don't even have to sleep with me."

She groans audibly, lifts her dress, and slides down her underwear. Then she turns and kisses me. "Some people don't believe in AIDS," she says, raising an eyebrow. "Some people believe it is witchcraft. That those who get sick have been cursed."

"What do you believe?" I ask her, slowly positioning myself behind her, slowly remembering how to fuck a pregnant woman.

"That it doesn't matter," she gasps as I slide into her. "That either way the funeral is the same."

I surprise Kwendo, which I did not think was possible, when I tell him I am staying on here for a few days. He is in no hurry and is more than a little suspicious of the white man who is far too comfortable being taken advantage of.

This is not exactly what he had planned. Especially when, on the third day, I announce my intention to marry his sister. Which I do— in broad daylight, so as to avoid the evil spirits that come to weddings held after dark.

Tradition. Family. Free will. And now, on top of all that, evil spirits to answer to as well.

And so I get a tour of the real Uganda and part of Kenya. And instead of a mask or drum or some other tourist trinket, I get a wife. Which in Kenya means a lot and not very much at the same time. I make promises but I don't take her with me. It's the promises that count and the rest that doesn't mean very much.

Back in Kampala, Nikudi, the hotel concierge, helps me arrange for a real house in Kisumu city center for Oma and her children, and for a bank account that will support her and pay the children's school fees and her medical costs when she gets sick. The total cost is the equivalent of a new Honda. I add a little for emergencies.

The bank manager, a young, balding Brit, fills out the paperwork haltingly. He examines and reexamines the wedding license. He is sweating through his seersucker jacket. I make Nikudi a cosignatory on the account and entrust him with making sure Oma gets her check every month. Nikudi, the hotel concierge whom I have known for only a few weeks. But what choice do I have? Am I really going to oversee this responsibility myself? A ridiculous notion. And if some of the money makes its way into a different "charity," it's still doing more good here, in this place, than it would be in my pocket. Promising to take care of Oma was a good idea. I've worked it out to the best of my abilities under the circumstances. I simply can't worry about the details after I leave.

I am checking out of the hotel. Nikudi hails a taxi and then stares at me, shaking his head.

"What?"

"When I say I could not guarantee your safety, this is not what I . . ."

"You just make sure Oma gets her check on the first of every month," I say.

He nods, shakes his head solemnly again. "For as long as she lives . . ."

"And after that, all those kids."

"Yes, right. All them kids." Nikudi rolls his eyes. As if just the thought of Oma's inevitable orphans is exhausting. "You one crazy motherfucker. You got a death wish—you know that, right?" he whispers, checking to make sure we are out of earshot of the other hotel staff.

"That's really no way to speak to a hotel guest . . ." I pull the name tag pinned to his uniform close to my face. "Nikudi."

"No, sir. Sorry, sir," he says with false sobriety. Then he cracks up. "Well, maybe if you are lucky you'll get knifed to death in Nairobi before you have a chance to die of AIDS."

"I'm not generally a lucky guy." I shake his hand. "Thank you for an extraordinary stay."

As he puts me into a taxi headed for the airport, I press a hundred dollars into his palm and he makes a gesture of refusing it. "You have done enough," he says. But we both know a hundred dollars will go a long way here, so when I stuff it in his pocket he doesn't resist. "May God bless you," he says instead.

He stands there waving as I drive off. When he is out of sight, I slide the gold band off my ring finger and deposit it in the taxi's ashtray. I have done enough.

Nairobi is big, ugly, dusty, and above all, crime-ridden—making it the perfect and logical next step in my descent into hell. But hell comes in many shapes and colors, some very tempting. And so I choose the Norfolk, the oldest, most colonial hotel in Nairobi. More than likely built on the broken backs of black Africans, I think as I ascend the steps into its grand lobby, passing the ranks of uniformed bellboys. It's hard to convince myself I am not on a soundstage of some Hollywood studio where some sweeping romantic period epic is shooting. Easier to believe that than to buy that all this could be real. The cool stone courtyards and shady gardens block out the dirt, the reality, the hostility of the street—of the real Nairobi.

I arrive at dusk, settle in, and head immediately to the outdoor bar overlooking the spectacular gardens. I imagine ninety years ago, when the place first opened, you could probably see the beggars at the gates from here. Now there are twenty-foot-high shrubs strategically planted to keep out such unpleasantness.

Though I am in the mood for something harder, I order a Tusker beer—a tribute to the brewery's famous founder who was killed while hunting elephant. When in Nairobi, I think, raising my chilled glass to him. For most Westerners, Nairobi is a stopover on the way to or coming back from safari. But I don't feel like moving. I certainly don't feel up to chasing lions or elephants. Like Lord Tusker. So I stay in Nairobi. And watch as things begin to happen.

I am becoming my own safari. My own hunt. Some days I am predator; some days I am prey. And then I begin to get confused. Because some days I am both. The space between inhale and exhale disappears. Time stops. I forget how to breathe. Just for a moment. But it's happening more and more. So I have another beer. Tusker. And another. Tusker Tusker.

I think I am growing them. Tusks. No one else has noticed. I shave them off every morning. Pressing the razor hard into my face where they are sprouting, making deep cuts, covering them with Band-Aids I have sent up from the front desk. So no one has noticed. Maybe if I switch to another beer. Avoid the elephants.

The hotel people—which is to say, the people in the hotel—they are looking at me. The Band-Aids, the tusks, I don't know. So I go out on the street. The street is loud. I go to the markets where black women in white skirts sit on mats in parking lots, weaving baskets and selling baskets. But I don't want baskets. I want quiet.

The day I stumble into Comtewa Stationers, a tiny antiquarian bookstore, I find what I am looking for. Metal utility shelves crammed with everything from military history to maps to mysticism, religion, archeology, local authors, and Western favorites like Sidney Sheldon and Danielle Steel create aisles so narrow it is impossible for one customer to pass another.

I spend most of my time with the older hardcover editions—old enough to preclude me from attaching my own egocentric imprint to their publication dates. The more esoteric the better. It doesn't matter that most of those books are written in a language I cannot read. I like to stand in the narrow aisles, pulling them from the shelves, smelling the ink and the dust. Something about the way the pages smell—ink, paper, bindings.

Once I discover Comtewa, I am on a mission. I visit every bookshop in Nairobi. It doesn't take long. There aren't more than a handful and at least half of those carry crap catering to tourists—old dime-store paperbacks bought in American or European airports and discarded in local hotels, obviously purchased for a shilling or two by booksellers from the hotel maids and bellboys who find them in vacated rooms.

A few shops, though, become my friends—Estriol, Prestige, the little shop without a name behind the Stanley Hotel. These small storefront bookstores provide hours of calm in the Nairobi storm. Because every day when I wake up, the clouds gather, a little darker each day, and I feel less and less equipped to do anything about them. To go anywhere. To make a change. To speak more than the occasional sentence. So I go to the bookstores.

I do not want to speak and I do not want to be spoken to. I find it hurts my ears. My head. My skin. And people are quiet in bookstores. I like the anonymous, mute companionship of my fellow browsers.

I am at Comtewa, my favorite bookstore, when the incident occurs. I can't say I remember very much, only that I have been feeling increasingly restless and agitated. For days. Weeks? I have lost track of how long I have been here.

Either things are moving too slow or I am in a panic to keep up. Sometimes I don't know which; often the sensations seem to coexist. Everyone around me is in my way all the time. The bookstore clerk, a young man with long, graceful fingers whose pink fingernails stand out against his dark-brown skin, is having an endless conversation with a large-breasted woman who holds two dingy, worn books in her hands.

I can't understand what they are saying, but it is fairly obvious. She raises one book and then the other, weighing their respective merits and asking him endless questions. And he, knowing I've been standing there for-fucking-ever, not only patiently but enthusiastically continues to carry on this third-world literary salon.

I really and truly don't remember the rest. From what I understand, I verbalized my impatience and offered to buy both books for the lady. But not in those words. And apparently, in my frustration, I pushed over a bookcase. Or two. Apparently there was a sort of domino effect. The police came and I was arrested. That part I remember. I couldn't think of much to say in my defense. So I resisted. And was quickly introduced to the policeman's nightstick. A single efficient blow that brought me to my knees. The U.S. Embassy was called but there was only so much they could or would do. I was a tourist who had without provocation vandalized a local business and assaulted one of its customers, who, it turns out, happened to work for the Kenyan Ministry of Education. The books were first editions by beloved African poets.

On the advice of the embassy's legal department, I did what I could to make amends. I supplied the funds to renovate the bookstore, donated livestock to the district of Subukia, tried to convince the injured parties that my behavior was an anomaly. But I had the feeling I was lying.

I decide to leave Nairobi and return to Kampala, vaguely remembering things were better there. Thinking I knew people there and they knew me. Not remembering who. Hoping familiar surroundings will restore a sense of equilibrium. But knowing I am probably wrong.

After three weeks in Kampala I am becoming a superhero. Except I haven't done anything heroic. Nor do I intend to. But recently I have started developing superpowers. Supersensitive smelling capabilities and ultrabright-light sight receptors. But my most super powerful sense is my souped-up hearing. I hear everything. All the time. The sound of bus exhaust. Ringing telephones and telephones that have not yet rung. The gears of the hotel's elevators moving between floors and cockroach feet tap-dancing over bathtub porcelain and the scratch of waiters' pens on their pads and all the music playing on all the Walkmans in every pedestrian's headphones within a square mile of Me Central.

All of it.

All at once.

And everywhere, always the growling, grinding, wheezing of all the air conditioners and ceiling fans in Kampala desperately, hopelessly, uselessly trying to take Africa down a degree or two.

In the beginning, I was fascinated by my powers. And for a while I was obviously pretty fucking fascinating too. If you can judge that kind of thing by the ease with which genuinely excellent pussy seemed to fall from the sky and land on my dick with very little effort on my part. That was fun. While it lasted.

But it didn't.

It never does.

And now, *it*—all of it—is too much. Too hot. Too bright to hear. Too loud to see. And with no way to turn it down, there is no sleep, nothing to stop the onslaught.

Now I am sitting at my favorite little round stone table in the lovely garden bar of my international hotel, surrounded by voices that, in their foreignness, all sound the same—shrill, irritating, grating. I want another vodka. Another 'nother vodka, I guess.

Across the lawn, half a football field away, a hotel gardener wielding a power saw trims the towering, well-groomed wall of hedge that protects the paying guests from what's *out there*.

Buzzing. Buzzing. Buzz. Zing. Wave after wave of shimmering rainbow-colored vibrations fly off his magic Black & Decker wand. The vibrations roll toward me, breaking like giant waves, and I feel my chest tighten as I wonder how close they will get. Should I duck or take cover? I am relieved when they dissipate before becoming a serious threat. Crisis averted. But the uncomfortable tightness lingers. Need another vodka.

I rub my hands over the smooth table. It is porous and miraculously cool. I lean over and lay my cheek down next to my hand, pressing my ear hard against the table, hoping to dim the buzzing. This table, I decide, is the only cool place in Africa. I let my eyes roam over the rest of the bar, covering as much territory as I can without actually moving any body parts. Smoking cigarettes. Smoked fish. Buzzing flies. Buzzing. Endless. Buzzing. And Pulsing. And Vibrating. Living. Alive. Banging down my door like the Big Bad Wolf. Driving down my intersecting, interchangeable super highway of fucked-up, misfiring, hydroplaning neural pathways. And there is nothing super about it.

It is Just Fucking Irritating.

I lay my empty glass down on the table next to my face and use my tongue to fish out an ice cube. Held prisoner between cheek and gum, it melts quickly. I slip my tongue through my lips and stretch it out flat like a paintbrush on the table. I lick up and down and around my fingers, tracing the outline of my hand. But I run out of saliva before I can complete the project.

And frankly, I am disappointed that the table—the stone—does not have a more unique taste, something more intrinsic to its stoneness. I sit up, fall back into the big wicker armchair, and take a deep breath—only to find my mouth filled with the sickly sweet aroma of gardenias budding but not yet in bloom. Want vodka.

The woman at the table next to me bursts out in a high-pitched cackle and I dig my fingernails into my forehead to keep from throttling her.

Yessssssssss. For a moment I am distracted by the pleasantness of the pain.

I let my head fall back onto the tabletop and think of things I'd rather be doing. Running naked through heavily thorned shrubbery is the first thing that comes to mind. But it doesn't have to be thorns. Almost anything sharp would work. Anything sharp enough to provide some kind of equally intense but opposite sensation to counter the effect of my supersenseless senses. I probably should have stayed upstairs in my room—away from things. And people. But I've been trying to carry on a normal life—despite my developing superpowers. And so far I don't think anyone has noticed.

But today feels different.

And with each new addition to the already cluttered cacophony—spoon clattering onto slate floor, waiter chewing out busboy in Swahili—I know I am coming closer to the edge.

"Sir? May I bring you anything else?"

Without bothering to open my eyes, I pick up my empty glass and rattle the quickly melting cubes in the waiter's direction.

"Very good, sir."

A moment passes before I realize I still have my glass raised. I open my eyes and examine the hand wrapped around the tumbler—mine, I assume, since it is attached to my arm. But not exactly the hand I remember. It is puffier, meatier than any hand I remember having. I lay it flat on the table in front of me. I stare at the thick purple vein that rises like a mountain range out and over the top of my hand.

The woman—that fucking woman laughs again. It is an assault. I am sure I can see my pulsating purple vein pick up the pace. I turn and glare at the witch but she is oblivious. Her companion—a fat, pasty turd with an impressively three-dimensional mole on her upper lip—leans in and whispers to her. German. They are German. Nazi German bitches. Pig-fucking Nazi bitches. The women drinking tea at the next table are responsible for the deaths of millions.

A distant voice in my head tells me I should turn away. Because I've been known to act impulsively. And then regret it later. Although right now I can't think of a single example of that. And anyway, this situation is entirely different. These Nazi pig fuckers are guilty of genocide. My homicidal rage is completely justified. I mentally bury the little voice under a pile of biochemical landfill and continue to stare at them, idly turning the hotel silver over in my hand and letting the heavy dull knife and fork clatter onto the table. Picking them up, letting them fall. Picking them up, letting them fall. It is gratuitously obnoxious. Irritating and annoying. At least I hope so. Why should I be the only one to suffer?

The witch shouts something at me in Nazi. Which I neither speak nor understand. Then she spits—just as the waiter is crossing between our tables bearing my drink. The viscous glob lands on his black trouser leg.

He is speechless. She is shocked, appalled, and, screaming at the waiter in German, points a gnarled red-tipped finger at me. Her turd companion is mortified and apologetic and jumps from the table to wipe at the bubbling spot on his pants with her linen napkin.

I smile. I have willed it into being. I have another superpower.

"Madam, please," the waiter says, trying to shake the prostrate turd-woman off his ankle, "that is not necessary."

He puts my drink and a bowl of salted nuts down in front of me.

"Will you be needing anything else, sir?"

I have been pressing the heavy, three-tined fork against the bulbous purple vein on my hand, watching, fascinated at how its weight, pressed at just the right angle, forces the one vein to become two—forces the blood to flow otherwise. I poke one of the thick tines into the outside of my even thicker purple vein. It makes a benign indentation. Like poking the Pillsbury Doughboy. How far from the surface could the blood be, I wonder. It is purple enough to see. Purple and pulsing.

"Sir?"

"I'll have the shrimp cocktail," I answer without looking up.

The cackling woman has left. Fled. But her cackle has stayed behind. An aural parasite, it has taken up residence in my chest. Like millions of tiny cackling wings all flapping inside me. I can feel them. Cackling, buzzing, building a hive in my chest. Bees. Buzzing. Inside. A giant, humming cancer filled with buzzing, stinging, cackling, crackling insects, angry and desperate to break through the cramped confines of my chest wall. When I put my hand over my sternum I can feel it getting bigger, strangling my heart every time I try to breathe.

The waiter returns with four perfect shrimp—cleaned, peeled, and hung over the side of an ice-filled silver bowl at the center of which is a little dish of cocktail sauce. When he sets them down in front of me, I spin the plate around several times, check under the paper doily, and finally tear it apart, sifting through it all with my hands.

"Sir?"

"Where's the damn fish fork?" I ask. I am furious. My hands are shaking and covered in cocktail sauce.

"But sir, the shrimp have been peeled, they don't require . . ." He stops talking and looks at me. Then, taking my linen napkin, he wipes my hands off—gently, carefully, completely. Cradling first one and then the other in his large, cool, dark hands, he takes his time. As if this were a normal part of his job. Like preparing Caesar salad tableside.

I should be angry. But I'm not. I should feel embarrassment and humiliation. But I don't. I want to cry. But I can't.

When my hands are clean, he makes the dirty napkin disappear behind his back.

"Fish fork. Very good, sir. Right away."

The moment he leaves, the bees are back. Buzzing. I breathe in and feel their tiny feet in my bronchi. Buzz. Wings beating in my alveoli. Flutterbuzz. He is back in a minute. He sets the fish fork on a clean napkin. Then he nudges my vodka toward the far end of the table and puts a very tall iced tea that I did not order in front of me.

"Just brewed," he says. "Very refreshing."

"Thank you."

"Not at all, sir."

Flutterflutterzzzzzzzbuzzzzzz. I have to do something to make it stop. I have to feel something simple. This—flutterflutterflutter-buzzzzz—is too complicated. Too confusing. I want to feel something about which there can be no argument or debate. Something about which everything will be known. Here. Now. Something that will make all the rest stop.

There is an exquisite and audible pop when the hooked tip of the center tine of the fish fork punctures the fat purple vein. I have enjoyed every delicious second leading up to the final breaching of inner and outer—the sharp poke of the tiny dagger pushing, pushing, pushing. But now that it's in and the blood is leaking—slowly at first, then faster—the sharpness of the pain has receded to a dull ache. And I am aware once again of the fucking bees. The buzzing that is every-where around me, inside me, all the time, all at once. I want it gone. I pull the single tine out of my vein but have to tug a little when the hooked edge gets stuck inside. The nearly translucent skin tears easily and the gush that follows brings a windfall of unexpected sweet relief.

It is good. It is a beginning. But it is not enough. So I lay my left arm flat on the table, palm facing upward, and squeeze my fist open and closed. Open and closed. Watch and wait. I sigh, relieved, as my hot, swollen veins finally rise to the surface—the fattest, purplest ones just at the inside of my elbow. So that is where I plunge the fork.

Yessssssssssssssssssss.

For a moment the pain is blinding. Wonderfully, beautifully blinding. I feel the smile spread across my face as my brain scrambles to readjust and rewire its sensory priorities. This pain is precise and delicious and totally satisfying. It is exactly what I have been craving.

Leaving the fork just where it is, and thankful that the perfect shrimp are in fact already peeled, I pick one up, bathe it in cocktail sauce, and lower it into my mouth. The flesh is sweet and tender and has just the right crunch when my molars come together on top of it. And the sauce, redolent with horseradish and fresh lemon, has just the right bite. I eat the second and the third and by the time I get to the last shrimp I have run out of sauce. I hate that. Also, there seems to be a puddle of blood covering the stone table and threatening to run down the sides.

Someone screams. But the sound is fuzzy, distant, cottony soft. I raise my hand to signal for more cocktail sauce and notice the fish fork sticking out of my inner elbow like a harpoon.

Oh yeah, that, I remember distantly. That was a little dramatic. But it worked. Stopped the buzzing.

I yank the fork out of my arm. There is a sudden spray of blood. Like from a drinking fountain. Then it subsides to a generous trickle. There is a commotion behind me, and when I turn I see my waiter running toward me, a stack of clean white napkins in his hands.

My waiter kneels beside my chair and presses the napkins gently but firmly against the oozing punctures.

"Sir?" he asks. His eyes search mine for an answer.

But I don't know what he wants to know.

Behind us, back toward the hotel, there is more commotion—a siren, some men in white uniforms wheeling a gurney. But none of it bothers me. It is all gauze and honey and a distant wind and I will ride it.

Floating. Held. Safely in safety. Until I feel falling. The panic of the fall. Not me. I am—was—on my feet. Running. To get there. To stop her. Falling.

My feet cannot move fast enough.

"Hold him down." There are voices and clattering.

Over the green grass. Across the playground blacktop. To catch her falling body.

"Restraints, now!"

She hits the ground.

"No!"

It had seemed so simple—a Sunday, a park, a family. And now all I can do is run with her held against me—red seeping into white—and drive. And make promises to God about everything I will do from now on if He makes her okay.

The happiness of a simple Sunday crushed under the heel of an accident that was no one's fault but will be riddled with guilt and blame anyway.

God made her okay. But I let go and now I am falling.

"Noooo!" Panic rising. Overflowing. Into consciousness.

"Can you tell me your name, sir?" a female voice asks.

Who wants to know? I think, awake now, eyes still closed. There is noise and bright lights shine through my eyelids.

"Sir, open up your eyes for me and tell me your name."

What's in it for me? I think, still shaking from a nightmare I don't recall. But I don't ask. It's not a good way to begin a negotiation.

"His vitals are stable." This time it's a male voice—with an African-British accent. "He's just being difficult."

Fuck you, I think. If he thinks I'm difficult now, just wait. I feel my personal space is being violated when, without my consent, the asshole shoves his thumb in my eye, pushes up the lid, and shines a penlight around.

"Jesus Christ, what the fuck," I mean to say. But apparently I have grown an extra tongue or three. "Eeezz Cryy, whaaa" and some drool is what actually comes out of my mouth. My head feels as if I've been dropped on it. From a third-floor window. This feels familiar. Like Stanford. Like Thorazine.

I try to shield my eyes but find my hands are inconveniently tied to the bed rails.

"See, his pupils are reactive," the asshole says.

The woman rolls her eyes at the asshole and shakes her head. "Page Dr. Mijumbi. Tell him his patient is awake."

"Mr. Dowd? Mr. Dowd?" I feel a cool hand lightly tapping my cheeks. "Wake up, Mr. Dowd."

"He was awake a minute ago."

At the sound of the asshole's voice, I open my eyes.

"Ah, there he is. Welcome back, Mr. Dowd."

And for a brief moment I experience consciousness in a vacuum. There is no place. No time. No identity. Only the awareness of Is. It is the single most stress-free instant I have ever known. And it is over far too quickly.

"Come on, Mr. Dowd, wake up. Stay with us."

Dowd. Mr. Dowd. Nope. I am drawing a blank. But the metaphysical ground has shifted. Now I know it is me, Greyson, who is blank. How disappointing. Why, when there are so many other, better choices, am I back to this again?

I feel the gentle tapping on my cheek again. I open my eyes. Because I must have closed them again.

"Mr. Dowd?"

So if you go chasing rabbits and you know you're going to fall . . .

Wait. Maybe I do know that name. Dowd. Elwood Dowd. Seer of large white rabbits. Named Harvey. Nice guy. People think he's nuts.

And then I remember: As far as the hotel is concerned, as far as Africa is concerned, and now as far as the young man sitting in the metal chair next to my bed is concerned, I am Elwood Dowd.

"I am Mr. Dowd," I say as clearly as I can, which is not very clear at all.

"Mr. Dowd, I am Dr. Mijumbi. You are in Mugali Hospital. Do you remember what happened?"

I think. No. Nothing. "Ra-b-bit?" I ask. Because I have nothing else to offer.

The three doctors exchange looks.

"You see a rabbit," the asshole says.

I struggle to peel my tongue off the roof of my mouth. "Mo. I she an ashhole."

The woman doctor giggles. She is pretty. I like her.

"Sense of humor. Very good, Mr. Dowd," says Mijumbi.

"Yes, very funny," the asshole says. "But what does the rabbit have to do with it?"

I shrug my restrained shoulders. They hurt. I hurt. All over. Consciousness is overrated.

"He's hallucinating," the asshole says to Mijumbi. He doesn't even bother to whisper.

Mijumbi shoots him a warning look. "I don't think so," he says and turns to look me in the eye. "I think the very powerful drug we gave you is still clouding your mind a bit, hmm? And your memory maybe?"

His voice is soft and slow and it feels good in the heavily trafficked spirals of my cochlea. Dr. Mijumbi sits back down in the metal chair, scoots it up to my bed, and pushes his little gold-framed glasses higher on his nose.

"Mr. Dowd, I want you to think back if you can, to earlier today. You woke up. You had breakfast, maybe? Hmm?"

I nod, remembering none of that. "Good, okay, and after that, can you tell us what happened?"

No. There is nothing.

"You don't remember how you got here? You don't remember what happened?"

Nothing happened. But I don't like the way he's saying it. Not only like something did happen and not only like I should know what, but like it's bad. Really bad. He knows. He knows something bad happened. But he won't tell me.

Willa.

And suddenly, panic starts to seep out of all the cracks and fissures of my drugged-up, numbed-out insides. Before I can stick my finger in the dike, all the empty spaces are flooded with loss. Before I can take a breath, I am drowning.

"What is it? What happened?" Mijumbi asks, concerned.

"Willa?"

I am twisting and turning, trying to get up, but nothing is working right. Grunting and twisting and the pain that rips through my right shoulder is sharp and searing.

"It hurts."

"Where does it hurt?" he asks, racing to my bedside.

"I don't know," I lie.

Everywhere. All the time.

"What does it feel like?"

"I. Don't. Know," I sob, lying again.

In the mornings, it is an endless ocean of bottomless loss. By late afternoon, every cell in my body has a bleeding hangnail. But I don't say that. I never say that.

"Mr. Dowd, who is Willa?"

"I don't know." The biggest lie.

I feel sick. I turn my head away from Mijumbi and try to vomit over the other side of the bed, but my arm gets in the way. Cocktail sauce and bits of shrimp splash everywhere. On me, on the bed, on the floor, and on the asshole's shoes. Every cloud has its silver lining.

I think I am crying, but I am not sure.

"Un-die my fuck-ing hans!" I try to scream.

"Of course." Dr. Mijumbi, despite the crushing heat, wears a crisp white shirt and navy blazer. He unties one arm and then calmly walks around the bed through the muck to untie the other. The asshole looks horrified. "Dr. Ngasi, would you please go find someone to clean this up and bring Mr. Dowd some fresh bedding?" The doctor, who upon closer examination looks like a kid in an expensive prep school uniform, helps me sit up. "Why did you try to hurt yourself?" he asks.

I glance over at my bandaged hand and arm. I carefully lift the white gauze and look underneath at the mess of crisscrossed black stitching. "Chrisss, I'll ne'er be able 'a wear a stra'less dress 'gain."

"You almost bled to death, Mr. Dowd."

"Really?" I try extremely unsuccessfully to snap my fingers. "Bud almos' doden' coun' does it?"

"Was that your intention?" he asks gently, laying my arm back on the pillow.

"No," I say sincerely, "I wuz. Trying to. Kill. The bees."

Dr. Mijumbi quickly scans the brief report in front of him. "There is no mention of bees at the hotel from the rescue workers or hotel staff or anybody who—"

"No," I say and point to my chest, "that's because they . . . they live in here."

The doctor nods. I take his hand and place his palm on my sternum. "They . . . they are quiet now. Because of the pain. But," I close my eyes and whisper, "if you concentra you can still feel the buzzing. Nothing like before. They are res-ing."

The doctor nods again and withdraws his hand. "So, you stabbed yourself to stop the excruciating internal pain?"

I nod and feel a tear form in the corner of my eye.

"And I'm guessing you haven't slept in days? Maybe longer?"

"Can'd rememba," I say groggily.

"Take him off the Thorazine," Mujimbi tells his minions. "He's not schizophrenic."

"Then what—" the asshole challenges immediately.

"I believe Mr. Dowd has had an acute mixed manic episode. I doubt it's his first. The psychosis is just a symptom. Start him on lithium, six hundred milligrams."

New York, 1994. We are a no-touching unit. We have a no-touching policy. No touching, no hugging, no violation of personal space. Glenda does not feel this policy applies to her. Watching her violate the no-touching policy provides endless minutes of fun. I don't report her when I am the one being violated. Lately she has begun tracing her index finger up and down my chest, my back, my thigh, my ass—usually first thing in the morning while we are standing in line waiting to have our vitals taken. She stands on her tiptoes and with minty fresh breath tells me what she'd like to do to me as she runs her index finger along the waistband of my pajamas. Lately my blood pressure has been higher than normal. Just a little higher. They wonder if it could be some rare side effect of the shock. They don't seem to notice that the huge hard-on I have corresponds to the increase in blood pressure. They are idiots. No touching, my ass.

TENTH

When I think about it, this is all Ellen's fault. I think. I am here because Ellen gave up on us—on The Team. Stopped caring. Or maybe that was me. Actually, I don't remember. But I remember the team. Us. Or the story of Us. The ad campaign featuring Us. Us the united front. Us on the same page. Us finishing each other's sentences. Us liking the same movies, the same music. Arlo Guthrie and the Byrds and Zeppelin and the Who and Mama Cass. It Never Rained in California. Until Mama Cass choked on a ham sandwich.

But why can't I remember who we really were? The real us. Maybe we were those people. I don't remember now. I miss that memory. Actually remembering us is unfathomable. Like trying to smell chimney smoke from an autumn fire when you're standing on a beach in August. It can't be done. There is an ocean of time to cross, and the dizzying scent of sand and salt and melting ice cream. And no matter how much you want it, you will never find your way back to that smoke and that chimney. You will only feel the empty space and not know why you are so sad. Especially when the day is sunny and the ocean is warm and the sand is soft under your feet.

You won't know why because you won't remember what belongs there. You will only feel the ache of absence and know something unnamable is missing.

Beverly Hills, 1961. Ellen. I'd called and canceled our date to Alan's pool party. Pop. Sears. All those boxes. So I'd had to cancel. The day before our first date. And every excuse I could come up with sounded like a lie. This was my one chance. Now she probably hated me. I wouldn't blame her if she did. And if she knew the truth . . .

By noon I had returned the first load and was backing into our driveway. Looking into the rearview, I saw Ellen Goodman sitting on the curb outside our building reading *The Stranger*. She was little and had wavy dark hair and green eyes with ridiculously long eyelashes. And a great ass.

"Ellen, what are you—"

"Well, I thought we had a date. Am I wrong?"

"No. I mean, I thought you understood. When I called . . ."

Ellen smiled. "You said you had to do something with your family. You didn't say I couldn't come along."

I didn't know what to say. I didn't want to explain. So I just stared at the cracks in the driveway. And her legs in the cutoff shorts she was wearing.

"Grey?"

Shit. Fine. "This isn't some barbeque or my grandmother's eightieth birthday and it's certainly not a damn pool party." The words came out sounding angry. I hadn't meant them to. But I was. Just not at her. I was screwing this up completely, blowing any chance I ever had. But she didn't even blink.

Instead she threw her head back and laughed. "You think I would've come if I thought it would be anything as boring as a stupid pool party?"

Malibu, 1976. Ellen groaned as I took her hand and hoisted her out of the car. "I can't believe you said we'd come."

I stood back and admired the job I'd done squeezing the Jaguar into the tiny legal-ish spot I'd found only five houses up PCH from Didi and Hugh Lazar's spectacular wood-and-glass beach house. "As opposed to what, sitting around waiting for you to go into labor?"

Ellen stopped walking and put her hands on what used to be her hips. "Screw you, Grey, you know that's not what I meant. Three nights ago a cop brings you home because you can't remember where you parked your—"

"I'm fine now. Okay. I'm fine."

"You're not fine. You wanna lie to yourself, go ahead, but you can't lie to me. I've seen this movie more than once and the ending never gets any better. So don't try to convince me—"

"Okay, Ellie, you're right. It's just—it's the stress—which I know is bad. I've been under a lot of it lately—"

"You're not the only one," she huffed.

I ignored the accompanying eye roll. "Between the studio stone-walling on Victor's deal and—"

Ellen smiled and waved as a couple passed us on their way to Hugh and Didi's. "And it's always going to be one goddamned deal or another," she said, lowering her voice. "That's not going to change unless you change it."

"I get it, I get it. Please, Ellen, for today, just lighten up, okay? Dr. Taysen said I should relax. This'll be relaxing. And you know you'll end up having fun."

"What I know is you'll end up doing business."

There was no point disputing it. I had made and broken too many promises to the contrary. I'd also hammered out some major deal points on Didi's deck that couldn't get done in studio offices.

Didi was a full-time friend. She had hundreds of them. And she loved them all and made each one feel special. It was the same with her dogs. There was always room for one more.

"I swear to God, if Jimmy or DeSanto or McNulty or any of your other wacko clients touches my stomach I'm gonna cut their friggin' hands off," Ellen said, resting for a minute to catch her breath. "No belly-rubbing. I don't care how many Oscars they've got."

Didi—olive-skinned, dark-haired, and long-legged—was still talking over her shoulder when she opened the door.

"He's really old, sweetie, so you have to pick him up gently and you have to keep the diaper on or he goes wee-wee on the rug."

When Didi turned around and was confronted by Ellen's stomach she gasped and reverently put both hands to her heart, just above her macramé bikini top.

"My God, El," she said, "look how beautiful you are!"

I couldn't remember the last time I'd seen the kind of smile that broke out on Ellen's face. I certainly didn't remember the last time I'd been the one who put it there. Didi reached her hand out tentatively in the direction of Ellen's belly.

"May I?"

Ellen took Didi's hand in hers. "Of course."

I found Victor sitting cross-legged in a corner playing Mastermind with his two younger kids and balancing a bottle of Labatt on his knee.

"Jesus, Greyson, where you been? My legs are numb."

"You're a big boy, Victor. You don't need your agent to help you mingle."

"Mingle. What the hell does that even mean? I want to go for a goddamn walk on the beach."

I looked down at Lilly and Thomas. "He's kind of cranky, isn't he?"

"He hates parties," Lilly whispered.

Victor looked exaggeratedly irritated. "Now you have to tell him why."

"Because," Thomas said, leaning in to make sure no one else could hear, "he's really a pirate."

I looked to Victor for a cue.

"It's true. And we're a very antisocial bunch. Now don't tell anyone or I'll have to kill you, right, Lil?" Lilly nodded solemnly and ran off.

"I'm fucking Didi," Victor said when we'd gotten all of five yards from the house.

Victor had a very dry sense of humor. I didn't always know when he was kidding. We kept walking and I just watched his face for a while.

"You're not going to say anything?"

"No, I just . . . I wasn't sure if—"

"Christ, I'm not fucking around."

"You mean you are?"

"Don't be an asshole, Greyson."

Victor stopped walking and his feet sank into the wet sand. "You realize you can't tell Ellen."

I wouldn't. But I'd be tempted. Ellen was always holding Victor up as the perfect husband. Kate and Victor as the perfect couple. Married since they were kids, since they were poor. They'd stayed devoted, grounded, unsullied by Hollywood.

In Ellen's mind they were the golden couple. Never mind that she and I had been married since we were kids. Since we were poor. That we were devoted and, as far as I could tell, grounded. Still, I paled by comparison to the formerly blue-collar couple that'd had fame reluctantly thrust upon them.

So, as Victor's agent, I kept my mouth shut—about the one-night stands and meaningless flings he indulged in while on location. Not just because he was my client, but because he was a good man who loved his wife and kids. And because he couldn't help it. He was an actor, and like many of the best, he was disciplined when it came to his craft but lacked a shred of will power when it came to what and whom he did after he wrapped for the day. It was SOP that what happened on location stayed on location.

But this was different. Too close to home. Shitting where he ate. Screw the trysts with Didi—Victor was courting disaster.

"So Kate doesn't know?"

"Oh God, no," Victor said. "What a fucking disaster that would be."

"And Hugh?"

"No! I don't know. I don't think so." Suddenly Victor looked worried.

"But, it's not . . . serious? You're not—" I was trying to tread carefully.

"Oh for Chrissake, Greyson, do I look like I'm in fucking high school?"

"So things with you and Kate—?"

"Are fine. They're fine. It's just not as much . . . fun."

"Fun."

"Yeah. Didi throws a fuck like she throws a party."

"Victor, you don't like parties."

"Yeah, but I like fucking."

I couldn't help laughing. "Okay, Victor, agent-client privilege has been invoked."

We started walking again. The tide was rising. We'd have to dodge the jetty to get back without getting soaked—time it just right and run between the waves.

"Actually, the sex is fine, but when I think about it later it's never as good as I thought it was at the time."

"With Kate? Or Didi?"

"Didi. Jesus, Greyson, keep up."

"Just want to make sure I've got my facts straight."

"So every time I'm fucking her—Didi—I'm also telling myself it's not worth it—swearing to God, Kate, and myself I'll never do it again."

"You sure you're not Jewish?"

"Wanna see my dick?" Victor asked, going for his belt.

"You don't do full frontal," I informed him. "It's ironclad. In all your contracts."

"Really?" Victor seemed genuinely surprised.

"Really," I told him.

We kept walking. The waves broke farther up on the beach. Cold water foamy on top, clear underneath, and filled with pebbles and shards of shell rushed over our feet and ankles and rose to our knees.

We grinned at each other like psychopaths.

"Cold, huh?" I said through clenched teeth.

"Fuckin' A."

We turned around and headed back. For a while, neither of us said anything. I just watched over and over again as my feet made depressions in the sand that disappeared almost immediately. It was like I was weightless. I looked behind me. I'd left nothing behind. Nothing. Had I ever been there at all? Where was the proof?

"Greyson?" All I heard was static. I went back to my feet, my footprints, appearing and disappearing. Appear and disappear. I tried leaning into the sand; really pushing my weight into each step. They'd linger maybe a second longer, maybe two. And disappear.

"Greyson, you there?"

I looked behind me. Nothing.

It was as if I was leaving almost before I got there. The more I watched it happen, the more anxious I became. I told myself it was crazy and tried to look away. And the panic rose. I couldn't stop thinking, if that mark, that proof of my existence, could be erased so quickly, what would be next?

Victor shook my shoulder gently. "Greyson! You okay?" Victor was next to me. We were talking and walking. Our pants were wet. And cold. Victor could see me. For the moment, the disappearing hadn't spread beyond my feet.

"Uh, yeah, just thinking."

"I must be getting old. It's the after-sex fun I miss," he said.

"Uh-huh." What were we talking about?

"That's what's so great about Didi. That's the party. We lie around in bed. We laugh and she cooks and we watch old movies."

Right. Victor. Didi. Affair. "And you can't do that with Kate?"

"Nah. The sex is still pretty good but the second it's over she's stuffing Kleenex up her pussy and talking about the menu for some god-awful dinner party she's planning for next week."

I put my arm around him. It was important that he feel like he could depend on me. That they could all depend on me. All the time. I was the rock to which they clung. I could not falter. Ever.

"Can you schedule an emergency meeting for us at Fox so I don't have to go?"

"Can't," I said. "I have to go to your god-awful dinner party."

When we got back to the house, Victor turned on the hose at the bottom of the stairs and rinsed the sand off his feet. Then he tried to hand it to me.

I jumped back, away from the running water. "No. Thank you."

"What? Jesus Christ, Grey."

"Go ahead, I'll be up in a . . . I just . . . I thought I saw a house for sale up the beach," I said, hoping I sounded convincing. "I want to take a look."

"You want me to come with you?" Victor sounded concerned.

"No, go be with your kids. I'll be right back."

My feet were still there. So far so good. I looked over my shoulder. Victor was halfway up the stairs. He waved. I waved back like a fucking Mouseketeer.

Just get in the goddamned house, Victor.

When he was finally out of sight, I climbed up and under the house next to Didi and Hugh's. Like a lot of houses in Malibu, it was built on enormous wood pylons and sat eight or ten feet off the ground. I sat down in the soft, damp sand and tried to will this reality away—tried to replace it with the one I knew should be there. The one that had been there. I'd just had it. Which meant I had only misplaced it. Like I do with my car keys all the time. And I get pissed off and yell and swear. And then Ellen finds them for me. And it's always somewhere I should have looked. But didn't. That's what this was. I buried myself in sand so I wouldn't blow away. But I left my feet sticking out.

When Victor came back alone, Ellen knew something had happened. She also knew she couldn't tell anyone. So she took a flashlight from the Lazars' utility closet and trudged up the beach by herself. It wasn't hard to find me shivering under the neighbor's house like a wounded animal. With great difficulty she lowered herself down next to me and wrapped her shawl around me.

"Grey, sweetheart, I think we all feel that way sometimes," she said when I explained about my footprints and fading existence. "You just feel it louder and bigger. The first thing we need to do is get you on solid ground. So you can feel your feet." That's when I knew I was going to be all right. I had misplaced myself for a little while and she had found me and put me back in the world. Simple as that.

Ellen went back inside and made our excuses. In the car, I rubbed one bare, sandy foot over the other and it started to snow. A fine, white dusting that settled into the black carpeting of the floor mat. The car wash guys would have to use the Power Vac on it. I'd swing by in the morning before my eight-thirty breakfast meeting. No one would know.

No one but Ellen. And she would never tell. She would make it okay. She always had.

Beverly Hills, 1961. Before I could say anything to stop her, Ellen was dragging a carton toward the back of Van Gilder's truck.

Jesus Christ. Some first date.

"Well," she said, breathless and bossy, "don't just stand there. Help me!"

I ran over and lifted the thing onto the flatbed.

When I turned around, she was standing so close I could feel the heat coming off her skin. I looked her in the eye and she didn't look away.

"Sorry," I said, suddenly self-conscious. "I need a shower. I probably stink."

She inched forward and stood on her tiptoes and I felt her breath on my neck.

"I like the way you smell just fine," she whispered. Then she smiled shyly and walked toward the pile of Sears merchandise, swinging her hips. "Well, are you going to help or do I have to haul this canoe myself?" she said. But I wasn't sure I could walk just then, much less carry a canoe.

It wasn't the beginning I had planned. But in a way I had never imagined, it was turning out to be better.

Beverly Hills, July 1981. "Ellen—Forever My Love—Grey." I'd paid Cartier an extra $350 on top of the cost of the watch for same-day engraving. I'd have paid $1,000, I thought, as I waited for the girl to wrap it. And I would have paid for a much more expensive watch. But I knew my wife.

"Are you sure?" the sales girl had asked that morning. "We have some lovely new designs in. Delicate with diamond bands."

"I'm sure. I know what I want," I told her.

"If it's a matter of price . . . ," she went on.

"Money is not the issue," I said. "My wife is not some Beverly

Hills JAP. She wouldn't wear a diamond watch if you gave it to her for free."

So she rang up the watch I'd chosen, the signature Cartier: octagonal, white face with Roman numerals, 22 karat gold wrapped around beveled edges, a black crocodile band. Simple, elegant, not at all ostentatious. Classic Ellen.

"Gift card?" the girl asked and without waiting for an answer handed me the little Cartier-embossed ecru square and matching envelope.

But I had nothing to say for myself. The expensive watch was supposed to do the talking for me. And the begging and apologizing and promising that it would never happen again. Because the night before, almost but not quite out of nowhere, it *had* happened. Again.

I remember coming home from work late, but not in a bad mood. I was buoyant actually. I'd just signed a new director and couldn't wait to tell Ellen the news. When I came in, she was lying across the couch with a book across her stomach. She didn't even bother to get up.

"Hi, Greyson, how was your day? Can I get you a scotch?" I yelled and then threw my jacket at her.

Without saying a word, she got up, made the drink, and handed it to me. Then she asked. But not like she meant it. She listened and then, instead of congratulating me, what she hit me with was, "Why is it nothing I do or think is worth asking about?" And that knocked the last breath of victory out of me. "It wasn't always that way," she went on. "You used to at least allow for the possibility that something interesting might have happened to me."

"You just crapped all over my A-plus day, you know that?"

"I'm sorry, I just had some news too. But I didn't mean to—I mean, it's great that you signed Bromwell."

"Burnwell!"

"Burnwell, sorry." Ellen was shaking a little now.

"Stop apologizing. Jesus." And that, I think, is when I threw my drink at the wall.

"Greyson, what the hell?"

"I'm sorry. I don't know. I just. Shit! I was in such a fucking good mood."

"Grey, you still signed the damn client. That didn't go away."

But it felt like it had. And in place of all that joy was this roiling funnel of black rage. I poured myself another drink and swallowed it quickly to try to force the black back down with it. "What did you want to tell me?" I asked Ellen, trying to fake casual conversation. She looked pale.

"Nothing. It can wait."

And now suddenly I needed to know immediately. Nothing was more crucial.

"No, tell me. Now. What is it?"

"Not when you're like this. You'll get angry."

"Oh, so now you're in my fuckin' brain? You know how I'm going to react?"

"No. I'm just saying I don't think this is the best time—"

"Don't fucking manage me, goddammit!" I screamed.

"Okay. Fine. I went by UCLA today and registered for classes for next semester. To finish my degree."

It was like a slap in the face. Like what we had wasn't good enough. "College? Why the fuck would you do that?"

"Just to finish up my degree."

"You have a child."

"Who's in school most of the day."

"So what? What? You're telling me you're going to take this degree and go get some fucking job? Is that it? You want people to think my wife has to work?"

After that, I was out of the gate like a champion. Rage fueled by the same energy that fueled the euphoria I'd felt just moments before—out of control, electric, and limitless, but mean. And everything fell away but the target of my anger.

I did not even register that Ellen looked scared. And at first she did not know how scared she should be. "I deserve this opportunity," she said. "Dr. Brody says it's my turn. I put you through law school. It's only fair."

I was incapable of setting an object down; shoes had to be hurled, books torn from the shelf, wedding photos ripped from albums. Shredded. The energy was too much; it had to come out—too mean, the vitriol too had to come out. And it spattered all over the room like blood.

"You want to be paid back? Is that it, you nickel-and-diming little bitch?"

"Shh. Please. Willa's going to hear."

I slung my money clip at her and it took a chip out of the paint on the wall behind her head.

"Okay, that's it. Calm down. I won't have a discussion with you when you get like this."

"Fuck you! Like what? Does your bitch shrink have a diagnosis for your ingratitude?"

"Why are you yelling? And who made the mess?" Willa stood in the doorway, and the moment she entered the room, Ellen was on her feet, pushing Willa behind her, out of the way, out of my way. Like I might hurt my daughter. I waited while Ellen put her back to bed, but Ellen stayed—locked in Willa's room with her. I banged on the door and hurled accusations and called Ellen names normally reserved for X-rated movies and the asshole who cuts you off on the 405.

I woke up naked in a chaise longue by the pool. I don't remember how I got there. I only remember the rage and, before that, walking on air. And the split second it took for there to be nothing in between. And then the endless expanse of remorse. Again.

Because I always wanted to take it all back. But there was an irrevocable rupture—raw and still bleeding where the dam had burst inside. And the damage was done.

I had never hit either of them. I was sure I would never cross that line. Wasn't I? And so all I could do was apologize. Watches, earrings, bracelets, necklaces. Velvet boxes filled with remorse. Ellen had at least a dozen. And tonight, after a client dinner, I would go home and give her one more.

The house was completely dark and very quiet when I got there. Usually Ellen left the light in the front hall on for me when she knew I'd be home late. The long narrow bedroom hallway was dark too, but there was a sliver of light coming from under our door. I'm not sure why but I knocked before entering my own bedroom. When there was no answer, I slowly, carefully opened the door. What I'd expected to find was Ellen asleep with the TV and lights still on. Instead, she was wide-awake, sitting on the edge of the bed. Her eyes were red and swollen. She hadn't done anything to hide the fact she'd been crying. Maybe all day. I probably should've canceled my dinner.

"Hey," I said gently and leaned in to kiss her. But she backed away. "I know. I was an asshole. This can't begin to make up for it, but ...," I said, pulling out the box from Cartier.

She opened it silently, then turned it over and read the inscription. And laughed.

"*Are you fucking kidding me?*" she whispered and threw the watch against the wall.

"Ellen, come on—"

"No, you can't buy me off. I don't want your expensive guilt jewelry. I never wanted it." She went to her dresser, picked up her jewelry box, and dumped the contents on the floor. "Haven't you noticed I never wear the shit you buy me after one of your Jekyll and Hyde moments?"

She kicked at the pile and began to sob. "I can't do it anymore, Grey. You're up, you're down, you're fine for weeks or months, and then suddenly the ground shifts under my feet. I never know who I'm going to wake up with or how long it's going to last." She sat down heavily on the bed.

She was scaring me. Things had been bad before. Much worse than this. Hadn't they? But she sounded ... I was on my knees in front of her, pulling her hands away from her face.

"Please, Ellen. I'm so sorry. I love you. I love Willa. Don't—"

"I know," she said, continuing to cry, "but it's not enough. You're not good for her and you're not good for me. And you won't get help."

"I will, I will, I'll get help, I promise." And I meant it this time. I really meant it.

Ellen laughed. It was a nasty, bitter laugh. "That's what Dr. Brody said you'd say."

"Brody? Your shrink told you to do this?"

"She didn't tell me to do anything."

"Who does she think pays her fucking bills?"

She stood up. "I want you to leave," she said calmly. She wasn't crying anymore.

She pulled open the double doors of one of our huge bedroom closets, wallpapered—at the insistence of Deena Divac, coveted decorator—in the same tasteful jungle-floral print Deena had chosen for the other walls. And the bedspread. And the armchair and the love seat and the curtains. I felt like I was sleeping on the set of South Fucking Pacific.

"Ow! Shit!" Ellen yelled from inside the closet.

"You okay?"

"Fine," she snapped, clearly not.

I stood just outside the door, not knowing what to do. I wanted to know how she wanted me to be. Then I would be that way and this would stop. My job was convincing people to do what I wanted, but now . . . now I couldn't think of a single word to close the zero-gravity galaxy that had just opened between us. It was infinite and unreal and I hadn't seen it out there on the horizon. Not even a little.

She picked up the biggest suitcase, pushed me out of the way, and threw the bag onto the bed.

"Pack."

"What?"

"Pack. Pack some clothes and leave. You can come back for the rest later."

"But . . . Ellen . . . It's almost midnight."

"Oh come on, Grey, you're an important guy. I'm sure the concierge at the Beverly Hills Hotel can make room for you at the inn."

When I left my own house that night, I was the one who was crying. "I know this is hard but it's better this way," Ellen whispered. Then she kissed me on the cheek and shut the door.

I sat in my car at the bottom of the driveway of the Beverly Hills Hotel. I had driven there like a robot. Not thinking, not feeling, just following the same route I always took, the same shortcuts and side streets until, in less than twelve minutes, I found I'd arrived at the last place I wanted to be. And I didn't know what to do. In the past I'd zipped right up to the valet, exchanged my keys for a bright orange stub, which I slipped into my breast pocket as I strode briskly into my breakfast/lunch/drinks meeting.

But there was no meeting. It was a Tuesday night and my wife had thrown me out. Pull one thread and the sweater unravels. I couldn't breathe. My hands were sweating. I saw myself pulling up to the valet, taking my orange ticket, checking into one of the beautifully appointed Beverly Hills Hotel suites and using my necktie to hang myself.

"Good evening. Checking in, sir?" I was so startled I leaned on the horn. "Sorry sir, I didn't mean to sneak up on you. I just noticed you've been here a while and I thought I'd see if you—"

But I didn't let him finish. I put my foot on the gas and flew past the red-carpeted entrance to the hotel and out the other side, swerving left onto Sunset, my heart racing even faster than my car.

By the time I got to Victor's I was ascending the peak of a full-blown panic attack while at the same time trying to rationalize my appearance well past midnight at the home of my favorite client—a client with whom I had a friendship of sorts. The kind of friendship that would allow him to show up on my doorstep in the middle of the night, no questions asked. But not the reverse. Sure, our families socialized and we had a history—insofar as anyone in Hollywood has history—but I was the confidant, the caretaker, the troubleshooter. I had kept his marriage together, made his son's DUI disappear, got rid of the bogus paternity suit. That's the way it was supposed to work. Not the reverse.

And so I stopped for a moment as I walked up the stone path toward his giant Beverly Hills Tudor mansion, took out my handkerchief and wiped my eyes. Then I stuffed it back in my pocket and straightened my tie. I'd left my suitcase in the trunk of my car but I carried my briefcase. I hoped I looked like I was on my way to a meeting. That it happened to be 1:00 A.M.—well, there wasn't much I could do about that.

I rang the doorbell. It wasn't like ours, the normal ding-dong kind that chimed twice and was done. Victor's went on and on like a god-damn church organ. Eventually the tiny eye-level door within the giant door opened. Then, seeing it was me, Victor's maid opened it. She was wearing a robe and had one curler in the middle of her forehead.

"Good evening, Mr. Todd."

"Hello, Zelda. Sorry to wake you."

"No trouble. Please come in."

Zelda closed the door behind me and reset the alarm.

Victor came creeping down the stairs, hair standing on end, holding a baseball bat.

"Greyson?"

He put the bat down. "Zelda, you can go back to bed. Thank you for . . . just—"

"Yes," I said. "Thank you, Zelda."

"It was no bother. Good night."

Victor watched until she was out of sight. Then he turned to me. "What the hell's going on? Why are you—?"

"Well," I said, popping open my briefcase, "there are a few things in your contract I wanted to go over before I meet with—"

"Greyson, what are you doing at my house at . . . ," he said and looked at the clock on the mantel, "one twenty in the morning?"

"Ellen . . . uh . . ." I felt pressure behind my eyes, tears building. I cleared my throat, trying to force them back.

"What? Ellen what?"

"Threw me out," I whispered.

Victor and Kate insisted I sleep in their guest room for as long as I wanted. For the first few days I was able to play the part of the merely despondent, recently separated spouse. But then I stopped being able to sleep. At all. And I couldn't control the crying. Every day the feeling of profound loss and overwhelming panic, feelings which existed concurrently, ate me alive. And the only person I could tell—the only person I'd ever been able to tell—wouldn't talk to me.

And so, late at night, when Victor and Kate and the kids and Zelda and the live-in nanny were sleeping, I would walk the grounds and halls of Victor's mansion wearing a borrowed bathrobe and sobbing, begging Ellen to take me back. And in the morning I would shower and shave and make sure no one knew. Until I got caught.

I was huddled in a corner of Victor's kitchen. As if I were talking to Ellen. Crying and talking. And rocking back and forth, because the motion—I don't know why—created a tiny buffer against the panic. It was a particularly bad night.

That's bullshit. If I'm honest, it was a night like any other during that time.

"Jesus, Grey." When Victor turned on the bright overhead light, I turned my face to the wall. I was humiliated. He walked over and pulled me up and I leaned on him, shaking. I wanted to give in; to let myself fall apart and be held by him, by this man I knew wanted to be my friend. I wished more than almost anything that was an option. Instead, I did my best impression of someone who was pulling himself together.

"I'm fine," I said, quickly turning to stone. "You can't tell anyone about this."

Victor put his hand on my shoulder. "Grey, it's perfectly understandable, you just—"

"No!" I shook my finger at him and left it suspended in the air pointing at him. There was a fine but noticeable tremor in my hand. We both saw it and I lowered my arm to my side. "Nobody! Do you understand?" I stood inches from his face. He didn't move and his eyes didn't leave mine.

"I think I do," he said, nodding. "Nobody. I promise."

I nodded back. And then I let him hug me. Because I knew he needed to.

Beverly Hills, 1961. On the ride out to Sears, Ellen actually got me to tell her a little bit about Pop. Not a lot, but more than I'd told anyone else except Alan Rothman.

At one point when we were stuck in traffic, she turned to me and put her hand on my knee. "You know, Grey," she said, "I haven't met your father, but you've never met my mother, and trust me when I tell you she is a ball-busting bitch on wheels. On a good day."

I was so stunned I almost rear-ended the guy in front of us. And that's when I knew I was in love.

By the time we got back, the pool party was over. I took her to see *Touch of Evil* starring Charlton Heston and Janet Leigh instead. Then I drove her home in Van Gilder's truck. We sat on the hood down the block from her house and I kissed her good-night. Not such a bad day after all.

I felt pretty great all night and even woke up smiling, until I heard the sound of a loud, persistent car honking. I tried to block it out and replay the date. Ellen. And for a moment the noise went away. But it wouldn't stop. I went to the window and leaned out. There was my father sitting outside our house in a light-blue Eldorado, leaning on the horn. Neighbors be damned. My mother came rushing outside in her bathrobe.

"Well, whaddaya think?" he asked, with a manic grin on his face.

My first impulse was to get as far away as I could. But I knew I would never do that. There was my mother and Hannah and Jake and Ben. And now there was Ellen. I wondered if there was any way I could keep her from ever meeting him.

Beverly Hills, June 1982. I'd made a reservation at the Polo Lounge in the Beverly Hills Hotel. They had an enormous Swedish apple pancake that Willa loved and an enormous Bloody Mary that would get me through Father's Day brunch with Ray. My first Father's Day without Ellen. Without Ellen to act as a buffer between my father and me. To hold my hand and reassure me for the millionth time. And I needed it this year more than ever. Because six months earlier I had accepted Sydney Freeman's offer to come work for him at the studio. He'd been bumped upstairs and needed a new President of Production. I couldn't pass it up. And I was terrified of running the place into the ground.

No one but Ellen knew how frightened I was of getting close enough to catch what my father had. As if failure were contagious. I'd thought about asking Ellen to come today but I knew she wouldn't. Despite the fact that I had met all of her demands—medication, therapy, all of it—she still wouldn't let me move back in. Those were the requirements for seeing Willa, she said, not her. I wasn't going to go looking for more rejection. So I didn't even bother to ask.

Willa and I climbed the stairs to the outdoor balcony that led past apartments 2A through F and down to the corner unit where Ray lived. Some of the doors were closed but most were wide open, the screen doors providing a sort of Emperor's New Clothes nod to privacy. I should have told Willa not to stare in, but I couldn't help looking myself. Old people sat in front of their TVs eating alone, being fed by an aid or feeding their own rapidly degenerating spouses. We stopped in front of Ray's door.

I rang the bell.

I was feeling guilty and defensive. Which was absurd. Hannah, Ben, Jake, and I had looked for weeks before I signed the lease on this place.

I knocked.

So, it wasn't Club Med. But it did have a central courtyard with a pool. And there was a senior center across the street that did mixers, outings, and Trivial Pursuit parties for single seniors. It wasn't my fault if he didn't go. Was I supposed to drag him there myself?

I knocked again.

Not to mention it was in Beverly Fucking Hills. This was no goddamned nursing home. I refused to feel guilty.

We waited.

"Maybe he's asleep," Willa said, setting down the Saks bag that held the expensive overcompensation gift I'd bought my father.

I looked at my watch. "No, sweetie. Grandpa knows we have a reservation. And he can't wait to see you."

I took out my keys and sifted through them, looking for Ray's. It was shiny and bright and unused. "Okay, we're goin' in," I said, trying to make the familiar dread, anxiety, and disappointment I felt sound like an adventure.

The apartment was dark and silent. The sharp slivers of sunlight that managed to sneak through the closed blinds did nothing but illuminate the layers of dust and lint that had settled on every surface. The place smelled of dirty laundry, bad breath, and sour milk. Shit. Either the cleaning lady I'd hired was falling down on the job or she and my father had had a falling out. Some time ago.

"Daddy, it smells in here," Willa said, burying her nose in my cashmere sports jacket.

"I know, baby, but I'm going to clean it up, okay? I just have to say hello to Grandpa first."

"Can I come with you?"

Let's see, how much trouble would I be in with Ellen if—worst-case scenario—Willa saw Grandpa lying in a pool of his own blood? "Why don't you wait here? Grandpa might not be dressed yet."

"Mmkay."

I left her sitting on the living room couch with the TV remote in her hand and her nose stuck down inside the collar of her pink-and-white dress.

I turned hesitantly toward my father's bedroom. I pushed the door open and the putrid smell got stronger. I walked into the room and stood at the end of the bed. It was really dark but I could make out a form, a lump lying on the bed buried under the covers.

"Pop?" If he were dead, it would probably smell even worse in here, I thought.

"Pop, come on, it's Grey." Something moved. I went around to the side and pulled a fistful of covers back.

I had to fight the impulse to run. I so wanted this—him—not to be my problem. Undershirt stained with food and sweat, pajama bottoms stained with urine, red-rimmed eyes, greasy hair, yellow teeth, dirty fingernails. I desperately wished Ellen were here to help. She was always so good with him. And then I stopped and looked at him again. Had I ever been this bad? Was I ever this much of a burden to her? Bad, yes, but *this* bad?

And suddenly I was very glad she was not here. "All right, Pop, up an' at 'em," I said, looking into vacant eyes.

"Nnooo."

His voice was ragged. Lack of use. Crying. Probably a combination.

"Yes. I'm gonna help you. We had a date today, remember?"

I took off my sports jacket and rolled up the sleeves of my dress shirt. I kept talking to him from the bathroom while I turned on the shower.

"A date?" he mumbled.

He was using words. Progress. I pulled him into a sitting position.

"Sure, it's Father's Day. We're going to the Polo Lounge. You and Willa and me."

"Willa?"

"She's right here in your living room, waiting for you." I hoped knowing that his only grandchild was sitting in the next room would provide incentive. Instead, Pop started to cry.

"I can't, I can't," he sobbed.

This was not the particular kind of shitty I was expecting today. I sat down on the bed next to him and put my arm around him. He leaned his greasy head against my shoulder.

"Yes, you can, Pop. I'm going to help you. I'm going to help you feel better, okay?"

He looked at me with the scared, watery eyes of a child lost in a department store. I hadn't done this in a long time. It's nothing like riding a bike, but it does come back to you just the same.

I spent the next twenty minutes helping my sixty-year-old father take a shower—making sure he washed his genitals and shampooed his hair and cleaned his nails. Then he sat on the toilet seat while I shaved him.

Some people learn to bake by watching their mothers. I learned this.

When I went to check on Willa, she was sitting in virtually the same position I'd left her in.

"Sweetie, you could have turned on the TV."

"I have to pee."

There was a bathroom right off the living room. "Well go ahead. You don't have to ask."

Willa shook her head.

"Why not? What's . . ." I flipped the light on in the bathroom and found myself staring into a toilet bowl full of festering excrement. Apparently, even flushing had been too much of an effort for Pop.

We had long since missed our reservation by the time Pop got around to putting on the new clothes I'd bought him. Willa was starving. I poked around in Pop's cabinets hoping for an unopened box of crackers but came up empty.

Willa opened the refrigerator door before I could stop her. The smell nearly knocked us both over. I slammed the door shut and rolled my sleeves up for the second time in an hour. I took a deep breath and opened the door again. Christ, the contents of the vegetable drawer had liquefied. It was impossible to tell what had once been what. I pulled out the whole thing and poured the rotten mess into the trash.

On the top shelf, a distended plastic bottle of milk struggled to hold its shape against the gases building inside.

And then I realized it was pointless. Even if I cleaned out his refrigerator and threw out the piles of moldy takeout containers and detoxed his bathrooms, my father still couldn't stay here alone tonight. I was going to have to take him home with me.

A surge of acid shot up from my gut into my esophagus. Thick metallic-tasting saliva filled my mouth. My esophageal sphincter began to spasm. I dropped the sponge I'd been using and clawed at my sternum.

Willa looked up from the TV. "Daddy, you don't look so good."

"Fine . . . sweetie . . . jacket . . . please?"

There were four Rolaids left in the package I carried in the breast pocket of my sports coat. I ate them all. By the time I finished chewing the chalky white tablets, I looked like a rabid dog. They barely took the edge off. I was going to have to get something stronger.

My father shuffled slowly into the room just then, looking remarkably normal. Except for the fact that he was effectively doing fifteen in a sixty-five-mile-an-hour speed zone. And the fact that he'd neglected to take any of the tags off the new clothes he was wearing. And that he was wearing slippers. Other than that, he was good to go.

I put his toothbrush and some clean underwear and pajamas in the Saks bag. Anything else he could borrow from me. As soon as we got home I would be on the phone with all three of my siblings, reaming them out for not living close enough to deal with this shit. One of them would be on a plane first thing in the morning to take over. There would be no negotiation. Tomorrow I'd have my secretary get a professional cleaning crew in here. Or maybe I'd just torch the place. In the meantime I had to find us someplace to go for Father's Day lunch. Someplace we didn't need reservations. Someplace that served enormous goddamned Bloody Marys.

We went to the Hamburger Hamlet. Nothing fancy. And Willa was happy because, as far as she was concerned, they made the best root beer float in town. But little by little, I could see that Pop was starting to scare her.

"Is he sick?" she asked.

"Well, kind of."

"What does he have? Is it catching?"

"No, sweetie, it's not contagious."

"Why does he look like that? Why do you have to feed him? Why is he crying?"

She started to shred her napkin and stopped eating and I knew it was time to go. And when we got back to my place, the last thing I wanted to do was pick up the phone but it was the first thing I did.

"El?" I had only meant to ask her to come pick up Willa—to spare her having to witness any more of this.

"Grey? Hello?"

But when I heard her voice, all I could think of was everything I really wanted but hadn't dared to ask for. There was too much to say. I wasn't allowed to say any of it. So nothing came out. It had begun as such a simple request.

"Greyson? What's wrong? Is Willa hurt? Is she sick?"

"No. No, no, God no. It's nothing like that."

"Well, then what? You sound . . ."

I sighed. I started to speak and my voice broke. I cleared my throat to cover it. "Shit. It's Ray, isn't it?"

"I'm sorry," I said when I opened the door to let her in a half hour later.

"Jesus, Grey, how many times do I have to say it," she said, hugging me. "Your father is not your fault."

"Say it again?" I whispered into her hair.

"He's not your fault and you're not him."

"Thank you. Again."

"Anytime."

After seventeen months, Ellen let me come home. Just in time for Christmas. I made sure it looked like something out of a Bing Crosby movie. I bought an enormous tree, strung lights across the roof and in the trees outside, and bought out half of Saks and most of Toys "R" Us. Other than the fact that there was no snow and it was seventy-eight degrees, it was a perfect white Christmas.

Things at work were less than perfect. I was constantly being disappointed. By my team, by everyone. Assholes. I was surrounded by assholes.

"No, Marvin, the *problem* is that you're someone's nephew with a degree in business from Cal State who doesn't know shit about movies. Making them, marketing them, or watching them for that matter." I paced a straight line the length of my office, back and forth in front of the floor-to-ceiling windows that looked out onto Burbank—olive trees and gargantuan billboards advertising the studio's latest movies. "The problem, Marvin, is that you have no taste. Uh . . . Huh. Huh. Well, you go right ahead and tell your uncle if you feel you need to. Oh . . . okay, Marvin, I don't think you want to threaten me, you two-faced conniving little shit."

I slammed the phone down. Who the fuck did that little cocksucker think he was? More to the point, how could he not know who he was dealing with? Hanging up on Marvin Jacobs didn't make me feel any better. Just caged. I rifled through the carefully constructed piles of scripts on my desk, scattering them.

My secretary, Rene, came in and closed the door behind her. Stood there with her arms crossed. "Well, that was special. What was your strategy? Bad cop, bad cop?"

"Not worth my time or breath."

I walked over to the door and yelled down the hallway to Christine, my VP of Production. "Where the hell is Zantaugh's rewrite?"

She walked briskly out of her office. "Uh . . . Grey, it's not in yet."

"What? Why the hell not? Lean on him."

"Well, it's not due for another week."

"Fucking writers. Whiny, overpaid. What do they have to do except sit in front of the goddamned keyboard?"

Christine laughed. I thought I saw Rene shoot her a look.

"What's funny?" I asked.

"You always say you could get offered the biggest box-office draws in town and you still won't make the movie unless the script is there. You sort of need writers for that."

"Doesn't mean I can't hate the pasty-faced, sensitive, artistic assholes."

The smile fell off Christine's face. "Jesus, Grey. You okay?"

"*I'm* fine. Just tired of being the only one who's getting anything done." I yelled down the hallway again. "Zach, when am I going to see a first cut of *Comes a Stranger?*"

Nothing.

"Zach!"

The young creative executive came jogging into my office. "Sorry. I was on a call. I—"

"*Comes a Stranger.* I should have seen first cut weeks ago. I've been too fucking indulgent at staff meetings. And you've been too fucking vague." I ignored the terrified look on his face. "Do we have a problem? Is it Leland?"

Zach looked quickly at Christine and then Rene, who both stared at the floor.

"They don't know the answer, Zach. It's all you. Do we or do we not have a problem?"

Zach spoke softly. "Editing is taking longer than we thought. Leland sits there and agonizes over every frame. I mean the movie's great but it's long. Too long. And he won't let the editors do their jobs."

"Apparently you haven't been doing yours either, have you?" I snarled. "You told me you could handle Leland. You should have come to me weeks ago. And I should have known better."

The kid looked pale, sweaty.

"I'm sorry, Greyson. I thought if we could just get past this one section . . ."

"Where's he working?"

"On the lot. In one of the editing suites in the Bogart Building. But he's gone for the day."

"Good." I grabbed my jacket off the back of my chair. "Call the picture and sound editors back in. And show me."

Christine, Zach, Rene, and two or three of my other executives who were still in the office struggled to keep up with me as I zigzagged across the lot, cutting through buildings, past the commissary, the soundstages on which America's favorite sitcoms were filmed, and through the streets of a permanent set that was made to look like Anytown, USA.

"Do you want me to show you what we have so far?" Zach asked. His voice was trembling a little as Jerry Nunez, the picture editor, arrived with a key and opened the door to *Comes a Stranger*'s editing suite.

"No. You can go. All of you. Jerry and I are going to finish this goddamned movie." But no one left. They just stood there, watching as Jerry and then Bertram Doyle, the sound editor, and I sat at the Steenbeck, expertly making the cuts I demanded.

"Greyson, you can't do that!" Christine hurled herself between me and the massive flatbed editing machine. "Leland has final cut. You can't just go in without his permission and cut his picture."

"Watch me."

"But . . . Leland's . . . he's the director. That's like—"

"Leland works for me. If he can't get it done, I'll do it myself."

"But you don't know what he wants."

"It's not about what he wants anymore. This is business. Besides, I know this script inside out. I can do this."

"He has a contract. He could sue and he'd probably win." She knelt down beside me and tried to take my hand, but I shooed her away. "Greyson, you're not thinking clearly. This isn't good business."

"Go to hell," I told her.

The next morning, I found a cease and desist letter on my desk. Leland threatened to sue me if I didn't hand over his movie, and the studio said contractually I had to. Their fucking loss. If you want to get anything done you'd better damn well be prepared to do it yourself.

And even then, the assholes will bring you down.

In February, Taysen said my blood test showed my lithium was below the therapeutic level. So he increased my dose. And within a week I became a lumbering, inarticulate idiot who nodded off in any meeting that started after 2:00 P.M. In the mornings, my hands shook so badly I had to hide them under my desk. I told everyone I had hay fever.

After I burned my hand pouring coffee because I couldn't hold the pot steady and then dropped the mug and the rest of the coffee on my bare feet, Ellen decided she was going to have a word with the doctor.

"He can't live like this! He can't do his job like this!"

If I'd known she was going take my side, I would've poured coffee on myself weeks before.

"Ellen, the tremors, the fatigue, most of the side effects will probably dissipate."

"Probably?" She looked at him incredulously.

"What about my memory?" I asked.

I'd had a reputation, ever since I was an agent, for knowing every deal point word for word after reading through a contract just once. Now every negotiation became another test, another minefield. I was a fraud and it was only a matter of time before I got caught. Last week I'd been heading out to a lunch with the ridiculously large entourage of agents, publicists, and lawyers that represented a young actor with whom I wanted to do business.

"And where do you think you're going?" Rene asked me.

"Lunch with Giordono's people at . . . at . . . shit, where again?"

Rene looked concerned. "That was pushed to next week. We had a long conversation about it yesterday. You're having lunch in the commissary with the producers on *Sleepwalkers.*"

It was all news to me.

"Greyson?" Rene felt my forehead. "Maybe you should sit."

"What? No! I just wrote it in my book wrong. It's nothing." I pulled off my tie and changed gears, heading for the commissary.

"*I* wrote it in your book," I heard Rene say, "—correctly."

Rene would keep her mouth closed. Out of loyalty. But she knew something was up. One more slip like that and she'd go to Ellen.

"I'm afraid the memory issue will likely stick around," Taysen said. "It's hard to know to what degree. Everyone's different."

I stood up and walked over to the window. His office overlooked the UCLA campus.

Ellen stared at Taysen, shaking her head. "Jesus, what a fucking nightmare."

"We'll monitor the level," he said. "Keep it as low as we can. But there's a very fine—"

"Line between the therapeutic dose and the toxic," Ellen cut him off. "Yeah, yeah. I know."

"In time, some of these side effects will dissipate or at least become tolerable," Taysen said.

"So you're saying they won't go away," Ellen said flatly.

"Some might. I don't know. We just have to wait it out."

Ellen nodded silently. After a moment she leaned forward toward Taysen. "Dr. Taysen, do you understand what would happen if . . ."

"If what, Ellen?"

Ellen looked at me like she was asking my permission.

"Go ahead," I said. "It's not like we haven't talked about it. Ad nauseam." I went back to the window. The grass looked incredibly green and the brick-and-sandstone buildings—many of them domed with gentle curves—were in a way friendlier, more welcoming than their colonial and Gothic Eastern counterparts.

"Well?" She threw up her hands.

"I understand Greyson's position requires discretion."

"That's one way of putting it. Do you understand what would happen if anyone found out? Anyone? They don't let people with . . . *this* run studios."

"I understand the stigma is . . . a tremendous burden to bear," Taysen said. "But the fact is, untreated manic depression gets worse. One in four commit suicide."

Fourteen floors down, there were coeds biking to class along the wide path that cut through the center of campus.

"So," Taysen said firmly, "do you want a medicated studio executive with side effects that may or may not go away or do you want a dead studio executive? Because one in four is not a bet I'd be willing to make."

Still more kids were lying on the green, green grass. Eating pizza. Reading. Playing Frisbee.

I wondered if the windows opened.

Ten days later, on a Monday morning, I was sitting at my desk going over memos for the weekly meeting with my core staff—the six men and two women I'd handpicked to head up the Production divisions, Domestic and International Distribution, Marketing, Accounting, Development, Casting, Postproduction, and In-house Packaging. They were my cabinet advisors. They gathered the intel. I made the decisions.

I willed myself to memorize every tiny detail. Production costs, coverage of the scripts up for discussion, replacement options for an actor whose drug habit might make it necessary to replace him a week before shooting began—I wouldn't even have to look down or turn a page.

"Meeting in five, Grey," Rene said, setting a stack of scripts down on my desk. Rene had been with me, or, more accurately, had put up with me, for fourteen years—ever since I first got my own desk at Franklin Morton. At the time she was a single mother in her thirties working a full-time job and taking care of two young children. And me. Now her kids were in college. Now it was just me.

I picked up a yellow legal pad and the Montblanc pen Ellen had given me and walked out of my office.

"Grey," Rene said, rushing up behind me and handing me a file, "the meeting memos. Your notes."

"Don't need 'em," I said, waving her off. "But I'd love another cup of coffee."

"Good morning," I said cheerily as I made my entrance into the conference room where my staff was already assembled. I took my seat at the head of the table. "Okay, we've got a lot to get through," I said, writing the date in the upper left corner of my blank yellow pad. "Shall we get started?"

I looked up at the people seated around the table and froze. I couldn't remember a single one of their names. I began to per-spire and suddenly it was as if I were looking through the wrong end of a telescope. I had to get out. I smiled weakly at the group of familiar-looking strangers, stood up, and immediately fell onto the floor.

The studio publicist called it food poisoning and managed to keep it out of *Variety.*

That night, I cut my dose in half. After a week, most of the side effects were gone. Ellen and I celebrated having dodged a disastrous bullet.

After that, every night before my monthly blood test, I would sim-ply triple my dose. Taysen and I celebrated my miraculous progress. And everybody was happy.

Even the studio.

New York, 1994. It is difficult, I am finding, to make friends on the psych ward. Certainly we all have something in common. But usually, I find, it's just the one thing. And mutual insanity is not a good foundation for a friendship. Or maybe I'm overly demanding. But I am more delighted than a grown man should be when I discover that the beautiful and maniacal Glenda loves movies almost as much as I do—that she can quote dialogue from *The Maltese Falcon*, *North by Northwest*, *The Rocky Horror Picture Show*, *Last Tango in Paris*. The difference between us is that, for the time being anyway, I have a grasp on where the movie ends and reality begins. But no one is perfect. Glenda may be certifiable but she knows her cinema and she has earned my respect. And so we have become friends. And then some.

The then some really started because of *Basic Instinct*.

Glenda is not the only patient with issues that might induce the staff to monitor our viewing a little more closely. But despite the various pathologies wandering the ward, they let us watch virtually anything on TV—sex, violence, the abuse of small animals—particularly on the weekends, when group activities are pared down to a minimum and the depressive doldrums kick in.

And so, one bleak Saturday afternoon, eight or ten of us—patients and staff members alike—found ourselves watching *Basic Instinct*, a film which Glenda has seen thirteen times.

"I fucked Michael Douglas," she blurted out at one point. "But he disrespected me so I broke it off."

Five minutes went by.

"He begged me to take him back. Practically stalked me."

"Shut up, Glenda. You're full of shit and we're trying to watch," said Esther, an Orthodox ECT patient who, on top of everything else, had to suffer the indignity of wearing a bad wig. I wondered, though, if for Esther watching movies like *Basic Instinct* was the next best thing to eating lobster.

"I don't appreciate that coarse language, Esther," Glenda said, twisting her long, wild, dark hair into a bun. "And I'm not full of shit. I had to get a restraining order against Mr. Michael Douglas."

"*SSSSHHHHHHHHHH.*" Eight people simultaneously shut Glenda down. I smiled at her.

"Are you laughing at me?"

"Not at all," I said, "I believe you. One hundred percent. I've worked with Douglas. I wouldn't put it past him."

She dragged her folding chair so that she sat directly across from me. "You have?"

"It was years ago."

By the time Catherine Tramell was getting interrogated by Detective Nick Curran, Glenda had slipped off her underwear. Using a crayon as a cigarette and reciting Sharon Stone's dialogue word for word, inflection for inflection, she let her hospital gown ride up and her paper-white thighs fall apart until I was staring directly into her pussy.

She left her mark on the vinyl-covered chair. After that, the ball was in my court. But it is not easy to have an affair on a psych ward. It may be even harder than killing yourself.

ELEVENTH

I can't help wanting to fight back when they try to put me under. Because as much as I want to padlock what is left, I know I can't. I know they will creep in and steal more. What I ate for dinner last night, the name of the first girl I kissed. And I do not know how much is left. What I remember now mostly are words—the ones they say endlessly, the ones that make me want to do something that would get me thrown in the Quiet Room: "Most likely," "Eventually," "We don't know," "Wish we knew more," "Wait and see." Failed attempts at reassurance, they are empty, mean-ingless, insubstantial, placeholders for what is missing.

I feel the pinch of the first needle. Pot roast, I think, and tuck the memory away in a dark corner. I hide Emily Sachs away someplace I'm sure they'll never look. I won't know for sure until I wake up. But for now it's the best I can do.

New York, 1992. "Sir?" I open my eyes and see the Pakistani cabbie looking at me in the rearview mirror.

"Where we going this evening?" he asks in English so heavily accented I can just barely understand him.

Shit. I hadn't really thought about it.

"You pick," I say. His brow knits into a perfect V.

"Sir?"

"Central Park South. The Sherry-Netherland." It's what I always said when I got into a cab at JFK.

The drive from the airport along the Van Wyck and the BQE is one continuous stretch of drab—Woodhaven, Kew Gardens, Rego Park. I stare out the window straining to catch a glimpse of a garden or a park. Anything that could even in the broadest sense be construed as haven-like. But there is nothing. I've seen third-world countries make more hospitable first impressions. I close my eyes.

"Wake me up as soon as you can see the skyline."

"Oh, yes sir," he says enthusiastically. "You don't want to be missing that. Very beautiful, very dramatic. Just like it looks in the movies." His accent has a singsong quality to it which, after a while, I find oddly soothing.

I wonder what it means that I have just had the same thought as my Pakistani cabbie. Perhaps nothing more than that we are both cinephiles. He could in fact be the next Satyajit Ray. Or Quentin Tarantino. I lean forward and take a good look at his taxi operator's license. Savijii Sengupta. Eventually Savijii's going to have to lose the turban.

Eventually he'll have to water down everything that drew Hollywood to him in the first place. And he'll do it. Give in. Sell out. What choice does he have? Like he's going to spend the rest of his life driving this fucking cab. Not when all he has to do is lose the turban.

But I digress. I was thinking about the Manhattan skyline. About the fact that there is something deeply, fundamentally satisfying—inspiring, exciting, and at the same time comforting—about reencountering that view. Because it doesn't matter what season it is or whether I'm sneaking in at dawn after taking the red-eye or how many years I've stayed away; everything is where I left it.

The Chrysler Building, the Empire State Building, the Twin Towers—always there waiting for me. Faithfully. Watching for me. Standing tall. Like the proud, lonely, loyal wives of sea captains.

L.A. has no skyline—no elegant bridges or buildings that soar toward the clouds. Shopping centers, nondescript office buildings, and citywide, event-themed decor (The Olympics! The King Tut Exhibit!) go up and down like sets on a soundstage. Nothing lasts. From one trip to the next. One day to the next, L.A.'s slapdash, easily impressionable landscape changes as hastily as the events on its civic social calendar.

Most of the time, you drive by without even noticing there's nothing to look at. Unless you're in one of the canyons or out at the beach. But L.A. can't really take credit for that. The Pacific Ocean, Topanga Canyon—that kind of thing is just dumb luck. A gift. It's only a matter of time before the well-intentioned people of Los Angeles fuck it up.

"Sir?"

"Mmmm."

"Sir."

I open my eyes and the drab is gone. We are crossing the Triborough Bridge and the sun is glinting off the swells in the East River. And suddenly I am seeing my little yellow taxicab from above. I am seeing the opening credits roll. I am orchestrating the establishing shot. Not as gritty as *The Asphalt Jungle*, not as gauzy as *Manhattan*. I am still deciding. But it is the same landscape, the same city.

When we get to the hotel, I realize I have only Kenyan money in my wallet. Now my cabbie is not so cheerful.

"Keep the meter running," I say. "I'll go to the currency exchange inside."

I turn toward the hotel.

"Wait," he calls out his window. "Leave your bags in the trunk."

The bellhop—a man of about sixty, wearing a maroon tux and tails with brass buttons down the front, white gloves, and a little hat held on with elastic that cuts into the pillow of fat under his neck—has just finished loading my luggage onto a cart. Three heavy suitcases, a guitar I had custom-made for me in Brazil for $30,000 (I don't play), a rug stitched from the skins of African water buffalo, a set of two-dozen hand-carved ivory chopsticks, and a giant brass Tibetan gong.

"You, bellboy! Put those bags in my trunk."

"You don't order *me* around. I don't work for you." The bellhop turns to me. "Savages, every one of 'em. Hardly speak the language."

My cabbie throws open the car door and stands next to the taxi, one hand resting on his trusty yellow steed.

"You bastard! You think you can insult me. You think you better than me?"

The bellhop holds on to the cart with one hand and gestures dramatically with the other. "See what I mean?" he says to me. "Savages."

My cabbie walks toward us menacingly.

"Why don't you go back where you came from," the bellhop says, shoving the cart toward the cabbie, "before you have an accident."

"You shouldn't start a fight, old man. You might get hurt," my cabbie says, stabbing his index finger in the bellhop's direction.

That kind of behavior could get you kicked out of Africa, I think, and deciding it's really not my problem, I go inside the hotel to change my money.

As soon as the revolving doors spit me out into the lobby, I know I've made a big mistake. Luxury hotels in foreign countries are one thing. They provide a kind of privileged anonymity. But this is just the opposite. The circular velvet couches, the white marble staircase, even the clinking of glasses I hear from the mahogany-paneled lobby bar. The smells, the sounds—it is all nauseatingly familiar. Only this time I am not a VIP. This time I do not even have a reservation. My heart begins to race.

I should have known. How could I not? And when I see the couple ahead of me hand their passports to the woman checking them in, I realize how truly stupid I have been.

"I won't be staying," I tell the bellhop, who's patiently waiting to follow me to my room after I've checked in.

"Sir?"

"Put my bags back in the trunk and tell the driver I'll be right out. Please."

Crimson-colored anger appears at the top of the bellhop's collar, travels upward, seeps into his neck fat, and spreads across his broad face.

"Certainly, sir." He smiles with tight lips and a clenched jaw. When I get back in the taxi, the cabbie is wearing a shit-eating grin.

"I gave him a hundred dollars," I say, and then wonder if that was enough to compensate him for his trouble and the inevitable shit he took from my cabbie.

Savijii's smile fades quickly. "Where you want to go?" he asks.

"I don't know."

Savijii bangs his fist on the steering wheel. He's muttering to himself in some third-world language. I don't need to speak it to understand he's pissed.

"I need a place to stay. Nothing fancy."

Without another word, Savijii burns rubber out of the Sherry-Netherland's cobblestone driveway and heads downtown, quickly leaving Central Park South in our dust.

"No hot plates, no music, no guests. You pay a week in advance."

The ancient black man behind the desk at the McBurney YMCA has been rifling around the same drawer of loose keys for ten minutes. He is thin and bent and wears an orange Teamsters baseball cap, though knowing the details of the Teamsters retirement package as I do, I doubt that if he were an actual card-carrying member he'd have to work at all.

"That's fine," I say. He looks up at me and then past my shoulder to my belongings.

"Can't leave anything out in the hallways. Violation of the fire code."

"Okay."

"Room ain't big," he says. Like it's a threat.

"That's fine," I say. He goes back to rifling. "Laundromat's around the corner on Seventh."

"Fine. You do have a room, right?"

"Yeah, I got a room. Just opened up this morning."

"Could that be the one you're looking for?" I ask, taking a step forward and pointing to the lone key hanging on the bulletin board behind him."

"You gotta stay back a' the yella'!" he says, pointing to the broken line painted on the floor. I do what I'm told. He turns and pulls the key off the wall. "Two hundred twenty-two dollars. You pay again Friday before five if you want to stay."

"Thanks, but I don't think—"

"That's your business. I'm jus' informing you of the policy. Policy is you pay Friday before five if you plan to stay."

"Okay. That's fine." I peel off the bills and he hands me the key.

"You damn lucky," he says as he watches me fill out the dog-eared registration card. "Mr. Meyer just passed this morning. Well, we found him this morning anyway."

I glance up at him. "Lived in that room for thirty-four years."

"He lived at the YMCA for thirty-four years?"

"You got good timing. Before today I ain't had a vacancy since 1978. I left you a fresh set of sheets."

"Thanks, I appreciate that." I am in the right place at the right time. I can't remember the last time that happened, I think, as I drag my shit up three flights of stairs. And I have to admit, I feel only slightly guilty that Mr. Meyer had to die to make it happen.

The following Friday, I am standing at the desk handing over another two hundred and twenty-two dollars. I see now how this could easily turn into thirty-four years. The majority of the all-male residents here are either gay or over seventy. And so far everyone I've met has been quiet, clean, and discreet. Tony—I think that's his name—scrubs our open communal shower stall with Ajax at least daily.

Staying at the Y is much like living at a monastery. Without the sex.

Chelsea is loud and bustling and there is very little green. I don't know what to do with myself, so I look for bookstores. In the six years since I left the States, the smaller independent bookstores have been mostly replaced by big chains. I don't mind. It just means I can be even more anonymous. I find myself gravitating to the Parenting section at Barnes & Noble, flipping through books with titles like *Helping Your Child Through Divorce* and *The Divorced Dad*. As if I am a responsible parent. As if I am a father who is going to have weekend visits and pay doctor bills and attend Christmas pageants. Every day, in every branch, pregnant women holding stacks of baby books look at me with contempt. The impending split must be my fault. How could it be otherwise? That poor woman, that poor child, they think, as they lay a protective hand over their ballooning stomachs.

Sometimes I take Willa's picture out and look at it in front of these women. I keep it with me. It came off the cardboard key chain long ago. I have re-glued it over and over but it keeps falling off, so I carry the whole thing around in a Ziploc bag. The tacky, mottled blue background of her first-grade school picture makes her look ordinary. Her hair is combed back and kept neatly in place with a red floral headband that matches the dress she is wearing. This is my picture-day daughter, not my real girl.

I drift from Parenting over to Psychology/Self-Help. The titles run together like raindrops on a windshield. Glossy pictures of confident, self-satisfied experts stare out at me. For $16.95 they promise to change my life, solve my problems, increase my concentration, improve my memory, manage my time, fulfill my potential, discover my sexual self. They all have the answer.

My eyes fall on a small pink book—no author's picture on this cover. I pull it from its snug place between *Beating the Blues* and *Be Your Own Therapist*. The pages of the pink book are made of cream-colored parchment paper, the edges uneven, like the ones in those leather-bound volumes of Dickens and Chaucer people keep on their bookcases but never read. I let the thick, soft pages stroke my thumb as I flip through the book. The pages stop turning and fall open. The words fly at me: "I have felt the wind of the wing of madness." I slam the book shut and shove it back onto the shelf.

That night I take two sleeping pills. I wake up a little after 3:00 A.M. My heart is racing. My mouth is dry. The sheets are cold and damp. There is sweat in the creases behind my knees and on the insides of my elbows. I go into the bathroom, run the cold water in the sink, and put my mouth under the faucet. I walk back to my room and stare out the window at the streetlights and the traffic on Twenty-third Street. The grimy, ugly street has grown on me. Like mold.

I open the window and stick my head out to make sure it is all still there, that I am still here. Bodega, Chelsea Hotel, stained mattress left sagging at the curb four days ago. My world is as I left it. But when I close my eyes, all I see are images from my dream.

My daughter is three, maybe four. She stands over me with a giddy look on her pink-cheeked face. She is wearing a party dress—one of those frilly things that stand out at the bottom—and patent-leather Mary Janes. I reach out to hug her, to tell her I am sorry, that I've missed her. Her lips part, revealing little cat-like white teeth. She raises her arm and in her tiny, dimpled hand she holds a gun. She raises the other hand and waves at me. "Bye-bye, Daddy," she says in a tiny voice. And she pulls the trigger.

A breeze blows across my face.

The wind. The wing. I can feel it coming.

I do not go back to sleep.

I do not go back to Barnes & Noble.

Lately no one and nothing can keep up with me. Not traffic or store clerks or elevators or the old lady with the walker in front of me on the sidewalk. Especially not her. Her I want to kill. I try to pass her on the right but her walker is too fucking wide. I try to pass on the left but a woman with a double stroller the size of a goddamn Winnebago beats me to it. She flashes me an insincere "I won this round" smile. The kind of victorious New York expression reserved for total strangers.

That I have been forced into a holding pattern causes rage to rise in me. My tsunami. My chest constricts and I am painfully aware that suddenly, inexplicably, there are tacks and shards of glass circulating through my veins.

I slip between two parked cars and walk briskly down the street. In the street. No pedestrians to worry about, to slow me down. Except now and then when I encounter another fast walker like myself—someone who has abandoned the sidewalk for the fast lane. And then I am relieved. Because everyone in New York is impatient and irritable and agitated. So there is nothing wrong with me.

The Piccadilly is the answer to my prayers. I discover the enormous used bookstore accidentally. Apparently I am the only person in New York not already familiar with "the Pick," as it is known.

It is easy to get lost in the Pick—not just in its famously daunting miles of labyrinthine aisles, but to lose track of time, of proportion, of perspective, of oneself. It is a drug. And within a week I am a junkie.

At first I need help navigating the Byzantine shelving system and outdated store maps. When I first begin coming here, spending long, languid hours during which time finally slows down for me—the only time during which I can finally take long, slow, albeit musty breaths—I am as lost as anyone else who first wanders into the Pick. And so it annoys me when, seeking help, service, or aid of some kind from the sales staff, I find a young man wearing a bright red Piccadilly shirt, his "Pick My Brain" badge pinned over his heart, hiding in a secluded corner of the Military History section. He is wearing a Walkman and shamelessly filling up multicolored note cards with information from books he obviously can't afford to buy or isn't allowed to xerox.

"Excuse me," I say loudly. But since he doesn't hear me, I walk up, grab a hold of the ladder on which he is perched, and give it a good shake.

"What the hell, man?"

"What's your name?"

"Cecil, why?"

"You work here, Cecil?" I ask, as if the answer isn't completely obvious.

"Yeah?"

"I thought maybe you were a customer impersonating a salesperson."

He pulls his headphones down around his neck. "Can I help you with something?"

"Yes, actually. John Berryman. *Dream Songs*."

He points in a general direction. "Poetry. Aisle 18b." Then he puts his headphones back on.

Not that the aisles actually have numbers on them.

"Thanks for your help, Cecil."

But I am only annoyed with Cecil until I don't need him anymore. Which isn't long. Very quickly I find a much more dedicated salesperson who, as luck would have it, also has breasts, which she has done a wonderful job of showcasing. She has customized her child-sized Piccadilly T-shirt by taking scissors to the neckline, *Flashdance*-style, so that it now hangs provocatively off one olive-skinned shoulder.

Now, after months of trying to navigate its topography on my own, Nicki—that's her name—has become my own personal Beatrice of the Piccadilly, taking me by the hand and guiding me through every nook and mouse-friendly cranny, explaining the nuanced maps, even teaching me the secrets of the aisle numbering system.

She too has a tag pinned above her heart. And though by now I no longer need her assistance locating books, I often ask if I can "pick her brain." But Nicki, who is studying Library Science at the New School, takes her job very seriously. So she only helps me on her lunch hour. Usually downstairs among the ergonomics textbooks or in the Typography section. Rare Typography. Nicki once confessed that she finds the old letters and typefaces to be quite a turn-on. She likes to put on the special cotton gloves used for handling rare books and, bending over so that her nose is almost but not quite touching the pages, she inhales their smell while slowly turning the pages.

I have not yet confessed to Nicki that I find her turn-on quite a turn-on. As do I the Technicolor bras she wears underneath her Pick T-shirt, their straps always visible on one shoulder or the other— fuchsia, lavender, aqua, fire-engine red. Never beige. Always something cheerful and impractical. One day maybe, one day. For now, admiring her ass as I watch her inhale antique ink is enough to get me through the day.

Cecil's lack of work ethic no longer bothers me. Now I find him endearing. Technically, Cecil works at the Pick inventorying and shelving. But what he really does for at least ninety percent of his shift is research for the dissertation he's writing as an NYU graduate student in American History.

He's passionate about his dissertation topic on the three thousand Jews who fought for the Confederate Army, and I admire that. Now when I see Cecil's pale, skinny arm peek out of the Military History aisle, his ink-stained index finger pointing unhelpfully in some vague direction of the cavernous store, I wait for the disgruntled customer to emerge, usually muttering obscenities. Then I help them find what they're looking for. Because I really don't want Cecil getting in trouble with Tina and Terri.

I've seen the owner's identical twin daughters (porcine women whose behavior seems to indicate they have their periods all the time) yank a salesperson into one of the store's dusty, less-traveled corners—Art: Printed Ephemera or History of Aviation, for example—and ream him or her out for not providing an adequate level of service.

"It doesn't do much good to tell them we have what they're looking for if they can't fucking find it, does it?" one of them—I can never tell which—asks in a tone reminiscent of the Wicked Witch of the West. Usually the beleaguered, uninterested, occasionally intimidated sales associate nods and vows to lead the customer by the hand until the actual sale is made. Often, when the lecture is over, an eye roll or a barely audible "suck my dick, bitch" lingers in the air as Terri/Tina makes her way to the front of the store.

And so I feel terrible when it happens because I absolutely, positively do not mean to get Cecil fired. I have only been trying to help—showing his exasperated customers exactly where to find the book, edition, or translation they are looking for; helping them back to the register when they get lost. Which is where my plan backfires. Because the now-satisfied customer asks Terri/Tina who the useless kid in Military History is and why the excellent middle-aged salesman isn't wearing a red shirt so he can be more easily identified.

And that's it. Because of course it isn't the first time Cecil has been called useless. Among other things. But training people to work at the Pick is a bitch. So Tina/Terri has let him stay. Until now. And now he is done.

"I'm really sorry," I say.

Cecil and Nicki and a few other Pick staff are in Cecil's apartment in Hell's Kitchen, getting stoned and eating pizza.

"It's not your fault, man," Cecil says generously.

"What are you gonna do?" I ask, looking around at all the half-packed boxes.

"I'm moving in with two other guys. In Brooklyn. Fuckin' sucks."

I look around the place. It has a kind of turn-of-the-century, poverty-stricken Jacob Riis charm to it. "Nice place. Do you know if it's been rented?"

Cecil glares at me. "You get me fired and now you're going to steal my apartment."

One week and a new coat of paint later, I move out of the Y and into my new apartment.

I hoped having my own home, a more permanent living situation, would make me feel more grounded, less weightless and insubstantial. Like a hot-air balloon without the sandbags. But I am wrong. Again. Nothing can hold me down.

I hardly sleep anymore. Not much, I mean. People who say they don't sleep at all are lying. But I sleep less and less. I move purposefully around my apartment with the energy of midmorning while the hands on my cheap wall clock glide stealthily through 1:00 and 2:00 A.M. They are dipping deep into the three o'clock hour before I notice it is getting late. I know it will be an hour or more until I can unwind enough to fall asleep.

I watch the twenty-four-hour news networks. I don't keep track of which hours. The tiny store of sleeping pills I was able to get at the neighborhood clinic is long gone. Apparently the emergency rooms don't consider insomnia to be an emergency. I could go to a real doctor, but then there would be real questions, and just the thought of those make it harder to sleep. I need a drug dealer. I splash water on my face from the tap in the bathroom and stare into the medicine cabinet mirror. I look like shit. "You talkin' to me?" I look over my shoulder and back to the mirror. "I said, you talkin' to me? Well, fuck you." I aim with my hand and shoot the man in the mirror.

I wander through my railroad apartment, its narrow hallways piled high with stacks of books I've bought at the Pick. I buy novels, poetry, philosophy, history, medical texts, scientific journals, and erotica. I am indiscriminate. I have several spinning towers of CDs planted like saplings in my living room. I spend my days in book and record stores, browsing, collecting, trading, discarding—hoarding words and sounds—so I can consume them later. Gorge on them in private.

Once a week, a Polish girl comes in to clean. I pay her extra to sleep with me. We fuck and then she changes the sheets. She doesn't seem to mind that I can't remember her name from one week to the next. Every Wednesday at nine, she introduces herself all over again. Sort of like a perpetual first date.

At twenty after nine, the buzzer downstairs rings and I push the Enter button without asking who it is because the intercom doesn't work for shit and no one but the housekeeper and the delivery guy from Szechwan Dragon Garden ever comes over. A few minutes later, she is standing in my doorway panting from the hike up the stairs.

"Good morning." She waves girlishly. "Here is Marsienka."

She is pale and petite and has short burgundy hair. I look up from where I am—where I have been since *Letterman* ended—lying on the couch reading Patton's diaries. I smile at her and wave back. Girlishly.

Regardless of the season, Marsienka always comes to work in some version of the same outfit: miniskirt, tight shirt made of some stretchy, shiny material with a plunging neckline, brightly colored tights— usually fishnet or lace—and a pair of ankle-high stiletto boots. I wonder whether the outfit is just for me, but since I don't really care that much, I'd rather not know.

After we fuck, she puts on sweatpants, an oversized T-shirt, and rubber sandals.

I will pay her twice what she normally gets for cleaning toilets. And she will be able to take her asthmatic kid to a real doctor instead of some filthy clinic. I enjoy doing charity work. Marina? Mareska? Marinka?

I am not so pathetic that I don't know just how pathetic I am. I am pathetic but self-aware. And Wednesdays with what's-her-name are all I can count on to punctuate the passage of time. The time. My time.

They are no longer the same. Because my time has become unreliable. The days have become a blur. I am exhausted but on edge, revved up, impatient. Nothing is fast enough. No one walks fast enough. Gets out of my way fast enough. Objects have begun to shimmer and shine.

I need to move faster to break out of the shiny, shimmery fog. So I buy an expensive bike. So I can get around the city. Faster. The guy at the store tries to sell me a helmet. But I pass. It will only slow me down.

I ride everywhere—in bike lanes and bus lanes, darting in and out of traffic, steering with one hand because the other is always busy flipping off the cabbies and truck drivers and pedestrians I've cut off, sideswiped, nearly hit. I am impatient and can't be bothered with stop signs and red lights. And now I am in the park riding fast, passing anyone and everyone. I am lightning. Except there is one guy who is riding faster. Faster than me. And that is not okay. So I give chase. I try to close the gap between us, pedaling hard—on and off the bike path, dodging nannies pushing strollers and dogs on retractable leashes and girls with triple-wide asses who take up the whole sidewalk.

He is heading east, cutting across the park toward the Met. Maybe. I don't know. I am losing him. I am having trouble keeping up. So much trouble it hurts. But I push. And pump. And pedal harder. My heart pounds. And I manage to keep him in sight. Just. I don't know why, but it feels important. I lose sight of him for a moment and get a sick feeling in my stomach. I catch a glimpse of him and ride harder, faster to catch up. I can't tell if he knows I am following him. He cuts easily across all four lanes of the park drive and hops the curb, but by the time I get there, a riding club is making its loop around. I weave in and out, nearly killing myself and several other riders.

"Fuckin' tool."

"Get your ass outta the park, dickhead."

"Fuck off," I call breathlessly over my shoulder as I desperately try to make up lost time and space.

And then I see him, mounting a hill on a no-bikes-allowed path. He is wearing a red biking jersey. Just like mine.

I can't tell if he is trying to get away from me or just doing his own thing. But he sure as shit is oblivious to my near-death experience. To me and my need to catch up. Suddenly he stands and jerks his bike off the bike path onto a lawn and then rides headfirst down some stairs and back onto a pedestrian path leading to Fifth Avenue.

I follow, nearly falling off my own bike with each awkward switch-back, barely making it onto Fifth, where I see him heading north. Finally he looks at me over his shoulder.

When I see his face, the sweat coming out of my pores turns to ice. I assumed, when he finally looked back at me, he'd be laughing. All along, I assumed this had been a game for him. But he's not smiling. What I see when he looks at me is the same thing I see every time I look in the mirror lately.

My face. Terrified. Terrorized. Persecuted. Pursued. Paranoid. Apocalyptic.

Me.

"Excuse me, sir, can I see some ID please?"

"Huh?'

I whip around to see a Central Park police officer wearing his aero-dynamic NYPD helmet and sitting astride his NYPD bike. He is hold-ing a summons book in one hand and biting the cap off the pen he's holding in the other.

"Sir, you broke like four really serious laws and six or seven moderately serious ones. Did you not hear the whistle?" The officer picks up the silver whistle hanging around his neck and blows it in my ear.

"I was trying to . . ." I point to the space in front of me. It is empty. There is no one anywhere near us. I collapse on the stone bench and let my bike fall to the ground. I still haven't caught my breath. Chest heaving, gulping mouthfuls of air, I look up at the cop.

"You ever have those days where things are moving so fast you can't keep up with yourself? Literally. Like you are a just blur passing through yourself until you can't keep up and your outside slips off? Almost like a snake shedding its skin. It's just hanging by a fuckin' thread and if you don't haul ass and catch up, that part of you is going to split off and just blow away for good? And then it's gone. You'll never get it back. And maybe it's just one piece to begin with. One day. But if you have enough of those days . . . how many pieces can you lose? Before you're just fuckin' gone? And they're fast. So fast. Like a blur. You ever feel that way?"

The cop has taken a few steps back. He says nothing for a while, then puts away his summons book and pulls out his radio.

"So, you were following your blur?"

"Yes, officer, I believe I was."

More nodding and this time head-scratching as well.

"You sit tight, buddy, okay? Can you do that for me?"

I nod.

"I'm gonna be right here. Just need to make a quick call."

His radio makes some beeping noises and he turns away from me while he talks into it. Then he turns back to me.

"Sir, is there somebody I can call for you? Your wife maybe, or a family member?"

"I don't have any family."

"A friend then?"

"Look, just give me the damn ticket, okay," I say, getting up from the bench and reaching for my bike.

"Actually, sir, my, uh, CO thinks it would really be best if you were checked out. You know, at the hospital."

"That won't be necessary. I'm fine. And besides," I say, picking my bike up and getting back on. "I can't. I'm in a hurry."

It's 2:00 A.M. when I reach into the drawer in the little table next to my bed and take out the small teak box I bought at a street fair to benefit the Little Red School House. It's just the right size and shape to hold my pipe, my lighter, and my film canister with a half-ounce of weed. When I light up and inhale a lungful of ashes, I kick myself for not refilling the bowl when I finished smoking last night. I dump the film canister upside down into my hand and find that it too is empty. I zip into the kitchen and pull open the freezer. I feel around, roll the vodka bottle out of the way, and feel nothing but the indentations it's made in the accumulated frost, which I have no idea how to get rid of. I'm looking for a Ziploc bag of pot I'm hoping I may not have smoked yet. The bag is not squished between the cans of Bacardi frozen margarita mix, which are standing in a neat line on the shelf in the freezer drawer.

I'm not hopeful. The truth is, I think I finished off the last hit of the pot I bought from Cecil before he vacated the apartment last night and now I have nothing. And now I am more anxious, more wired, more racy. All the things you don't want to be at four o'clock in the morning. Sleep is definitely out of range now. At this point I'll settle for anything that will take the edge off. I fly around my apartment, looking for my address book and the phone. I punch the numbers so fast I misdial twice. Then, finally, he picks up and I'm talking so fast the words come out almost as one:

"Cecil, buddy, how you doing? Great. Listen. I was wondering if you could help me out, I'm kind of in a jam here . . . what? Oh, were you sleeping? Sorry buddy. It's just if you could spare a little weed I'd be willing to come to Brooklyn to . . . Hello? Cecil?

SHIT! The phone makes a visible indentation in the wall when I throw it across the room.

Shimmer, glimmer, higher, faster, shatter, break.

Fall.

Every day rainy, cold, grey. Regardless of the weather. I don't read. I don't taste. I don't fuck. Who has the energy? Or the interest? But I get through the day. So gold star for me. Sometimes I even leave the house. Today I sat on the floor in one of the aisles at the Pick. Staring at book spines. It was exhausting.

Now, back at home, all I want is to go to bed. But when do I ever get what I want? "Hey, mister," I say, this time loud enough for people walking by to hear. "I've had three birthdays standing here waiting for you to get your mail."

Old guy is bent over his mailbox, blocking access to my building's narrow entry. I know my neighbors only by the labels I've given them—depressed single mother, great tits/no ass chick, Christie Brinkley wannabe, kid who smells like curry . . . At the moment, old guy is jabbing haphazardly at the lock with his key—like a fifteen-year-old virgin who can't figure out where to put his pecker.

If I thought this inconvenient twitching were a Parkinson's thing, I'd probably be more sympathetic. Maybe. Hard to say. Phil, the guy who owned Phil's Fish Store on Beverly Drive where Ellen bought the most incredible Dungeness crab, came down with it. Phil was a good, solid working guy. I always admired him. So I have good associations with people who have Parkinson's.

But old guy does not. A few months ago, not long after I moved in, I came down the stairs and found homo couple and compulsive recycler talking about how they couldn't believe he was eighty-one and how he looked like an older Jimmy Stewart. When they started speculating on what kind of fitness routine he must follow to stay in such good shape, I got nauseated and left the building.

Soggy copies of the *Times,* the *Post,* and the *Daily News* stick out of the faded canvas Planned Parenthood bag that hangs from his arm. He's either oblivious or indifferent to the slippery-when-wet spot spreading out in all directions from his New York Public Library umbrella that lies on the tile floor, shedding enough water to irrigate the Sudan.

Pro-choice/anti-neighbor seems to be old guy's platform, because he's bent at a right angle in the narrow vestibule, completely blocking my entry into our building. Either he moves or I knock him down and step over him.

"Look, I'm cold and wet and I live on the fifth floor, so I've got miles to go before I sleep," I say in my last attempt at quasi-friendly banter.

"Frost. I'm impressed," old guy says, not looking up. "But I figured you more for the 'Good fences make good neighbors type.'"

"And you'd be right."

"Ahhh," he says, straightening up and looking at me with a kind of wild-eyed fervor almost never evoked by Robert Frost. "Something there is that doesn't love a wall," he booms. "That wants it down."

When he leans in and whispers conspiratorially, I can see little flecks of foam in the corners of his mouth. He smells strongly of the same mentholated cough drops my grandfather used to suck on. I always hated those.

"I could say 'Elves' to him," the old guy says in a stage whisper and goes back to jabbing at the lock. "But it's not elves exactly, and I'd rather ..."

I grab the little key out of the old guy's hand. "You ever think maybe it's time for reading glasses?"

I open mailbox 3c, pull out the underwhelming contents, and lock it up again. I slap the key into his palm and try to get around him, but he's not budging.

"I can read fine, Mr. 5c." He grabs his mail and pokes me in the chest with his key. "I'm just a little too stoned to get the teeny-tiny key into the teeny-tiny lock."

He turns and unsteadily starts toward the narrow staircase.

"Excellent shit, too," he says without turning around.

This unexpected revelation knocks me off my game and now I am stuck behind him. I feel like a Porsche following a tractor on a one-lane highway.

Somewhere between the first and second floor, he stops to admire the tacky Sears light fixture on the ceiling.

"Now that is beautiful workmanship. I'm guessing belle epoque. But probably a reproduction," he says, bending his head back so far he almost tumbles backward down the stairs. He doesn't say anything when I put my hand on his back to prop him back up. A few steps later he stops to pet the polished wood banister. "No seam. All one piece. You don't see carpentry like that anymore." And a few steps later, to appreciate the dark red paint on all the second-floor apartment doors. "Have those always been that color? What would you call it?"

"Red."

He turns around and, without actually focusing his eyes, gives me a dirty look.

"Philistine." He stares at one of the doors, tilting his head from side to side as if he were looking at one of those blinking Jesus holograms. Fuck, I am never getting home tonight.

"Okay, fine," I say. "What would you call it?"

"Burgundy maybe? No, more of a Chianti or—I know, claret."

"So really any shade of red with an alcohol content of fourteen percent."

"Claret, definitely."

"I don't know about you, but I was fuckin' terrified we weren't gonna solve that one. Can we move *on*, please?"

Lucky for me, the numbered floors start at street level. One more and we'd be camping out on the landing overnight. When we reach three—approximately twenty minutes after completing the thirty-minute mail retrieval mission—he stops in front of the apartment at the top of the stairs. He keeps his back to me while he fumbles with his keys.

"I don't put out on the first date," he says over his shoulder.

"Don't flatter yourself. I like 'em a little higher up the actuarial table. I just wanted to make sure you could get in."

"Bullshit. You want to smoke."

"What? No!"

The plan is to protest, but not so much that he can't actually see right through me.

"I mean I might. You know, once in a while. But I'm not going to smoke yours. You probably need it for your . . . and don't they ration you?

"My what?"

"Your—well, don't you have . . ."

"Cancer? Do I look like I have cancer?"

Old guy, thinning hair, getting high regularly? Pardon me for jumping to conclusions. I shrug.

"No, I do not have cancer. Shit, I look a helluva lot better than you. I work out, you know. Weights."

"So I've heard."

"You don't believe it."

"Sure I do. I bet you can bench-press your own weight."

"Asshole."

The old guy picks up the stroller parked outside the apartment next door and hoists it over his head. A shower of Goldfish crumbs, petrified Cheerios, and animal cracker amputees rains down on him. He stumbles backward a few steps, loses his grip on the stroller, and it goes bouncing down the stairs. Most of it comes to a stop on the landing, but one wheel continues down to the first floor.

The old guy stares over the railing at it. I stare at the apartment that belonged to the stroller.

"Depressed single mother?" I ask.

"Uh-huh."

"Leave her a note. I'll take care of it."

He's still staring into the abyss when I notice that his Planned Parenthood bag, deflated and empty, is hanging limply from his wrist, one strap dragging on the floor. The contents—more than just a bunch of soggy tabloids—have spilled out and there must be a dozen little plastic containers of weed, all neatly labeled, scattered across the hallway floor.

I bend over to start picking them up and suddenly the old guy whips around, knocks me out of the way, and snatches up every one. He readjusts his bag onto his shoulder and looks at me bashfully.

"I just had lunch with my dealer."

"You do lunch with your dealer."

"We're very tight."

"You know," I say, "I don't think we've ever been formally introduced. I'm Greyson Todd."

"Walt Fischer," he says, shaking my hand. "Wanna get wasted?"

I know exactly what to expect when I enter Walt's apartment. Cabbage boiling on the stove, plastic runners to protect the high-traffic areas of his beige wall-to-wall carpeting, econo-size tube of Preparation H on the bathroom counter.

But I am wrong. Very. True, the peeling paint and ceiling cracks are just where I thought they'd be, and the wood is stained on the floorboards around the radiators. But repairing those obvious signs of wear and tear would be a mistake. Apparently, our landlord agrees.

Wear and tear is the foundation upon which Walt has built his castle. Through the doorways of the railroad apartment, I can see that room after room is filled with what are either family heirlooms or, more likely, carefully sought-out treasures picked up for nothing over years of dedicated flea-marketing.

I do not expect to be invited into someone's home. It has been a long time and I am unprepared. I am searching for feelings I cannot name. Like trying to identify the spices in a new version of an old recipe.

Walt peels my coat off without asking me and hangs it carefully on a brass coatrack. He tosses his keys and mail on an old silver tray monogrammed with someone else's initials and then bends to squint at an invisible spot on the narrow oak table it sits on. I smile for the first time today when he licks his thumb, rubs the spot, and then polishes it with the hem of his sweater.

I wander around Walt's living room: grandfather clock, well-worn kilim rugs, antique mirrors, rolltop desk, velvet armchair, faded leather sofa. The combined alchemy of these objects gives off the warmth and peace of mind Beverly Hills decorators have struggled for centuries to replicate.

Beyond the living room, a streetlight shines into Walt's bedroom, illuminating a collection of little colored glass bottles on the windowsill. Those bottles. Something about them makes me want to put my arms around Walt and hold on very tight. Because old guys don't have little glass bottle collections. Teenage girls do. Willa does. Probably.

I am in Walt's house, looking into Willa's room. I am in Walt's house, standing in my house, looking into Willa's room from my living room with the grandfather clock for which we overpaid because Ellen fell in love with it at the Santa Monica Antique Show. I fell in love with the deep reverberating sounds it filled the house with every fifteen minutes. The chiming that eventually made Ellen regret we'd ever bought it in the first place.

I taste home. And for that, I love Walt.

But I think I will save the hug for another time.

"Pretty swingin' bachelor pad, huh?"

"You've got quite an eye, Walt."

He walks over to an antique wooden icebox—the kind that used actual ice to keep the food cold. "Had one just like this when I was a kid."

The advent of Freon has freed up Walt's icebox to accommodate his large and varied selection of booze. He pulls out an excellent bottle of Hennessy and two old-fashioned-looking snifters.

"Are you sure you're not a gay man from West Hollywood?"

"This," he says with a sweeping gesture, "was a hobby born of necessity."

"Fire or divorce?"

"My ex-wife got every fucking stick of furniture," he says, handing me my drink.

"If I didn't hate her so much, I'd thank her. I didn't realize how ugly that shit was. It was kind of a toss-up which one of 'em I was happier to get rid of."

Walt unlatches the old pipe rack that's sitting on the coffee table, and as soon as he cracks the lid, the thick aroma of fresh, sticky pot leaks out.

"Give yourself a tour while I roll us a joint."

The kitchen is narrow with doorways at both ends and the appliances are ancient—the downside of living in a rent-controlled apartment. Walt's refrigerator door is covered with photos: a boy around seven and a girl of nine or ten. In one, the children are younger. They sit together on Walt's lap eating ice cream cones, dripping chocolate and strawberry all over Walt, whose head is thrown back midlaugh. I lift the corner to look at the photo underneath it. A much younger Walt—probably in his forties—stands with his arm around a young man in a cap and gown. A pretty, young woman stands on the other side of him smiling.

I am halfway out of the kitchen before Walt's art collection catches my eye. Layer upon layer of crayon drawings, macaroni collages, and construction paper snowmen are taped to the side of the fridge facing the wall. Secreted away like treasure. These I remember. These I know. Our Sub-Zero was Willa's private gallery. The exhibits changed, but Ellen kept them all. All of the fall leaves pressed in wax paper, all of the cotton-ball bunnies, all of the four-fingered, pickle-nosed self-portraits.

I feel tiny beads of sweat form on my forehead. My heart is racing.

Why didn't I take one with me? How stupid. Just one to tape on the side of my refrigerator. I am convinced that everything would be different if I had slid a crayon landscape with a rainbow out from under the Pepsi bottle magnet. Or taken one of her early works from the giant plastic storage box Ellen kept them in under her bed.

I can't stop it. I press both hands over my mouth to muffle the unplanned sob that escapes. Just one. I wipe the tears away with a dishtowel. I'm fine.

"I didn't realize my kitchen was so interesting," Walt yells from the living room.

My first impulse is to run. I've been caught standing in Walt's kitchen staring at his grandchildren's artwork like it's porn.

I remind myself that it's possible I'm being paranoid. That most likely Walt has no idea what I've been doing in here. I stick my head out the door so I can see Walt.

"Those your grandkids?"

"No, I just like to hang out near playgrounds with a telephoto lens."

I can see the little glass bottles. Just over Walt's shoulder. In Willa's room. I'm sure there is a plastic storage box under the bed filled with her artwork. I look at the art on the fridge again. I'm sure it's just like what's in the box under her bed in her room.

So I take one. A macaroni-and-lentil collage in the shape of a heart.

"And your daughter and son?"

I roll it up very carefully and walk to the other side of the kitchen, which opens onto the entry hall.

"Uh-huh. She's an astrophysicist at Cal Tech. He's . . . a Republican."

I gently slide my heart into the sleeve of my jacket.

"Makes me sick. But Richard, my son, lives in Westport, so the upside is I get to see my grandkids. I read to them from *The Communist Manifesto* when they come to visit."

I sneak back into the kitchen and walk out through the other side into the living room, where Walt is carefully licking the edge of the paper on a perfectly rolled joint.

"Soup's on," Walt says, handing me the joint and a sterling silver cigarette lighter circa 1940.

I am still stoned when I leave Walt's and walk down the street to the twenty-four-hour drugstore on the corner. I am cradling my jacket as gently as I can. When I get back upstairs to my apartment, I spread the jacket out on the kitchen counter and gently work the collage out of my sleeve.

Then I take out the Elmer's I bought at the drugstore and carefully reglue the macaroni pieces that broke off.

New York, 1994. I wake up feeling lost, empty, as if I have given too much blood. Or all of it. But Glenda is there to cheer me up. To make me forget what I can't remember.

The day after Glenda's cinematic come-on, I more or less invited her to watch me jerk off—an invitation some girls might actually balk at. Dragging my blanket behind me, I came into the dayroom, lay down on one of the couches, and, making sure she could see, put my hand down my pants. While the other patients watched *Jaws,* Glenda pulled up a chair and watched me. We went on like that for days, eventually getting each other off under the table at breakfast, lunch, and dinner.

Still, we're adults. We want to fuck. But the logistics of psych-ward fucking are tricky, to say the least. For one thing, it is difficult to find a loophole in our unit's no-touching policy that allows for penile-vaginal penetration. So we, Glenda and I, have chosen to disregard this draconian rule entirely. True, there are no locks—anywhere, at anytime. But we have found that the unlocked showers of our unlocked rooms afford us the most privacy. For at least a few minutes at a time. Then again, it's not as if Glenda worries about things like consequences or getting caught or even being watched while we're going at it. Sometimes I think she hopes we'll be seen. I never know from one minute to the next what her desires will run to. It is like fucking a different woman every day. A different paranoid, psychotic woman who mumbles under her breath about government conspiracies. But beggars can't be choosers and my potential dating pool is limited.

Besides, Glenda would kill me if I cheated on her.

TWELFTH

This is it. The last one. The one that will put Humpty together again. So they say. But how will I know whether or not I am whole now that I have lost so much? It seems an endless cycle—losing and gaining parts of myself. Gaining my sanity; losing the ability to hold on to five minutes ago. It can drive a person crazy. This endless loop. This crazy loop. End-less. Maybe I am just keeping them in business.

If that's the case, I could almost respect the marketing strategy.

New York, 1993. I knew it would happen eventually. It was inevitable. There are only so many people in the world.

I am in the Jazz section of the Sixty-Sixth Street Tower Records when I first catch sight of her standing at one of the listening stations across the store.

The ambient sounds of riffing and scatting muffled through abandoned headphones, of shopping bags rustling, and the tail ends of passing conversations all erupt, blossom, and wither like some great acoustic time-lapse photograph. In the microsecond it takes me to recognize her.

She looks different than I imagined. I guess I thought my leaving would have done more damage—something that I could see just by looking. Tattoos, a nose ring, some ugly form of rebellion. But she doesn't really look any different. Older, but not different. Her hair is still long, shiny, and blonde, like the little girl who hugs her mother in the hair color commercial.

My first impulse is to run and hide. I'm not sure why. Maybe fear. Fear of what I want.

She smiles as she talks to the sales guy. He has a tattoo—it looks like barbed wire circling his bicep—and an artificial body, constructed by machine at a gym. She tosses her hair. Is she flirting? Jesus, he must be ten years older than she is.

"Can I help you?" A pale boy with unnaturally blue-black hair and lipstick to match has come up behind me.

"No, I'm just . . ."

The boy walks away.

I look down. My feet are moving—following her. I walk up one aisle and down another, pretending to browse. She joins some friends. They all stand with one hip cocked, wearing more or less the same thing—low-cut jeans and too-small hooded sweatshirt jackets. They all wear flip-flops on their feet, presumably to show off the hideously colored polish they wear on their toes. One girl is too chubby to pull off this uniform. Baby fat hangs out over the top of her jeans, which cling too tightly to her thighs. But she seems oblivious. They are giggling. My daughter and her friends shuffle down the aisles—talking, laughing, shopping, laughing; stepping on the backs of their too-long jeans, which are frayed and dirty on the bottom. Why are girls that age always laughing?

If I were still her father, I could ask. I would know her friends' names. I would take them out for pizza. Do sixteen-year-old girls eat pizza or just salads?

I look up. I am standing in Rap/Hip-Hop. A middle-aged white man with thinning hair, wearing Timberlands, browsing in the Rap section. Not the least bit conspicuous.

One of the girls looks over and catches me staring. I panic, look away, study the fine print on the parental advisory sticker on the CD I am holding. She whispers to the others and they all look over. I can feel them. I know I shouldn't look up, but I can't help it. I need to see if there is anything at all in Willa's face. Anything. I am older, I have grown a beard, but she would have to know me. I look up for an instant, lock eyes with her, and see nothing. She laughs and puts her hand over her mouth the way young girls do and turns away. She whispers to her friends and they turn to face me.

"Pervert!" The chubby one yells at me, and they all laugh and run down the aisle. My face burns. My stomach lurches. I walk quickly and calmly to the back of the store, hoping to find an employee restroom. Nothing. And no one around to direct me. I panic and run to the stack of boxes I'd seen one of the sales kids unpacking earlier and, bending over it, I vomit onto Garth Brooks's latest release.

Willa and her friends are still there when I collect myself and return to the front of the store. I feel somehow stronger now, purified, ready to face her head-on. I stride over to the Employee Picks station where they are sharing earphones. At the final moment, though, I freeze, and instead of closing the last few feet between us, I stop at the end of the rack and pick up a CD.

"Look, guys," says Chubby, "the Perv's back."

I look up at her. Cunt. Bitch. Cow. I know exactly what she is going to be in twenty years.

"Now listen here, young lady," I say in an entirely unconvincing parental tone of rebuke that none of us believes. "I don't know where you learned your manners, but—"

"Why are you following us? Why are you, like, staring at her?" one of them asks, pointing to Willa.

"I'm not . . . I . . . I . . . I'm . . . because I'm her . . ."

Willa looks at me, her eyes searching. "My what?"

"Your father."

There is no sound. At least I don't hear any. Willa looks confused. Her friends are stunned; their mouths hang open.

"My father," she says. It isn't a question.

I nod. "I know this must be . . . I mean, after such a long time, this isn't . . . Do you think we could go talk somewhere?"

"Um . . . I don't think . . . ," she begins.

"You are fuckin' nuts, mister," says Chubby. "You better get the hell away from her."

"Pardon me, but what goddamn business is it of yours?"

"I'm her SISTER! And you're not our fuckin' father. So fuck off."

So. Fuck off. Not our father. Fuck. Off. My Sister. Not. Her Father.

It's like they are all very far away. Like I am looking through the wrong end of a telescope. And silence. Someone has pressed the universal mute button. I don't know for how long.

I am looking at Willa—staring, squinting. Until my eyes sting.

"Willa?" I ask desperately.

She looks at me and sadly, slowly shakes her head. "Sorry," she says, and means it.

"But I . . ."

"I'm from Wisconsin. My dad's a dentist."

Chubby grabs her arm and pulls her away. The other girls follow, giggling nervously.

Willa looks over her shoulder at me as she is being led away. "I'm really sorry."

Something is wrong. I stand there, going over the calculations: height, weight, age, eye color. I had been so sure this time. I had made a mistake in Chelsea. And in Tampa. And Stockholm. And Berlin. I am willing to admit that. But this time I had been sure. Absolutely.

Maybe she was just afraid. That would be understandable. I am sure there was something in the way she looked at me, spoke to me. I look around the store. She and the others are at the register paying.

"Can I help you?" A skinny kid with odd facial hair and a small silver hoop through one eyebrow steps in front of me.

"No, I can't see my—" I try to get around him.

"What? I don't understand. Can I help you find something?"

"I don't want any—just get out of my—"

"Okay man, just chill."

I push him out of my way. I can just see Willa and her friends going through the revolving door out onto Broadway, where another group of kids and three adults stand. One of the kids wears a brand-new T-shirt from a current Broadway musical. The adults—two women and a man—study a Manhattan Streetwise map. They look like sensitive progressive schoolteachers who go by their first names and sit cross-legged on the floor talking honestly with kids about sex. The whole group starts down the stairs into the subway.

I push through the revolving door to run after Willa.

I don't realize I am holding the CD until the alarm goes off and I am standing on the sidewalk. I feel the security guard's hand on my shoulder. Tight. I look at the CD. Notorious B.I.G. The kid with the facial hair jogs up behind me. "Hey, Mister," he says. "You can't just walk out without paying."

The security guard and the kid argue for a good ten minutes over whether or not to call the cops. The guard locks me in the tiny employee break room where I sit in a plastic chair decorated with anti-Reagan graffiti, staring at a wall covered in posters of popular female vocalists caught—of course, completely unexpectedly—in obvious states of dampness and chill.

The longer I sit there, the more scared and confused I get. I begin to wonder if someone or maybe some organization is planting girls who look like Willa in cities all over the world. That somehow they know where I will be when. That they are trying to drive me crazy or get me to do something. I start to panic. I tell myself I need to calm down. Because the guard and the kid could be involved. I clear my throat.

"Excuse me, could I please use your phone to make a local call?" I ask, and then wonder if they notice how much I sound like a robot.

They look at each other. The kid shrugs.

"Sure. But make it short."

"Cool," I say, trying to compensate for the robot thing. My hand trembles as I dial Walt's number. I am in the principal's office because I was in a fight. I am in the Beverly Hills Police Department because I TP'd a neighbor's house. I am in the Tower Record's break room mistakenly accused of shoplifting. I am in trouble. I don't know if Walt will come. Why should he? We hardly know each other. They look over at me—the guard, the kid—and I lower my head. In shame. There are specks of vomit on my shoe. Walt answers and I struggle to tell him everything at once. That I have been falsely accused at Tower Records, that I threw up and passed out and don't want to impose but . . .

"It's gonna be okay, son," he says. "I'm on my way."

And Walt comes and gets me. On the way home, we stop for pastrami sandwiches and cream soda. I never tell him about the girl. Willa.

It is long past dark when we get back to the apartment. Walt follows me up to my place, sits down on the sofa, and kicks off his shoes.

"Let's see if there's a decent movie on," he says, without turning around to look at me or asking if I want him to stay. I don't understand. It's late. I know he must be tired.

And then it dawns on me. I am being taken care of. Someone is taking care of me.

I sit down on the other end of the couch. "Thank you."

He nods, barely, and aims the remote at the TV. "*African Queen*, it's our lucky day."

New York, 1994. I am walking home from the Pick, one of three places I go when I leave the house these days—the other two being the liquor store and the video store—when I see a small crowd gathered outside my building. As I get closer, I see what looks like an ambulance but it isn't pulled up onto the curb. "Medical" something is written on the side. I can't see the rest. There are too many people standing around blocking my view. And still, for no good reason, I begin to walk faster. And to feel slightly ill. I push my way to the front door and get there in time to see two men in white uniforms trying to fit a stretcher through the narrow entryway, tilting it this way and that—a body, zipped into a black plastic bag, rolling precariously with each attempt.

I can tell, without even unzipping it, who is in the bag. Time slows to a crawl. My breath is gone. I blink, but the scene around me does not change. Something is off. I blink again. And still, crowd watching, men in white clumsily, almost comically, failing at their macabre task. Employing the same failed strategy over and over. Not understanding the square peg will never fit through the round hole.

There are movies where this would be funny—Chaplin, the Keystone Kops, the Marx Brothers. I have laughed at those movies—the absurdity, the gallows humor. But I am not laughing now. Now I am wondering what the Marx Brothers are doing in my tragedy. I drop my leather messenger bag and rush toward them screaming.

"Stop! Just stop it. Put him down!"

"'Scuse me, sir," the older bulky one says, "but who are you?"

"I'm . . . I'm . . . his . . . son." Some of the neighbors exchange looks.

"Oh, well, very sorry for your loss, sir."

"Why don't you take a moment?" the younger skinny one offers.

They put the stretcher down inside the entryway. On the floor, underneath the mailboxes where Walt and I first met almost two years ago. I unzip the bag so that I can see his face. He is and is not still Walt.

I sit down cross-legged on the cement floor and lift him into my lap, cradling him in my arms. Was it his heart? A stroke? An aneurysm? And if I had been home could I have saved him? What if I could have saved him? I could have saved him if I'd been home. I pull Walt closer and hold his head to my chest. He smells faintly of aftershave and pot. My tears fall onto his cheeks. Now we are both crying. Maybe, I think, it means he will miss me too.

"Sir, we need to take him now," the big one says to me.

"No, please," I am begging. "I . . . I don't have . . . anyone else." I'm sobbing in front of my neighbors. I am ashamed but I can't stop. "He . . . He . . . took care of me."

The big man kneels down and puts his arm around me. "It's tough. Losing your dad, even at our age. But think of it this way, you're lucky you had as long with him as you did. That you and your old man were so tight. Not everyone's so lucky."

I look up at him and nod. And then he zips the bag closed, takes him from my arms with the help of the skinny one, and carries him out the narrow entry of our building and over to the truck. "Medical Examiner" is what's written on its side. The two men take Walt and lay him on a gurney in the truck and hand me some papers to sign. Which I do with some indistinct mark. And then they drive away.

I do not think I have ever been more alone.

Somehow the fact that I feel more pain over the loss of a man I've known for a couple of years than I did for my own father strikes me as not the least bit strange. In fact, I have to concentrate to remember Ray's death. What year was it? Does it matter if I remember? It hardly mattered then.

Los Angeles, 1983. "He has a large abscess in his left lung. And pneumonia. Normally we'd do a surgical procedure, but there's no chance he'd survive that. We're treating with an antibiotic and we'll know more in twenty-four hours or so."

The doctor gave my shoulder a squeeze.

He had a mustache and wore a bow tie. No white coat, no

stethoscope. He looked more like a guy who made ice cream sodas at the Woolworth's counter than a guy who specialized in death by cancer.

"Okay, well. Thank you, doctor." I shook his hand, but instead of letting go he brought his other hand down on mine, turning my exit attempt into a sympathy sandwich.

"I believe in being honest with my patients. And their families."

"I appreciate that, Dr. . . ."

"Neiberg."

"Right, Dr. Neiberg. I certainly appreciate that."

He continued talking as he held my hand between both of his, cupping it gently as if holding a small, wounded rodent.

"Even if he survives the infection, the MRI we took yesterday shows the cancer is working its way up his central nervous system."

I pulled my hand away. "Jesus Christ. He was only diagnosed five weeks ago. How—"

Neiberg took a deep breath and sighed. If I didn't know better, I'd have sworn he was about to tell me he was out of fudge ripple.

"Your father has stage-four lung cancer with metastases to the lymph nodes, spine, liver, bladder, and more than likely, by next week, the brain."

I stood there looking past Neiberg, nodding. I stared at the nurses and orderlies and physician's associates. "How do they decide who gets the ugly salmon-colored scrubs, who gets the purple ones, and which poor sons of bitches get stuck wearing the pastel-colored cartoon teddy bears to work?" I asked Neiberg.

"Excuse me?"

"Well, I mean, is there some kind of pecking order or does it go by department? Is it just random? Luck of the draw? Matter of choice?"

Neiberg stood there for a moment blinking at me. Silent. "I . . . I'm afraid I can't . . . I don't really . . ." He cleared his throat. "Mr. Todd, even with all the pain medication, your father is fairly coherent. These next few days are going to be the last lucid ones he has. If there are things you want to say, things you want him to hear, now would be the time."

Neiberg handed me his card and gave me one last arm squeeze.

"Call me if you have any questions. About your father."

I walked down the carpeted hallway looking for room 401 North. This was the most expensive ward in the most expensive hospital in Los Angeles. Insurance didn't begin to cover it. I couldn't give two shits if Pop kicked at County, but that wouldn't look right. Sons like me paid for their fathers to die well. So, Pop, here you are in the VIP wing at Cedars, next door to where Charlton Heston is convalescing.

401 North. I stood there for a minute deciding whether to knock or run. I pulled open the door and stepped inside. The room was bright and sunny and clean and filled with French reproduction antiques— good ones. Apart from all the medical crap, it looked like a standard double at the Four Seasons.

My father dozed in his hospital bed under Ralph Lauren sheets while monitors flashed like video games and an IV pumped him full of some milky white cocktail. His face was yellow, his stomach was distended, and his arms were just wrinkled flesh that hung from the bones. I stood there repulsed and tried to summon up some sympathy. I had resented, despised and been disappointed by my father for over thirty years.

During the years since my mother had died, my contact with Pop had gradually diminished. Now I had one, maybe two brief phone conversations with him a month—mostly at Ellen's insistence—and saw him rarely if ever. But I paid his rent and sent a check every month. Partly for my mother's sake and to play the good son, but mostly to remind him that I could. That I had succeeded where he had failed. He was never anything but grateful. Grateful and proud. As if he'd forgotten the first two decades of my life.

I stood around while he slept. I didn't want to wake him, but I wanted him to know I'd been there. Otherwise what was the point? So finally I just "bumped" into the bed. Gently.

His eyes fluttered open. He looked up at me and smiled. I smiled back. The good son. "Hey, Pop, how you doing?"

"I'm good, I'm good," he said in a low, dry voice. He beamed at me and the guilt kicked in. "You didn't have to come all the way across town. Traffic's hell this time of day," he said.

"C'mon, Pop. Don't be silly. I *wanted* to see you. You have every-thing you need? Are the nurses treating you well, because I could—"

"I'm fine, I'm fine," Ray said and took my hand. "Sit down for a minute. Tell me about Ellen and the baby. Do you have a picture? I'd like—"

"She's not a baby anymore, Pop."

"Right. Sure. I guess it's been a while. When I get outta here we should—"

Shit. They haven't told him. Fucking Neiberg. He wasn't putting this on me.

"Listen, Pop, I didn't want to wake you before, and now . . ."

"Have you talked to the doctors, Grey? Because I can't get a straight answer from any of 'em. This one says he's gotta confer with that one and that one's gotta confer with this one."

Dammit.

"Sure, Pop. I'll get it all straightened out," I said, heading for the door. "I wish I could stay longer but I've got a meeting at three so I should probably—"

"Oh sure. Yeah. You get your ass back to the office. You got things to do." He laughed, but it stuck in his chest. He started coughing and couldn't stop.

I stood there and waited, but it just went on and on. Finally, I called for the nurse. She shoved past me, pushed the button to raise the back of the bed, and held a mask to his mouth. The coughing began to subside. Pop pushed the mask away and waved me out.

"I'll be fine, don't worry about me," he said, smiling and coughing.

"Okay, Pop. Well, I'll call you tonight then." I walked out of the room backward, smiling cheerfully until I was sure he couldn't see me.

A few days later, he died. The tagline of our relationship: He was an asshole. And then he was dying and I was an asshole.

New York, 1994. For days after Walt's death, I wait to hear when and where the funeral will be. I don't go to the Pick or the video store. I don't leave my apartment except to check the mail and the bulletin board in the lobby for some announcement about the funeral. I think maybe the super will know. But there's nothing. And when I ask the super, all he says is, "The family is very private."

And so, after ten days, I finally have to admit to myself that they've had it without me. I tear up the eulogy I spent days writing and throw it in the incinerator. I consider following behind it. A sort of cremation/self-immolation form of protest. But I can't. Because whether by accident or design, the chute is far too small to accommodate a human body.

Ten days later, I'm collecting my mail when I see a large black Mercedes—anomalous for our little strip of Hell's Kitchen—parked outside the building. Illegally. Ricardo the super is sitting on the stoop reading the *Post*. I jut my chin out toward the car.

"The family come to clean out Walt's place. The son paying me to watch his car."

While I know in theory they are within their rights, I also feel quite strongly that Walt is being violated, that only I know what was truly important to him, and that it is my duty to protect Walt from his asshole Republican, Westport, Connecticut son whom, while he didn't come right out and say it, I know Walt hated.

And so I bolt up the three flights of stairs and let myself into the apartment with the set of keys Walt gave me.

A tiny blonde woman wearing a headband and an Hermes scarf around her neck is tossing things into garbage bags. "Oh my God!" she yells.

"What do you think you're doing?" I yell back.

"Richard!" she screams.

"He better not have thrown away the little glass bottles," I threaten.

"Who the hell are you?" she asks, suddenly more outraged than frightened.

Richard, tall and skinny like Walt but with none of the Jimmy Stewart charm, rushes into the room. "You must be that guy," he says.

"What guy?"

"I think he's that guy, honey," Richard says to Blondie. "I told you there'd be a problem with him some way or another."

"Which guy do you think I am, asshole? And did it ever occur to you that Walt might have friends, neighbors who would have wanted to go to his fucking funeral?"

"See?" he says, smiling smugly at his wife. "Problem."

"The problem is you're an inconsiderate dick, Dick, and you're gutting Walt's place. You have no idea what some of these things meant to him."

"You know," Richard says, "I could have had you arrested for signing those papers. For claiming to be me the day my father died."

"I *never* claimed to be you," I say with as much disdain as I can manage.

"You claimed to be his son."

"His son, but not you. Not the same thing."

"Is it money? Is that what he wants?" Blondie interjects.

When I realize how pointless this is, when I realize for the four hundred millionth time that Walt is gone and with him the unfamiliar feeling of safety and friendship I was just beginning not to doubt, a wave of exhaustion and grief washes over me and I stumble backward onto Walt's couch. I let my head fall back and I close my eyes.

"Look, I understand what you're going through." I force my eyes open and look at him. "I didn't give a shit about my own father either. But Dick, I gave a shit about yours."

"Where the fuck do you get off telling me how I felt about my own father?"

"You're right. I shouldn't. I was extrapolating from what Walt said about you."

Richard points toward the front door. "Get. The. Fuck. Out. Before I tell you what he said about you."

I know he's bluffing. He has to be. This is just sibling rivalry shit. Because I know Walt loved me more. On my way out, I walk past the kitchen. Blondie is pulling all the macaroni collages and cotton-ball snowmen off the refrigerator and stuffing them into the garbage bag. The bag is getting full. To make more room, she sticks one foot inside and steps down hard and I hear the cracking of uncooked pasta, lentils, and hardened glue.

Now I am done.

I go for days without speaking to another human being. Maybe weeks. The conversation in my head seems to suffice.

Today I woke up to discover I have become a ghost. I have disappeared. I come and go in public, in broad daylight—crossing streets against traffic, slipping in and out of nearly closed subway doors—never once getting handed a supermarket circular, discount offer, or trial membership to a gym. I have fallen off the radar. No one makes eye contact. Not with me. I am invisible. I walk among the living but exist on a different plane. Distanced, as if I am at a remove. Or rather, as if I am as if. Imaginary.

The sensation is strange. Not to feel nothing, but to feel *like* nothing. I am light and cold. I can feel the wind blow through my empty veins. I do not exert enough gravity to keep my feet on the ground. So I hover, suspended. I am somewhere between now and when, between here and just beyond where. I am halfway there. I have had enough. More than enough. But I have tried and failed to go the last mile. I have stood at the edge of the subway platform leaning into the oncoming light. And stepped back. Because I am a coward. I need help. With my exit.

So I decide to consult the experts. I flip through the yellowing yellow pages, write the address on my hand in ballpoint pen, and leave the apartment. It is cold. I don't know what day it is. Or what season. I am not wearing a coat. I notice only because other people are. I can see them but I am certain they cannot see me. There's nothing here to see. It has come on gradually, this apartness I feel. Little by little, thread by thread, I have been coming untethered. From things. From people. From voices and meaning.

For a long time—for as long as I could stand it—I tried to make the effort. I tried to wear the face of a functioning member of society. But when I woke up this morning, it had happened. It was done. And now, while I am not yet dead—already almost, but not quite dead— my ability to pass as living, to function among the living, is gone.

This morning I woke up a ghost. Frosty air follows me into rooms overheated by prewar radiators. And my hands—large, grey, and cold—are going numb. I must remind myself to blink. To look human. *Blink,* I think. But they know. Everybody knows. Now it is just a matter of time. And of how and where and when. Now it is a matter of getting it right. I want to get this right. So I will consult the experts.

It turns out I don't have a lot of options when it comes to suicide advice. Prevention, sure. How-to, virtually none. But there is the New York chapter of the Hemlock Society. So, with much effort, I take myself to its small, windowless office located on the fifth floor of an ugly white limestone building on First Avenue and Thirty-Eighth Street. I'm not sure what I expected, but this cramped, dingy, fluorescent-lit, linoleum-floored hole-in-the-wall isn't it. Frankly, it's depressing. Then again, I suppose they don't really care much about first impressions given their lack of repeat business.

I don't see anyone sitting behind what appears to be the bulletproof glass that surrounds the tiny reception desk, so I ring the little bell on the white linoleum counter. The plastic at the corner has peeled back and someone—one of the Hemlock staff—has restored it with silver duct tape. I read the entire Hemlock Society brochure, find out they're opposed to euthanasia but in favor of assisted suicide, and decide that the subtlety is lost on me but I don't really care. What is beginning to annoy me is the fact that it's taking so long to get any kind of assistance at all. So I knock on the bulletproof glass.

"Hello? Hello? Excuse me, anybody back there?"

"Coming," a shaky voice calls back. "Be right there."

The woman who comes out is neither young nor old. She has on one of those long flowered jumpers that leave everything to the imagination. Her long reddish-blonde hair is done in a complicated braid and she is using the kind of metal crutches you have to put your arms through—the serious kind. From where I'm standing, I can't see below her knees but I can tell it's been a long time since there was a bounce in her step. When she finally reaches the counter, she rests against it and takes a deep breath. Then she looks at me and smiles. "We don't get a lot of walk-ins." Her lipstick is seashell pink.

"Oh," I say, "do I need to make an appointment?"

She laughs and has to grab the counter through her crutch to keep from falling. "Gosh, no. Most people just call in. Never mind. How can I help you?"

It occurs to me that despite her disability she has a demeanor far more suited to offering advice on seasonal planting in a flower shop or on vitamin supplementation in a health food store.

"I want to die," I inform her.

Her pink mouth stops smiling.

"What do you mean?"

"Which part didn't you understand?"

"Well, are you sick?"

I think about that for a long moment. I certainly feel terrible. Close to death. In pain. Unbearable pain. And nothing, nothing makes it better. It is only getting worse. Helping me to die would be an act of mercy.

"Yes," I say.

She looks skeptical. "I don't mean to pry, but . . . you don't look . . . Have you gotten a second opinion? Whatever you have may not be as advanced as you've been told."

"Trust me," I say. "This is the end. I can't live like this anymore. Just tell me what to do. I don't want to screw it up."

"Uh-huh. Again, forgive me for . . . What exactly is it that you're suffering from?"

"Depression. I'm depressed."

And when she laughs, her pink lips open so wide her face disappears and I can see her uvula dancing in the back of her throat.

"I'm glad I could make one of us laugh," I say.

She stops laughing. Stops smiling. She leans across the counter and pokes her crutch at me menacingly.

"You think this is a joke, mister? You know how hard it is for us to keep this place open? For people with real illnesses? Real pain?"

"But I am in—"

"Oh screw you, mister. I'm going to be dead in two years. And not because I want to be. If you want to die now, why don't you go jump off a building or slit your wrists or jump in front of a subway?"

"Because," I say, "those things don't always work. Things can go wrong."

As she drags herself back to the office, she stops and looks over her shoulder. "Well, you know what they say, if at first you don't succeed . . ."

I stare at her, shocked, shamed. Unassisted.

I don't know how I get to Penn Station. I am just there, staring up, unblinking, captivated by the clacking, perpetually shape-shifting Amtrak departure board.

I have the fantasy that I am going to ride the rails. See the good old U.S. of A the old-fashioned way. I am filled with romantic anticipation of train travel fueled by dueling images of Old World opulence from *Murder on the Orient Express,* American ingenuity from Ford's *Iron Horse,* and danger from *North by Northwest.*

I pull out of Penn Station aboard the Amtrak Crescent bound for New Orleans, immediately enter a long, dark tunnel, and emerge into fields of wildflowers. There is a beautiful blonde woman in a sundress running toward me. I open the window and breathe in, not caring that flowers will no doubt aggravate my allergies. The smell of long, uncut grass is intoxicating. I reach out the window to grab a handful of yellow flowers.

Suddenly, though, it is dark. The flowers are gone. And when they come back, when the lights come back, my flowers have been replaced. By fake, two-dimensional paper ones. And a two-dimensional paper girl who smiles because she can breathe freely again due to the contents of the bottle she displays.

My perfect world is gone. Just like that. I turn around, look over both shoulders. I am on a subway. Attracting attention. I search my pockets for my ticket. To New Orleans. Because I'm sure I bought one. That I got on that train. I'm so sure, so sure. I would swear to it. But my truth, like my time, seems to be fungible, capricious. The ground under my feet is eroding. Soon there will be nothing solid left to stand on. Soon there will only be shadows. Shadows and whispers. And I will mistake one for the other.

I spin around, hoping to take him by surprise. "TAKE ONE MORE FUCKING STEP AND I'LL FUCKING KILL YOU, MOTHERFUCK-ER!" I scream.

There is no one there. Just the crowd of anonymous commuters who expertly and efficiently divide themselves in two in order to give me wide berth. Moments ago I felt someone sidle up behind me. Saw his shadow rising up over my left shoulder. Heard him exhale in my ear.

The light changes and, aside from two or three impatient pedestrians who have risked death crossing four lanes of oncoming traffic, I am left alone on the corner. My heart is still pounding from my encounter with the phantom assailant. Only a bottle of Hurricane shattering at my feet, spraying the bottoms of my pants with drops of malt liquor and shards of glass, reminds me that I have been standing in this spot for a suspiciously long time.

I scan the collection of teenagers on the street corner but cannot identify my sniper—the one who launched the bottle at me. The light changes again and suddenly I am in the way. The looks I'm getting from passersby are not friendly and I feel shoulders and sharp elbows pushing, prodding, and buffeting me around.

I don't know how I got here. I remember a bus. And lights and tunnels. Crowded staircases that smelled like sweat and piss and doors opening and closing like mouths, spitting out miserable, angry people. I followed one. To see where she was going. To see if it would be better for her when she got there. She had been trying to tell me something. The whole subway ride, I could feel the effort she was making. I could see the message she was trying to send me spark in the backs of her eyes and struggle to catch and take hold. She was like Lassie, barking at Timmy's father so he'd follow her to where Timmy had fallen off a cliff or into a well.

So when she got off the train, I got off too. And when three blocks up and one block over she boarded a bus, I got on behind her and dumped a pocketful of change into the machine and stood there listening to it chew up my money until the driver told me to move to the back. And when I stood next to the seat where she was sitting and she looked up surprised, I knew she was happy to see me. So I smiled and got off at her stop. And when she went into a little bodega to buy milk and cat food and batteries and tampons, I waited outside and watched her shop and pay. And when she came out, she started walking faster and crossed the street and I had to run after her to keep up. And she started running and yelling for help.

"What is it, girl? What's wrong?" I shouted.

But she wouldn't tell me. She just kept running and looking over her shoulder. I tried to stay with her. But we got separated. And now I am lost.

There are numbers on the streets and names on the avenues. I should know where I am. This should feel more or less like a place feels when it's where you live. But the coordinates are off. The city is not where I left it this morning. I look over and see the entrance to the 125th Street station and the stairs leading to the raised platform. I'm guessing that is where I came from. This shouldn't be so hard for me. I know that. But the last few days, no matter how hard I try, I can't seem to come up with a better version of myself.

The noise in my head is like a radio. Constant. It skips quickly from station to station. And then back again. Trying to find a frequency. Meantime, it's all-in, all the time, all at once. Whatever's out there's in here. Skidding, shouting, banging, laughing, *Don't-be-that-way-baby*, *Don't-fuck-with-me-asshole*, *Don't-know-why-I-bother*, Don't Walk, Don't Walk, Don't. Walk. Walk. Walk on by. Bye-bye baby bye-bye. Wet. Wet. What? Drip. Wet? Fuck. Wet. Drip. Drip. Fuck. How many drops are dripping from this goddamned scaffolding? 1-2-3-4-5-6-7-8-9—drops or seconds? I've lost count. Start again. No, stop. Stop! StupidBoringCrazyLazy. Get outside your fuckin' head. Look outside. Look. Liquor store, laundromat, chicken shack, Dunkin' Donuts, hair weave palace. Wish they'd stay still. They switch places when I blink. Just to fuck with me. Donuts *blink* chicken. Chicken *blink* laundry. Laundromat; hair palace; liquor store. Liquormat Laundropalace. Shell game. Musical fucking chairs. Just to fuck with me. I walk away. Walk this way. Walk away, Renee. And my feet take over. The sound. The rhythmic clip-clop on the blacktop. *The boom-clop, click-bop.* Stop. Can't stop. *Clop-boom-skip-stop chick-a-boom bop.* Miles Fuckin' Davis. John Fuckin' Coltrane, jazz man. I'm the man. I'm the anchorman. News and weather on the eights. All the eights. That's a lot of eights. It is tedious, monotonous, onerous listening to my own news and weather all day, all night long. On the eights. And underneath the sound of my own voice in my own head is the rhythm of my own feet on the ground. The containable soft-shoe that escalates into the full-blown percussive jazz rat scat that will not be tamed—the unlikely soundtrack to my interminable A.M. radio anchorman monologue. I am fascinated by my ability to syncopate, enumerate, ruminate, calculate, self-flagellate. It occupies every millimeter of available space in my head. I want to take a broom and sweep it out my ears like dust out an attic window but there will be more. On the eights. Every eight. All day, all night. No matter how much or how often I sweep it away, the noise will always come back.

I know enough, am aware enough, to know that what I'm hearing—or thinking—which is it? Don't know—does it matter? Doesn't matter—is crazy shit. Or rather, it is the shit that fills the heads of crazy people. But I should get points for self-awareness. Because if I know it then I'm not. If I were really crazy, I would think I was God or Jesus or Mick Jagger. That's what crazy people think. But I don't. I know who I am. Which is a relief. Because I was getting worried. Not really. But a little. Because of the noise.

I've spent too much time alone lately. Too much time in my own head. Thus the noise problem. I'm out of practice with words. Need to use them out loud again. I decide it would be a good idea to have a conversation with someone. Nothing too hard or too big. No politics or religion. Not even the weather. Just a verbal exchange. A verbal transaction. Maybe an actual transaction. I look up: chicken, donuts, laundry, liquor, hair weave. Not a tough choice. As long as they stay still.

As I walk past the bums huddled under their filthy blankets, shopping carts tethered to their ankles, the dirty bastards tell me to stop kidding myself, that there's a puddle of piss waiting there with my name on it. *Lie down. Make yourself comfortable.*

I spit on the ground in front of one of them and get in his face. "Someday, the skies will open, and a flood will come and wash all the scum like you off the streets."

"Huh?" He looks at me, confused, scared. Like I'm the crazy one. Like I'm the one with the problem.

"Don't fuck with me, asshole!" I scream at him.

He looks up. "Okay, man, okay, whatever you say."

Then I head across the street toward the friendly pink neon sign happily buzzing the word "Liquor." It's right where I left it.

I feel better already.

I point to the largest bottle of scotch I see behind the cashier and pull out a wad of balled-up cash. I am sure the cashier is watching me, looking at me. I leave the store and, having no idea where I am, chart a random course. Sounds and colors are bright, blurred, inseparable. I cannot tell "Walk" from "Don't." And so I keep walking until the scotch runs out. I know it is time to go home, but I would have to know where that was in order to go there. *Walt,* I think.

Walt. I cross half an avenue and sit down on the bench in the middle. *Home. Willa.*

By the time I see the shadow behind me, it is too late. And I'm not sure that I care anyway. Maybe he is doing me a favor. What I haven't been able to do myself. But I want to see him. And so I turn around just as the towering bearded man in the filthy clothes raises my empty scotch bottle over his head and brings it down on mine. Once, twice, hit the bench on the way down, sharp, hard kick in the ribs, head pulled up and back and dropped hard onto the bricks, final kick in the jaw. *The pain,* I think, *the pain is truth.*

It is dawn when I wake up shivering, throbbing, still bleeding. Coat and shoes gone. Pockets empty. But cold is the central issue now. I raise my head and see steam coming from a grate across the avenue and a third of the way down the block. It may as well be a hundred miles. But when the light changes, I begin to crawl, and when I get there, collapsing on that heating grate is one of the highlights of my life.

I fall asleep immediately and wake up far too soon to the inconsiderately thunderous footsteps of weekday commuters. By now the pain of last night's shenanigans has spread throughout my body like a virus. I look up at the passersby from my position on the grate and could swear that every one out of ten is a wolf in a suit, furry and fanged. I blink only to see the flesh slowly melting off the face of a man dressed in a Brooks Brothers suit. I wonder if the blood I'm covered in—my blood—is real. No one stops. No one even seems to see me lying here, so maybe it isn't real. I am invisible. So maybe I'm not real. Maybe the only thing that's real is the pain.

I don't know if I wake up because I want to scratch the uncomfortable itch below my left eye or if scratching the itch is the first thing I want to do when I wake up. I don't have time to fixate on the question: both my arms are tied tightly to a wheelchair. There will be no scratching whatsoever. My eyelids fall shut, but I will them halfway open, manage to drag my chin off my chest, and force my eyes to move back and forth for a few seconds, looking for information. The effort is overwhelming, but before my head drops and my eyes fall shut again, I am able to ascertain that I am, it seems, sitting in the wheelchair to which I am tied and that the wheelchair is facing a sign that reads: NYPD: NO LOADED FIREARMS PERMITTED BEYOND THIS POINT.

The itch becomes secondary.

The words roll around in my head and eventually a red flag goes up. My vision is a little blurry, particularly around the edges, but this time my eyes stay open. I have an excellent view of the floor from this position, and this time I notice that my ankle is handcuffed to the crossbar of the wheelchair. Or foot-cuffed, as the case may be. I wonder if the police have special ankle cuffs or if standard-issue handcuffs are designed to expand to accommodate lower extremities. I kick at the restraint and the metal bites into my bare skin. When did I lose my socks? I kick again and try to get some forward momentum going on the wheelchair. It occurs to me this whole thing is overkill on someone's part. Whatever I did, I have less neck strength than a newborn, so I'm probably not much of a flight risk.

Slowly, as the blood rushes forward, I become aware of a dull ache on the left side of my mouth. It throbs rhythmically as if it has its own pulse. My tongue is thick, dry, and it would help if I could use a finger or two to peel it off the roof of my mouth. But I concentrate on sucking and swallowing and eventually produce enough saliva to wrench it free. And to notice the distinctly unpleasant coppery tang of recently shed blood.

A wave of nausea sweeps over me. I reluctantly allow the oral exploration to continue and almost immediately regret it when the tip of my tongue encounters a large gap occupied by teeth last time I checked. Now it is just a big empty parking lot haunted by soft, sore gums. The handcuffs, the wheelchair, the sign, the missing teeth—as the fog begins to lift, I am starting to get the feeling something bad has happened.

A second wave of nausea hits and this time there is no turning back the tide. There is also nowhere to go except maybe six inches front and center, give or take. I pitch forward and projectile vomit the nearly day-old contents of my stomach—mostly alcohol, stomach acid, and the remains of a McDonald's Quarter Pounder, which, if not upchucked, might have remained in my colon undigested for years. I lurch forward with such force that I actually achieve the forward momentum I was seeking just a moment ago. The chair falls forward and I fall face-first onto the black-and-white-checkered linoleum floor and into the pool of warm vomit I've just deposited there.

New York, 1994. Viagra guy is already waiting in line for dinner. Even though there is no line and there is no dinner. But when it gets there, he will be first in line. It's like this at every meal. We call him "Viagra guy" because that's what his shirt says. It is bright yellow with blue lettering. On the back there is some information about Viagra in red letters. Viagra guy wears his T-shirt every single day tucked into his hospital-issue paper pants.

I've never heard him speak. Just the occasional grunt. Bald on top but with more hair on his arms, hands, and knuckles than I've ever seen on a human being. I believe Viagra guy may be the closest thing science will ever get to a living, breathing specimen of the missing link. When Glenda and I walk by the dining area, Viagra guy has one hairy arm crossed over his belly. That arm supports the other so that he can pick his nose for extended periods of time without fatiguing the picking arm. Viagra guy doesn't read, watch TV, or participate in group activities unless forced to. His chosen form of recreation is nose-picking.

"You are revolting," Glenda says as we walk by him.

"FUCK YOU!" he yells.

"So you do speak," I say. "Way to go."

The dinner cart is wheeled in and Viagra guy grabs a tray. "Don't you think you should wash your hands?" Glenda says, curling her lip at him in disgust.

"It's none of your damn business," he says, flicking what I can only imagine is a tiny rolled-up ball of snot in her direction.

"It *is* my business, you filthy illiterate cretin."

"FUCK YOU!" he yells at her.

"LIMP DICK!" she yells back and takes her place at the back of the line.

AFTERSHOCKS

New York, 1994. I'm thinking about moving. From this chair. I've been thinking about it all day. Thinking that if I concentrate—really put my mind to the task, give it a hundred and ten percent—I could do it. I could move. But then, I think, that would probably be it. Today's activity. And what if I want to move later? What if there's a fire and I *have* to move later? I'll be fucked. More fucked.

They have started me on lithium and something called Zyprexa. But lithium, they say, is the first line of treatment. This from the people who call ECT the gold standard. They make it sound so VIP. So why is it my muscles are filled with something heavier than lead and I can't keep my hands from shaking? I'm thinking I want my money back.

But my brain trust is optimistic. They stand around in their white coats conferring and consulting and continuing to throw around phrases like "gold standard" and "first line" like we are in the throes of deal-making and these are perks, negotiating points. I begin to feel I stand to make big money if I concede. Apparently there was no decision to be made about the shock. They told Hannah it was the only thing that would work—and, of course, that it was the gold standard. So she signed the papers. And though my memory has more holes than that kind of cheese they make in the country where you get those clocks with the little birds that come out and . . . Oh fuck it.

After I am all done with shock, they say, the drugs will keep me on the straight and narrow. But I will have to take them for the rest of my life. Hard to imagine since the lithium makes my head heavy and my hands shake, and the Zyprexa causes confusion, constipation, weight gain, and more memory loss. God knows what the others might do. But if these don't work, there are lots of others to try. In literally dozens of combinations. So not to worry, my doctors say.

I wanna do business with these guys, but so far they've been all pitch and no product, and frankly, I'm beginning to think they're blowing a lot of sunshine up my ass. But that could just be me being negative. Or maybe having no memory and no cognitive skills to speak of is what's causing the negativity. Could definitely be a chicken-and-egg thing.

Regardless, when Ted, an orderly clearly hired more for his brute strength than for his sharp wit, comes to tell me I have a visitor, it's tough to muster up any enthusiasm, let alone the momentum required to get myself out of the chair in my room where I'm installed in front of my teeny personal TV with my supplemental premium cable and VHS player. Especially since "You have a visitor" is what they say when your shrink has stopped by unannounced. I choose to ignore Ted and continue watching *Easy Rider*.

"Come on, Mr. Todd, don't you want to know who's here to see you?" Ted sings this to me as if I were a baby and he were an idiot trying to feed me mashed peas.

"The possibilities are extremely limited, Ted," I say.

It couldn't be my sister. Hannah called from California yesterday. Or maybe the day before? Well, I'm sure it was a Tuesday. I think.

Anyway, eliminating her leaves only my shrink, Dr. Knight. Nice guy. Funny. Almost worth getting up for. But not quite. "I'm afraid dangling the carrot is a very bad strategy, Ted. You'll have to try again."

"Aw, come on now, Mr. Todd. Don't be like that. You don't want to get me in trouble, do you?"

After extracting the promise of an extra package of cigarettes (the drive to negotiate is either deeply ingrained or genetically determined), I shuffle into the visitor's lounge and collapse into a deep, soft armchair near a window overlooking the street in front of the hospital. Outside, the sun is melting what little is left of an unseasonably early snowfall. Though the storm ultimately dumped only two inches of snow, the sky was fierce and blew icy forty-mile-an-hour winds. Or so I heard. But that was yesterday. Today it's warm again—so I hear—nearly fifty degrees. Maybe nature is bipolar. That would explain a lot.

The walk here has taken nearly everything out of me. I take a quick survey of what's left. I can move my eyes in my head. I can move my diaphragm in and out. I can push air through my lungs. But that's about it. I am hollow and with each breath out I deflate further. I am not tired. "Tired" is for marathoners who hit the wall at mile twenty or ER doctors who pull thirty-six-hour shifts. Tired is for sissies. I am an oxygen-starved climber of Everest forced on to ever higher altitudes by dangerous weather conditions; stranded for days in a dark little ice cave, supplies exhausted, with no hope of rescue. Or something like that. Must tell the brain trust a new cocktail is in order. This shit's a deal breaker.

I stare absently at the stains on my grey sweatpants and try to remember how many days it has taken me to accumulate them. I try to remember the last time I went outside, the last time I read a sentence I understood. The last time I took a crap. I try to remember what day today is. I try to remember when I started feeling so fucking sorry for myself.

I hear that last thought circling my mind like the last bit of dirty bathwater rounding the drain before it's sucked down. And when it's nothing but meaningless residue, I look up and see Knight through the glass wall of the activities room. He smiles and nods. He is talking to someone. From here all I can see is a pair of legs. Not Knight's. He is a tall man, a little on the doughy side, with circles under his eyes that bespeak chronic sleep deprivation. He wears heavy, lug-soled hiking boots with his wrinkled khakis and is oblivious to the dirty snow he tracks into the lounge. I find this eccentricity amusing; the orderlies who have to mop up after him, less so.

The legs in front of Knight are long and slim and are dressed in a pair of lived-in jeans. The feet on the ends of them are wearing brown leather boots. Cowboy. From the look of the dark stains around the edges, clearly not waterproof or built for snow. Even an early November snow. There is a fine-boned hand hanging down next to each of these legs. Pale skin. Long, thin fingers. Short nails. Bitten maybe.

A girl. The legs belong to a girl. In one hand she holds a bulky pair of ski gloves and earmuffs. Overkill. Even with the snow. This girl has overdressed for the weather but she has gotten the shoes wrong. Typical of people from California who've only recently moved to the East Coast.

She raises one little hand, puts it in Knight's big meaty paw, and they shake. Then they leave the activities room and walk in my direction. I continue my exploratory analysis. A ridiculously puffy blue down jacket balloons out from the narrow hips, creating a mushroom effect.

The ass, however, is spectacular. Round. High. Ripe. Like a piece of summer fruit. There's a red JanSport backpack hanging off one shoulder. Resting on the ass. Juicy. Sweet.

I feel a hand on my arm. I look up and see Miriam, one of the few nurses here I actually like. She is from Trinidad and has very cool hands.

"Greyson, Dr. Knight has a special visitor for you. Would you like to come into one of the conference rooms?" Miriam's voice is quiet and gentle and I like the sound of her words. Their meaning is lost on me, but I like the sound. There is music in her voice. She smiles at me and I smile back.

"No. I am very, very tired. I would like to stay right here."

And then the wrinkled khakis enter the frame, obscuring my perfect view of the perfect ass.

"It's okay, Miriam. We'll sit out here. Thank you," Knight says. "How are you feeling today, Greyson? A little bit foggy still?"

"Little like a fucking zombie still."

"It takes a few weeks, maybe longer, after stopping the ECT, but that will wear off. Your memory will get better too. Meantime, we'll get a lithium level. See if we need to adjust the dose."

I'm not really sure whether he says this for my benefit or that of the girl who stands several feet behind him uncomfortably shifting from one foot to the other.

"Listen, I want you to meet someone," Knight says casually. "You might remember her, you might not. Either way, it's okay."

He waves the girl over. We stare at one another.

I turn to Knight. "Well, I failed that test. Want me to take another?"

The girl hangs back, looks at Knight, then lets her gaze drift slowly my way.

"No, let's stay with this a little while," he says patiently. "Greyson, this is . . . Willa."

"Nice to meet you, Willa." *Willa,* I think, *Willa.* "That's a nice name."

Knight smiles. "I'm going to let you two talk for a while."

"But . . ." The girl turns to him.

"Just talk to him. We're not expecting a miracle in one visit." Knight starts to walk away.

She grabs his sleeve and I can just make out what she's saying. "Dr. Knight? He obviously doesn't know me, and frankly I hardly know him, so . . . I mean, I really don't think there's going to be a next time."

Knight is soft, gentle. "Why don't we just see how it goes today?"

I am baffled by the whole exchange.

She comes back and looks around at the empty chairs and couches, deciding where to sit. She chooses the far end of the sofa across from me and burrows into the corner.

We are silent. I assume she is new and suffers from depression or paranoia or OCD or one of the other quieter pathologies. And while I am an electrified, burnt-out, post-paralytic zombie, she is extremely attractive and I do remember how afraid I was when I first got here, so I make an attempt to form a reassuring sentence.

"He's actually a better shrink than most of the assholes in this place."

She nods. "That's good to hear." She nods again.

Knight passes by and she jumps up and runs over to him. She comes back with a tense smile on her face.

"So, he says I'm supposed to tell you who I am."

I wait. "Okayyyy . . ."

"Okay?" She repeats, as if it's not. "This is so not okay. You don't even look anything like what I remember."

"We've met before?"

The girl, Willa, laughs but it is joyless. In fact, despite the pacing, nail-biting, and hair-twisting she has employed to try to distract herself, she is having to wipe away tears she's pretending not to shed.

"It was a long time ago. I wouldn't expect you to remember."

"Please don't take it personally, I don't remember five minutes ago." That is my attempt at being charming, and it falls flat. I don't know what I've done to piss this girl off but her contempt is profound. Frankly, I don't need this shit. I'm about to fabricate an excuse for leaving when she finally speaks.

"So. Wil-la," she says, stretching the word out and leaning toward me. "The name Willa means nothing to you?"

"Actually," I say, "when Knight said it, I was thinking how I love that name. I have wonderful memories of that name."

Her face lightens just the tiniest bit. "You do?"

"I do. I just . . . I don't know what they are."

"Your mother was named Willa," she says.

"Yes! That's right," I say. "How did you know that?"

She rolls her eyes. "And I'm named Willa."

"That's quite a coincidence," I say, "because it's not a very common name."

She looks at me, expressionless. "Wow."

"What?"

"How much of this is permanent? What they did to you?"

Knight comes over and puts a hand on Willa's shoulder.

"Um, maybe not the most helpful approach."

"What did you do to him?" she asks Knight.

"I know it can be frightening. That's why I explained about the anterograde amnesia before you saw him."

"I wasn't expecting him to remember," she says, looking up at Knight. "But I thought if I gave him the numbers, he could do the math. Very basic math. And you know, I could finally have a conversation with him. But he's not even in there anymore."

"He is. He's there. This is temporary. The anterograde issues should be gone in a few weeks."

"Why didn't you have me come *then?*" the girl asks Knight.

"Because Greyson is also experiencing some retrograde amnesia— gaps in his past," Knight says in a low voice. "I don't think it's gone, it's just misplaced. He needs help finding it. And the sooner he starts, the better."

"Oh Jesus. I don't think I can do this." The girl is agitated. I wonder what meds they've got her on because they don't seem to be working. "I don't know how to—" She stops midsentence and stares at me. Knight's gaze follows hers. It is the first time I realize this angry, high-strung, overwhelmed but beautiful young woman has come here especially to see me.

Lately I have become more than a little slow on the uptake. Something else I hate about the new me.

"Please," Knight pleads with her, "just be straight with him. Just . . . tell him. And see where things go from there."

"Tell *him* what?" I say, now annoyed and fully tuned in. "I've been beaten, degraded, electrocuted, and tranquilized, but I'm not deaf. Yet."

"Sorry, Greyson." Knight turns to face me. "His thinking may be a little fuzzy right now, Willa, but Greyson is still sharp as a tack."

I change positions so I can assess him more closely. Tilt my head from one side to the other looking to see whether he might have had a nip of something before coming to work this morning.

"What?" he asks.

"Sharp. As. A. Tack," I say, hitting the consonants hard enough to break a tooth. But he doesn't even flinch. Empathy—it is both his best quality and his Achilles' heel. He will never survive this place.

"I only meant," he says, tapping my forehead with his index finger, "that *you* are in there somewhere." He pokes my chest where my heart would be if I had one. "There too," he says.

"And so," he says, pointing at Willa, "is *she*." He smiles at the girl and walks away, leaving us alone again.

"Well?" I say, with more hostility than I intend.

"I'm your daughter," she says. Just like that. No preamble. No emotion.

"My daughter." Suddenly the interior architecture of my brain shifts several degrees. The walls, floors, staircases, and hallways change position. She sits there patiently while I go from room to room, searching my memory.

It is like trying to find a single date buried in a world history text-book somewhere on the shelves of the Library of Congress.

"My mother's name was Willa," is all I am able to come up with.

There is a flicker of encouragement on her face before disappointment settles there. Right century, wrong decade.

"You named me after her," she offers. A clue. Yes. A dog-eared page I can turn to.

I nod again. "She was wonderful, my mother. She died before you were born." And we're both surprised. Because that is . . . something.

Milton comes around announcing the end of visiting hours. The girl is on her feet instantly.

"Well," she says, "I should go."

"It was nice to meet you," I say and awkwardly shake her hand.

She laughs at me. Or maybe in spite of me. "Right. Well, good luck, I guess."

"Will you come back?" I ask, suddenly anxious I might never get to see this girl again.

"Maybe," she says, looking at the floor. "I'll try."

But when I see her rush to the head of the exit line and bolt for the elevators as soon as she has escaped the double-locked doors, I decide that I should try very hard to remember her face.

"Your daughter is here to see you."

I look up into the expectant faces. Miriam, Knight, Milton, and a beautiful young blonde girl who must be at least a decade older than Willa.

"I'm sorry, have we met?"

Her face falls. "Yes. You said . . . you asked me to come back," the girl says.

"I don't think so. I have a daughter, but she's much younger. Just a little girl."

The girl's eyes fill with tears. Her mouth contorts in an angry grimace.

"*I am* Willa, you asshole. You don't have a little girl anymore. I'm all there is, the only Willa left."

That can't be. I remember a lot about Willa. The name. But I confuse what I remember. What I know. Because the fundamentals are so similar. Love, loss, guilt, regret, ache, comfort, more loss.

And yet, if I am honest about the details? There aren't any. Sometimes I think maybe there is a glimmer, a flash. But it is gone before I can get a good look. It is like trying to catch fireflies in broad daylight. With no jar.

Still, even though the memories haven't come back, the feeling attached to them has. I had a daughter. And I loved her. And I remember how it felt to have a little girl. It is for her that I feel the love, the loss, the regret, the guilt. But she is gone now and cannot be replaced.

I am dopey and out of it the next time she comes. I open my eyes and see her sitting just a few feet away from me. She is reading and tap-tap-tapping her yellow highlighter against the wooden arm of the chair. I recognize her, but I do not have good associations. She is that girl who reminds me how much I dislike myself. I don't remember why.

"What are you doing here?" My voice is gravelly and not particularly welcoming.

She smiles. "You're awake. How do you feel?"

"I said, why are you here? What do you want from me?"

She looks frightened. And like she is searching for an answer. "I ... I've always thought I might be missing something. And I ... I just wanted to find out."

"You ... You're ..."

"Willa. Your daughter."

"Right." The pieces are beginning to belong to the same puzzle, even if they don't quite fit.

"I wanted to see if you were worth ..."

"Worth what?"

"My time."

This is very much like a blind date. My daughter is coming, they've said. So I have put on pants with a zipper and a shirt with buttons and I am sitting here waiting. Going over the terrible sketch of her I drew after she left the last time. Reading the notes I made about how she speaks and moves and laughs. So I will recognize her when she comes in. Because while my memory of her is frozen—like a picture of a missing child on a milk carton—as this fog clears, I am beginning to believe that she is the real thing. I have no right to the real thing, but that doesn't stop me from wanting it.

And so, when I hear a girlish laugh that sounds like the tinkling of piano keys, I sit as still as I possibly can and do my damnedest not to move, blink, swallow. I'm afraid if I do she'll turn out to be a delusion. Or a side effect. The rantings of my fucked-up neurotransmitters. Not the real thing.

"How 'bout you give me that big coat and I'll hang it up for you, sweetheart?"

I hadn't realized Miriam was standing behind me.

"Oh, thank you. That would be great. I totally overdressed for the weather," Willa says, handing over her jacket, scarf, and gloves.

"You get yourself comfortable. I'll bring you two some coffee."

"Okay. Thanks," Willa says quietly. She looks at me warily and extends her hand. "Greyson? Hi, I'm—"

"Willa, I know," I say, beaming with pride.

"You remembered!"

And all I can do is nod and stare. At my daughter. Or the girl who looks like the sketch I know is my daughter. Close enough. I forget to inhale. I close my eyes and, like a swimmer coming to the surface, gasp for air.

When I open them again, I take a good, long look at the rest of her—long neck, hazel eyes flecked with green and gold, high cheekbones under cheeks still padded with a trace of baby fat, short blonde hair that makes her look just like Jean Seberg in *Breathless*.

"You're so . . . beautiful."

She turns her face to one side and looks down, biting her lip to keep from smiling, but she can't keep the pink from creeping into her exposed cheek and ear.

"Thanks," she says. She looks around at the options and sits down tentatively on a little flowered love seat opposite my chair.

I am a terrible host. That is, if one can be considered a host while at the same time undergoing inpatient treatment at a mental institution. And she is nervous. Her left knee is bouncing and she is biting at the cuticle around her thumb. She's been taking inventory of the room—of the "residents" who, I suddenly realize from her perspective, must look like extras from *Invasion of the Body Snatchers*—but then she sees me still looking and catches herself. She pulls her hand away from her mouth and sits on it. She is looking anywhere but at me.

If I don't say something now, I'm afraid she will leave.

"Say something," is what comes out.

"What?"

"I want to hear you talk."

"Okay, how about you're creeping me out a little?"

"I'm sorry. You're right. You don't have to say anything."

"It's alright. I mean, you're mentally unstable so I'll cut you some slack."

I laugh, pleased to discover grown-up Willa has turned out to be a bit of a smart ass. "Thanks. I appreciate that."

A self-satisfied grin crosses her face. Then she laughs nervously. I smile. She looks at the floor, looks back up, smiles uncomfortably, clears her throat.

"So how did you, um . . . find me? In the first place?" My voice sounds like I haven't spoken in weeks. I try to clear my throat. Instead, I gurgle.

"Aunt Hannah. She called Mom."

"Hannah?" I'm confused.

"Yeah. Your sister. Hannah. She called after they found you."

"Oh." I nod. "You've been . . . in contact?"

"Well, yeah. She's my aunt."

I am overcome with jealousy, fury, and rage at Hannah's betrayal. How dare she stay after I left? How dare she get to keep what I abandoned? My losses should be her losses. Of course I know this is irrational. And insane. Of course I realize that I cannot customize the destruction and devastation I left behind. And of course I know that what I really feel toward my sister is gratitude.

"Right, right, sure. And so you came from Los Angeles to see me."

A single guffaw erupts from Willa. The hand she's been sitting on escapes and flies up to cover her mouth. I smile and try not to look hurt.

"I'm sorry, that's not funny. I mean, I don't know why I laughed."

"It's okay."

"No, I mean, not that I wouldn't have. I mean, come from L.A. Shit, I'm sorry. That was mean."

"It's fine. Then where did you come from?"

"School," she says. And then, as an afterthought, hitchhikes her thumb over one shoulder as if to indicate she's matriculating at the visitor's lounge handicapped restroom. We nod. I offer her tea. I am thrilled when she accepts because it gives me something to do while I try to think of a sentence to utter, a question to ask.

"So, you're a freshman?"

She seems surprised I would know this. That I would know my daughter's age.

"Right."

"Where?"

"Princeton."

Some biological sense of pride takes over and I beam. "Impressive." I can't resist asking, "How many schools did you turn down?"

She tilts her chin up and tries to sound cocky despite the bright pink that has flooded her cheeks. Blushing is her tell. I didn't remember that. "All the others."

She is alarmed when I laugh, stamp my feet, and even briefly applaud. But I am overwhelmed by joy at her achievements, her diligence and hard work and talent and humor and sensitivity. I am overwhelmed by what a great kid I think this girl, my daughter, probably must be.

Then the adrenaline dissipates and we are silent again. It is awkward again. Willa starts chewing on her thumb.

Once again, I scramble for something to fill the silence. "I'm sorry the first few times you came to visit were so difficult. That I wasn't at my best."

"Your best? It was kind of like *Groundhog Day* meets *One Flew Over the Cuckoo's Nest*. No offense."

The cinephile in me feels a rush of genetic pride—my DNA is there—but I keep it to myself. "Dr. Knight shouldn't have put you through that."

"I volunteered. And it's not like I'm used to being foremost on your mind anyway."

"That's not true, you know. Though I can certainly see why you'd—"

Willa lets her head drop, and even though she's looking at the floor again, I can tell she is smiling. "You think I'm still holding a grudge because you abandoned me?" She is being glib, obnoxious. In a nasty, ironic kind of way.

I am not smiling. "I think you'd still be very angry."

"Nah. I was never angry at you," she says. "I was precocious. I mean, not totally. I did denial, but I skipped anger and moved right on through to acceptance. Drove Mom and the shrink crazy."

The whole talking-to-the-floor thing is driving me crazy, but I don't know that I'm in a position to complain or nag. I'm not sure what I'm in a position to do. So I make a polite request.

"Would you mind terribly if we sat up for this conversation?"

Willa giggles, and as she throws herself back into the deep cushions of the loveseat, her hand comes up to cover her mouth again.

"Why do you do that?" I ask seriously.

"What?"

"Cover your mouth when you laugh."

She blushes and looks away.

"Willa?"

She shrugs but stays silent.

"I'd understand if you were angry."

"At you?" she asks, as if it were the most ludicrous question ever posed.

"Yes. At me."

"All of a sudden you know who the hell I am and you think that gives you the right to start analyzing my childhood? Awfully presumptuous, don't you think?"

"You're right. I'm sorry. I didn't mean—"

"Don't be sorry! Look, Greyson, I had a fucking excellent child-hood. You leaving—probably way better than if you had stayed."

Sucker-punched. I am unprepared for the pain and loss of breath.

"I mean, you don't, you know—you shouldn't feel guilty. I was like the happiest goddamned kid in the world."

"Oh. That's good. I'm glad things worked out."

"You and Mom never would have stayed together. You would have had one of those horrific Hollywood divorces. It would have been a disaster."

"You're probably right."

"I had a better childhood than most of my friends," she says, start-ing in on her thumb again. "When their parents were in the middle of heinous divorces and custody battles and moving to shitty little houses south of Olympic, my parents were blissed-out newlyweds." She lets her hands fall to the edges of the couch cushions, holding on as if she's afraid it might take off any minute. "Our family never had to deal with exes or child support or alternate weekends. I'm lucky. I have an amazing family. Amazing parents." She lingers on the word "amazing" to make her point. "So, no, I'm not angry. How could I be angry?"

And there it is—the feeling that I'm seated across from a woman who's telling me she's found someone else. But I want her to be happy, so I smile encouragingly.

I see the blood flow back into her paper-white hands when she finally lets go of the cushion she's been gripping. I see her chest fall as she exhales the useless air in her lungs. I see her give in to the urge to bite the skin on her thumb again.

"Gee whiz, I never thought of it that way before. Boy, it certainly does relieve me of that crushing guilt and overwhelming regret I carry with me like a rotting albatross. I'm sure I'll sleep much better tonight."

She rolls her eyes. "God, everyone always assumes . . . I mean, what's to understand? You were sick. You couldn't help it. I've spent my whole life being told not to take it personally. So I didn't. Now everyone is acting like I should."

She looks up at me and shrugs. "Sorry I don't hate you. Besides," she says, examining her cuticle, "Mom had enough anger for both of us." She is a terrible actress but has clearly had enough therapy to believe her version of the story—her bullshit. Because how could it be true?

I want to reach out and touch her—just her hand, a sleeve—but the voltage running through her, the stored current is so powerful (I can almost hear the hum), I have no doubt I would get burned, and I am still recovering from the last jolt that shook my system. I blink hard several times, hoping this will clear the fog in my head. Instead, when it clears, I'm left watching me play out a scene from *The Deer Hunter*. Seated at a table between Robert De Niro and Christopher Walken, I am holding a loaded gun to my head. And inside the chamber are all the wrong things I could say right now. All the possibilities for killing my chances with her are contained in that gun, and it's only a matter of time before one of them shoots out my mouth.

It occurs to me, my odds of succeeding with Willa were probably better when I didn't recognize her. That may have been awkward, but this—this is a bloody mess.

I have had a setback. If the depression does not resolve on its own, I will have to undergo more ECT. But it may just be drug related—a bad reaction. It's really too soon to tell. No one who has been depressed has ever used the phrase "too soon to tell" when describing what it feels like. "Too much," "too hard," "too painful to go on." Yes. But never "too soon to tell." That is doctor bullshit.

Knight has changed my medication. He says the new drug might "sloooow" me down for a little while. I don't like the sound of this.

"How slow?"

"Don't know," he says.

"How long before it works?"

"Not sure," he says.

"Who the hell put you in charge?"

"I ask myself that question every day," he mumbles to himself. He writes the prescription and hands it through the window to the duty nurse.

Before I swallow the first tiny, benign-looking pill, I think about calling Willa. But we do not have that kind of relationship. Certainly not yet. I would not even know what to say if her roommate answered and asked who was calling. I lie in bed until the days run together. And then when the haze finally begins to clear, when I can speak in full sentences again—albeit with a residual slur—and remain conscious for more than a few hours at a time, I venture into the dayroom.

"Boo!" Not a single one of my muscles moves. Not a twitch. "Wow," Willa says. Coming around from behind me, she holds her palm in front of my mouth. "Checkin' for signs of life," she says. "Yep, still breathing."

"Sorry," I say. I want to think of a joke but nothing comes to mind. Perhaps because at the moment I don't have one. It's still only been a few days since I've been back in circulation and I am nowhere near "normal." I wish I could will away the dullness but it won't budge.

She takes a closer look at me and lets her backpack fall to the floor. "Jesus, you really look like shit," she says quietly and sits down next to me.

"Candyman." I smile weakly. She reaches over and touches the baggy material of the sweatshirt covering my arm. Her touch is so light I barely feel it through the heavy cotton. But the gesture is everything. It is empathy. Exactly what I want and precisely what I do not deserve. The truth is, I have no idea what I deserve.

"You don't have to do anything," she says. "I have a surprise for you."

Unzipping her backpack, she takes out a small pink photo album. The spine is cracked with age. She opens it up and on the first page is a picture of me sitting on the edge of a hospital bed next to an exhausted, annoyed-looking woman. I am holding a newborn wrapped in a hospital-issue blanket. "That's me," I slur, surprised.

"Bingo," she says. "And I'm the baby. And that's Mom."

"Mom?"

"Ellen."

Ellen, I think. And I feel a rush of warmth and comfort and loss and regret all at the same time. "Ellen."

She shows me more photos. Birthday parties and family get-togethers and one of the girl when she was three or four asleep in my arms in a big unmade king-size bed.

And little by little the memories that have scattered come together and begin to shuffle like a deck of cards, arranging and rearranging themselves until every once in a while I see one and am momentarily struck by the depth of its meaning. And when I remember, it is not just a fuzzy fragment but a full-body experience. Short-lived but complete. As if I were there. As if then was now.

I touch the photo and the sounds of the hospital recede. I close my eyes and hear my daughter's small, quick footsteps crossing the hardwood floor to my room. She struggles with the doorknob. She is barely three and it doesn't turn easily. She pushes open the door and uses my sheets as a tether to help pull herself onto my bed. She does all this with her eyes only half open.

She has always preferred to sleep naked. Ellen wrangles her into a Pull-Up at bedtime but it's pointless. In the morning, wet or dry, we always find her bare-assed. Now her small body is soft and warm. I curl myself around her and think sleeping with her is like sleeping with a puppy.

But now I am awake. The soft-glow numbers on the titanium Hammacher Schlemmer clock that sits on my dresser tells me it's 2:37 A.M. Willa has been climbing into bed with me more and more frequently lately. Ellen, who's been known to sleep through earthquakes, never realizes it until morning. Then she gets mad at me—says I am encouraging bad sleep habits.

But I like it. It is my favorite time to spend time with her. I can give her what she wants—be the daddy she wants. No phone calls to return or meetings to go to. No reasons to tell her to be quiet or leave me alone. At 2:37 A.M. I am Willa's hero. So I run my hand lightly over her impossibly soft skin—her back and perfectly round butt—and I hold both of her tiny feet in one hand. And I wonder how much longer I'll be able to do this before it isn't okay anymore. I assume Ellen will tell me. I assume she knows these things.

Willa. Ellen. A world in two words.

"Show me more," is all I can manage.

She turns the page. My stomach seizes but I don't know why. There is a broad expanse of green lawn, a big oak tree, and a tire swing. I am pushing Willa on the tire swing. Her head is thrown back, her long blonde hair falls almost to the ground. She is six, maybe seven.

"That's the house on—"

"Sand Dune Road."

"You remember the name of the street, but three weeks ago you didn't know who I was?" she asks.

"Things come back in bits and pieces."

I look at the picture again and can't help associating that house with the beginning of the end. Even though I know I'm probably telling myself another lie. But it felt that way. Every time I turned onto our new street, I felt mocked.

The house we bought was a block north of Sunset in a very nice but not overly ostentatious part of Brentwood. It had a swimming pool and a huge backyard. The school district was excellent. The drive into the office was fifteen minutes instead of forty-five. It made perfect sense. And I hated Ellen for making me buy it. For making me give up our little place in Malibu where we went to sleep every night with the waves breaking outside our bedroom window.

I knew it wasn't really her fault. If we'd stayed, Willa would have turned into just another beautiful surfer girl who hardly ever went to school, spent most of the day getting stoned, and ended up working at the Fred Segal in the Malibu Cross Creek Mall. No, there was really no other way. But the street name. I couldn't help experiencing it as a not-so-subtle "Fuck you."

"What's wrong with it?" Ellen screeched, exhausted from finally getting me to admit what it was I was pissed off about.

"Sand Dune Road?" I yelled back.

We were standing in the street in front of the house, watching Willa play on the picture-perfect tire swing. I looked up and down the perfectly manicured, perfectly flat, perfectly green street. "Why don't they just call it Constant Painful Reminder?"

"Oh grow the fuck up, Greyson," Ellen said. "Not everything is about you. We're doing this for her."

She was right. But I never stopped missing the beach. And then Willa started having nightmares. There'd been a robbery on our block. So I installed an alarm system. But still, Willa didn't sleep through the night. She missed Shadow, the enormous German shepherd technically our neighbor's dog but really the unofficial mayor and the only security system we ever needed on Beechwood Shore Drive, the little cul-de-sac we lived on in Malibu.

Willa was sure there were men hiding in the bushes outside her bedroom windows. I wasn't sleeping much then—couldn't sleep— and so I'd stay up watching old movies. Willa would wake up from a nightmare at two or three in the morning and come find me and climb up into my lap and watch with me.

"Remember when I was scared of the robbers?" she asks. I remember. After four or five nights without sleep, I would be seeing shadows, hearing noises. I would be convinced our house was being cased. I kept thinking there were men outside coming to get me.

"We went to the lumberyard and bought planks," I say, wishing this was not coming back to me so clearly.

"And you boarded up all the windows in my room," she says wistfully.

And now I remember. That was also around the same time I had my office swept for bugs. And when I started buying the guns.

"You made me feel safe." Willa is lost in her completely bogus memory. "Really safe. Mom thought you were nuts, but I thought I had the perfect dad."

I look up at Willa and try to smile. "Sweetheart, I *was* nuts."

"But I don't—you were fine when I was little. I remember. Everything. Vacations and holidays and—" She turns the pages of the photo album and points to a picture. Ellen, Willa, and me smiling, tan, vacationing on St. Barts. Less than a year before I left.

"Look," she says. Her voice is beginning to shake. "I remember you like this. Before."

My throat tightens.

"What?" she asks.

But I don't know what to say or how to say it.

"What?" she asks again, anxiously, impatiently.

I point a shaky finger at the man who looks like me. "*That* is not before. It just looks like it." Willa examines the photo, searching for clues.

"But you were so—I mean, I would have known. I would have noticed. Something. You read to me and took me to the pony rides they used to have in the parking lot at—"

She stops midsentence. Her eyes drift past my shoulder and settle on a group of patients who are engaged in some kind of art therapy. One young man has done an excellent job capturing the anguish of a woman who, for the last three days, has done nothing but push herself—forward and back, heel to toe—in a rocking chair, and sob. It appears the boy may have found his true calling.

Willa turns back to me. Confused. And sad. Like I've taken her memories apart and reassembled them in a way that makes no sense.

"When did it start?"

I want to give her an answer that will help. I want there to be an answer. But there isn't one.

"I don't know. I suppose there was a beginning. But I don't remember there being a before anymore. I only remember trying to pretend. I remember the trying."

Willa thinks about this. Her elbows rest on her knees, which she's let fall wide apart.

She stares down at the freshly waxed wood floor. It starts small. Just a tiny rhythmic bobbing of her head. She is nodding. Little by little, it becomes a nod of true understanding and grief. I watch helplessly as it becomes a committed nod that engages her shoulders and upper torso. Her tears hit the floor—one, then two. And then they are falling too quickly for me to count.

When she looks up, I can't read the expression on her face.

"I used to have these dreams about you when I was little," she says quietly. "I still have them—sometimes. They're all basically the same—they just come in different flavors. In one the police come to the door in the middle of the night to tell Mom and me you've been killed in a car accident. And then there's a version where you die really heroically saving a little kid from being hit by a bus. And one where you're the victim of a random act of violence. In my favorite one, I find out that you're dying of cancer. I go to the hospital and sit by your bed and read to you and I'm there holding your hand when you die. The cancer one is the best because I get to say good-bye."

The tears are careening down her cheeks and she wipes at her nose with the back of her hand.

"Those dreams always feel so fucking real, you know? And . . . every time . . . every goddamn time, I dream you died—that you're dead, no matter how it happens. Daddy, I'm—I . . . always feel so . . . I feel so relieved. But then I wake up. And I know it's not true. I know you didn't die. That really, you left me. And every time is like finding out for the first time. Over and over and over again." She is gasping, choking on her sobs. "But that—that doesn't mean I'm angry. I'm not angry. I'm not."

I want to die. Again. I *could* have died then. Way back then. It's not like I didn't think about it. I don't know, would that have been better than leaving? Or just a messier form of the same thing? But it doesn't matter. Because suicide is not one of the flavors her dream comes in.

Maybe it's not too late to die heroically. I could loiter near a school crosswalk and wait for some asshole to run a red.

Miriam comes by and quietly deposits a box of tissues next to Willa. She pulls several from the box but is crying too hard to do anything but wad them up in her fist. No one in the lounge so much as glances over. If it ain't psychosis, it ain't worth the effort.

I feel useless. I pull another tissue from the box, lean forward in my chair, and hold it up to her drippy nose.

"Blow."

She stops crying and looks at me wide-eyed. Then she bursts into stuffy-nosed laughter. "*Blow?* What am I, three?

"Are you okay?" I ask.

She is standing in line with the other visitors, waiting to be frisked and sent out one by one through the glass cage with the double-locking doors. Her face is pale, her eyes are red-rimmed and swollen.

"Yeah. Why wouldn't I be?" she says.

I stand next to her until it is her turn to enter the cage. I want desperately to ask when she's coming back, to hear that it will be soon—a few days, not more than a week. But I can't. Who am I to ask her to come back?

I am shocked when she reaches up and gives me a hug. I hold on, trying to memorize the way her hair feels against my cheek, the smell of her shampoo. Then she pulls away. I am sure that after today she won't come again.

I am convinced our last visit was more than Willa could handle. I give up and commit myself to wallowing. But as with most things, I am wrong.

"Just because *you* leave doesn't mean everybody else does," Willa says when she shows up and finds that I haven't shaved, slept, or eaten in almost a week. I showered only because Milton threatened to bathe me if I didn't.

She sits down on the couch. But when I make a move to sit next to her, she stops me. "No no no," she says, shaking a finger at me. "I am going to wait here. You are going to go back to your room and you are going to lose the Wolfman look and the skanky sweatpants. When you come back looking like the father who inflicted irreparable trauma on me, I will be here. I promise."

And she is. I have no idea why. Or why she comes back the following week. But she does. And that weekend she shows up for an unscheduled Sunday visit because, she says, her roommates are driving her crazy and she can't concentrate on her work.

"Right," I say, taking her backpack from her, "because an insane asylum is so much like a library."

"Well, there's a book I need to pick up at Columbia anyway," she says. "I need it for a paper and it was assigned for a whole course, so they're totally out of it at our campus bookstore."

I nod, thinking I've never enjoyed being lied to more.

An hour later, Willa kicks me under the table in the dining room where we are playing Scrabble. "Um, I think your girlfriend wants in on our game."

I look up and see Glenda dash into the activities room and duck below the big glass window. "She's not my girlfriend."

Willa raises her eyebrows. "Whatever."

"Glenda!" I yell over my shoulder. "We've had this conversation. Many times."

Willa giggles. I shoot her a narrow-eyed look. "It's not funny."

"Oh it is *very* funny." She is enjoying this way too much.

"Glenda!" I yell again. "Would you please come out?"

Taking tiny steps and with her hands folded demurely in front of her, Glenda comes out of the activities room and over to the table.

"Oh, why hello, Willa, what a pleasant surprise. I didn't know you were visiting today. How nice. You know, your father is always so much more cheerful after one of your visits."

Willa smiles and nods. The effort of trying not to laugh is causing a sweat to break out on her forehead and upper lip.

"Glenda. Stop," I say. "I thought we had an agreement."

"Yes, Greyson, yes, we did."

"Oh really? What's your agreement?" Willa asks.

"Don't! That's—" But before I can stop her . . .

"I leave you two alone during your visits or no sex for me."

"Glenda!" I yell and she flinches.

Willa swallows hard and then whispers to Glenda. "I think you just violated the terms of your agreement. Big time."

Glenda turns and with a shriek runs toward the dayroom.

"You realize your girlfriend's a psycho."

"I know. And she's not my girlfriend."

"Whatever. You gotta get out more."

"More?"

Willa puts her letters on the board. "P-R-O-V-O-K-E. Triple word score." She leans back in her chair and grins, smugly. "Ha."

And before I can even attempt to recover my dignity, Milton is walking around with his bullhorn calling an end to visiting hours.

After nearly two months in this place, I have procured a coveted two-hour pass. I am out in the world. Sort of. Willa and I are sitting on the upper level of the hospital lobby. That's as far as I'm allowed to go. Willa has brought Chinese food and chocolate cake. I am fascinated just watching the people below us walk in and out the front door.

Anytime they want. No restrictions. In and out, back and forth, coming and going. Or just going. We have not talked about the going and I have to ask.

"What do you remember about the night I left?"

Willa looks up from her cake. "What?"

"What do you remember about it?"

"Um, pretty much every detail," she says.

"Tell me," I say.

"It was a warm night in September. I know because I had just started third grade." She begins to tell me the story and then the story tells itself.

It is a warm September night when I leave my wife and eight-year-old daughter.

"I'd made you a present in school that day—a key chain with my school picture glued in the middle of it. You acted like you couldn't give two shits when I gave it to you, but I really wanted you to use it for your keys. Your jacket was hanging on the back of your chair and I slipped it into the—"

"You were wearing a blue dress with pink and green flowers on it," I say without thinking. "And a headband."

Willa puts her fork down. "How do you—?"

"I don't know." I am as mystified as she is. "I just do."

Her eyes wander to the people around us, to a group of doctors standing by the elevator bank, to the cashier at the coffee stand. As if maybe one of them has the answer.

Her hand lies limply on the table. I put mine on top of it and she looks back over at me. "Go on," I say. She pulls her hand away.

"That night after dinner you promised to read me a story. Right after you finished cleaning up the backyard. I waited and waited but you never came."

I tell my wife I'm going out to the backyard to clean up the dog shit.

"So I went outside in my nightgown—the purple one with the giraffes. The garage door was open and the light was on and all your dog crap equipment was lined up against the wall."

She stops. "None of this sounds familiar?"

"Vaguely. I don't know. Go on."

"Your car was gone. You were gone. I ran to the end of the driveway. I yelled for you. I remember the feel of the gravel on my bare feet. I opened the big gates at the end of the driveway and ran into the middle of the street in front of our house looking for you."

"Where did you think I'd gone?"

"I knew you hadn't gone to the market or the video store or back to the office. I don't know how, but I knew you'd left. Period. That's when Mom came out. And told me to calm down. To stop crying. That you'd just gone to the market or the video store or back to the office. But Greyson, it's not like it was the first time you'd taken off. I mean, I didn't know that until much later. Do you remember that? Those other times?"

I shake my head. No idea.

"Mom was pissed as hell when you didn't come back the next day, but she wasn't scared. She didn't get scared until, like, day five. And then she called Aunt Hannah and Victor. And after that there were people from the studio. And then the police. Lots of police. And random people I didn't know bringing platters from Nate 'n Al's and giving Mom Valium. Lots of Valium. And everyone kept telling me not to worry. That you'd be home soon. But I knew they were lying." She looks at me, crosses her arms over her chest, and sits back in her chair. "That's what I remember. What do *you* remember?" she asks pointedly.

"It's kind of a blur. A haze."

The story tells itself.

It is a warm September night.

Willa nods.

I leave my wife and eight year-old daughter. I promised to read her a bedtime story. Charlie and the Chocolate Factory.

I attempt a smile.

But I leave before I can make good on the promise. Doesn't matter. It's only one of many I've broken. One of many times I've disappointed her. She'll fall asleep before she realizes I've failed her again.

Neither one of us says anything. Willa goes back to her cake. I go back to the ward before my two hours are up. But Willa has to take me. Because I am not allowed to go anywhere unaccompanied. I walk a few feet behind my angry, silent escort. Just in case I don't feel small enough, humiliated enough, powerless enough already.

Just in case I wasn't sure where I stood.

Despite all the drugs, I do not sleep. Instead, I ruminate. Which is both what cows do to their cud and the bad habit practiced by depressives of turning things over and over in their minds. Ceaselessly, relentlessly. Until the thoughts themselves are enough to drive them over the edge.

In the morning, I ask to see Knight. As soon as possible. An unscheduled session. An unprecedented request.

I am pacing, agitated.

He looks at me, concerned.

"Everything okay? Well . . . I mean relatively speaking."

I tell him about my triumphant return to the outside world.

"Oh. Well, that's some heavy dinner conversation," he says.

I stop pacing. "I know. I pushed too hard. Things were better and I fucked it all up."

"One bad night does not mean you fucked it *all* up. We've talked about—"

"What is my best-case scenario?" I interrupt, still pacing.

"In what sense?"

I slam my fist against the wall. He doesn't flinch. "Come on. Don't bullshit me."

"I always tell you the truth, Greyson," he says calmly. "I just need a little context. Why don't you sit down?"

I nod. Pull out a chair and try to gather my thoughts. No small feat for me these days. I take a deep breath and try again. "What is . . . the treatment goal for people with . . . with what I . . ."

Knight leans across the table toward me. "Bipolar disorder type I."

"Yeah."

"Okay . . . well, we want to stop the extreme mood changes. Bring down the ceiling on the mania, bring up the floor on the depression." Knight uses his hands to illustrate the shrinking space. "Put more time between the episodes. And make the medication regimen as tolerable as possible. Stability. That's what we're aiming for."

I nod, get up, head for the door. Knight looks perplexed.

"Was it something I said?"

"No. I mean yes. You just confirmed what I assumed."

Knight rolls his eyes and rubs his hand over his face. "Which was?"

"Stability. The best-case scenario is stability. Not happiness, not passion, not joy. Best-case scenario: a flaccid fucking life of stability. A living flatline."

Knight stops rubbing his face and lets his forehead fall onto the table with a thud. "That's not what I said, Greyson," he says facedown into the table.

"Yes, it is," I insist. "That's exactly what you said. The treatment goal is stability."

He takes a deep breath and pulls himself into an upright, seated position. "Okay, maybe that is what I said, but the truth is, without stability, there will be no room in your life for happiness. Real, non-manic, nonhallucinatory happiness that doesn't inevitably eventually end in suicidal depression. So without the doctors and the pills and the ECT, I would say your chances of having *any* happy in your future is pretty close to zero."

I would like to get angry at Knight, but unfortunately I am struck by the fact that when I think about it—and I do, a lot—I realize I have had very little happy over the past three decades. Not none. But not a lot. "Go on."

He sighs. "Once we get you stable—and I have every confidence that we will—then and only then—you might get the chance to experience those unexpected minutes or days or, if you're really lucky, weeks of honest-to-God happiness. And Greyson, if you think the rest of us so-called normal people get any more than that, I obviously need to prescribe you a stronger antipsychotic."

He is not bullshitting me. He is not even talking to me like a shrink. My shrink is talking to me like a friend in need of a friend. And apparently I am so touched by the gesture that I have started to cry. Without pausing, he hands me the ubiquitous box of tissues.

"We are all of us—well, with the exception of people who have just fallen in love and those lucky demented few who see life's glass as three quarters full—we are just getting by. We do our jobs and love our families and take pride in our kids' accomplishments. Some people believe in God because that makes watching the nightly news a little easier. But our ups and downs stay within a manageable range. That's what I want for you."

I nod. "But what if I want more?"

Knight gets up and comes around to my side of the table so he can sit directly across from me. "When you got here, you were half dead." His tone is far more serious than I'm used to. "Mostly from the illness, and the damage you inflicted on yourself, but also from grief and guilt. And loss."

"I don't remember. Anything."

"I know," he says. "And some days I think it's better that way. But I don't know. Because when you got here you remembered Willa. And in making you well, we took away what little you had left of her. I'm sorry you don't have those memories. But she's here now. Which is kind of a miracle. She may be angry and conflicted and resentful, but she wants to know you. Even if sometimes it's just to rub your nose in the terrible thing you did to her. So you should let her."

I pound my fist against my forehead. "It just sounds a little too much like a cheesy Hollywood ending to me."

"Trust me," Knight says, "no one is handing you a happy ending. At best you're being spared a Shakespearean tragedy." He puts a hand on my shoulder. "Let me work on the stability. You spend your time on the happiness part. "

"You realize I have a terrible track record in that department."

Knight smiles at me. "Past is past. Consider your record expunged." He gets up to leave the room and pauses at the door. "By the way, did I mention she's a terrific kid?"

My team and I have decided the best thing for me to do when I get out of here is to transition to the outpatient program—at least for a while. Until I figure out what I want to be when I grow up. It's kind of anticlimactic. But it's either that or go to live with Hannah in California. Away from Willa. So I will explore my options while receiving four hours of treatment and Group every day, five days a week. I might also enroll in some extension classes at NYU. In film. Because what I really want to do is direct. And all my favorite directors are bipolar.

I am looking through the NYU catalog, reading course descriptions to Willa, who is rummaging around in her backpack pretending to listen to me. I guess I should take that as a sign of progress—each of her monosyllabic responses a little trophy of normal father-daughter relations. I guess I should. But I find talking to her back annoying. To be fair, though, it is the end of the semester. She is supposed to be in the library studying for finals, but she has come to see me anyway. I am not no one to her. I decide to be helpful.

"What are you looking for?"

"Oh . . . nothing . . . I can't believe I . . ."

Once more, with feeling. "Maybe I can help."

"No, I'm sure it's here. I just . . ."

She continues to rummage, increasingly frustrated. She is yanking books and loose papers out of her backpack, and as she tugs at some stapled pages, a large corner section tears off.

"Fuck! No! Shit! Great, that's just fabulous."

The nurses within earshot look over. I'm sure I see one or two raised eyebrows when they find the source of the river of expletives is my daughter—beautiful, brilliant, mouth like a toilet. I am surprised at the embarrassment I feel.

"Willa, please," I whisper, "a little decorum."

She stops, stares at me drop-jawed.

"You used to say that to me all the time."

"I did?"

"I was like seven years old and we'd go out to dinner. You and Mom would let me bring a friend and it was always someplace like the Jetty or the Chart House where the wait was like an hour and Lauren Fineman and I would be running around playing tag or something and you'd be like, 'Ladies, a little decorum please.'"

"Jesus, really?"

"Really. I was the only kid in second grade who knew what it meant. Then it showed up on my SATs and I stared at it for five minutes before I filled in the bubble."

She shoves her backpack onto the floor and collapses onto the couch. I can tell she is close to tears. I cross the expanse of linoleum between us and sit down next to her. I want to put my arm around her, but I am afraid.

"What were you looking for?" I ask gently.

Her voice is hesitant, halting. "I can't find the plane ticket. That Mom sent me."

Ah. That. I'm guessing it's the one I've been staring at with dread. The one that means she'll be gone for over a month. The one I've been staring at while her back was turned, hoping if I concentrate hard enough it will spontaneously combust. The one sticking out of the inside pocket of the very grown-up-looking black wool coat with the red lining—a gift from me via the Bloomingdale's catalogue. Which is lying over the arm of the couch we're sitting on.

"And while I was looking," she continues, "I tore my French Lit study notes, which I spent like five hours—"

"Willa?"

"What?"

I point one finger at her coat. She gasps, grabs the ticket, and hugs it to her chest.

"Oh my God, I'm such an idiot. Thank you so much. Mom would have killed me."

"I seriously doubt that," I say.

"No, really, I'm so relieved. Thank you." And then she throws her arms around my neck. I inhale deeply, hoping to fill my lungs with enough of her essential Willa-ness to keep me going while she is gone.

"Okay, I'm going to get some tea and then deal with the next crisis," she says, releasing me. "Do you want some?"

I shake my head and continue circling courses in the catalog, pretending not to feel the pit in my stomach where Willa will have been after she goes.

And trying not to look up every thirty seconds during the five minutes she is away.

"I made us hot chocolate," she says, handing me one of the two Styrofoam cups she's holding. "But I had to make it with water. The only milk in the fridge had Glenda's name on it and I just couldn't deal."

She hands me the cup and I stir the thin hot chocolate and mini-marshmallows with the red plastic stick Willa hands me. I blow on it and take a small sip. It is sweet and wet, not particularly chocolaty, more vaguely cocoa-like. I open my lips a little wider and several of the tiny, slippery marshmallows swim into the warm cocoa pool. When they catch under my teeth, I feel the pop. They are sticky like candy, not soaked through.

At that moment, for a split second, time stops. I feel it. I wonder if Willa has felt it too. Or is it just me? After all the ECT, could I have built up residual stores of electricity that are setting off random charges? Am I shocking myself?

"Hello?" Willa is waving her hands in front of my face. Apparently she has been talking. "Tape? For my notes? Do they let you have tape or are they afraid you guys will try to make a noose out of it?"

Tape. Tape. I close my eyes and it is like pulling up an anchor. One that was dropped from a ship abandoned decades ago.

Willa leans in close. I inhale. Breath. Skin. Hair. And whispers, "Uh, Greyson? Daddy? Are you okay? Should I . . . call someone?"

Daddy.

And then, finally, it comes to the surface. Past and present connect in one moment, one memory, one human being—bridging time and distance.

I remember.

I remember.

"What are you grinning at?" Willa asks.

"I just remembered something—"

"What?"

"You were so little, I don't think—"

"Tell me."

"For a little while, when you were still in nursery school, your mom and I split up."

"Yeah?"

"We took a trip. Just the two of us. We drove up north?" I search her face. Nothing. She doesn't remember.

Miriam walks by and Willa jumps up.

"Excuse me, would you happen to have some Scotch tape I could use?" She holds up her torn notes as if to prove she isn't planning anything sinister.

"Sure thing, come with me, sweetheart."

I tell myself it's enough that I remember. More than enough. That it is everything. Almost.

Willa comes back with her notes patched together just as Milton announces the end of visiting hours.

I get up and help Willa on with her coat. As if I were a real father. As if this weren't a psychiatric hospital. She turns toward me, but is focused intently on buttoning her coat. "You were totally bullshitting me about Cassiopeia," she says casually.

I am incredulous. I wait. Hoping she will unwrap another gift I do not deserve.

When she looks up, I can tell—we are in the same place at the same time.

"We were lying on top of Leland Costa's RV looking at the stars and you were pointing out the constellations. As . . . if . . ." She smiles at her own Valley Girliness.

I look into my cup. "And you wanted to sleep up there."

Willa laughs. "Yeah, I said we should tape ourselves to the roof so we wouldn't fall off."

"You remember."

"*You* remember," she says.

Milton walks up behind us. "Visiting hours are over. Got to go now."

"I'll walk you to the door," I say, lifting her backpack onto my shoulder.

"I'll call over break," she says.

Five weeks. I can't say good-bye. I hand her backpack over, nod and try to smile.

"I'll come visit as soon as I get back," she says. "I promise."

I am still afraid, but I wrap my arms around her and hold her tightly. "I love you, Willa," I whisper.

"I believe you," she says.

I was hoping for an "I love you too, Daddy." But that would be the cheap Hollywood ending. And I've always hated those. I may want the

Hollywood ending, but I know it's not real. At least real is something I can work with.

I realize that I am feeling a tiny glimmer of something. Something good. I cannot remember what it is because it comes from someplace so far away and so deep inside that I cannot place it or put a name to it.

Maybe someday it will come to me.

ACKNOWLEDGMENTS

My heartfelt thanks:

To Mark Doten, my editor, for his incredible vision, patience and persistence.

To Bronwen Hruska, my publisher, for being the book's greatest champion.

To Paul Bresnick, my agent, for being in my corner every step of the way.

To John Oakes for his invaluable guidance and wisdom.

To Jennifer Belle and Tim Tomlinson for showing me how it's done. I couldn't have asked for better teachers.

To Michael Sears, Desiree Rhine and Sherri Phillips for their essential input throughout many, many drafts.

To The Virginia Center For the Creative Arts, The Vermont Studio Center and Carol Levine and Melissa Slaybaugh for providing welcoming places and the head space in which to write.

To Professor Richard Goodkin for introducing me to Proust and the magic of the Madeleine so many years ago.

To Diane Colman for being my very first reader and copy editor (thanks Mom!).

To Richard Roth for his boundless generosity and creative input.

To Jack Levine for his unconditional support.

To Albert Colman, Karen Finerman, Janet Eisenberg, Donna Broder, Gavin Polone, Monica Cohen, Karen Levine, Lisa Garey, Sharon Hayes Roth, and Jonathan Reiss for the many and varied ways they supported me as I made my way down this very long road.

To Dr. Elizabeth Fitelson, Dr. Christina Matera, Dr. David Printz and Dr. Margaret Spier for saving my life.

To Gabriel and Emma for being the most compassionate, awe-inspiring, wonderfully eccentric, genius children I could ever dream of. You amaze me every day.

And finally, to Michael—for more than I can possibly say here, but especially, for always (and often) saying "when" and never "if." It made all the difference. Thank you.